# A Country of the Mind

## Yugoslavia in Six Tales

### David Fulton

**Brigand**
London

Brigand Press
All contact: info@brigand.london
www.brigand.london


British Library Cataloguing-in-Publication Data
A catalogue record for this book is
available from the British Library

Printed and Bound in Great Britain by
Datum Creative Media Limited, EN6 4RY
www.datum.agency

ISBN: 978-1-912978-39-7

For Min, the *sine qua non*, and, of course, Kath.

Many thanks to Phil, Nigel and Rob for
reading early drafts and making helpful
suggestions.

*A Country of the Mind*

# Contents

*A Country of the Mind*

## Rough Guide to the Pronunciation of Serbo-Croat Words in the Text

**c,** for instance 'Sitnica'('Out of Mind'),
should be pronounced 'ts' as in 'spots'.
**č,** for instance 'lozovača'('Out of Mind'), should
be pronounced a heavy 'ch' as in 'charm'.
**ć,** for instance, 'Milošević'('What Was Yugoslavia?') should
be pronounced with a lighter 'ch' like the 't' in 'feature'.
**š,** for instance 'Priština'('Serbia's Guts'),'
should be pronounced 'sh' as in 'show'.
**j,** for instance 'Biljana'('First Light'), should
be pronounced 'y' as in 'yard'.

*A Country of the Mind*

# Out of Mind

*Maybe you're a troubled wife,*
*But you can sidestep strife*
*And live the life, live the life.*
Mary was waving her arms up and down, like a handball goalie desperately trying to save a penalty, her red topknot bobbing crazily, when the phone rang. *Damn! Just as I was getting going!*
*Live the life, live the life,*
*All you gotta do is live the life.*
She sighed, squatted to press Pause before padding across the carpet in tiger leotard to snatch the receiver up. 'Yes?' breathlessly loud.
'Mrs Radford?' momentarily taken aback.
'Correct, who is it?'
'The Foreign Office....' The speaker halted to let his words' full solemnity sink in, but Mary was more concerned with how genuine they were.
*Those plummy tones! Can they be real or is it just one of my friends having me on? If someone's winding me up, who can it be? Definitely not Roger. I'd always spot his voice, no matter how well he tried to hide it. Fred, no....*'Oh yes.'
'We're calling about your husband ....'
'Haven't got one.'
'Apologies, I mean, your *estranged* husband, Jack. You are still married, aren't you?'
'Technically, yes, but I haven't seen the scumbag for years, don't want to either – not ever again.'
'Well, you might not.'
'What do you mean?'
'Mrs Radford, we've got some rather disquieting news for you: your husband – your *estranged* husband, that is – has gone missing!'
'Is that all? Look, he's probably got drunk and fallen into some coal bunker and is still struggling to get out.'

'Well, if he did, it's unlikely he's still alive. You see, it seems the university last sighted him over two months ago!'

'Oh!' in angry surprise.

'The local police have combed Kosovo, but found no trace. He seems to have vanished. There are no clues as to his whereabouts either in his flat or university office, and no one – colleagues, students, neighbours –has any idea where he might be.'

'How do you know he didn't leave the country? It's – what? – September. The summer break can't be over yet, can it? I wouldn't be surprised if he hadn't gone to Bulgaria or somewhere like that – you know, one of those sad Eastern-bloc countries I was always having to veto as holiday destinations – and now he's on his way back.'

'We think not. You see Michaelmas term started two weeks ago, so if he did go abroad, he should have contacted the university to tell them where he wanted his things stored. No, we think he stayed in the country. While it's true his passport's missing, we know he was more or less penniless when he disappeared.'

'Maybe someone lent him money.'

'But there are other factors: everything you'd think he'd need for a journey – everything, that is, except his passport – was left in the flat.'

'Maybe he was travelling light.'

'And then he didn't apply to the Yugoslav authorities for an exit-entry visa, as he should have, and his name doesn't appear on any plane-passenger list. We know: we've checked them all. Of course, he could have adopted an alias and forged a passport, but we see no reason why he should.'

'Not unless he was doing undercover work for your boys in Belgrade.'

'I'm sorry, I don't quite....'

'It's alright, I was only joking.... So, he's still in Yugoslavia – no doubt staggering down some country lane, a little merry and completely lost.'

'Mrs Radford, you don't seem to be taking this very seriously.'
'Look, if you'd been let down as often as I have, you'd feel the same. He was always like this, always running away. It's what made it hard – no, impossible – to live with him – well, that and other things. First time I got so worried I couldn't eat or sleep. I imagined all sorts of horrors: a hit-and-run, a fall down a ravine, a crash, trapping him in a burning car. I panicked, rang round all the emergency services, but they hadn't heard a thing. And then he turned up three days later without so much as a word of explanation. He just seemed to have no feeling for what he'd put me through. So I thought, *Sod you! If that's how you want to play it, you can bloody well worry for yourself in future.* After that, whenever he went missing, I started caring less and less. In the end I suppose I just got blasé, maybe slightly amused even: that a grown man could act like a little kid – pathetic!'

'On this occasion, however, we think he's not acting. Mrs Radford, we've reluctantly come to the conclusion that your husband – *estranged* husband – must be dead!' She let her breath out slowly and glanced across to the bookcase, now less than half-full with the absence of his many books. 'And as you're next of kin, we'd like you to take charge of his effects.'

'Yes, but what about his mother?'

'Oh, didn't you know? She died almost a year ago.'

Mary looked along the hall and out through the kitchen window to the back garden where Linda and Peter were playing, lost in their separate adventure, yet still very much part of her. She was shocked, not so much at the woman's death – she'd never really warmed to her – but that Jack had so coolly decided not to tell her, had, all the time he was over for the funeral, made no attempt to contact her or the children, had returned without so much as a phone call or letter. Such active passivity! Nothing, not even death – he seemed to be saying – could break the silence between them. The rift was final. Linda and Peter, as far as he was concerned, no longer existed.

'Let's get this straight. You want me to go over to Yugoslavia and collect his things. Is that what you're saying?'

'Well, not everything, just what you want to keep. Given the delicacy of local sensibilities, we'd pay for the flight, hotel and transportation costs – even the expenses. We'd account for you as a visiting lecturer ....'

'Me give lectures! You must be joking!'

'Oh, don't worry: it's just an accounting procedure. You won't be asked to do any teaching.... All you have to do is go on two short plane journeys there and back – oh, and two even shorter internal ones – and make your selection of his things and agree for the rest to be disposed of. It could all be done in – what? – three days. Naturally, we will arrange for the chosen items to be shipped back.'

'Look, it's not as easy as that.'

'No?'

'Well, for starters, I haven't got a passport.'

'Haven't got a passport!' in astonishment. 'But everyone does nowadays, don't they?'

'Well, I don't.'

'Whyever not?'

'Well, to have a passport would mean I recognise the British State.'

'Oh, I see.' *One of the awkward squad, eh.* 'Well, perhaps you could compromise on this occasion.'

'But I don't know I want to. I could, I suppose, call myself a citizen of the world and make my own documents.'

'I don't think that would do.'

'And there are other things. I can't just swan off from the hospital at a moment's notice. You see, I've already used up my holiday quota – then I've got two children to think of.'

'Don't worry, Mrs Radford. That can all be taken care of.'

'Really! Well, the thing is ... I suppose I just don't want to go.'

'Think it over, nevertheless. If you decide not to go, his possessions will be disposed of – well, that is, they'll all be burnt. But if you do change your mind, you can contact us at

4

the Foreign Office. Ask for Extension 658.'
'OK, but I'm sure I won't.'

After lockers and seatbelts had snapped shut, bilingual instructions vied with chatter, and piped Mozart strove to reassure the nervous, all noise was drowned in the engines' piercing engagement. The slow, swaying, slightly-bumpy progress along the tarmac had ended in a leftward veer and now the jet was starting to race the runway's lines down its black length. Full power came with the flick of two switches, converting a whine into a wind-tunnel roar. What had been smooth acceleration was now headlong rush. Tremendous forward thrust was meeting tremendous resistance. One would have to give way. Passengers, pinned back in their seats, wondered if they were being punished for aping birds. Certainly, the plane's avian body seemed to be suffering as much as theirs: alarming creaks and rattles suggested some vital piece of fuselage might be torn off at any moment. This scheduled fight against gravity was not to be easily won.

The knot tightened in Mary's stomach. Here was the moment she dreaded most: the point of no return. Her pilot, so noisily committed to take-off, could no longer pull out. If the plane now failed to leave the tarmac, there could be, for her, only one outcome: a slicing through bushes, a shuddering slide into ploughed fields, explosions, fire, and, then, a smouldering wreck, charcoal and charred bodies.

*If I'm going to die, please make it painless and quick.*

In truth, she was worried less for herself – she'd already had a sort of life – than her children. Peter and Linda were effectively fatherless. What would happen if they lost their mother as well? But these thoughts were short-lived for after a heart-stopping scrape the plane shuddered off the ground, cleared the vegetation beyond the runway by what seemed to be inches and began sharply rising into a grey London sky.

*Is our angle too steep? Will we spin out of control and nose-dive into those fields below? No, it's OK, the pilot knows what he – she? – is doing, doesn't he ... she?*

The plane climbed away from the conning-tower's restless scanner, the grey terminal buildings, rank on rank of parked aircraft, cars streaming in and out of the airport like circulating blood, and acres of depot, suburban estate and shrub. Mary noticed how quickly everything fell away, how thick wedges of people, buildings and problems so rapidly disappeared. A London without urgency or threat was vanishing beneath her feet as the plane rose through wisps of cloud, then dense bands of white. Nothing seemed able to touch her now – she was so high above. The airliner banked, straightened and, after taking bearings from a blackly-glistening Thames, shot through the cloud barrier. And she was Empress of Cotton Wool, sole ruler of the soft silent canyons over which she sped. The dull light of an English autumn had given way to crystal clarity; every colour, every tone gained its full value: the white ranges beneath sparkled or dipped into hard-edged shadow, as ice-mountains must on cloudless Arctic days, and a light-blue atmosphere above radiated a purity that made her long for origins.

Life's normal functions began to return: lights came on above seats, allowing passengers to release their belts. Some smoked, some stretched their legs, while others merely chatted. And as if to signal the tense moment of take-off had truly passed, the first drinks were wheeled in.

'Oh, tea, please ... white,' after scrutinising the cabinet. *Something warm and soothing. That's what I need.*

Mary took a sip and looked down from her porthole. On a plane bound for Belgrade was where she least expected to be. A week ago, after replacing the receiver, she'd felt sure that was the end of the matter and, two days on, still felt the same. However, later, memories of Jack tugged, unbidden, on her thoughts and, early one morning, just before dawn, she dreamt of his funeral in the snow. A black, teak coffin with his bloodless face staring dolefully out of a small window at the top slipped down icy slopes with the speed of a toboggan, forcing the mourners to ski recklessly to keep up. How the old priest managed to stay level with the box and, at the same time, chant the requiem she couldn't imagine. The speeding service shot over bare mountain-sides and through wooded combes till, at last, it came to a ledge, over which coffin, priest and mourners all disappeared into the dark.

She'd awoken, sweating. What might have been comic set her heart thumping. Perhaps this latest disappearance wasn't just another stunt, but a conclusion – his end – at last. And though this thought didn't grieve her deeply, it made her feel, more and more, that attention ought to be paid and if she didn't do so, no one else would. A sense of duty, surprising in its pit-bull strength, gripped her and wouldn't let go. None of her resentment could shake off the beast. She began to think of her own life, the struggle it had been: a tough council estate in Bermondsey, dad's early death, mum scraping by on social security and the odd charring job; the early years with Jack, when he was more out of work than in; then alone with two young kids and mum looking after them while she trained to be a nurse; and now on the wards, a grind – though a rewarding one – what with the long shifts and hard physical labour. What had happened to those dreams she'd nurtured as a child – a life of excitement, fulfilment? So gradually, imperceptibly she started to feel that although this trip to the Socialist Federal Republic of Yugoslavia would have its depressing side, it might also offer the chance of adventure. Didn't she deserve a few days of freedom, a short time when she could rid herself of the worries of work and children? Wouldn't it be great to be selfish for once, not on the margins helping others, but centre-stage? Eventually, despite herself, she gave in. The children had been packed off to her sister in Corby; Roger had been told she wouldn't be around for a week or so; the hospital – with help from the Foreign Office – had been persuaded to grant her 'compassionate leave'; and Petty France had had her passport ready for collection the day after she'd submitted form and photo.

*Amazing what you can do when you know the right people!*

So here she was, gliding over soft white canyons towards a Balkan rendezvous. At the airport she'd be met by a Hamish Brewster from the British Embassy, who'd put her on a domestic flight to Priština. There Nuhi Islami, a member of the University's English Faculty, would be waiting. Everything had been arranged; all she had to do was sit back and relax. And as soon as she'd swallowed her last mouthful of tea, that's exactly what she did. After setting the plastic cup down, pressing the chair's incline button and easing her body back, in no time she fell asleep.

Mary woke with a sinking feeling as the plane plunged through cloud-cover towards Belgrade; but the landing proved uneventful. Soon she was semi-sleepwalking behind other passengers down to a blue bus. After collecting her heavy case from a carousel, she stumbled past custom officers, who showed not the least interest in what she might be carrying. Then, pushing through exit doors, she moved from a tight corridor to an impressive expanse of hall and a curving barrier, against which were pressed lines of people, three-to-four deep. Many held up cardboard placards: 'Cecily Fairfield', 'Darko Suvin', 'Hotel Turist' and so on. But where was 'Mrs Radford'? She struggled through the crush, looking from side to side, without seeing her name.
*Oh God, British incompetence again! Can't even get one man to arrive on time to meet a flight. So, what do I do now? Sit down and wait, I suppose. They didn't even give me the Embassy number.*
She was turning towards a row of red plastic seats, dwarfed by high windows, when an authoritative voice, assuming deference, boomed down onto the back of her head.
'Mrs Radford?'
'Yes,' spinning around. She looked up, then up again. A giant – six-foot-four, six-foot-five, he must have been, and at least

18 stone – seemed to scrape the ceiling above her. 'You're from the Embassy, I suppose,' trying to recover her poise through bluster.

He nodded.

'But you weren't carrying a sign or anything.'

'Oh, I don't need all that,' he drawled. 'I had a description. I knew it would be unlikely there'd be more than one unaccompanied woman in her mid-thirties with flaming red hair!'

'Oh yes, of course,' she replied, chuckling. *I stand out wherever I go, but then so must he? He couldn't exactly carry out undercover work here without being noticed!*

'Let me introduce myself: Hamish Brewster,' shaking her hand vigorously.

'Pleased to meet you. Very Scottish name, but you don't sound a bit Scottish.'

'Well, I am, but then I've spent most of my life abroad: boarding school in England, the Guards in London; embassy postings to Abu Dhabi, Algiers and now Belgrade.'

*If he's a spy, he's not exactly a tight-lipped one.*

'But your home's in Scotland?'

'Oh yes, the Highlands.'

'So what does your family do?'

'Nothing much really. I mean, we own a grouse moor and part of a salmon river ... oh yes, and we have a rare breed of Highland cattle. My father's the local laird, you see, and when he passes on, I'll be the next one.'

*Another man of the people for the Foreign Office. Well done, boys!*

'Now we need to sort some things out. Let's find a quiet place to sit.' And with that he lifted her case as if it were a light hamper and strode towards a cafe at the end of the hall. She skipped behind him – ridiculously, it seemed to her – like a child running after a father's long legs. Finally, with the case deposited next to a table, her scampering came to an end.

'What will you have?'

'A coffee, I think, to bring me round.'

'Dve Turske cafe,' he boomed imperiously to a bored waiter, who gave him a look before shuffling into obedience. 'What a country! Even the waiters can hardly deign to wait; sometimes you almost have to negotiate.'

Mary looked round sympathetically at the man's slumped back.

'I can remember one absurd situation at a fish restaurant, forty miles up the Sava from Belgrade. There was a large expanse of outdoor tables, stretching down to the river. Four men arrived, deciding not to sit in the shade with the rest of us, but round a table right at the water's edge. They called for the waiter from the blinding sunshine, oh, three or four times, but he feigned deafness and attended the tables nearest the restaurant. Finally, after they'd appealed to the other customers, the waiter informed them they wouldn't be served unless they came and sat within easy reach. They threw hands in the air and uttered the usual oaths insulting his mother, but to no avail. The waiter refused to back down. They sat it out for, it must have been, at least five minutes, but in the end their resistance weakened and they left, though not without firing a further volley of abuse at the waiter, advising him to have sex with himself and other anatomically impossible feats, as well as casting doubts on the legality of his parents' marriage.'

*Good for you, waiter: independent, self-respecting. After all, who wants to be servile, even if you're paid to be? As a nurse, I don't serve my patients, I help them – it's a partnership, a pact of equals. In fact, where I am in maternity, with the ten days postnatal lying-in, the mothers often become friends. I keep in touch with some of them after they've left.*

'Was that waiter an odd case or pretty standard?'

'Oh, it's typical of state-run restaurants: the waiters have a fixed wage, no matter how many customers they serve or how well, and tipping's not a custom; so they've no incentive to do their job properly.'

*Good for them! I bet they all pull their forelocks up in the
Highlands, though.*

'However, let me at least *serve* you in some small way, Mrs
Radford,' he smugly offered. Reaching into his jacket, he
drew out a thin bundle of hundred-dinar notes. 'This should
cover your day-to-day expenses.'

She quickly surveyed the restaurant. If the secret police were
trailing them, they might have thought the money was cash
for some spying mission. But, to her disappointment, no one
in the half-empty room was paying them the least attention;
all she could see were well-dressed people, often in the latest
Western fashions, enjoying their drinks, and, beyond the café
in the hall, a number of reasonably well-stocked shops. The
uniform drabness she'd expected was nowhere to be found.
Indeed beyond the high windows there was even a crush of
taxis and cars.

'If you get through these, just go to the branch of Beobanka
at your hotel; the British Council have arranged for you to be
able to withdraw more funds, should you need them, up, that
is' – with a wry smile – 'to a certain ceiling.'

'Don't worry. I won't be wasting taxpayers' money.' *Unlike
some of Her Majesty's servants abroad, no doubt.*

'Good. Here's your ticket. The return date's left open, so you
can fill the box in when you're surer of your movements. A
hotel room's been reserved for five days with an option on a
further three.'

'Oh, I won't be staying that long.'

'Well, if you do, it's all set up. Your plane leaves in, let's see,
forty minutes. I haven't heard the call, but I think we'd better
drink up and make our way over to the exit lounge.'

Again with a decisiveness born from never having your
actions questioned and never doing so yourself, he downed
his coffee in one, rose abruptly, picked up her bag as if it were
a toy and marched towards the lounge. Again she had to rush
off, leaving her half-finished coffee behind, stumbling, almost
running to keep up.

*God, this man would be a nightmare patient, wandering out of his bed when he's not supposed to, waving the nurses over every other minute, ordering them to do this or that, even telling the Matron off! But, come to think of it, he probably wouldn't be seen dead in an NHS hospital among all those 'common people'. He'd go private, I'm certain of that.*

For a second time that day Mary came down through clouds, but not to a busy airport with highways leading off. No large town bristled on the horizon. Instead she descended into what seemed a place of desolation with the strips of tarmac surrounded by endless grey fields. No sign of habitation, no arterial roads, no speeding cars could be seen – just a modest concrete building, not much bigger than a local flying club, a tiny scanner on top. The aerodrome was devoid of civil craft, but, barely camouflaged in one corner, Mary could make out a wedge of army fighters, guarded by the small dot of a single soldier, alone in that immensity.

*Who's he guarding the planes from?*

The hills rolled away as far as the eye could reach, to all appearances empty of threat, although Mary had heard Albania was not far away.

*Who would this firepower be used on? Enemies from outside or within?*

As the planes loomed larger, she noticed on the nearest rust and ingrained dirt on its fuselage and wondered if they merely acted as totems, scaring off whoever dared approach, or whether they could actually splutter off the ground. Nearby, she could also make out tanks and jeeps under cover of trees, but could see no other soldiers.

Mary looked down behind the terminus for evidence that today at least it was a proper airport, but the car park stood empty, apart from four cars and a concatenated bus. They seemed to have been dropped from the sky into a world where hope was left behind with the misplaced luggage and aspiration turned round on itself like a baggage carousel. Was this the end of

Europe where all the West's talk of freedom petered out in dull field after dull field? Did Jack sense that from here there was no way out? Did he feel this was the final bolt hole?

Nuhi Islami waited with one other man in the arrival lounge. There were no barriers as there'd be no crush of passengers He clutched a piece of cardboard with '**MRS RADFORD**' in bold capitals – no doubt, a redundant gesture. Surely her foreignness would be immediately obvious – from her style of clothes, cut of hair, or paleness of skin. He made out on the other side of the empty customs desk a pile of cases dumped on the floor, as if their owners had been dematerialised and this was all that was left. Where was the airport bus? He'd seen the plane land over five minutes ago. No one would be taking the passengers on a guided tour of the aerodrome, that was for sure.

He was about to light another cigarette when he spotted the first straggle of passengers emerging from the far doors. Eventually, forty or so presented themselves, huddling round the pyramid of cases. His eyes moved from one woman to the next. There were a dozen or so. Several could be immediately discounted because of their traditional Albanian dress; a couple were clearly too old, and one – a teenage girl – far too young. Of the rest the most obvious choice was a woman with red hair and very white skin. She couldn't be Serb (the red hair would have clashed with an olive complexion); and though Albanian women could be as dark as Turks or as fair as Swedes, they almost never had auburn hair. This redhead, having found her bag, was taking in every detail of the hall as if this were the first time she'd seen it.

*Yes, that must be Jack's wife. Oh well, here we go.* He raised his sign and began to wave it from afar. The woman didn't seem to notice and, instead, continued her scanning. *Am I too far away? Or perhaps she's short-sighted. She doesn't seem to be wearing glasses. Contact lenses?*

Finding nothing, the woman gave up her scrutinising and

struggled with her case up to and past the empty glass box of Passport Control. Nuhi instinctively began to move towards her to help with her load. They met in mid-lino.

'Mrs Radford?' holding up the card as well as if she might not understand his slightly-accented English.

'Yes. Are you the person meeting me from Priština University – a Mr Islami, I think?'

He nodded. 'But please call me Nuhi.'

'And you must call me Mary.'

Both kept a steady gaze as they smiled at each other, hers eventually making Nuhi look away, but not before he'd got a sense of her luxuriant chestnut hair and pale, incredibly pale, skin. Though his fellow Yugoslavs would probably say she looked anaemic, shocked by life almost, Nuhi thought her complexion suited her.

*Well, Jack! You lucky man, to have a wife like this! So why couldn't you get on with her? Strange! Maybe she's not so easy to live with, but if you carried on in England like you did here, it'd be you who was the difficult one.*

'Let me take your bag. My car's just outside.'

She thanked him and sneaked another look as he picked up the luggage.

*What an intriguing mixture: hair black; swarthy as if he'd have a five o' clock shadow right after shaving; medium-height; sturdily-built; standing up straight (he's obviously done military service, yet doesn't seem macho). He eventually turned his head away when we were eye-to-eye. He speaks quietly, almost shyly. Yes, there's also something pleasantly old-fashioned about him – the last of the gentlemen perhaps. I get the feeling if he were a patient, he'd be no trouble at all. In fact, it'd be a pleasure to nurse him.*

The pace at which they set off was comfortable for her. He strolled and chatted, apologising for the lack of this or that, constantly trying to see things from her point of view. She walked easily beside him, taking in the sparseness of everything they passed. As all the other passengers had made straight for the airport bus, Nuhi and Mary walked to his car in splendid isolation. After removing certain items and trying a number of angles, he finally managed to fit her case in the boot of his small green Zastava. Soon they were bumping out of the airport onto an almost-deserted B-road that cut straight across a vast, bare valley. Not another car was to be seen, going either way, but, after a couple of miles, Mary noticed a black speck on the horizon, which slowly grew bigger and bigger.

*We're not alone, after all? But if that's a car or lorry, it's really dawdling.*

As it came closer, the dot became a horse-drawn cart, seemingly occupied by only a driver with a white skullcap, sitting at the front.

*Maybe a farmer returning home from selling sheep at the local market – wherever that could be in all this wilderness.*

Just as the cart was passing, Mary noticed – with a sudden start – two women, an older and younger one, at the back, squatting as best they could on dirty floorboards.

*Are these the unsold 'livestock'? Why is there no seat for them up front?*

The car went by in a second, but Mary retained an image of the women, hair covered by scarves, coarse dresses hoicked up from ankle-socks by their hunched position, exposing thick bloomers beneath.

*Mustn't show a bit of leg, obviously – or any other part of the body for that matter. Can't have any man, besides the husband, seeing uncovered flesh and getting excited. God, how they must fear women! I know I've come many miles to get here, but it looks like I've also travelled far in time – back to ... what? The Middle Ages?*

Nuhi seemed to intuit what Mary was thinking and, tactfully, tried to distract her with pleasant, innocuous talk. Their light words relaxed him as well, taking his mind off the moment when the conversation would come round to her husband. Carts gradually gave way to cars, but not many. Mean straggling dwellings thickened to hamlets, hamlets to towns or, at least, overgrown villages. Mary was moving back to the twentieth century – or was she?

*God, there's some real poverty here. Makes Hackney look well-off.*

Eventually, the car entered the suburbs of what must have been a sizeable town. Beyond the small cottages of whitewashed walls and red-tiled roofs Mary could see a cluster of tower blocks thrusting improbably into the sky.

'This is Priština, though we – the Albanians, that is – call it Prishtinë!' The narrow winding roads widened to a main street with multi-storied buildings asserting their status by mere size: Germija Department Store, Beobanka and, last of all, the Grand. 'This is where you'll be staying,' he announced as he turned into the hotel car park.

Mary looked up at the structure whose phallic thrust had at least been split into three smaller erections, the central block being the tallest. The style had no smack of locality: International Modernism, she'd heard it called. The building could easily have been standing in Tokyo, Chicago or Singapore. However, she froze in mid-wince, when, glancing at Nuhi, she noticed how proud he seemed of it.

*We're just the opposite in England, I suppose. We want to knock down high-rises and build something more human; but here this sort of thing must be excitingly modern, a sign of progress.*

'I expect you're tired after all your travelling, but if, after some rest, you'd like to dine out this evening, I, as representative of the English faculty, would be pleased to invite you.'

*God, that was some mouthful.* 'Not for yourself.'

'Of course, Mrs Radford, for myself as well. No, no, I was just pointing out that as our guest, you wouldn't have to contribute anything to the evening.'

'Oh good, I'll order all the most expensive dishes then.'

Pause.

'Oh, I'm sorry, Mr Islami....'

'Nuhi.'

'Nuhi, I was only teasing.'

'Go ahead; have all the jokes you want; I don't mind, Mrs Radford.'

'Mary.'

'Sorry ... Mary. Now would 7.30 be a good time?'

'That would be fine; see you then.'

As water coursed down on her head in warm lines of pleasure, Mary let out a long sigh. By leaning slightly backwards, she could make the jet hose her shoulders and breasts, stream down her torso and slap on the tiles between her legs. Half-blinded by the surge, she groped her way to the soap dish, picked up the small bar and savoured its lavender scent. Having wetted and worked it to a lather, she stepped back from the jet and coated her body in a soapy layer, which the water then satisfyingly washed away.

How good it felt to rinse dirt and tiredness from your pores, to melt your numbed body till it was fully there! How great to be aware of every part again, to have each responding to the soapy touch of hands, to sense the blood beneath the skin surging again round its circuit, joining brain and ankle, palm and palm! She was alive again, touching, tasting, hearing, smelling, seeing and, above all, thinking – yes, thinking, among other things, just how much life was worth living. How could Jack ever think otherwise? Then, as if she'd become a camera pulling away from the scene, she imagined her shower cubicle widening to the three-star room beyond, the modern hotel, the row of slick high-rises, Priština, and then the surrounding countryside that was not, and perhaps never would be, modern. So was her shower unit, her luxury mattress, her room service all that Kosovo was, or a sign of what it should be?

She turned off the shower and wrapped herself in a bath towel. Her pleasantly-flushed skin seemed to breathe a warm, scented air of well-being. She smiled: yes, now was the time to ring the kids.

'How's it going, Sal?'

'Fine, fine: your two have been great: haven't squabbled with our lot at all, as we thought they would; eaten everything we've given them; done what we've told them to do.'

'Has it been hard keeping them amused?'

'Not at all! They've been down the park already – to the play area. They love that. Then, when they're here, they watch telly, play board games or run round the garden. In fact, that's where they are now.'

'Could I have a word?'

'Course.' Mary could just detect her sister summoning the children from afar. After what seemed a long wait Peter arrived, breathless.

'It's not fair, Mum! We're playing Cowboys and Indians and I've just captured Linda, but she says I cheated. She's the cheat!'

'It was him who cheated!' His sister had joined him, equally breathless. 'You can capture someone only after the game's started. He sneaked into my tent, tapped me on the shoulder and said, "Got you!" That's so stupid: we're not playing It, are we?'

'No, it's not stupid. You're stupid!'

'No, you are.'

'No, you are.'

'OK, break it up, you two.'

So, instead, they told her about sausage and chips for tea and the swing in the park which you could get to go really high by kicking your legs out and the funny thing Valerie Singleton said on *Blue Peter* and the car Aunt Sally drove, which was better than their old banger, but never once did they say they missed her or ask when she was coming back.

Nuhi readjusted the tie gripping his neck like a noose, fiddled with his cufflinks, juggled the coins and keys in his pockets, and put the weight first on one foot, then the other.

Mrs Radford would soon turn up, they'd soon be seated and she'd start to ask the very questions he didn't want to hear. The subject of her husband was one the English department studiously avoided. Nuhi welcomed this restraint more than his colleagues as he was the one who'd simply rubber-stamped the British Council's choice. Perhaps he should have done more background checks. In that sense what later happened was partly his fault, but, initially, things had gone so well: in fact, for the first six months Jack had been a model teacher – punctual, well-prepared, diligent, energetic. This good start had been enough to earn him a new contract in the summer and, after that, it'd become increasingly difficult not to renew – just as long as he requested it, which for the last three years he always had. However, yes, Nuhi should've faced that problem head on and terminated the contract at the end of the second year. Pretending nothing was happening only allowed the situation to worsen.

Immersed in such thoughts, he didn't sense Mary's presence till she was almost upon him. He turned and an unexpected woman filled his eyes. The faded jeans, grey T-shirt and sloppy cardigan had become a pink dress with bare shoulders and – for Kosovo at least – an adventurous neckline. The red hair that had hung loosely was now neatly pinned. Everything that had been casual was now smart.

*How unsettling! You build up a picture of a person, think you're getting to know them, then, in a blink, they're someone else. I thought she was casual, jokey, uncomplicated, but is she?*

Mary, for her part, was pleased she'd put her glad-rags on. Most of her days were spent in uniform: a white frilly cotton cap, an open-necked, short-sleeved blue dress under a starched white apron, all held in place by a tight black belt, and, below, black stockings above flat black shoes. Hardly any of her red hair was allowed to peep out; no showy make-up, no jewellery, just a fob watch pinned on her pinny, and when she went out, a thick blue cape covering all but her cap and shoes. She did like the way those work clothes made her feel as if she was in disguise, another person. Yet for that reason she wanted to be herself for once, herself at her smartest, or – dare she say? – at her most glamorous.

'Mary, you surprised me!'

'Not in a bad way, I hope.'

'Oh no, certainly not.... Now, would you like to eat here – they do international dishes – or try something more local?'

'Local sounds good.'

'Splendid. Let's go to the Rugova then.'

After a short drive along the high street – so brief Mary wondered whether it would have been better to have walked – Islami pulled up outside a traditional building. It was wedged incongruously between taller, plate-glass structures, with the look of an alpine chalet, its sloping, red-tiled roof not only covering the rooms, but reaching down on the far side to a line of columns, creating a veranda that might shade the customers in summer. Through those columns and into the restaurant the couple strolled. The tables, chairs and cutlery were all modern, but little else. Every wall was crammed with mounted samples of local handicraft (rugs, inlaid slippers, swords, daggers and musical instruments). Folk patterns on the rugs were echoed by the tablecloth's edges and the waitresses' aprons. Mary noticed how the white, red and black motifs rearranged themselves strikingly with each step the girls took, bustling from kitchen to dining room and back. Mary and Nuhi had their pick of half the tables and they chose a small, round one near the window which afforded a clear view of the street. For a while Mary scrutinised the menu, its Albanian and Serbo-Croat providing few clues of what to expect, then, with a sigh, gave up.

'Any dishes you'd recommend, Nuhi?'

'Well, Tavë Cosi's my favourite: it's, basically, lamb, eggs and yogurt, baked in an earthenware dish; and it comes with vegetables. Really tasty, it is ... similar to quiche, I suppose, but not so firmly set. And for afters I'd suggest Shëndetli. It's a dark, nut cake, soaked overnight in a special syrup, and served with cream or a slice of lemon.'

'All sounds good to me.'

'Would you like a local wine with the meal – Kallmet, for instance? It's a red wine.'

'Go for it. I like red best.'

While trying to gain the attention of a waitress, Nuhi couldn't help noticing Albanian men round the room, slyly eying his companion and looking at him with seeming envy. Though content to be so assessed, the smile he presented to surrounding tables wasn't one of pure pleasure. The onlookers only saw the surface – a lucky Albanian man entertaining a glamorous (doubtlessly foreign) woman. What they didn't, couldn't know was that the woman in question was the wife of a colleague, presumed dead, that he was acting in a wholly-professional capacity, and that beneath his smile lurked niggling worries about the route their table-talk might take.

Having finally flagged down a waitress, he started to order. Mary, meanwhile, oblivious of the glances cast in her direction, entertained herself by inspecting the densely-decorated walls and, when she'd finished examining every object, turned to him with a quizzical look.

'So this is the real Kosovo then?'

'It's the side we want visitors to see.'

'And what's the other side?'

'Well ... mountain villages without connecting roads, electricity or proper sanitation, for instance.'

A red-cheeked waitress, looking as if she'd newly arrived from the countryside, brought across a bottle of wine, uncorked it ceremoniously and, with one arm behind her back, poured Mary a taster. She was being put into a role she'd never assumed before. Bluffing would be the best way forward, she decided. So she sipped the red liquid and swirled it across her palette as she'd seen people do in films. Apart from realising the wine wasn't gut-rot, she was clueless, having no idea whether it was good or not. All she knew was that she liked the taste.

'How do you say "very good" in Albanian?'

'*Shume mire.*'

'Yes, *shume mire, shume mire*,' smiling like an idiot at the smiling waitress, who then proceeded to half-fill her large glass, then Nuhi's.

'*Gëzuar*! It means "to your health", Mrs Radford.'

'Mary, please. And to yours.' Their glasses and smiles chimed, but, behind the smile, the fatigue of a long day's trek was threatening to overwhelm her. She therefore drank a couple of quick mouthfuls and soon found the full-bodied wine was just what she needed to keep tiredness at bay.

'OK, so it's tough up in the villages, but what about life in the towns? It doesn't look too bad.'

'True, particularly the bigger ones like Priština, but that's the problem. The villagers don't like townspeople, think we don't work, not real work, yet get all the money, all the privileges, while they're forgotten.' Recalling the cart near the airport, Mary could see why they might feel that.

'Now Priština ... that's the capital, right?'

'Yes, of Kosovo.'

The waitress returned with two gently-steaming, garnished 'quiches'.

'This might sound silly, Nuhi. Look, I know Serbia, but Kosovo? What's that, exactly?'

'Oh, it's a long story. Sure you want to hear?'

'Sure, but if it goes on too long or gets too complicated, I'll ring a bell or something.'

'Well, Kosovo's part of Serbia, the biggest republic, the one that's dominated past Yugoslav federations.'

'OK.'

'After the War of Liberation Tito – he's not a Serb by the way – decided to weaken the Republic of Serbia by making the Hungarian bit in the north and the Albanian bit in the south semi-autonomous provinces, calling them Vojvodina and Kosovo. Three-quarters of people living here in Kosovo are Albanians; most of the rest Serbs.'

'So the Serbs don't have much of a say in Kosovo?'

'Well, ultimately they're in control, but Belgrade's a long way off and we use our majority in the local parliament to get some of what we want.'

'And what's that?'

'Albanian-language radio-and-TV stations, an Albanian newspaper, lessons in Albanian in schools and colleges – oh yes, and some representation in the police, army and civil service.'

'Talking of the army, when I was landing at Priština airport, I saw quite a few tanks and jeeps, hidden at one end – and there were fighter planes too.'

'Yes,' looking round to see if anyone could overhear them, 'they're everywhere in Kosovo – well, in all the possible trouble-spots. That's the big problem: almost all the soldiers here, from officers to privates, are Serb.'

'To keep you in your place?'

'That's right.' He leant forward to whisper confidentially. 'They think we want to break from Yugoslavia and become part of Greater Albania, but few of us do. We know all about Enver Hoxha, how strict he is. You know, he's the hardest of hardline communists, quarrelling with the Soviets and calling them "bourgeois revisionists". Do you know who his only friend is?'

'No.'

'Chairman Mao. Well, we don't want a Cultural Revolution in Kosovo! Anyway … the Serbs are still worried about us and they've got army units just outside every major town. For us they're – what do you call it? – "an army of occupation".'

'I see, but what about the border with Albania? Is that far?'

'About 70 kilometres.' His head inclined towards Mary yet again. 'You know, at the end of the Liberation War Priština was just a village, but Tito chose it as capital over historical towns like Peć or Prizren. You know why?'  Mary shook her head. 'Geography! It was right in the centre of Kosovo – the other towns were too near the border.'

'If it was only a village, I suppose it hasn't got much of historical interest.'

'Not really. There are a couple of mosques – three or four hundred years old – but they're in need of repair.'

'And nothing around Priština?'

'Ah, now you're getting into history again. Are you sure you want to go there?'

'Sure.'

At this point the waitress arrived to clear the plates away and bring the second course. Nuhi followed Mary's thumbs-up by half-filling her glass, then topping up his own.

'Well, a few kilometres out of town – maybe eight or nine – you come to Kosovo Polje. It means "Kosovo Field" and it's where one of the big medieval battles took place. The Serbian Kingdom made its last stand there, trying to stop the Turks invading Christendom. They lost, of course – they were totally outnumbered – but they did manage to kill two of the Turks' top commanders. You can still see their mausoleums near the old battlefield.'

'And when did all this happen?'

'Oh ... 1380s, 90s, I forget, but, you know,' with a chuckle, 'the Serbs still haven't forgotten.'

'What do you mean?'

'They still sing ballads, praising battle heroes and cursing the traitors who betrayed them, and still dream of making Kosovo Serbian again. I suppose they feel the same as you do about the Battle of Hastings.'

'Not me. I'm no Anglo-Saxon, I can tell you! My parents were Irish, Catholic Irish.'

'OK, but it was harder for the Serbs than the Saxons. After a century or so the Normans became part of English life, didn't they? Same religion, same Northern-European origin. But the Turks were always alien – different religion, different culture – and the Serbs had to put up with over 500 years of them.

That's why they don't like the Bosnians – or us.'

'Whyever not?'

'They think of Bosnians as traitors: they are Slavs, just like them, but while they were busy resisting the Turks, Bosnians gave in and converted to Islam – simply for money, position, they think – and as for us Albanians, they see us as Muslims the Turks brought in to do administration and trade, a buffer between them and the locals – you know, just like your British Empire did with Indians in Africa and Hong Kong. But that's where they're wrong. We were here before even the Slavs came down from the Russian steppes. We are the Illyrians, mentioned by Romans like Pliny and Livy, and this,' spreading his arms wide, 'is Illyria – you know, where Shakespeare set *Twelfth Night.*'

*One national myth rubbing against another, so....* 'Good. Thank you, I think that's enough history for one evening.'

'Yes, agreed. Lesson ended.' Nuhi drew a fat cigar from his inner pocket with the conspiratorial air of a conjuror pulling a rabbit from a top hat. 'Do you mind?'

'Not at all. Go ahead.' Though she knew, as a nurse, smoking was harmful and would herself never smoke, she'd always rather liked the smell of tobacco – those old, properly-made cigarettes and cigars. They reminded her, she supposed, of her father. After taking a long, satisfied drag, Nuhi blew the smoke as far as he could away from her out of the corner of his mouth.

'Would you like some coffee?'

'Thanks.'

'Funnily enough, even the Serbs call it "Turkish Coffee". You pour it from a small pot with a handle – a *xhezve* – into a little cup and drink it black and very strong. It's guaranteed to set the heart racing.'

'Mine should just about be able to stand it,' smiling, while patting her left breast with theatrical exaggeration. As Nuhi tried to attract a waitress' attention, Mary finished her cake and cream without the usual worry of the number of calories

going down. 'Look, I don't want to embarrass you, but I can't help noticing how good your English is. In fact' – laughing – 'it's a good deal better than some of my friends. How come?'
'Well, I am an English professor, you know, but, yes, I suppose, beyond that, what helped was the year I spent in England – a Visiting Scholar at Brunel University. For a whole twelve months I spoke, thought, even dreamt in nothing but English. And then I "keep my hand in",' looking round the restaurant once more, 'by listening to the BBC World Service at night.'
'Well, it certainly pays off.' Nuhi smiled in response – with pleased discomfort, Mary thought.
'You'd have been in London the same time I was visiting, yet, of course, we didn't know anything of each other's existence then. Funny thing that, isn't it? You know, parallel lives.'
'Yes, but no good for the plot of a novel.'
'No, unless it was an experimental one – or the plot was extended up to the present day, since we've now met.'
'We almost didn't. I had to find a place for my kids and get time off work at pretty short notice.'
'I seem to remember Jack once saying you were a nurse.'
'I still am for my sins: at the Mothers' in Hackney. Funny place that: used to be a Salvation-Army hospital for unmarried mothers, but now it's part of the NHS, though we still have hymn-singing and sermons on Sunday evenings. The holy rollers arrive and I make myself scarce.... So, yes, I'm in maternity. Haven't the stomach for the other side of nursing: all that blood, those fouled beds, the bodies broken by accidents, eaten by disease. I admire those who do it, but I couldn't. Helping bring new life into the world suits me better.'
'But maternity can't be – what do you say? – all "plain-sailing".'
'God, no: the torture of childbirth, every time, even with epidurals; sometimes the labour going on hour after hour and never seeming to end; the mothers and babies – very, very few, I have to say, but still some – who don't make it through; the babies that come out ... not quite right; the girls sobbing as

they give up their babies for adoption right after birth – you get quite a lot of those in Hackney, poor dears. It goes on and on, but I wouldn't do anything else; it's just so rewarding. Looking at the mothers in their flannel nighties, smiling, despite all they've been through, as they rock their babies in their arms or breastfeed them, makes you feel – I don't know – happy to be alive.' She smiled in reminiscence and her smile was prolonged by the wine's happy warmth, now spreading satisfyingly through her. 'You're a Muslim, right?'

'Well, yes. With a last name like mine I'd have to be.'

'But you don't seem a strict one.'

'What do you mean?' Instead of replying, she simply pointed at the cigar and wine glass. 'Ah yes, of course, but what does your Bible say? Something like: "the heart is willing, but the flesh is weak". My flesh is very weak.'

'And is your wife as easy-going?'

'How did you know I was married?' Again she said nothing, but simply indicated the ring on his marriage finger. 'Yes, stupid! My wife, she's ... stricter. She wants our kids to live good Muslim lives.'

'And how many have you got?'

'Three: Sami, Lulzin and Valbona – nine, six and five.'

'And are you as easy-going a father as you are a Muslim?'

'I suppose so,' smiling.

'In other words, very. Good, that's what I think as well: best to set broad limits, then give them room to find themselves within them.'

'Are yours about the same age?'

'More or less: Linda's eight and Peter six. But how did you know I've got children?'

'Jack used to have a photo on his study desk. He'd sometimes show it to his colleagues.'

'That's very unlike him!'

*Oh dear, mustn't let Mary think too much about her husband. Change the subject, Nuhi, change it quickly.* 'So, what did you think of the meal?'

'Very rich. Just as I like it.'

To Nuhi's great surprise, though their ensuing talk – encouraged by a further bottle of Kallmet – ranged widely, it never returned to Jack. After the wine had warmed his blood and eased his fears, he found himself enjoying the occasion. What made it special was its rarity. There wasn't a single Albanian woman he could think of who could go to a restaurant with a married male stranger and be such relaxed company. Oh, why couldn't it always work out like that? Why did it have to be that an Albanian woman in this situation would be so scared it might provoke gossip that she'd freeze from head to toe like an ice sculpture? Though a Serb woman would do better, she could never look at Nuhi the way Mary looked at him: as an equal, someone from a community as interesting as any other in Yugoslavia. No, history would always come between and she'd view him as an alien in the Serbs' ancestral land, in the majority only because his people bred like rabbits, member of the country's poorest nationality, which, wherever it went, generally found itself at the bottom, the blacks of the Balkans. No, Mary treated him with respect, but also someone she positively enjoyed being with, someone she could even play little verbal games with – in a perfectly harmless way, of course.

'So, shall we go then?'

They rose, happy, replete. Outside grey skies had long given way to the black of night. Islami held the car door open for Mary.

*The last of the gentlemen. Ahhh, sweet!*

The Zastava returned to the hotel by a longer, back route.

'Why aren't we going along the High Street?'

'Well, during the late afternoon-early evening the *korzo* more or less makes it into a pedestrian way.'

'*Korzo*, what's that?'

'A sort of promenade. It gives people, mostly young people, the chance to meet each other.'

'So, they all mingle together, do they?'

'No. It's more ordered than that. They link up with their friends in the city centre and move in lines of people up the right hand side of the main street and down the left, chatting about the latest news, but, all the while, eying the opposite sex in the rest of the parade. I like to think of it as a slow turbine, gently generating sound and energy.'

'So it's a kind of outdoor dating agency?'

'Well, I suppose so, in a way, but not just that.'

After entering the Grand at the back and coming round to the front, they caught sight of orderly lines of mostly-young citizens, snaking past the hotel.

'Thank you, Nuhi, for taking time out to wine and dine me. You're a good host.' Again she detected a pleased embarrassment, but he recovered quickly.

'I expect you're feeling tired after such a long day.'

'I am actually, now I come to think of it.'

'So, goodnight. I'll come round tomorrow at about 10.30, if that's alright, and take you to the English department. We've moved virtually all of your husband's things from the flat to a basement at the bottom of the building for safe-keeping.'

'OK, thanks. See you then.'

After pulling the nightdress over her head, Mary got into the strange bed. Its clean smell and the sheets' crispness reassured her, but there was something not quite right: the mattress didn't mould itself around her body like her treasured one at home. Now that Linda and Peter had learnt to sleep on their own, she, usually, threw her clothes unfolded on the chair and leapt naked into bed. Clothes, particularly in the sack, made her feel constrained. Why not free yourself from them whenever you could? That didn't mean naturism, which she thought a puritanical way of taking all the fun out of nudity. But in the hotel she'd have to be more wary. You never knew who might knock unexpectedly: room service, perhaps even a member of the faculty ... Nuhi! She suddenly felt self-conscious as if her cheeks had slightly reddened. *Was it all that wine?*

Before switching the light off, she turned to her travel clock on the bedside table.

*God, look at the time! Ten. When have I ever gone to bed at such an ungodly hour? Probably not since childhood. Well, Mary, you certainly are living the virtuous life here in this Muslim province. I suppose all the other Kosovan women – wives, mothers, daughters – are doing the same – or are they? They've probably got no choice, particularly the wives. Who was it told me a Muslim man can get a legal separation from his wife by merely repeating, 'I divorce you' three times? Then when he dies, the wife must hide away in the house for half a year, mourning, letting her looks go to ruin. Some might say I should be acting more like a widow, tear-stained, in black, all waking thoughts on Jack, but no .... For a start I don't even know if he's dead. What did Wilde say in that play of his? It's absurd to mourn for someone who's still alive – something like that. Anyway, it should really be me, not him that people are grieving for: a woman left to bring up two young children all by herself! Not that he was much use when he was around. I know it's not fashionable to say this, but I do think a woman on her own can't bring a child up, particularly a son, properly. Kids in their early years do need a man, as well as a woman, in the house. They might end up rejecting him, but at least they have him there. Jack was certainly someone to reject, though you could say he was so rarely present or so quiet when he was that there was nothing much for the children to push against. Just a void. Thin air.*

*The air round here doesn't seem that good. There's a definite chemical smell in the town. I've only been out a short time, yet already my lungs and eyes feel a little sore. This isn't what I'd call an industrial town – you know, smoking chimneys, factory after factory. No. I suppose it's all those coal fires in the houses. Is Nuhi raking his now? Is his wife, like a good Muslim woman, already in bed, having tucked her children in hours ago? Perhaps she's even asleep, presenting to Nuhi, as he climbs in, a gently-heaving back. I wonder what she looks like. Is she large or small, plain or pretty? If she did have a little beauty, maybe it was stretched out of her by childbirth? Is she a housewife or does she have a job? It'd be funny if she's a nurse as well – but surely Nuhi would have told me when I said I was. If she is, though, I bet she didn't give birth in the same hospital she's now working in, as I did. Well, when I had Linda and Peter, I never knew I'd become a nurse, now did I? And if I had, I wouldn't have known which hospital I'd end up at. Fortunately, most of the nurses at the Mothers' were recent arrivals when I joined and the two older ones that I remembered didn't seem to remember me. Well, they never let on, if they did.*

*So, Nuhi and his wife: was theirs a love match or one of those arranged affairs Muslims seem to go in for? Nuhi, he's certainly a character. That sharp suit he wears makes him look a bit like a gangster or a fifties spiv. You have to laugh. And yet he has manners like one of the old school. Was that put on just for me? Is he, behind all that, a so-and-so with his wife, kids, and colleagues? His rubbery clown's face makes you want to smile every time you look at it. But, like a clown's, when it's not lively, it can seem sad. The Hamlet thing. Hamlet cigars? No, don't think he was smoking those. They grow their own tobacco around here, he told me. Probably a local make then, though it smelt alright.*

She yawned. Bed warmth joined wine's relaxing power to let the long day's tiredness at last wash over her and shut her eyes in sleep.

*Smoke, autumn leaves, the kids' den. Linda stands with Peter at the lawn's edge, satisfied with what they've built. There's a mosque towering over the fence behind them where there never was one before! Its minaret is lit up, though in the garden it's still day. A man's melismatic chant, sad and sharp, cuts through the daylight night. As Linda and Peter run towards her in slow motion across the lawn, she glances up at the tower again, spotting a muezzin calling believers to prayer, but not in Arabic. Every word he sings is in English.*

*Looking more closely she notices a familiar face in the chanter: Brewster! Hamish Brewster, summoning Hackney's faithful! But her children continue to race across the bright grass away from the minaret, smiling, lips moving, yet silent, as if they are in a movie, whose sound's been muted. They throw arms wide for her welcoming hug. She stretches hers in response, but just as they are about to reach her, they trip over something that wasn't there before. Falling heavily, they are winded and in their shocked state it takes time to recover enough to cry. She leans over and scoops them up, all the while looking down at the obstacle: it's the body of a man lying face down. She doesn't know why, but senses it is Jack. Suddenly, she feels great anger. What is he doing, tripping their children, making them cry? She wants to kick him, prop him up, do anything to roll him out of the way, so she sets Linda and Peter down; but just as she is about to grab hold of Jack she finds herself over-balancing, falling down what seems an endless windy space till something finally catches her dress, slowing her fall, then, as if she's on a lead, jerking her up towards the light. On turning, she sees, caught in her dress, a hook that's reeling her in. Though her weight bends the rod almost to breaking, it doesn't break. She is swung up towards the bank, laid in a net, then lifted to the triumphant face of ... Nuhi, who murmurs, 'What a catch!'*

Nuhi, half-awake, rolled to the left, but met no warm body, so reached out a hand to explore.

*Mmm, Luljeta must be up. What time is it? 9.30. Wow, strange: I must have slept through the alarm. Some feat that: it's loud enough to wake the dead! All that wine. Still, my head feels great. Wait till I get up.* He remembered a joke about the Queen that Mary told him the previous night and laughed again. *The evening wasn't so bad, after all. Quite the reverse. She's fun to be with. Today though's going to be grim. Sifting through Jack's things is sure to set Mary thinking and then she'll come to me with all those questions I don't want her to ask.*

32

Nuhi stumbled out of bed, threw some clothes over his long johns and shuffled downstairs. From the look of the breakfast table Luljeta and the children had eaten some time before. He called his wife, but there was no response from the kitchen or backyard.

*Stupid: no use calling! Of course, she'd be taking the kids to school. Must be because I'm never around at this time during the week – or maybe it's just that I'm not yet fully awake – all that Kallmet!*

He trudged to the kitchen, quietly humming an Albanian folk tune, and took yoghurt from the fridge, bread from the bin. He reheated kidneys in the pan. It was the same old food, eaten most days, but today – he didn't know why – it made his mouth water. How crisp that loaf looked! How juicy the kidneys!

*Will Mary be having her breakfast now, the usual international fare: a small pot of coffee, a couple of tiny rolls, butter, jam – or a croissant? That's no way to start the day.*

He set his food down and began to eat. How smooth the yoghurt was as it slid over his palate, making him forget the sharp under-taste! Shortly, he heard a noise at the back door and Luljeta's reassuringly-plump form emerged into the kitchen.

'Morning, dear.'

'Awake at last!'

'Yes, must have been dog-tired!'

'I'd say so: the alarm went on for a good time, but it didn't even half-wake you. So I thought – best leave you. Did it go well last night?'

'Not too bad, thanks, but it was a bit awkward, all the time trying to avoid questions about Jack.'

'Yes, exactly. But what's she like?'

'Talkative, yes, very talkative. She seems to be nice; I don't know why Jack couldn't get on with her.'

'I'd have thought it was more she couldn't get on with him.'

'Yes, you're probably right.'

'Pretty, is she?'

'Striking, certainly: she has long red hair and the palest skin you've ever seen. Makes her look a bit cold – even sickly.' *Now why did I say that?*

'Well, you never come across that sort of look round here.'

'No, she does stand out a bit.'

'And did she say much about Jack?'

'That's the strange thing: almost nothing. You'd think, coming over here, she'd be full of him – even though they've been separated a fair time. But, no, virtually nothing.' He finished the last kidney, wiped the juice from his plate with the bread and spooned down the remnants of yoghurt. 'Must get ready now, love, or I'll be late. I've got to show Mary Jack's things. It's going to be a tough morning – emotionally, at least.'

He rushed upstairs, brushed his teeth, washed, dressed and was down again in ten minutes. As he was kissing his wife goodbye, he closed his eyes and almost jumped when he glimpsed, like an image flashed on a cinema screen, the face not of Luljeta, but Mary, looking not at all cold or sickly, but as striking as she'd done the night before.

It was 10.25. Mary took a seat in the hotel foyer and looked round its somewhat-leaden attempt at style.

*Is Nuhi the type who's always on time or will he keep me waiting? He seems pretty laidback, so maybe the latter.*

Her introduction to Kosovo had been relatively painless. After the initial shock of endless plains, pre-industrial carts and cowed women, she'd been whisked to a modern hotel, had eaten a good meal and had, except for that unsettling dream, spent a comfortable night; but the difficult part was nearing fast. In looking at Jack's effects, she was bound to uncover memories long suppressed; whether she ditched or kept them, items would inevitably make her think of him. Why didn't she just get rid of the whole lot, stack everything in a heap and strike a match? Then every trace of him – barring a few photos back in England – would be burnt past recognition. Linda and Peter both looked more like her than him, so rarely triggered flashbacks, let alone nostalgia – heaven forbid. Though a big Kosovan bonfire seemed a good idea, why had she come all the way over when that could have been arranged from home? And, then, did she really so hate Jack that she had to obliterate everything of his? At one time she'd have said, 'Yes,' without hesitation, but now she wasn't quite sure. After all, he'd shared a fair bit of her life: to cut that out was to lose something of her own past and, far from wanting to deny former times, she'd rather face them, no matter how painful that might be. To keep some of Jack's things was a real sign of this resolve, like a skull in a hermit's cell. The holy man remembered death, while she'd remember Jack – at least, the part of him worth remembering.

Nuhi – unnoticed by Mary – entered the foyer and, having spotted her, came over, undetected.

'Mary.'

She jumped like a shoplifter caught red-handed.

'Oh, Nuhi,' hand to heart, 'I didn't know you were there!'

'Lost in thought, eh? Happy thoughts, I hope.'

'Well, not exactly.'

'Oh, yes, I see.... Shall we make a move then?'

'Let's go.'

The car trundled forward slowly, but inexorably, as fate is said to, along the High Street, through traffic lights, unjammed by cars, straight on up a steep incline before coming to a stop in front of the faculty building. Mary looked up at the four floors of the severely-functional structure. If human beings were robots, coming off a production line, this would, she felt, be a perfect building. Each floor seemed to be divided into seven identically-sized rooms with an identical balcony and recession to two windows. Such mathematical charm as the structure originally possessed had clearly suffered from yearlong bombardments of dirt and dust.

*Here we go. Cue: The Force of Destiny.*

Had she been a practising Catholic, Mary would have crossed herself before following Nuhi through the grey doorway. She felt in need of protection, a lucky rabbit's foot, a four-leaf clover, anything. He led her into a bare echoing hall with large stone flags on the floor and walls of an indeterminate cream. The only point of interest was a huge black-and-white photograph of Tito with a legend in two languages beneath.

'What does it say?' pointing.

'Oh, "Brotherhood and Unity" in Albanian and Serbo-Croat.'

'No, "Sisterhood and Unity" then?'

'Women are included in "Brotherhood".'

'Ah, I see.... And is "Brotherhood and Unity" what you have or what you aspire to?'

Nuhi put his right index finger to his lips. 'I'll leave you to judge that,' with an enigmatic smile.

He walked over to the caretaker's office, next to the entrance, to get the key, then led Mary down bare steps to a basement, dingier than the floor above. A long, dim corridor stretched away until it lost itself in shadow. Noises from upstairs percolated down in muffled ghostly versions. Here was no place to stay long in and certainly not to be left in overnight. As Nuhi conducted her down the passage, its end wall came dimly into view, but just before they reached that, he stopped in front of an unmarked door that looked to Mary no different from all the other unmarked doors, produced a key, turned the lock and lowered the handle. The door swung open with a groan. Nuhi reached into the semi-darkness and pressed down the light switch.

A bare bulb revealed a space, too big for a box-room, but not quite medium-sized. Piles of various heights, some almost reaching the ceiling, some scarcely getting off the floor, but all covered with white cloths, confronted Mary. Their pallid mass rose and fell like some huge ectoplasm about to emerge from the half-gloom.

*Will it grow and grow till it bursts out the room, filling this floor with its white horror, then the other floors above – the campus – the entire city?*

If ectoplasm it was, it was certainly a mouldy one, for a strong smell of decay began to emerge.

'There you are. I'll leave you to it. If you need me, I'll be up on the second floor, Room 241.'

'No, don't leave me alone,' she was about to cry out, but then told herself, *Come on, don't be silly. You're a grown woman. Pull yourself together.* So all she said was, 'Room 241, right, thanks'. *And, I suppose, if I'm going to tear up, it'd better be when I'm by myself.*

As the hollow sound of retreating footsteps faded, she began to stir herself. Slowly, carefully, she tugged the coverings off and laid them neatly folded on the floor. So these were the 'treasures' she'd flown across much of Europe to see, moving from one hostile bloc to another! Not Aladdin's cave certainly – just Jack's. Books, magazines, records, cassettes and clothes formed the largest piles; but as her eyes began to get used to the horde, she noticed other groupings: a folk-art collection (carvings, weavings, paintings, instruments) and, as expected, objects connected with drinking (patterned steins, some of glass, some of stoneware, but all with pewter lids and thumb-levers; decanters with stoppers; carafes without).

*Jack always loved his drink – sometimes too much, true – but he was no drunk.*

The rest of the effects appeared to be odds and ends, linked by no obvious theme (a bicycle, short-wave radio, files, and so on). Altogether, the collection startled Mary with its size. The room couldn't be called small, yet the objects filled it to quite a height. Indeed she had to stand on tiptoe to pull some of the cloths off. It mixed indiscriminately objects Jack must have acquired in Yugoslavia with old English things he brought back from annual visits.

*But did he still think of Britain as 'home'? Or could he have started to see Kosovo not as a place of exile, but his refuge, his final refuge? That might explain the English items. So ...*

*where to begin? Let's see – yes, books! They should be an easy way in.*

She surveyed the four columns of hard– and seven of paperback. There must have been – what? – a few hundred in all. She scrutinised the hardback spines.

*A hell of a lot of poetry! On our first date Jack told me he was a poet. I liked the sound of that: made him seem more interesting. Thought he'd be sensitive, romantic. Some hope! He was always scribbling things, but never seemed to get much published – and then only in small – very small – magazines that were there one day and gone the next. Certainly, he didn't have any well-known publishers knocking on his door. All that effort and nothing much seemed to come of it.... Let's see, what do we have here? Robert Lowell, Randall Jarrell, John Berryman, Theodore Roethke, Anne Sexton – who in God's name are they? Wait, Sylvia Plath, I think I've heard of her. Didn't she gas herself in London a while ago, stick her head in the oven, leaving her kids behind? And what's this? Bruno Bettelheim's* The Informed Heart. *That's not poetry, surely. What does it say on the back? 'The concentration-camp psychology of Buchenwald and Dachau.' Oh God, can't think of anything more harrowing. So something lighter maybe: novels! What's this? English, American, continental novels, all mixed up. Let's see. Hogg's* Confessions of a Justified Sinner; *Goethe's* Sorrows of Young Werther; *Conrad's* Heart of Darkness; *Dostoyevsky's* Crime and Punishment; *Hamsun's* Hunger; *Koestler's* Arrival and Departure; *Lind's* Soul of Wood; *Kosinski's* Painted Bird. *Blimey: just look at these dust-jackets! Madness, mayhem, atrocity. Jack, how could you get pleasure from such stuff? Fill your mind with depressing things and you'll end up depressed. Obvious, isn't it? But maybe the depression came first and then you looked for books to fit in with what you felt. Whichever's the case, these books will never interest me. Better give them to the faculty. In fact, unless I come upon one or two to keep – you know, page-turners, detective stories, thrillers, that sort of thing – why don't I just give them all to Nuhi and say, 'Choose whatever you want for the library – or your own use – and pulp the rest.' It can't be easy – or maybe it's expensive – to get hold of Western books like these.*

In her random sifting she spotted a book that caused her to suck in air: *The Collected Poems of Dylan Thomas* in hard covers. She quickly opened it, pulled back the tattered dust jacket and there it was: 'To My Dearest Husband, with Much Love, from Mary' – followed by six kisses.

*Six kisses! Oh my God! That must have been the first year of our marriage. I was no more than a girl then: naive, trusting, easily-fooled. 'Much Love'! It's funny: I've hated him so long I've begun to think I always did – hate at first sight. But, yes, I did love him once and that first year was a good one, now wasn't it? Not the honeymoon, mind you. We were both virgins. Hard to believe nowadays; probably hard to believe then. Well, I knew I was a virgin and he swore he was. I had this thing about marriage, can't remember why. I suppose it was all that 'keeping yourself pure', 'making it special'. Hard to get back to that way of thinking. Heavy petting was as much as you'd allow. He got so impatient, but, as it happens, on the wedding night he wasn't much better than me. It's a skill, isn't it? You need practice. We got better – well, we needed to. I guess I was glad he 'saved himself for me', but, maybe, it would've been better if he hadn't. He could have eased me gently in, by his assurance calming my nerves. Though we got better, we were never great. Funnily enough, while Jack liked to think he was oversexed, could never get enough of it, I think I was the more passionate one. Since then, other men have certainly been better lovers than him.*

For some temporary relief she turned from the piles of books to a stack of Yugoslav magazines and started to flip through them. Though they were all in Serbo-Croat, they had an English title: *Start.*

*Ha, just look at these! How bizarre! They have what look like serious articles – world politics, culture and so on – but all mixed up with girlie photos: bare breasts, hints of pubes. Hardly what you'd expect from an Eastern-Bloc country. Where's the puritanism?*

Gradually, though, as her smile faded, she felt sad.

*Why did he collect all these? For the articles? Maybe not, more probably for the pictures. Playing with yourself, were you, Jack? What did Woody Allen say? Something like: 'At least you're having sex with someone you love'; but did you love yourself, Jack? It doesn't seem so.*

As soon as Nuhi reached his room, he got down to work, setting a pile of departmental papers in the middle of the desk and running his eyes over them, page by page; but he found his concentration breaking as his thoughts drifted down to the basement below. What was Mary doing? Was she alright? He would have offered help, but felt she preferred to be alone: it was a very personal experience – a close communion between her and all that was left of her husband. Nevertheless, he still kept feeling he should go and give her a hand.

*Does she need a stepladder? She's not the tallest. Is it too soon after breakfast for a coffee? Should we give her a box to put things in or would that crowd up the space too much? Have some of the things stopped her short? Is she at this very moment standing in front of them crying? Does she need some comforting words – a comforting arm? On the other hand, she might just want to be by herself. Oh, I don't know.*

With a long sigh he tried to focus again on the papers. Though bureaucratic business had always been tedious, today it felt unbearably so. He couldn't get through more than a couple of paragraphs without his mind veering off. Yet it wasn't tiredness. He'd slept as deeply as a hibernating bear and had, if anything, more energy than he knew what to do with.

*Perhaps I should wait for half an hour or so, then see if Mary's ready for a break.*

He looked down at his papers yet again.

After finding the odd copy of Chandler and Hammett from the piles to put with the Dylan Thomas, Mary moved quickly through the grammars, dictionaries and pedagogical texts. *I'd no idea Jack took teaching so seriously:* The Communicative Classroom, Second-Language Interference. *What the hell's that meant to mean? And there are twenty or so others! Well, Nuhi's welcome to these without a doubt.*

Yet she was now held up by books on Yugoslavia, mostly written by Westerners or Yugoslavs living in the West. Perhaps they came to conclusions forbidden by the Communist government and so were dangerous for Nuhi to handle. *Phyllis Auty on Tito, Fitzroy Maclean's* Eastern Approaches, *Rebecca West's* Black Lamb Grey Falcon *and Duško Doder on the Yugoslavs. Then there's works by Djilas, translated into English. I seem to remember something about him. Wasn't he Tito's right-hand man during the War of Liberation? Didn't they fall out? Hasn't Tito put him under house arrest – or in prison – and airbrushed him from history as Stalin did with Trotsky? Obviously, not books Islami would welcome. Plain-cover, under-the-counter stuff. And there are these Yugoslav novels and poems translated into English? They'd be no use to Serbo-Croat speakers, surely. One of the writers seems to be called Kiš – now that sounds promising! A snogfest? No, wait a minute:* An Encyclopaedia of the Dead ... Hourglass – *'a man waiting to be sent to a concentration camp'. Oh God, not more gloom, Jack. Bulatović,* The Red Cockerel: *mischief in Montenegro; Ivo Andrić – 'Nobel-Prize winner', it says.* Bridge over the Drina. *Maybe, but it looks pretty heavy.* Serbian Heroic Ballads – *those must be the patriotic songs Nuhi was going on about last night.*

Hearing a noise behind her, she swung round, only to be confronted by the man himself. 'God, Nuhi, you startled me – again.'

'Sorry, but I thought you might be trying to deal with painful memories, so I tiptoed along the corridor and knocked as quietly as I could.'

'Nice of you, but there's no need. I'm a tough old bird, you know.'

This was the second time he'd caught her unawares. He remembered that look on her face, the panic that gradually relaxed into a broad smile. Had any of her past surprises ended nastily? Though the setting changed – dim basement instead of bright foyer; denim dungarees and free-flowing locks instead of evening dress and pinned hair – the expression stayed the same.

'I see you've gone through the books.'

'Yes, but I only found three or four to keep.... Nuhi, I wanted to ask you....'

'Yes.' *Oh no, the Jack question's coming!*

'Do you have a departmental library?'

*No, not this time, not yet.* 'Well, of sorts. It's not very good, I must confess.'

'I'd like you – and I know Jack would've approved – to take as many books as you want.'

'Are you sure?'

'Sure.'

'Well, that's very generous. I had a quick glance, after they'd been carried from the flat and they'd certainly help to fill some of the many gaps.'

'Why didn't you simply leave all the stuff in his place?'

'We've got to get it ready for the new lector.'

'But surely you wouldn't get a replacement till this case's been cleared up. I mean, Jack could still be alive, may even stroll round the corner in the next few minutes and say, "Hi," as if nothing's happened.'

'Yes, well, to be frank, the flat's not in a good state, so we didn't think we should show it you.'

'What? You must be joking. I *have* to see it. Nuhi, I *have* to.'

'Calm down, calm down. If you really must, you can, but my advice is: don't!'

'Whyever not! There's no deadly virus or killer dog inside, is there?'

'No,' smiling, 'none of that. It's just very ... squalid.'

'Oh, I see. Still....'

'Look, Mary, you must be tired after all that sifting. Would you like to take a coffee break?'

'Good idea.'


Seated on black plastic stools up against a strip of red counter, running round the walls of a small express restaurant across the road from the university, they agreed on Turkish coffee and thought about a snack.

'Have you tried burek?'

'No, what's that?'

'Fried pastry, filled with cheese or meat.'

'Sounds fattening, but who cares? I'll give it a go – a small slice, mind you.'

'Best to have it with yoghurt.'

'Fine.'

'Then some baklava?'

'Baklava?'

'Yes, pastry again, but filled with nuts, then soaked in honey. Very sweet and very tasty!'

'I'm sure, but the pie will be plenty, thanks.'

*Nuhi's offering might explain why local women, when they reach middle-age, are on the plump side!*

While Mary used a fork to pick at her small slice, which was a little greasy for her taste, Nuhi seized a generous helping in his hand and got stuck in. She enjoyed the unselfconscious zest with which he wolfed his food down. The constraints of the Rugova had perhaps hidden this for there was no pretence at table-manners in his vigorous onslaught, which he mixed with conversation from a mouth not always empty of food. He finished his burek and baklava before Mary had taken ten exploratory nibbles. Her finicky way of eating did irk him a little, he had to admit. It was as if her pleasing choice of local food over international fare the day before had in some way validated all things Albanian. Now this sudden squeamishness seemed more than just that: a reservation about the whole Kosovan project.

*Don't be so touchy! Wait, of course: what she looked through this morning must have upset her, put her off food. She's just being polite in accepting any.* 'Leave it if you can't finish it.'

'No, I'm fine, thanks. It's just I'm not very hungry at the moment. But the coffee's done wonders, really pulled me round.'

'Alert enough for more delving?'

'Just about.'

'Good. Shall we go then?'

Back in the dark bunker, Mary looked round for electrical items to save, salvaging a small Japanese eleven-band radio and a red music centre. An electric razor that had been too near Jack, hugging every contour of his face, was decisively set aside. She couldn't see, didn't want to see, Roger using it. For the same reason she discarded the clothes, even newish ones. *How could I let Roger walk around looking like Jack? That would seem a kind of haunting. No, Roger is what Jack wasn't. That's the whole point of him. There can't be any blurring of the lines.* Oddly, though, Jack's records and cassettes also troubled her, yet not because they'd been touched by him on an almost-daily basis, but, as with the books, because of their content.

*Again so bloody gloomy! Penderecki,* Threnody for the Victims of Hiroshima*; Schoenberg,* A Survivor from Warsaw*; Berg,* Woyzeck. *His idea of a feel-good musical:* Marat/Sade*! Even the pop music's downbeat: Roy Orbison, the Velvet Underground, Leonard Cohen. Dear, oh dear! Where's your old sense of humour, Jack? OK, life's shit, but you don't have to wallow in it. What about a bit of Morecambe-and-Wise spirit? What about some sunshine? Corny, I know, but at least it's positive. Or Hare Georgeson's sun that's come at last and everything seems alright? Or Cream with their sunshine love? Our love was sunny – wasn't it, Jack? – well, for the first* *couple of years at least.*

The Beach Boys, Buddy Holly and Tamla Motown were the only items she could find that would cheer her up. Though Yugoslav folk music was, no doubt, lively, it wasn't to her taste, and so was discarded, but she was unsure of what to do with Jack's collection of folk instruments: a one-stringed 'lute'; a kind of flute; a single-valve trumpet and a tabla-like drum.

*Jack used to be able to coax a tune from almost any instrument. One of these might remind me of better days. I could take it back and hang it on the wall, maybe. Just like in the Rugova, eh! But no, my flat's too crowded already.*

It was almost four. Nuhi hadn't been at all productive since leaving Mary; his pile of papers seemed as high as ever. *She must be getting thirsty with all that sorting out. I'd better take her down a coffee.* Five minutes later he was knocking on the basement door, but louder this time.

'Come in!'

'Thought you might be needing this.' He carried in the tray with its small steaming drink and, like a friendly waiter, served Mary with a smile.

'Ah, yes, thanks. Could certainly do with that.' She looked down at the tiny collection of things she'd set aside, then at the forbidding piles that still needed to be sifted through. 'Don't think there's any chance of finishing today. Five o'clock, you say, the building closes. Anyway, all these things are becoming a bit of a blur; I feel I won't be able to concentrate much longer. But what I would like to do, if possible, is see the flat.'

'It'll upset you.' *Then, no doubt, you'll ask awkward questions.*

'Don't worry: I can take it.'

'OK, let's go – that is, once you've finished your coffee.'

Nuhi turned off the main road, parking on an expanse of slightly reddish dirt. Once again he was quick to hold the door open for Mary. She climbed out and surveyed a newish, four-storey block of flats that climbed the hill and, like a string of dominoes resting lengthways, turned right, then right again, looking in on itself from three sides of an irregular trapezoid. As before, they needn't have used the Zastava, Mary felt, for the housing project was only a few hundred yards up from the faculty building.

*A car must be a status symbol here. So if you can afford one, why not flaunt it? Or does Nuhi want to make my contact with locals as distant as possible?*

They picked their way through litter that seemed to have been tossed from windows above. To the left a loosening, tightening knot of boys were hollering and laughing as they tried to get their feet on an old, half-punctured football. To the right two housewives were chatting, one with arms folded over large breasts, the other with hands on wide hips. Both had heads that were poised, ready to swivel to catch all that was – or wasn't – going on around them, yet never once stemming their spate of words.

*The estate gossips, I expect. Looks like a small-town mentality here, rule by rumour: Oi, did you hear what she did last night? Shocking, it was.*

They entered through a metal door, which clanged behind them. A smell of sour cabbage and kebab met Mary's nostrils.
'Teatime not far off!'
'But I thought tea was something you drank mid-afternoon – with cakes.'
'Oh, that's for posh people. For the likes of me it's an early-evening meal.'

They climbed two flights of stairs – there was no lift – to the first floor, then moved down a long stone passage with numbered doors facing each other at regular intervals. Just before they reached the end, Nuhi stopped as they came abreast of 254. After much fumbling, he produced a key from his trouser pocket.
'Are you really sure you want to go in?'

'Sure.'

Sighing audibly, he twisted the key, causing the lock to groan, as if in protest, but it did gradually give way and turn with an arthritic click. The door creaked open, releasing a musty odour, suggesting decay, which hit Mary so strongly it brought tears to her eyes. A hankie clamped to her nose, she followed Nuhi in, all the time breathing through her mouth. Room after squalid room greeted her: bottles – wine bottles, spirit bottles, but, mostly, beer bottles – lay everywhere (on tables, in cupboards, on chairs, in the fridge, on every ledge, under the bed, in the bath and so densely in the toilet they could hardly open the door. All were empty or almost empty, allowing blooms of fungus to grow along the insides.

Feeling the burek rising in her stomach, Mary rushed across the living room and threw the windows open so she could lean out and suck in fresher air. As soon as she'd recovered, she did the same to the bedroom and kitchen. As the flat's fustiness thinned and the air became more breathable, Mary was able to take in the full wretchedness. The light-brown carpet, which covered the whole apartment, was so stained that in places it was hard to spot an original pattern. So many bottles must have been knocked over, so many plates overturned and it looked – and smelt – in certain places as if disgorgings of sick had been allowed to seep into the pile. Then, in the living– and bedroom there were blackened areas where a dropped cigarette must have been left to smoulder and singe.

*Oh my God, Jack, you were lucky the place didn't go up in flames. This is awful, just awful. But when we were together, our flat was always tidy, wasn't it? I knew you'd find it hard, coping without me, doing the domestic things, yet I never dreamt you'd come to this. Even a pig would be ashamed to call this his sty. You've virtually made the place unfit for the living. And then the stink in here, even with windows open, is revolting, absolutely revolting. As a nurse I pride myself on my strong stomach, but this – damp mould, rotten food, dried sick, stale piss, dust – it's all just too much. My nose stings, my throat is clawed at, my guts juggled. I suppose in your drunkenness you sprayed your jet all over the toilet, your trousers, the floor. Did you never think of cleaning it up – later when you came round? But did you ever really sober up? That'd be the only way to explain how you could live like this – being constantly pissed.*

Hankie no longer over her nose, she explored the bedroom. The single bed had been stripped of its sheets, exposing a mattress almost as stained as the carpet. But as she was examining its headboard, the sun momentarily broke through the clouds, sending rays into the room which drew her eyes like a pointed finger to something on the wall above: marks, strange marks. Coming closer, she could see scratching, which seemed to have been carved with a knife. The marks crudely formed three English words: 'Gate', 'Water', 'Black'. *Whatever can they mean? Watergate? Surely not. That was – what? – a few years back.... Those scratchings, they're so spooky. Make me think of carvings I saw in the Tower of London – the scrapings of poor prisoners, condemned to have their heads chopped off on the Green.... What are you trying to tell us, Jack? That alcohol's pulled you through a Gate of No Return and now you're drowning in the liquid, spirit's fire-water; blackness, death, is the only way out! No, that can't be it.*

She pointed out the carved words to Nuhi, who simply shrugged.

'I expect he got really drunk and wasn't aware of what he was doing. It would have been more like automatic writing, straight from his dream world, not meant to make sense.'

'Maybe.' She started to cough and, having begun, found it hard to stop. The bedroom, like every other room, was layered with dust. Litter strewed the floor – scraps of newspapers, sweet wrappings, cigarette boxes. It might as well have been an unswept street. 'Nuhi, why has the flat been left in this state?'

'Well ....,.' Her host suddenly seemed to find his thumb of

absorbing interest. 'The police said they didn't want anything touched or moved till they'd completed their investigation. Then, after that, the department and the cleaners kept putting off when they'd go in. It was "maybe tomorrow" or "the day after" or "next week" and, in time, the flat became a place to be avoided as if some terrible crime had been committed there.'

'Perhaps it had.'

'Anyway, when we heard from the British Embassy that you were coming, we got a junior lecturer – he didn't have a choice – to put on overalls and take those of Jack's things that were worth saving down to a van. We gave him a pretty loose definition of "worth", so he chose quite a lot. We couldn't leave the stuff in the department building right away because it had to be disinfected first. It was so dirty and, in the case of some of the books, so mildewed the task seemed hopeless. The clothes that had stains or holes we threw out, but those that didn't look too bad, we took to the washing machines in the student hostels. It was, I have to say, not a nice business.'

'Quite…. Well, thanks, Nuhi. I can now see just why you didn't want me to come. Still' – gesturing at the flat – 'I'm glad I did. It explains a lot.'

As they were leaving, the door across the corridor inched open and an eye and sliver of head peered from the crack.

'Ah, Nikola!' The door opened wider.

'Islami!'

The two men talked at each other as rapidly as machine-gun fire in a language Mary took to be Serbo-Croat. Not a smile formed on either's lips. Eventually, Nuhi turned to Mary and with an arm outstretched announced in English, 'May I introduce Mrs Radford?'

Nikola stared at her coldly, gave a quick, half-military nod, which could, in Mary's mind, have been accompanied by a click of the heels, then closed the door firmly shut.

'Charming! And who's that?'

'Oh, a colleague – Nikola Mihajlović.'

'Not very friendly, is he?'

'Oh, don't worry about him. He can get a bit grumpy at times, but overall he's OK.'

While walking down the bare, draughty flights of stairs and out across the grassless dirt that surrounded the estate, Mary tried to process what she'd seen, but any sense she built up fell apart into stark images of Jack's last days. So, imagining all sorts of horrors, she ducked into the car.

'Nuhi ... how did the flat get to that state in the first place?'

He squirmed in his seat, glancing to left and right and back again. 'We don't know.'

'What do you mean: "you don't know"? Didn't you or one of your colleagues ever visit – particularly towards the end?'

Nuhi was looking more and more uneasy; his face had the drained pallor of a man about to face torture. 'Actually, no.' His eyes rolled like dice.

'But why not?'

'Well ... er ... he ... didn't want to see anybody at that time.'

'Did you try?'

'No ... I mean, yes.'

'Nuhi, I don't think you're being straight with me; you seem to be holding something back. Are you going to tell me what that is?'

'There's really nothing to tell.'

'Nothing?'

'No, nothing.'

'Right, drive me back to the Grand at once, please.'

They returned along the half-empty High Street in silence, entered the hotel car park and stopped.

'Goodbye, Islami. See you tomorrow,' slamming the door and striding rapidly towards the entrance, her red hair streaming behind.

To escape the images unsettling her head, Mary called Sal again and was gradually calmed by her sister's comforting words her about the kids. Linda and Peter, she said, had carried on their smooth transition to another house and all its different ways, and this was confirmed by talking to them. All she got was how much fun they were having, how great their cousins were, how tasty the food was. Not once did they ask her when she'd be back. After she replaced the receiver, she went down to a slow meal alone in the hotel restaurant and returned for a long soak in the bath. These completed the recovery and now she was stretched out on the sofa, letting the warmth of food and water spread gently through her.

*Well, if Nuhi doesn't want to say what really happened, so be it, but it's so frustrating. After all, from the state of the flat it's not hard to guess what sort of life – if you can call that 'life' – Jack led at the end. Maybe Nuhi's trying to save face. Maybe that's crucial here.*

So engrossed was she in her thoughts that a knock on the door made her jump. She padded over, but, before turning the handle, pulled her pink bath robe tightly around her neck and smoothed it flat so it fell well beneath the knees.

She opened the door to a man in his thirties, unremarkable, yet naggingly familiar. 'Sorry I was bit rude before.'

'Oh, yes, you're the man who put his head out of the door opposite Jack's. What did Nuhi call you?'

'In fact, Nikola.'

'Well, Nikola, you didn't exactly seem pleased to see me earlier. What's changed?'

'Can I come in? I explain all things.'

*I will be safe, surely. I mean, an educated man, colleague of Nuhi's. He wouldn't try anything, would he?*

'O ... K.' She moved aside to let him in. As soon as he'd entered, he set about searching under the bed, sofa and table. 'Whatever are you doing?'

'Just checking if there's any – what you say? – electric things for listening from outside.'

'Bugs! You must be joking. I'm no spy!'

'I know, but you can never be too much sure. Look, I can't

find anything, but I think it's good idea we have TV on.'
Without waiting for her reply, he switched the small set in the
corner on. Slowly, the screen settled into grainy black-and-
white pictures of what seemed a medieval battle.
*Kosovo Polje?*
He turned the yells, oaths and groans up loud and gestured for
Mary to sit next to him on the sofa.
*Should I? Well, you're in this far, might as well wade on.*
While he took a place near the middle, she wedged herself as
far away to the right as she could.
'So, what's made you want to come and talk?'
'Your friend not here? In the toilet ... somewhere?'
'Who, Nuhi? No, but I don't see what that's got to do with it?'
'Look, when you come to Kosovo, you have to make choice:
join either Serbs or Albanians. You can't choose both. You're
going round with one Albanian all time, so Serbs suspicious.'
'But that's ridiculous. Don't forget I'm a stranger here. I don't
know anything about quarrels between Serbs and Albanians.
I came on personal business. I've been with Nuhi because
he was the person your department chose to meet me and
show me round. But I can tell you I've grown to like him over
the past couple of days, so I won't take kindly to any nasty
comments.'
'Oh, he's OK, but he's still Shiptar.'
'What in heaven's that?'
'Our name for Albanians. They call their country Shqiptaria
– Land of Eagle with Two Heads. But we think, once Shiptar,
always Shiptar.'
'And once a Serb always a Serb, I suppose.'
'Look, I don't want to argue. I came because I like your
husband. He also started on Shiptar side, but by end he came
over to us and was good friend. Because of that, I'm here.'
'Right, I see.'
'Probably I know more than you, more even than police.'
'How come?'
'Well, they put two Albanian police on case, so we said

nothing. What has Nuhi told you?'

'Very little. He didn't even want to show me the flat.'

'Not surprise. You know, Jack gave Shiptars much pain at end.'

'But not at the start?'

'No, no, he was good boy then: gave his lectures, was polite with all.'

'So, what went wrong?'

'Beer, whisky, vodka, lozovača, klekovača.' The man made a drinking gesture with his right hand. 'All went down. Glug, glug. At first we didn't know what going on. We saw him nights in bars, staying till lock-up, but not too drunk. Still he was in control. Next morning he got in time to classes, looking not so good, I have to say, but doing his job OK.'

'He couldn't keep that up, I suppose.'

'No: bit by bit, slowly, slowly, he got worse. That's why not easy to see. Next step: when he came back from bars, he carried on drinking. Colleagues walking past 1, 2 in morning started seeing his light. He was clever, I give him that: changed classes with young lecturer, so didn't start till 11. By later morning he was in shape to work – more or less. He controlled lessons so long as he drank only nights, but then he started drinking after first class – just to keep nerves going.'

'Oh dear!'

'He was little excited in afternoon lessons, but not too much. Yet after while he started drinking soon as he woke. We noticed signs: red nose; unshaved face; smell of spirit on breath, half covered by mint sweets; jumbled clothes; not so sure on legs; but we pretend we didn't see. For time – two, three months – he kept together – just – by big, big effort. But in end it got too much. You see, he was drunk most of time, so couldn't come round – ever – and strange things start to happen.'

'Like what?'

'Well, his face was little red always, but now his eyes also red, really red, and his hands start shaking. Little while he kept rest of body still, but at last it would shake as well –all over – sometimes out of control – almost like epileptic. It was sad. He had loose walk; now he shuffled like old man, sometimes swayed to left, to right. He stood quite strongly, then for no reason began leaning to one side, almost falling. Soon it was hard to know what he was speaking. He mumbled, seemed to talk to himself, then suddenly shouted. He spoke at you, but you feel if you walked off, he'd just carry on. You weren't needed, you see.'

'Poor sod!'

'His clothes for time looked like he slept in them, but now had dirty marks all over; sometimes – pardon – he smelt like he pissed his pants. Around then he became really, really smelly – his clothes, his body. We here, especially those from countryside, aren't that clean, but to us even he smelt bad – like tramp. And things got worse!'

'Surely not!'

'Sorry to say, yes. Either he didn't turn up for morning class or turned up bottles sticking out of pockets, shouting bad words at everyone. His mind wasn't right: he said we wanted to kill him, so when we met, he'd roar and scream at us – colleagues, students. I say colleagues, students, but really it was mostly Shiptars. He got it in his head they wanted to murder him – you know, revenge killing between families is tradition; it can go for generations, many, many years. Anyway, he thought they thought he'd done something very bad, something against family honour. So when he went down college corridors, Shiptars would run into any room, to left, to right, just to miss him. It was too sad, but also funny in strange way.'

'Didn't anyone do anything about all this?'

'Department closed eyes as long as they can. Only when teaching broke down, they start to act. They moved his classes to afternoon and early evening. When that didn't work, they gave him less teaching, more making class materials. Islami tried hard to help him, but he got so bad all teaching was taken away. So he just supervised couple of theses of Serbian students, did more materials.'

'Why didn't anyone tell the British Council?'

'I think they're too shamed.'

'But didn't the British Council ever enquire?'

'Look, they don't care about us down here: they travel just between Belgrade, Zagreb and Ljubljana – only places they think of. One exception is holidays – to Adriatic. They don't come to Kosovo – unless they have to. Look, your husband – excuse my words – is maybe dead, but did we see British Council? No, it's just not interesting to them. They pity any teacher who comes here – I remember one telling me in Belgrade that Kosovo's more like Middle East than Europe – so they just leave him to it. It's always "him" by the way; they don't think job suited for woman.'

'Wouldn't there have been some sort of conferences every year, bringing all the teachers together?'

'Oh, sure, but Jack hated them. I guess, in the end, he got too scared to go. He didn't want them to find out, so gave excuses. In end Council used to him not there. Maybe it was joke in Belgrade. He showed me once this letter Council wrote. It said something like, "We are glad to see you've gone native" – that was it, "gone native" – "but if you ever venture" – yes, "venture" – "up to Belgrade, come and say hello". Funny! That didn't make you think they worry. They had somebody down in tough post; if he went bit strange, that's expected; but so long as he could do job, it was all that mattered.'

'So Jack was left at the end with the minimum of work?'

'No, he got worse even and wasn't given any and we had all his hours. That was last summer term. Jack kept flat, but understanding was he leave before next academic year. It was then, I guess, Islami wrote to British Council, told them he wants new lector.'

'And what did Jack do?'

'Well, he got paid still, but less – not enough for drinking, he said. Anyway – as you know – he was musician, good with violin. Well, this summer he started playing in Priština Radio

Orchestra. Not regular job; just when they need him. But then I heard he lost that too. That was time he go missing.'

'Did anyone see him during those last days?'

'Well, I drank sometimes with him, not ever heavy drinks. My stomach's not strong. But there was one he drank with often – Serb student. Maybe he knows something.'

'Is he still in Priština?'

'I think so. You want to see him?'

'Oh yes!'

'Look, I've got idea where he lives. If you want, I can show you.'

'OK. How about now? My time's very short.'

'Well, sure, but...,' gesturing at her bathrobe.

'Yes, of course,' smiling. 'If you wait in the lobby, I'll be down in a few seconds.'

Nuhi was unaccountably restless, rising from the sofa on numerous occasions to pace the room, sitting down again, pulling a cigar from the box, raising it to his mouth, then thinking better of it and putting it back. His wife would say things. He would see her lips moving, but somehow he couldn't quite follow her words. Other matters crowded his mind.

*Why was Mary so abrupt? Maybe I should have told her more, but, really, it's just too painful. I wonder if she acted like that because she was overtired – all that sorting out, all those heavy memories! And then the flat, the squalor of it and those imagined scenarios of the kind of life he led there must have torn through her head! She must have been so keyed-up a sharp response was waiting to happen. My silence was the cause, but it could've been anything – a tactless joke, a sign of prejudice, a comment on the weather even.*

'... so that was how it ended. Do you think he did right?'

'Er, um.' *She doesn't sound as if she does, so...,* 'No, dear.'

'No, he certainly did not. Enver told me that....'

*Phew! Good guess. Well, I hope Mary will get over things by tomorrow or the day's going to be a tricky one.*

'... but, you know, Violetta said, "That couldn't have been so because Dëde was away in Kosovo Mitrovica". And then....'

*Why am I feeling so uneasy? It's really unlike me. What I need is a nip of Skënderbeu. That should calm me down.*

While his wife continued her anecdote, he moved over to the drinks' cabinet and, with head slightly inclined towards her as if to catch every word, took the brandy bottle out and poured himself a double shot.

'... and then Mustafa ran out of the front door, shouting, "Fire! Fire!" You see, he'd woken in his chair, his brain still sleepy, and seen smoke and thought the whole house was alight, but it was just him dozing off with a cigarette in his hand and starting the newspaper in his lap smouldering. He hollered and hollered as if the whole town was burning. It was so funny. How his neighbours laughed! It took him a while to live that one down.'

Nikola glanced up as Mary, now suitably dressed in casual jacket and jeans, entered the lobby. She looked so determined to face the worst he felt sure he'd done the right thing in making contact. She could take it. She wasn't the timid type, teeth always nibbling her nails. Seeing the flat must have sent her brain into a spin, imagining all sorts of outcomes. Now, at least, it could be slowed by solid fact. These might at the start bring pain, but should in the end help set her mind at rest.

Once outside the hotel Nikola had no trouble finding a taxi: there was a line of six Zastavas, idling or parked. It was always like this and he'd sometimes wonder if there were more cabbies outside than guests within. Ignoring the first two because they were Albanian, he stopped at the third, who proved indisputably Serb.

'Ulica Bora i Ramiz.'

The car, like Nuhi's the day before, took a roundabout route to avoid the *korzo*, regained the main street further down and passed the university before entering the suburbs. After winding up a series of narrow, ill-lit backstreets, it came to a sudden halt on the top of a barren gloomy hill. Mary looked around. The place seemed devoid of everything you would usually associate with towns: street lights, pavements, buildings ... civilisation? All she could see was a stunted mulberry bush next to the car, besides which a rutted track ran away into the dark.

'I think this where he lives. Let's go.'

'Is it safe?' Mary looked doubtfully into the murk and instinctively zipped her scarlet jacket up to the neck.

'Don't fear. I guide you,' gripping her arm and tossing back over his shoulder a "Čekaj" to the driver.

As they moved away from the taxi's standing lights, Mary could barely see where she was going and sometimes stumbled or slipped on the uneven ground, but Nikola's strong arm always stopped her from falling. After what seemed to Mary more than a hundred yards of tottering an ominously-tall clump of trees suddenly materialised as if by magic. When they had all-but staggered round the roots, a dwelling's vaguely-lit back swung into view.

'This is it.' Nikola led her over to where a light leaked dimly from a narrow window. He gave the pane a couple of sharp raps and waited. Slow, heavy movements could be heard from inside as if a beast had been roused in its lair. Gradually, scattered sounds gathered to one source. The door swung open and a bull-necked young man blocked out most of the feeble light.

'Da!' a defiant bellow as if he were warding off an attack. While they couldn't make out his face, he could evidently see theirs for it seemed to dawn on him gradually that one of his Serb teachers and a female friend were paying him an unexpected visit. After a hearty 'Zdravo', he extended a hand of greeting, then ushered Nikola and his companion in.

'This is Mrs Radford – you know, Jack's wife,' in English.

'Aha,' blowing out his cheeks. 'Zdravo – I mean, Hello. I'm Slobodan,' crushing her hand.

'Pleased to meet you,' yet not so pleased about her fingers.

They filed into a ramshackle room with a discoloured iron bedstead, broken-backed chair and chipped washstand all crowded into the narrow space. The none-too savoury smell of boiled beans rose to Mary's nostrils. She looked down at the bare floor and saw the student's evening meal simmering on a one-ring stove. Raising her head, she took in the walls with their stuck-up pictures of Red-Star Belgrade, Bruce Lee and barely-clad, large breasted women, above a 'bookshelf' – an unvarnished plank laid on two piles of brick, the six or so titles lost along its wooden length. While she lowered herself gingerly onto the chair, Nikola sat on the bed and Slobodan stood, looking ruefully down at his beans. His large stomach would just have to wait.

'Don't you ever eat in student canteen?'

'Me? Canteen?' snorting. 'Pah, even pigs wouldn't eat there.'

'Look, Slobodan, Mrs Radford wants to find out what you know about Jack.'

'Ah, Jack,' chuckling at the memory. 'I am good drinker, 'specially slivovitz, but I even couldn't drink same as him. I guess, by end I didn't want to anyway: he was in bad state – body, brain, clothes. He didn't smell too good then. It was summer, so we drank mostly out of doors, but still it wasn't fun, 'specially if breeze blows at you. His shirt, jeans more and more got dirty. Then his mind stopped working right. You couldn't have good chats anymore. His words kept moving off – somewhere, I don't know. It was sad because before he was big fun – jokes, stories, gossip.'

'But did no one do anything to help?'

'To help Jack not easy – not possible maybe. By end he rowed with everyone, everyone – me as well. He swore at you, kept on giving you insults. Then he got – how you say? – *paranoja*.'

'It's the same in English: paranoia.'

'Yes, he was talking all time about "enemy"; he thought someone wants to kill him. At last, he said to world – excuse my words, "Fuck off, leave me alone." Everyone – friends also – were hurt, angry, therefore stayed from him. So he was drinking with himself in dirty bars, talking to himself, shouting, cursing – in Serbo-Croat, English.'

'I suppose, then, you didn't see him just before he went missing?'

'In fact, I did – one night in centre. Really I didn't want to talk. He'd shouted all over campus I was pederast, liking blond boys twelve years or so. Ha, ridiculous! Me: boys! Ha! Any case, you can't find blond boys in Kosovo, so very stupid rubbish to say. But as I spoke to him, I saw he didn't remember anything he'd said. Still, I wanted to get away before I punch him. I was still too angry. So I said very little words, just asked him couple of polite questions – like if he's doing anything for summer holiday.'

'Summer holiday! Did he say anything?'

'Well, I wasn't listening much,' stroking his beard as he replied to Mary, 'but I think, now I'm not sure, he said he go to Prizren.'

'Prizren! That's odd! Why not the Adriatic or somewhere abroad like Greece or Italy?'

'After he disappear, I thought on his words. Now I'm not certain – we drank helluva lot that night three, four months before – but I think he said something about woman he knows – that she lives in Prizren. Maybe he went to see her.'

'But how do we find this woman? There must be hundreds like her in town.'

'No. One only.'

'What do you mean?'

'Well, it's in my mind that Jack say she was Croat or Slovene, something like that – not Serb for sure. She went abroad, I think. New Zealand, could be. Australia? Anyway, married there, seem to think divorced, after came back.'

'If she was a Croat or Slovene, why did she land up in Prizren of all places?'

'Don't know, but I feel it wasn't work. Oh, yes, one more thing. It's funny: Jack used to joke how bad was my English and I

think he said this woman was only other person in Kosovo
to speak English well – better – sorry, sir! – than my college
teachers.'
'It's OK, he said same to me.'
'But do you think the police know about this?'
'Shouldn't think so,' shaking his large head. 'For me, I tell
them nothing.'
On their return to the taxi Slobodan led the way with a tiny
torch in his big paw, its pencil of light dimly suggesting the
terrain. The student waved them off and slowly turned to
make his way back to his beans.
'Do you think we can find this woman?'
'Won't be as easy as he says, but we should. Tonight I ring
my cousin – he lives in Prizren – get him to ask people. If he
has luck, I should know something tomorrow – afternoon or
evening.'
'Great.' In no time, it seemed to Mary, the car re-entered
familiar territory – the High Street. She was beginning to
develop a mental map of the way buildings, side streets,
crossings panned out from the Grand. As the taxi turned
into the hotel, Mary offered to pay the fare or at least split it,
but Nikola would have none of it, almost became angry as if
paying were a matter of honour.
*Is it because I'm a guest or a woman? Or both?* 'Well, thanks
for all your help. So, I'll probably be hearing from you some
time tomorrow.'
Nikola merely nodded, turned, then walked briskly away.

Mary was down in the lobby early next morning, hoping,
as there was so much to discuss, Nuhi wouldn't keep her
waiting; but he did. Indeed, after ten minutes he was starting
to be uncharacteristically late. She drummed her fingers on
the sofa's arms and looked restlessly around.
*Why do hotel lobbies always seem so anonymous? And why
are receptionists forever pretending to be busy, heads down as
if they're checking something really important? Oh, where's*

*he got to? Where is he?*

As soon as Nuhi came through the sliding doors, she was up off her chair and speeding over the carpet towards him. He seemed disconcerted by her animation.

'Mary?' cautiously.

'Look, Nuhi, I saw your colleague, Nikola. last night. We talked.'

'Oh yes.'

'He had so much to say about Jack. Why didn't you tell me any of that?'

'I, er, didn't want to hurt you.'

'That may have been so at the start, but after seeing the flat...?'

'What do you mean?'

'Well, after that, it was clear the sort of state Jack was in, wasn't it?'

'I ... I suppose I just didn't want to face it.'

'But why?'

'It's just too embarrassing. You see, when things started to go wrong, I tried to shut my eyes. I should've done something, I know, but it was easier to pretend nothing was going on. Then, when it got worse, it became too tricky to do anything – without, that is, calling in the British Council and that would have been a big loss of face. In the end I did, in fact, write them a letter, saying we didn't want Jack anymore, but didn't give any reason.'

'Wouldn't they need to contact Jack, though?'

'Yes, but after they'd failed to and turned to me, I could say he'd moved out without telling me where. I thought I'd be clear of the whole thing.'

'Well, it certainly hasn't worked out that way, has it? Jack hasn't turned up anywhere and the British Embassy have had to be called in.'

'I know. It couldn't have been worse: police, British Embassy, and now you – no, of course, it's been very nice to see you, but it would've been better in other circumstances.'

'Quite.... Look, Nuhi, from what Nikola and a student told me

I can see why you didn't want to talk. Jack, I hear, was very ... unpleasant to Albanians.'

'"Unpleasant", much more than that! In his last term he was screaming at every Albanian he met in the faculty. The women students were terrified. Then in the evening after more drinks he'd stagger to the halls of residence and shout— in English, though enough could understand. "You Albanian men" – excuse my words – "are a load of bum-boys, walking round hand in hand, arm in arm, handbags on wrists." These were ... unwise words. Albanian men can, you know, get very angry.'

'So I've heard.'

'I think the worse was a department party after the graduation ceremony. He hadn't been invited – well, he hadn't taught for a month or so – but he must have heard about it somehow. Anyway, he turned up – this was the afternoon – drunk, beer stains on his shirt, trouser buttons open. We didn't know what to do. Though no one wanted him there, for some reason – I don't know why – we never thought of showing him the door. So he stayed. First, he went straight to the drinks and gulped down a couple of lozovača. They hit him quite hard; he wobbled, but didn't fall. We were looking on with a mixture of horror and disgust. Jack turned on us and started leering randomly at the female staff, bothering one after the other. He smelt of alcohol, sweat and unwashed clothes, but still seemed to think it was good idea to lean into every woman's face and say – excuse me –, "Do you fuck? Do you fuck?"'

'Gross!'

'Yes. Now it wasn't a general question, but sort of grotesque invitation, said with aggression like a poke with a baton. To young teachers it was bad enough, but to the sixty-year-old senior lecturer he ended up with it was terrible, just terrible.'

'Oh no, he didn't! Look ... I'm so sorry. All I can say is he was never like that when he was with me. Drink, I suppose, brought out his worst side, a side I never – thankfully – knew.'

'It seems so. Well, everyone stood in shocked silence, while

Jack went on his round, totally blind to the effect he was having. But, in the end, we did come to life – as if a spell had been broken – and instead of asking Jack to leave, we all left. This may have been just what he wanted – to be alone with the drinks; but he only had a couple of minutes because as soon as I was in the corridor, I asked the cleaner if she'd clear the bottles away. That was the last time I saw Jack. After what he'd said and done, I didn't really want to have anything to do with him – ever. In fact, I even started avoiding the places he haunted in case he were there.'

'Totally understandable, totally understandable. Look,' placing a hand lightly on his arm, 'I can see how painful this is for you. Maybe we should get going.'

'Thank you, yes.' They left the lobby and ducked through fine drizzle before reaching the car. Its windscreen wipers moving rhythmically back and forth, Nuhi's Zastava pushed out into moderate traffic and headed towards the department. The nearer the car drove the mistier it got.

Just as Mary was, with great relief, starting on the final items, there was a knock on the door. Nikola entered, a rare smile on his face.

'Good news! My cousin found woman. You want to see her?'

'Oh yes!'

'Well, coach leaves for Prizren each hour. Decide the one you want and my cousin says he'll meet you and take you to her house.'

'That's great! Thanks a lot. Let's see: what about ... 10 tomorrow morning?'

'Fine.'

'But how do I get to the coach station?'

'*Nema problema*! I take you. I'll be in hotel lobby at 9.30. OK? But you mustn't be late or you lose seat.'

'Don't worry, I'll be on time. See you tomorrow and, again, many thanks.'

He nodded and left.

*Overall, Priština may be a bit lacking, but its people are so helpful, even the ones that at first look as if they hate you.... This woman tomorrow, I wonder what she'll be like. Well, at least we'll have no trouble understanding each other, if her English is as good as Jack said. Was that why he visited her – to have a relaxed chat without worrying about making his sentences as simple as he could – or was there another reason? Were they lovers? Hard to credit, given Jack's state at the end, but earlier? It'll be interesting to see what she looks like. Small, I expect, with short black hair and olive skin. Yes, I'm sure if he'd have wanted to get as far from my type as possible. She's probably demure, very quiet, a proper little woman.*

Another knock interrupted her thoughts. There stood Nuhi, holding a tray of coffee with all the patience of a waiter. She couldn't help laughing.

'I'm sorry, Nuhi. It just suddenly struck me you've, at last, found your true vocation.'

He looked crestfallen.

*Oh dear, my big mouth again.* 'Nuhi, I was only joking. Don't take it so seriously.... Look, you've been very kind over the past couple of days, and I'd like to repay some of that by inviting you to a meal tonight at the hotel.'

'Mary, you don't need to, you know.'

'Oh, but I want to. And it might make up a little for all Jack did.'

'None of that was your fault.'

'No, but Jack and I are still technically married, you know.'

'Yes, but separated and Jack was acting independently.... Anyway, it's very kind of you. I'd be delighted.'

'Shall we meet in the lobby at 7?'

'Fine.'

She turned and gestured to the piles rearranged around the room.

'Not much more now. Should be finished by two.'

'Good. See you then.'

*That cheered him a bit, cheered me too. All this stuff has stirred up so many feelings, feelings that war with each other. Yes, Jack and I were happy – weren't we? – at the start, but look how it ended. Oh, it's all such a waste! Well, maybe tonight I'll be able to forget for a while, forget before, I'm sure, more stress tomorrow.*

Back in his room Nuhi was again thinking of Mary. It almost seemed as if he'd been doing that and nothing else ever since their first meeting and this was no different, except now he was aware of his habit. How had this happened? It was strange, but he found the invitation and its meaning kept coming back to his thoughts. Was she just being polite? Or was it something more, a coded message? It implied she liked him, and not just as a sympathetic ear in stressful times, that she wanted to be with him beyond what was strictly required. He smiled as he realised that although he'd been looking down at Saussure's lecture notes, he'd not taken in a single word. Structural linguistics! Dry as the paper it was printed on. He'd better, more human, things to think about.

When he went down to the basement at a quarter to two, he was pleased to see that Mary had finished and was ready to go. Looking down, he noticed a vast disparity between the tiny heap of things she'd keep and the piles behind it, climbing high up the walls. 'Are you sure that's all you want?'

'Sure. The other things would depress me – or I wouldn't be able to find space for them in my flat. It's not very big, you know, and there are three of us.'

'OK, now you still have the afternoon left. What would you like to do? Rest? Go shopping? See the sights?'

*What would distract me best?* 'Sightseeing, I think. How about that battlefield out of town you were talking about? But do you think a taxi there and back would be very pricey?'

'Well, it might be once they saw you were a tourist. Look, I've no classes this afternoon; I'd be happy to show you round.'

'Oh, that's kind of you, Nuhi, but I don't want to put you to any trouble.'

'No trouble at all! But it won't be easy to see much of Kosovo Polje today – that is, unless the mist's cleared.' Yet when they left the windowless basement for the entrance, they found the mist had, if anything, thickened. With sinking hearts, therefore, they climbed into the car.

'I know the weather's not great,' with the air of a Polar explorer, 'but could we still have a look at that battlefield?'

'We could try.'

Swirls of grey silently bombarded the windscreen, one after another, as they drove carefully from town, headlights full on. Cars and lorries coming at them out of the mist seemed strangely disembodied as if colliding with them would be as harmless as cloud on cloud. The bare silver birch and odd house they glimpsed at the roadside appeared equally unreal – mere sepia prints from the old days, images of a past that would never come back. The outside's unreliability made the car's inside seem all the more trustworthy. Mary tried to forget her basement feelings with light chat and jokes; Nuhi chuckled and chuckled, finding everything funny, trying a few witty remarks of his own.

They were now past all habitation, snaking over a vast plain, which came in glimpses only to be snatched away by the next drift. Eventually, they drew up at a sign that pointed off the road into white nothingness. They got out and stared into the formless fluctuations.

'Well, we can see hardly anything, but it was near here, almost six-hundred years ago, that the battle took place. Two armies – about 20,000 Serbs, I think, and some 40,000 Turks – were caught between two rivers: Lab over here and Sitnica there, to the right. Though I'm no Serb and they'll never thank me for it, I must say they put up a good fight. They were defeated, of course, but still left the Turks with big losses: Sultan Murad and hundreds of begs and janissaries were killed. It was – how do you say? – a Pyrrhic victory. It really weakened the Turks; they only got as far as the gates of Vienna and were then turned back.'

Nuhi and Mary walked through the mist down a dirt path, sensing a huge tract of land beyond.

'It must have been a terrible sight after the battle: bodies and bits of bodies everywhere. No wonder they call this place the Field of Blackbirds. You can imagine the flocks flying down and pecking at the corpses. So much blood ran, it was said, the grass turned red and a few days later peonies grew out of the ground. Every spring you can come here and walk through field on field of red flowers.'

Suddenly out of shifting indeterminacy a square stone tower reared. The crenellations at the top and slit windows for archers at the side made it seem more like the corner of a medieval castle.

'How old is this?'

'Oh, only about twenty years.'

'What!'

'It was put up by the Serbs after the War of Liberation as a memorial to their heroes. The Muslim monuments are a little way over to the left.'

They moved off in that direction, the all-but-blind, led by memory, leading the blind. Soon a building looking more like a church with its square base, hexagonal roof and dome filtered into view; but instead of a gold cross on top, there was a crescent moon, pointing to the sky.

'They buried the Sultan's heart here, but took his body back to Turkey – to Bursa, I think. Can you make out that smaller mausoleum over there?'

'Oh, yes.'

'That's where the Turkish commander and his flag and shield-bearer are buried.'

They retraced their steps to the car and drove carefully back to town, Mary trying to imagine that ancient battle: the charging horses in different heraldic colours, swarms of arrows, hand-to-hand fighting with sword and mace. 'Infidel' against 'pagan', slaughtering each other, slicing off heads, arms, legs, unleashing streams of blood and all for gods they thought lived somewhere above the horizon. Or was it the desire to invade or defend territory that drove them on or, men being men, to kill everything facing them just because it stood in their way? Mary thought of the Balkans, so often, it seemed, the scene of slaughter, now unusually quiet, but for how long? The car drove tentatively through vast, impersonal skeins of mist, out of which medieval deadheads had once lunged and hacked. The Yugoslavs, the South Slavs – a warrior people. Slaughter-skills, once learnt, weren't easy to forget.

'Do you have national service here?'

'Yes, eighteen months, but if you're in university just twelve.'

'Only the men.'

'Yes, though the women do a short course, learning how to use guns.'

'So everyone's a potential guerrilla?'

'True, but we must be: we have enemies.'

'What – you mean the Soviet Union?'

'That's right. We're the part of the empire that got away. When they went into Czechoslovakia, their tanks rolled right up to the border. We all thought they were going to carry on into Yugoslavia. We were on red alert. Everyone rushed to the arms dumps, hidden in each town and village, claimed their rifles and took up positions, but nothing happened.'

'What about the Americans?'

'They wouldn't invade. Their empire ends in Western Europe. They encourage us in order to weaken the Soviets – anything to hurt "the commies" – but they seem to forget, we're "commies" as well.'

'Yes, but nicer ones!'

'Still, friendly as the Americans are, they're not real friends. We're stuck between two warring blocs. That's why Tito set up the non-aligned movement – you know, with Egypt, India and others.'

The plain's implicit vastness narrowed to avenues of trees, the odd house, then suburbs. Priština began to fill the windscreen, lent romance by the mist's soft suggestiveness. The car wound up narrow suburban lanes that seemed to Mary to be near Slobodan's digs and came to a halt on a hill that looked out on a city coming and going in the swirls. Blurredly monumental, a large mosque stood to the left, rectangular at its base, but covered by a dome and flanked by a slender minaret.

'This is the Fatih mosque – built, in around the fifteenth century by Mehmet II, more than a hundred years after the battle.'

They left the car, entered the porch and, at the door, took off their shoes. Islami searched round and found a cloth.

'Sorry, you have to cover your head.'

'Oh ... but why?'

'In here men mustn't have any thoughts that aren't holy.' Just as Mary was about to protest, a contrary impulse took her: she should, instead, respect local customs, even if she thought them wrong-headed. So, her red hair smothered in white, she let Nuhi lead her over to a spiral staircase to the left of the entrance. 'You can't go out on the main floor – sorry.'

'And why not?'

'Women aren't allowed there.'

*It gets worse and worse: gender apartheid!*

They reached the upper level and came to a wooden door with something in Arabic written on it.

'Here we are.'

Nuhi pushed open the door and they entered a darkened space with a large, closely-latticed screen at the far end. Mary picked her way between cushions to reach it and peered through narrow gaps in the wood. The floor beneath was bare now, but presumably during a service the women could see the mullah at the front, while men, if their attention strayed from the sermon, might turn and look up at the lattice, yet see nothing inside.

*Screened off. Religious purdah. Holy harem without the sex. Men, the important ones, commanding the roomy space below; women, their dependents, cramped and caged above.*

*Oh god, how depressing!*
Yet as she looked down, across and up, she found to her
surprise that the vast interior wasn't gloomy at all, was, in
fact, uplifting in its soaring sobriety. A huge empty space,
enclosed by light-brown stone, yearned for the sky beyond.
Sealed from the outer world, made austere by the absence of
human imagery, it reached toward the impalpable.
*Why are women wickered off from all this aspiration,
separated as if unclean? Maybe they believe women are of
the earth, not the sky. Maybe it's that Near-Eastern thing. I
remember a friend telling me Jewish women aren't allowed
inside synagogues during periods. Patriarchy! Patriarchy!
What are men afraid of? That the caged women will look up
to the ceiling and demand some of that spaciousness or look
down on line on line of praying menfolk, sticking backsides in
the air, and laugh? How could a Muslim boy learn to think of
women as equals when he sees his mother and sisters treated
like this?*
She turned with a sigh and followed Nuhi's back as he left
the room and descended the stairwell. Again she valued his
tact in saying nothing when he could see she was upset, for
knowing whatever words he used wouldn't be quite right.
Once they were a reasonable distance from the porch, she
turned and let out a sudden laugh of recognition as she looked
up at the mosque, shrouded in grey mist. For all its puritanical
disdain for human flesh, for all its shunning of any contact of
the sexes, the dome and minaret reminded her of nothing so
much as a breast and phallus. Her sense of the sheer irony of it
all so overcame her she just couldn't stop laughing. Nuhi ran
over and grasped her shoulders as if to stop her from falling.
'What's the matter?'
His eyes looked so genuinely concerned that she stopped
laughing and planted a kiss of gratitude on his lips. At first
he seemed taken aback. She, for her part, tried to sober up,
realising the gesture could be seen as meaning more than it
did. He clearly took the fullest sense for he returned the kiss,

adding extra of his own. She broke away, panting, trying to collect herself.

Mary's first thought was to protest, but when she recalled the kisses, she couldn't say they were unwelcome. In fact, they spoke to something in her, more strongly the more she thought of them. She did really like Nuhi, didn't she? More than like. And this was all harmless, wasn't it? So why not? But was it harmless? From that eager look in his eyes you could tell the kisses were for him just the start. And if they led to other things, what then of his wife? As a sign of solidarity Mary would never knowingly hurt another woman, but in this case would the wife be hurt? No, because she'd never find out: they could enjoy themselves and Nuhi could still get back home in good time. And in a couple of days she'd be gone for good. Everything over and forgotten. But what of her 'husband'? Of course, she hadn't exactly been faithful since the split, but why should she? It was Jack, after all, who'd walked out. So what was she supposed to do: devote all her life to nursing and the kids like some kind of secular nun? Then there was Roger, but they'd always had an open relationship. So why not? Why not let Nuhi do what he wants? There was no need to worry about getting pregnant. Her coil had worked for the past four years and would, no doubt, work again that afternoon.

Nothing seemed to be holding her back, so she put her arms round Nuhi's waist and let him kiss her again, not only on the lips, but also the cheeks, the forehead and, by lifting her hair, the nape of her neck. For her part she returned kisses of her own and thrust a thigh between his legs to feel his hardened aspiration. Out of the unreal mist here was something solid.

They lay side by side, breathing fast, smiling. Their clothes had been discarded or pulled off at various stages across the room like clues to a crime that was no crime, but such was the room's central heating and their recent activity that they were far from cold; indeed, their flushed bodies shone. Neither had made love so repeatedly and so enjoyably in the last year. Mary had been surprised at the potency of a man approaching middle-age; it made Jack's – and most of the British men's she'd slept with – seem decidedly low octane. And then, perhaps more surprisingly, there was his finesse. She'd expected a smash-and-grab, an all-out rush to get what he wanted and never mind her; in fact, he'd been as considerate as in everyday life, patiently waiting for her to be roused and open to whatever she wanted to try.

*Was he always like that in bed with his wife – oh dear, maybe I shouldn't have! – or is he on his best behaviour?*

Nuhi was equally surprised. He'd heard western women were very liberated, but he'd assumed that was in areas of attitude and social manner, that once they were in bed they'd be like his wife, lying on their backs, waiting for him to do his thing, as if his attentions were suffered, not enjoyed. But, no, Mary was as active as him, initiating as well as receiving, searching for her pleasure as well as helping him find his. And how she helped him! He'd never been in bed with someone like her. She didn't seem to have any inhibitions. What was Jack's problem, why couldn't he get on with her? She was everything a man could hope for: smart, lively and, on top of that, really good-looking!

So satisfied were they with each other, it did not matter one body was slightly flabby at the waist and the other had stretch marks on belly and thigh. These were honourable badges of experience that folk display in middle age. Who was it claimed only the young and well-proportioned could love? Who said like attracted like? Two bodies, one 'Christian', the other 'Muslim', lay side by side in a bliss that was beyond denomination, but not belief.

Nikola was getting anxious: it was already half-past nine. He paced up and down the foyer for a few more seconds, then strode over to the reception and asked if he could use the phone to call Room 351. He let it ring and ring, but there was no answer. She couldn't still be asleep, surely. He put the phone down and, seeing both lifts were in use, rushed up three flights of stairs to her floor. Mary was woken by some sort of loud sound; she reached out for Nuhi, then remembered he'd left her to get back to his wife before his absence became suspicious. As her head cleared, she decoded the noise as knocking. *Who can that be? A cleaner, but surely, she wouldn't carry on so or come this early. Nuhi? Can't be. It's – what? – 6 or 7.* She rolled over to one side and screwed her eyes up to read the clock. *God! Twenty-five to ten.... Nikola! Oh dear!* She stumbled out of bed and into the bathroom. The towels from their joint shower were all over the place. She picked up the one nearest and wrapped it around, mildly shuddering at its warm dampness. Having shuffled out into the bedroom and over to the door, she opened it just enough to peer out. Yes, it was Nikola!

'I'm so sorry, must've overslept – right through the alarm.'

'And through phone call too.'

'God, yes, I must've been well away: I was that tired, you couldn't believe it. Look, I'm not even up yet, so I don't see how I can make the 10 o'clock bus.'

'Don't worry; it's alright. We have to forget ticket, get another for 11. I'll go ring my cousin, tell him to wait for next bus.'

'Sorry, sorry – for all the inconvenience. I'll pay for both tickets, of course.'

'No, no, you're guest.'

By 10.40 they were down at the coach station. Mary was now seeing more of Priština's other side. Her route had taken her behind the high back wall of the Grand's car park to an area she had no chance to scan before as her room faced the main street. It was altogether less impressive. A huge wasteland of mud, broken by odd clumps of grass, stretched out before her like some Outward-Bound course whose footholds a fine rain was making ever more treacherous. She wondered how she could get across without caking her jeans when she noticed narrow paths, made out of discoloured planks, laid across the mire, which, though soggy, would at least prove less of a hazard than the mud beneath. Their wooden way took them past the international press block, a shell unfinished and seemingly abandoned, and on to a nondescript side road with crowds, largely of men and boys, trudging back and forth over its muddy surface. Three hundred yards along they turned into the most dismal bus station Mary had ever seen. On one side stood a row of three metallic boxes, like huge upturned coffins with windows, selling an array of sweets, magazines and nick-knacks that looked old or second-hand. Next to them a double box with male and female signs upon two doors signalled the toilets. The men's side seemed to have overflowed after a blockage, if Mary judged right from the seepage. She thought of temporary loos on a bad day at rock festivals. Overused, under-cleaned, their rank smell hit travellers as they bought items at the kiosks and stayed as they moved on to the ticket office, the largest metallic box of all. On entering, Mary was confronted with a space, empty of fittings, except for a circular booth in the middle. There was nowhere to sit and although the floor was covered with trampled dirt, scraps of newspapers and wrappings of grilled food, female travellers still squatted round the edge or propped themselves against the wall. Their menfolk were valiantly battling on their behalf at the small central hatches. A scrum had formed at each aperture selling tickets for a coach soon to depart, a scrum which refused to unknit. Men were pushing from the back and sides; others, having bought their prized ticket, were struggling valiantly against the oncomers to get out. No one wanted to give way because others would immediately move into the space you'd vacated. Around the edges men were waving arms in the air, shouting, trying to attract the attention of a friend near the front so he'd buy a ticket without them having to queue. It was an arena of pure strength; no wonder the women and children stayed out. The unluckiest were the men with cases, but with no one to guard them. When a new gap appeared, they were too laden to take advantage and, as a result, far from advancing, seemed to be slowly forced back.

'I show you how to get ticket. Watch!'

Ignoring the tail of the scrum, Nikola followed its edge till he was level with the ticket window. Every time a new ticket was bought he'd shove inwards, forming a wedge between the window and the strugglers. In a remarkably short while he'd prised his way to the ticket slot and, ignoring protests from behind, bought a return ticket and fought his way out.

'There you are,' proudly handing it over. 'You see: teachers aren't so useless – well, not useless like your Bernard Shaw said.'

'Oh, what was that?'

'Something like: if you can, you do; if you can't, you teach.'

'Ha-ha, very cynical! Still it doesn't apply to you, does it? Thanks for the ticket.'

'*Nema problema.* Oh, by the way return time is left open, so you can come back when you want. Coach leaves in ten minutes. Let's get out of here.'

Bora waited in Prizren Bus Station for the coach to come. It was called a bus station, though really – as he was reminded, looking round – it was no more than a patch of dirt where coaches stopped or turned round, a plot without facilities, which under a steady drizzle was now imperceptibly turning into a quagmire. He pulled his collar up, forced hands hard into his pockets and moved even closer to the tree trunk for extra protection.

He ought really to be back at his office in Jugobanka, but there wasn't much to do that morning or, indeed, any morning. Sometimes he wondered whether the bank really needed to open a Prizren branch; all the work could have been done from Priština; but who was he to argue with Belgrade's superior wisdom, particularly as it gave him a job in a beautiful and – despite the overwhelming Albanian presence – friendly little town. He hadn't bothered to learn Albanian, but why should he? This was part of Yugoslavia – wasn't it? – 'the land of the South Slavs'. So knowledge of Slavic should be enough. And then this city had been King Milutin's capital. If you couldn't speak Serbo-Croat here and be understood, where could you? The odd Western tourist wandering into the bank generally spoke German, so he rarely used English, which was just as well because his grip on that language was very shaky, unlike Nikola's. Now there was a linguist! He was always the brainy one, good at any subject.

*Luckily, the woman's house isn't that far from here, but this Mary and I are still bound to have awkward silences. How can I get round that? Tricky! Wait, why don't I point out places of interest as we go by? I do know the English for things like 'crkva' and 'džamija'. Yes, that should do it.... Well, I doubt the trip'll be of any value for this Mary. I mean, will she actually learn anything when she gets to the house? The Croat woman won't know much, surely. This Jack can't have visited Prizren that often or I'd have seen him or, at least, heard of him. Little happens here without me knowing it. I gather he was a good drinker and I myself like the odd tumbler of lozovača, but I've never come across him in any bar or cafe. And then he was meant to have been in a bad way, yet I've never heard talk of any stranger, staggering round the streets of Prizren, looking like a tramp. He could've gone straight to her house, of course, and stayed inside. Like a rest home ... a retreat ... a love nest? Surely not with the state he was in. And then her mother and daughter live there as well. Hardly the right spot for nights of passion. And with all that drinking I don't reckon he'd be up to much passion anyway. Maybe it wasn't any of these. Maybe it was a shared religion, maybe he was Catholic too. Or maybe it was just a cultural thing, similar Western values, or a family thing – him playing the role of father. Unlikely!*

He looked down at his watch.

*Already ten minutes late. What can have kept them? They've so few stops and, usually, there's little traffic? I could drive*

*here in something like thirty minutes without pushing it.*
Just as he was thinking that, a wet coach, its wipers slowly moving grime across the windscreen and back, inched into the station.
*Right: a redhead, Nikola said. That should be easy.*

Mary looked through lines of rain running down the window and out onto a barren tract of dirt. *So this is Prizren,* without much enthusiasm. Her delicious languor, on waking, had all but dissipated in the rushed rising, the muddy slog to Priština's coach station and the ticket office's challenging fug. Then there were the coach smells: unwashed bodies, unwrapped grills and a pregnant woman being sick into a brown paper bag. That wouldn't have been a problem had the windows not been clamped shut and firmly reshut whenever a passenger had the temerity to open one – 'breezes spread diseases', she presumed, was the local wisdom. The atmosphere was further thickened by dust rising from the seats. Mary prided herself on being a good traveller, but even she had on one occasion to fight back sick rising towards her throat. On top of this, she'd been unable to find distraction from her queasy stomach by noting the passing scenery. Condensation misted the windows and in no time, after wiping the one nearest her, it would cloud over again. In the end, she closed her eyes and tried to sleep, but the coach was more a country bus, rackety, uncushioned. So she sat there, bracing herself against the next jolt and breathing through her mouth.
Yet, the ordeal was over; she was thankful it had only been an hour. As she stepped down from the coach, refreshing rain replaced the fug, broad sky the cramped space. Where was Nikola's cousin? Hastily tugging at her anorak's hood, she looked from face to face, taking in the small knot of people waiting to greet passengers. A tall, middle-aged man, slightly detached, seeking cover under a tree, seemed to be staring intently at her. *Is that him?* The answer came almost immediately: he moved gingerly over the mud towards her

before inquiring, 'Mary?' though it sounded to her ears more like 'Merry'.

'Yes. That's me.'

'Bora,' pointing to himself.

'Pleased to meet you, Bora.'

'We go?' extending his right arm in the direction of the woman's place.

The couple carefully traversed the mire, tackier by the minute, until they reached the safety of a pavement. They set off down the road, but within a hundred yards Bora was pointing left, 'Church.'

Though still travel-dazed, Mary dutifully turned her head to take in a light-brown, stone basilica with five cupolas and a tall bell-tower. From the large lock on the gate that denied access into the open porch and the general dereliction she guessed it was disused. *Maybe the Communists have banned all religious worship. The mosque yesterday didn't exactly seem to be functioning. If they've imposed a blanket ban, good for them. The world has far too much religion as it is.*

Further down the street Bora again pointed to the left.

'Turk *hamman* – how you say?'

As he didn't know the word, he mimed washing his trunk and face.

'Ah, got it: Turkish baths!'

She looked to Bora's left at another light-brown, stone building, but much squatter this time with seven small and two slightly-larger cupolas rising just above the rectangular base like mushrooms from the forest floor. Again it was closed and appeared much in need of repair.

As they were crossing a quaint hump-backed bridge over the Bistrica, Bora pointed up to ruined towers on a hill, overlooking the town. 'Castel – Czar Dušan.'

*Comforting or ominous?* Mary wondered. *Did it protect the town or just keep it quiet?*

Once over the bridge, they turned off into narrow, twisting lanes past traditional homes with projecting upper floors.

Eventually, they came to a more modern, white-stucco structure, surmounted by a red-tiled roof, which was separated from the rest. What really distinguished it and gave it a touch of the West was a front garden. Mary couldn't help smiling as she looked across to a small rectangle of grass, surrounded on three sides by flower beds: it was so out of place. Bora stopped at the garden gate and extended his arm towards the house. 'This!'

He strode up to the front door and gave its knocker a firm rap. There were sounds of movement inside and in no time the door opened. The woman revealed was, as Mary predicted, very different from her: smaller, more formally dressed; wider-faced with black hair pulled back from the forehead in a tight topknot; but this slightly-severe appearance was allayed by gentle eyes and a broad smile.

'Hi, I'm Liljana.' The hostess greeted Mary by spreading her arms and hugging her.

After extricating herself at last, the visitor completed the introductions, 'And I'm Mary.'

'You must be soaked, both of you! Come on in and have a cup of tea!'

Bora lifted a hand like a policeman controlling traffic. 'Sorry. Must go. Have work in bank. Bye-bye!'

Mary was therefore led alone down a short passage and into the living-room. After gesturing for her guest to sit in the armchair nearest the fire, Liljana bustled off to make tea, leaving Mary free to take in the whole room at her leisure. Heavy, she would have called the table and chairs – almost Victorian, in fact. The walls were similarly dense in their cluttered decoration with folksy paintings claiming almost every available inch. Most were of mountains, islands, and men and women in the previous century's starchy clothes; but there was also a religious section with pictures of the Holy Family and saints she didn't recognise.

Liljana carefully carried in a large tray, laden with tea pot, milk jug, crockery and cake.

'I'm moving around as quietly as I can. You see, my mother's sleeping upstairs and she's not, generally, a good sleeper, so I don't want to wake her.'

'Should I keep my voice down?'

'If you don't mind.'

'And where's your daughter?'

'Oh, Ivana! She's off at school – junior school.'

Silence.

'I couldn't help noticing how many pictures you've hung on the walls.'

'All done by my great-grandfather,' with a smile of satisfaction. 'He loved to paint whenever he had a moment free. Our family used to live on the Dalmatian coast – in Split – so sea and mountains were all around.'

'You're a bit far from that now, aren't you?'

Liljana glanced up from the task of setting out cups and plates with a guarded look as if she suspected Mary of probing, but soon her face relaxed into its old smile.

'Here, try a piece of cake. It's a traditional recipe. We call it *Madjarica*, "Hungarian Girl". I've no idea why.... OK, so you'd like to know why we're here. Well, when my father was a hotel manager in Split, he had many difficulties with the authorities and wanted to get out. Then he happened to hear they were looking for someone to run Hotel Teranda, the biggest hotel in Prizren. It was a long way off and a very different culture, but – maybe in desperation – he applied and to his surprise got the job. So he and my mother moved down here, living first at the hotel, then in this house.'

'You weren't with them, then?'

'No, no, I was working in Australia ... Adelaide. In fact, I got married over there, but the marriage ... well, didn't last and around that time my father died, a sudden heart attack. Quite a year, that! My mother's health's never been good and I'm the only child, so I had to come back – along with my daughter. That'd be – what? – four years ago and I've been working as a secretary in Famipa, a catering company, ever since.'

Silence.

'I suppose it can't have been easy to fit in. I mean ... you're a Croat, aren't you? And you know the West. But here, it seems, it's mostly Albanians and Serbs who've never left the country.'

'Oh, you'd be surprised: many have. Unlike Eastern–Bloc countries, we're allowed to work abroad. I'm a case in point. But, yes, you're right: it wasn't easy, so you just have to make the effort. Me, for instance, I've been trying to learn Albanian. Hard, I can tell you. It's a totally different language from Serbo-Croat.... You know, I just feel that all the nationalities have got to find ways of getting on with each other – or the country will break up. I mean, it's so easy to be suspicious and then your suspicion turns to hate, but hate won't get us anywhere – except civil war.'

'Yes, I came across a Serb the other day who seems to hate all Albanians.'

'That's no good. Look, I'm not saying we Croats are any better. For instance, we have a proverb: "You can drink with a Serb, eat with a Serb, but you can't turn your back on a Serb".' Mary laughed. 'Yes, it *is* funny, isn't it? But we've got to get beyond that, we can't keep churning out the same old prejudices.'

Again silence.

*Friendly, welcoming and all that, yet a little reserved. It's as if she's not against letting go of information, but you've got to coax it out. Maybe she's shy.*

'Did you first meet Jack here in Prizren?'

'Yes, totally by chance. I'd just been shopping with Ivana in Liria and we were walking across the main square, speaking English because, then, her Serbo-Croat wasn't up to much. We were passing this man – blond hair, Western clothes, obviously a foreigner – and as we were going by, he turned with a smile and said, "You know, that's the first time I've heard English spoken properly in Kosovo." And then he added with a wink, "Even though it's with an Aussie accent." I liked his cheeky attitude: it reminded me of the banter I'd heard in

Adelaide. So, anyway, we got talking and I don't know how, but we found ourselves wandering back to this place. I invited him in for some tea – a bit like you, I suppose! But I can tell you that was the last cuppa he ever had in my house; he drank a lot of other liquids, mind you, but no more tea.'

'Yes, I wondered about that – the drinking.'

'Well.... Look, each time he came to me he seemed a little worse. I found it sad, so sad, but also – I must say – irritating. It was as if he wanted me to mother him: clean him up, wash his clothes, cut his drinking down and patch him up again for the road. But if I was his mother, I guess I was the mother he never listened to for as soon as he was back in shape, he'd be off and the drinking would get even worse.'

'That's it: Jack the rebellious son.'

'You know, in many ways he was just like a child. I tell you, asleep in bed, he'd curl up like a foetus as if he was dreaming of climbing back into the womb or he'd cling to me for dear life .... Oh, sorry, I didn't say: we got a bit ... close.'

'Oh don't worry about that: I've had relationships as well. In fact, I'm in one now, if you can call it that.'

'What do you mean?'

'Well, Roger and me have this "open relationship", but it's so "open" I sometimes wonder if it exists at all.'

'Yes, I felt that with Jack. Did he have deep feelings or was he just using me – a stop-off on his travels?'

'I'm sure he did love you; he just wasn't good at showing it. He was so wrapped up in his own feelings, he'd little time for anyone else's.'

'Then, last year, everything changed. It was no longer a question of him using me, but of alcohol using him. He began to lose control of his body, twitching and shaking, then of his words, speaking nonsense no one could understand. In the end his mind no longer seemed to know what was real and what wasn't, seeing things that weren't there. It was ... terrible. I told him he needed help, more help than I could give – that he had to go to the doctor's, the hospital, but, as always, he didn't listen.'

'And that was what he was like the last time you saw him?'

'Oh yes, so awful! I couldn't make a difference any more, couldn't set him back on his feet again and when he left, he simply mumbled, "I'll be away for a while. Away a while." That's what he always said, but this time I caught a look in his eye – resigned maybe, desperate certainly. It seemed to say, "This is it, this is the end; there'll be no coming back. This is the last time you'll see me ... alive."' She ceased with a gasp and the room fell into prolonged silence; but, just as Mary was about to go over and give her a hug, Liljana recovered and resumed in a steady voice. 'Then about a week after he left what should I find, but a cardboard box I didn't recognise, hidden at the back of a cupboard? I pulled it out, opened it and there inside was a desktop recorder, a pile of cassettes and an A4 envelope, full of poems.'

'And did you read them?'

'Some, and I listened to bits of the cassettes with their rambling speeches, but I soon stopped.'

'Why?'

'They were mostly so miserable I just couldn't carry on.'

'That's what I felt, going through his things in Priština. All the same, do you think I could have a look?'

'You can have them, have them all with pleasure, take them back with you.'

'What! Are you sure? He seems to have left them 'specially with you.'

'No, I don't think so. It would've been awkward to carry that box around and if he'd have left it in Priština and not come back, they might have fallen into – well, you know – the wrong hands. Just in the bits I've heard he's very rude about everybody, but particularly his colleagues. No, my house was the safest place for storage.... Anyway, you have them, if you want them. There's nothing there for me. It's not as if he wrote me any love poems or anything like that. And on the tapes ... I just don't know who he's talking to – probably himself, but certainly not me. Apart from all this, I guess, I just don't care to remember him that way.'

Mary's eyes, despite herself, started to mist. Though her feelings for Jack had started to unfreeze, here was a woman who clearly loved him more than she did, even though she'd known him in some of his most unlovable moments.

'Well, if you're really sure, yes, I'd like to take them. They won't be pleasant, I know, but I'm so far into this, I should really carry on to the end. Granted, it'll be Jack at his worst, yet I feel it'll set my mind to rest.'

'Good.' And with that Liljana was out of the room and back in no time, holding a box. She placed it on the table, pulled out its contents, then gestured for Mary to join her. 'Do you know how the recorder works?'

'Well, I've got a music centre back at home, but,' looking quizzically down at the small rectangular machine, 'it's nothing like this.'

'Oh, don't worry, it couldn't be more simple. Just press the window down to open, insert your cassette, then close; push this central button upwards to play, to the left for fast-forward, to the right for rewind; that red button on the left starts recordings and the small meter to the right gives you feedback; on the side you've got volume control and a socket for the microphone. That's basically it.'

'Not difficult at all.' Mary glanced surreptitiously at her watch and decided it was time to leave. 'Well, thanks very much for this and for all your hospitality, but I do have to move, I'm afraid: my coach leaves in half an hour.' She wolfed down the remainder of her third cup and rose. Liljana was on her feet almost simultaneously – a little relieved, wondered Mary, that the meeting was over.

'No need to panic; there's plenty of time. I'll walk you back to the station. First, though, let's get a bag for the box.'

'Thanks, and while you're doing that, I'll use your toilet, if I may.'

The two women stood next to the coach. The rain had stopped a while ago and the ground was firming up under a weak sun. Liljana bade Mary goodbye, kissing her on both cheeks in true Balkan fashion. Mary thanked her once again for all her kindness and, looking down at the address and phone number Liljana had scribbled on a scrap of paper, said they must keep in touch. Just as she was about to show her ticket to the driver at the door, Mary turned back.

'Oh, I almost forgot: you said Jack didn't let on where he was heading, but did he ever talk of any places he wanted to visit?'

'He was always ... secretive about his travels.'

'Yes, I can vouch for that.'

'But, let me see.... Well, the only thing I can think of is that, early on, he did once mention the Danube, said how he'd always liked the idea of a river trip; but that was when he was in much better health.'

'True, he'd have found it hard to cope with a rocking boat at the end. Anyway, thanks again, Liljana – I'll definitely write.' And with that, her show of ticket having got the driver's approval, she climbed into the coach and found a row of free seats near the middle. By sitting next to the window and placing her box on the inner seat, she discouraged late arrivals. Fortunately, there were none, so when the driver started the engine, she was still by herself. As the vehicle began to pull out of the station, she waved at a waving Liljana, the small woman getting smaller with each turn of the wheels till buildings screened her off from sight.

*Is that the last time I'll see her? Probably, but not the last I'll hear from her, I hope. We said we'd send each other Christmas cards. Then, of course, there's always the phone ... and we are already linked in a way – loving-loathing, loathing-loving the same man.*

The box sat next to her for the whole journey and two hours later, after a walk from the station and a quick meal in the hotel restaurant, it was sitting next to her on the bed. Back in her room she talked to the kids, who reassured her with their excited chatter they were still having a great time. Did they not miss her at all? Or was she so much part of their world, they simply took her for granted? The second option seemed the one to choose. Now free to explore, Mary took every item out of the box and carefully placed them on the coverlet. Where to start? Examining the cassettes carefully, she noticed they'd been numbered 1 to 8. *Must be in order of recording, surely. So let's try Number 1.*

She plugged the recorder in, turned up the volume control, slotted in the cassette and, before lying back on the bed next to the machine, pushed the Start button up. For a time there was nothing but static. It lasted so long she decided to stop the cassette, but just as she was about to do so there came the sound of someone moving about near the microphone and then a voice established itself – not slurred, nor manic as expected, but weirdly normal and so familiar it took her breath away, as it sped her back to their marriage's early years.

*Beer or spirits? Isn't that the big question in life? Trouble is you can't get proper beer here – no bitter, served at room temperature. It's all that sweetened, fizzy stuff – lager, bah! BIP.... Beogradska Industrija Piva – who wants to drink 'industrial beer'? Still, on a hot day what could be better than a glass of cool, smooth, pale-brown ale? Five, sometimes seven per cent, so not too bad. Trouble is, though, the hit takes a while. You have to drink and drink. Your bladder's forever under pressure, so you find yourself having to go to the bogs all the time....*

*No, spirits are the thing, get you feeling right so much quicker. Well, they're over forty per cent out here, after all – not to mention the home-made hooch that can strip paint.... Brandy, it's here with a vengeance. Brandy, brandy everywhere and many a drop to drink. Slivovitz – the old plum brandy; lozovača – grape brandy; klekovača – juniper brandy – gin really; kruškovača – pear brandy; jabukovača – apple brandy – their calvados; kajsijevača – apricot brandy; dunjevača*

*– quince brandy. What wonderful variety and each with the same burn! But let's not forget Albanian brandy, good old Skenderbeg, plum juice, mixed with grape and lemon. Tried them all and they're all great in their different ways. Oh yes, and there's medovača – honey brandy, souped-up mead that revs your head way beyond the speed limit. Oh and such pleasing colours! Reddish; whisky-brown; ochre; or colourless – transparent like water, firewater! How these spirits haunt my tumblers, waiting for my throat to lay them! Živeli! Gëzuar! Cheers! Bottoms up! Down the hatch! Down in one! That's the way – lovely heat surging through the body, telling me all's right with the world – after all....*

*Wet heat, so heavy all I can do is lie on my bed and pant – pant like a dog. Oh for a humidifier...!*

*No, here in South Slavia the only question is: not beer or spirits, but wine or spirits? Local wines, weighing in at ten or thirteen per cent, can slap you around a bit without knocking you out. Really cheap, though – a big plastic can of gut-rot costs less than a packet of fags. Even the good ones won't sting your pocket: Prokupac, Tamjanika, Krstač.... A tip, though, my friend: avoid Smederevka: neat, it tastes of vinegar; you have to treat it as you would spritzer and water it down, but then it loses its wallop.... But yes, I have to admit there's nothing better than sitting under an awning on a hot summer's day with a bottle of wine on the table before you, watching the world hurry past as you lazily sip one glass after another. Let them bustle by on their business, the fools – all so driven, all so serious – you have better things to do....*

*I'm lighting candles, but not as a romantic gesture. Ha, romance's furthest from my mind .... Electricity's gone again and I can already feel the cold air slowly creeping through the window frames and chasing out the room's warmth. So, early to bed – nothing else for it....*

*You go to a bar or you're drinking at home. You feel tense, you don't know why, but you do, so tense it seems as if your fears are closing in for the kill. Then you have your first drink and things still seem bad, but, slowly, after another glass or three, the worries start to wash away and you find the ground ahead's miraculously clear. And, suddenly, you're smiling, chuckling even, because, yes, the world is such a stupid place, isn't it? All those pushy people – competing, demanding, complaining – absurd, surely, aren't they? They're just background buzz – annoying, yes, but not worth paying attention to. .And you with your little worries are ridiculous too – now aren't you? Those so-called problems simply do not matter, nothing in the end really matters, does it? So, yes, you're high now, so high above it all, looking down, laughing. No worry can pull you back to earth. Fuck it all, fuck it all. Two fingers to the world below, that's all it deserves....*

*Course, next day you feel like shit ... your head throbs, throat's like sandpaper, you can't eat without wanting to throw up. But it's worth it – just for those brief moments of flight, those seconds when you break out, soar above the snares and realise existence isn't simply your little life down there. The world has other, better, broader ways.... If only those moments could last longer, last a lifetime....*

*Back to Priština, back to prison. Confined in a village, not a town – and a puritan one at that: no sex, no fun ... .At least I've got the booze. That'll keep me going....*

*What did Sir Henry say? If I had again the money I've spent on drink, I'd spend it all on drink....*

*Priština – where God left his boots behind.... Why did I ever come here – to this job, this appalling place? Simple, I came to Kosovo because I applied for the post and got it.... The British Council must've seen through me right away: a hopeless case, a bit of a risk, they must've thought, but they were desperate. No one else wanted the job.... Course, it was hardly ideal for me. I'd have preferred East Germany ... or Poland ... or Czechoslovakia – or, if I had to go to Yugoslavia, Belgrade, Zagreb, Ljubljana – but in my position I couldn't be choosy after six months on the dole....*

*John Berryman was once asked why he drank so much. He*

*simply spread his arms, as if he was saying something self-evident, and declared, 'But, my friends, have you ever seen the world sober...?'*

*As I join the table, two I know leave, repeating some words I used previously that are, in context, rude. Still I'm made to feel welcome by those that stay. I go over to the counter to order. The proprietor saws off a sizeable square from a long strip of food and puts it on the plate, but it's so slippery it keeps sliding off. None of the diners show the least surprise at this and continue eating. I pick up my piece, dust it off, skewer it with my fork and munch away at it. When I go for another large slice, one of the diners mimes nailing it to the plate. They all laugh....*

*Oh Alcohol, love of my life. Sorry, Mary, only kidding! Anyway, it's beginning to lose its sparkle, this long affair with booze. Things are turning nasty; signs are telling me I'm getting hooked....*

*Got out of Albion in the nick of time. Knew full well what they were going to do. I wasn't about to stick around to see the State I'd taken as a given shrunk to virtually nothing, the future abolished.   Public assets privatised at knockdown prices. Heavy industry destroyed to curb working-class 'militancy'. Trade unions neutered. A deregulated City, awash with dirty money and dirty tricks, allowed to run the economy. Council flats sold off to the middle-class. Hospitals, schools, colleges, universities deformed into competing businesses. The Great Degradation.   Albion wholly demoralised, a semi-socialist country sliding away towards America. Reaganomics running rife, polluting every public well.... So, Thatcher, your Reich won't last a thousand years, but it'll do the necessary damage. Can't have workers getting above themselves, thinking they can run the nation, can we? Will we ever see a Welfare State again? Not in my lifetime.... Monetarism, monetarism! Well, if that's what the Great British Public really want, they can fucking have it. Good riddance, UK, I'm staying here in this Workers' Democracy, despite its many faults....*

Mary stopped the tape.

*So politics was why you left, was it, Jack? Politics, politics – that's just what I'd have expected from you. You always did get round to politics in the end, didn't you? Look, we're all pissed off with Thatcher, Thatcher the Milk Snatcher, but we don't have to be thinking of her all the time; that way she wins – inside, as well as out..... But what an idiot you are, Jack! You can joke about booze till you're blue in the face, but, really, it's no joke or, if it is, the joke's on you.... Right, let's take a break. How about one of the poems...?*

She'd barely understood the ones he'd shown her back in London, but maybe his style had got simpler with the drink. She drew the thin wad of paper from the envelope and scrutinised the pages.

*The typewriter must have been pretty battered: most of the letters with circles or semi-circles have become dried lakes of ink. So... what have we here? 'A Question of Balance (Prizren)':*

*The high-rise staggered –*
        *it did not fall –*
                *but books on edge*

*took flight*
        *into an inner sky*
                *of plates and shirts,*

*all heading*
        *for the floor.*
                *I ran to door jamb*

*as the place to crouch*
        *in case an after-shock*
                *found strength*

*to bring the block*

*about my ears*
    *and pitch the carpet*

*eighty feet below.*
    *Waiting, but braced,*
        *I tried to see*

*if cracks had scrawled*
    *abjad warnings*
        *across my kitchen wall.*

*The bare bulb*
    *still swung,*
        *yet nothing really shook,*

*except my hands.*
    *The structure seemed to hold,*
        *but not my nerve,*

*for what if after-tremors*
    *struck with added force?*
        *Panicked past care,*

*I fled the flat,*
    *headlong as any sprinter*
        *from the blocks,*

*and skeltered down*
    *six flights of steps*
        *through swing doors*

*to dusty air below.*
    *Oh, that dingy square*
        *of dirt*

*had never felt*

*so welcome to my feet!*
        *How priceless, peerless,*

*each neighbour suddenly seemed,*
        *every last Albanian,*
                *Serb and Turk!*

*What revved voices,*
        *prodigious hugs*
                *greeted each prodigal 'son'*

*and 'daughter',*
        *emerging*
                *into moted light,*

*their lives*
        *unwasted.*
                *Shaking times*

*had made*
        *a family of us all,*
                *told how close*

*we'd come to burial,*
        *soft rubble*
                *beneath harder,*

*heavier stuff.*
        *True, our world*
                *had not collapsed,*

*but the building,*
        *still, had rocked*
                *beyond belief.*

*That our so-solid block,*

93

> *each monumental floor,*
>    *could sway*

*like saplings in the wind*
>    *was the awful puzzle!*
>       *So we stood around,*

*looking to recharge our trust,*
>    *eying the entrance*
>       *through deepening dusk*

*like bikers who,*
>    *having slid on ice,*
>       *reach the next bend*

*too scared to lean in.*
>    *And I, pleased to be upright,*
>       *feet firmly set on ground,*

*thought of my flat above,*
>    *its door ajar, the short-wave*
>       *trembling still as it told*

*news to no-one –*
>    *Bush House, vainly seeking balance*
>       *in our shaking world.*

*What was that at the start about Prizren, Jack? Maybe they
had an earthquake there when you were staying with Liljana
and you imagined the high-rise. Or maybe you did some
teaching in the local college and they offered you a temporary
flat. I'll have to ask Liljana about that when I'm next in touch.
Anyway, at least it's your body that's shaken in this poem,
not your mind. There's no sign of madness or despair here:
you're even happy to be alive. But you just can't end on that,
can you? You have to bring politics in. Typical! Now let's see.*

*How about another one? Ah yes, 'First Light':*

*Black sea, slate sky.*
*So much to terrify.*
*First light.*

*Dollar or you die.*
*'Evil axes' multiply.*
*First light.*

*Their charges permit no alibi.*
*Choose the prison where you'll lie.*
*First light.*

*Processed, packaged, ready to buy,*
*Their big words, lie on lie.*
*First light.*

*No more Eden, freedom no more the cry.*
*We saw the corpse of Albion floating by.*
*First light.*

*Nurture a lifetime to defy.*
*Know 'the self' that you'll deny.*
*First light.*

*Departing wings, the slow goodbye.*
*Look away when swallows fly.*
*First light.*

*So many gravestones crowd the sky.*
*Not to gibber when you die.*
*First light.*

*Well, Jack, you're still banging on about politics but not just that. You're unhappy with the state of things, for sure, yet don't seem suicidal, more angry – alarmed? And there is some hope, isn't there – that is, if I understand you right? You do keep repeating 'first light', 'first light'. Hoping for a new dawn, eh?*

Mary went over to the dressing table to make herself a mug of instant coffee. The powdered milk didn't exactly improve its taste, but she welcomed the caffeine jolt and the liquid's soothing warmth. Once seated in the armchair with her nightcap on the coffee table, she began to rethink tactics. If she listened to all the tapes from start to finish with barely a break, it would take – what? – well over ten hours; she wouldn't finish till breakfast-time or even later. Best, she decided, leave that for another time when she could do justice to every minute, every second. After all, what she really needed now wasn't each word, but little clues, pointing to where Jack might have gone. Was it the Danube or somewhere else? Those hints would most likely be found towards the end of the pile, so perhaps she should follow Liljana's precedence and skim through the early ones, but, unlike her, concentrate on the final two. As soon as she'd drained the last coffee drops, she went over to the cassettes, selected Number 3 and swapped the first one for it. She pushed the button up and lay back on the bed once more.

*Look, let's face it ... I hate, yes, really hate, teaching ... all teaching: school teaching, tutoring, college teaching, literature teaching, EFL teaching, the whole shebang .... Should never have started, but what else could I do? What, sit behind a desk from nine to five, Monday to Friday? Never, drive me mad. Well, I've managed to miss that – and I'm still mad ... ha! EFL's the worse without a doubt ... who really cares when you should use the past perfect – or is it pluperfect? And conversation classes – dear Christ! You've mastered English yourself, your one language, and all you get back is simple stuff, hardly worth saying ... and then there's all that playacting ... just to get the class' attention. You've got to bounce in and be an all-singing, all-dancing performer. You have to become a clown and who wants to be a clown? I'm tired of all that. More to the point, I'm too old. EFL's a youth racket and I simply don't want to – can't – do it anymore ... would rather be left to drink. Ah, yes, drink....*

*Turned on World Service last night just as they were playing 'Waterloo Sunset'. Started singing along in a loud voice, helping Terry and Julie to cross over the river – wise move, that, things always better on the north bank. Ray Davies, a Muswell Hillbilly, after all.... Thought I'd enjoyed my little sing-along, but when the music stopped, I found my cheeks were wet. Silently crying without knowing it – what was that all that about? Was it the words, Brother Dave's guitar solo or thoughts of North London ... East London ... how far off they were ... when, if ever, I'd see them again...?*

*To tell the truth, wasn't just Frau Thatcher that got me out of Britain.... Started to notice signs, didn't I? Drinking down the pub with mates no longer did it. Why did they down pints so slowly – and not enough of them? Had to sneak extra shorts at the bar, when buying the rounds, or have a couple of snifters before I left or take my own – a flask of whisky, vodka – to swig in the gents.... Could never get my fill ... started going off on benders, weekends during term-time, longer during breaks.... And when I crawled back home, Mary would meet me with that look ... what was it? Anger, yes – worry too – and disappointment, yes – but, underneath – and this hurt the most – love, the remains of it, mind you, but still there, just surviving.... It was awful, felt so guilty, couldn't look her in the eye, tell her where I'd been, what I'd done (I hardly knew myself), so I just slunk off and hid.... She cornered me once and I lied, of course, said I'd been hiking. Not a bad lie, I guess – I did use to go on walking tours before we met – but did she buy it? Couldn't be sure, could never be sure with any of my lies, and that made things worse....*

*Began hiding bottles case I needed them – behind the cistern – back of the clothes cupboard – out in the shed – behind the dashboard. They were never found ... well, I don't think so. Mary never let on, if she did ... but I did have some heart-attack moments when I couldn't recall where I'd put them – oh God, my heart pounding out of control, sweat pouring down my brow.... Mary never seemed to guess what was going on, but at that time it wasn't obvious – could still hold my liquor, stay sober... then one morning – can't remember when – waking with a bit of a hangover, a sudden thought hit me like a train: I'd started to become my father, my disaster of a father...!*

*He died when I was only five, so I've no clear memories, but Sis told me what he got up to.... She'd come home from school every afternoon, stomach churning, listening out for quiet ... check if he was sleeping it off or was ready to pounce? Then all hell would be let loose – shouting, doors slammed, things thrown at walls, at the floor, at her. And there were those times she and mum had to hide when the never-never man or local shopkeepers, came round, knocking on the front door, rapping the parlour windows, peering in, demanding to be paid. Not to mention the night she was sure they were all going to die when he drove the car blind drunk. Then the smaller things. The shame she felt when, in front of friends, he tried to act sober, but slurred his words, laughed wildly for no apparent reason, got up and staggered – his flies undone, glasses halfway down his nose.... It was so painful, she said – course, those friends never came back....*

*Worst still was the way he changed from an ordinary drunk during the day to a monster at night – shouting, screaming like a madman, hitting, kicking mum, doing the same to her.... Then he'd wake next morning and act as if nothing had happened....*

*He was a repeated car-crash for us kids ... injured us in so many ways. Sis always said that's what made her cold with other people. She could never trust them, and that's why her boyfriends didn't hang around for long, why she never married ... it's maybe why, in the end, she took her own life ...*

*oh Sal, poor old Sal!*

*I knew for Linda and Peter's sake I had to get away ... had to leave, leave Mary, a clean break.... Should've explained, no doubt, but at the time I thought it better this way – that all she could feel for me was hate, pure hate.... Just couldn't deal with her pity, her understanding – now it's too late....*

*She didn't know about dad ... family would never mention him ... if asked, they'd say he died early – no details given.... But seeing how it's turned out – like father, like son – makes you believe in an alcoholic gene.... No, no, that's not it. Sal was teetotal and I ... I could've stopped drinking, early on, if I'd really wanted to. Still, Mary, guess I should've said something – even from across here.... Sorry, love, sorry....*

After reaching across, Mary abruptly pulled the Play button down and let out a long sigh.

*Course, you should, you stupid sod ... you poor sod.... Yes, but maybe on my side I should've noticed what was going on. How could I have missed all those clues you were failing to hide? Some were staring me in the face, weren't they? Idiot! Idiot! I knew you liked a drink or two – that was obvious – yet I never guessed you were losing it. So I didn't search for hidden bottles; but – come to think of it – why should I? As you said, you always looked more-or-less sober. And when you went off for days, I simply assumed you were fed up – fed up with me – so felt bad about myself ... and angry with you. Just never dawned you were going off on long benders – well away from prying eyes, mine. I guess I trusted people too much then, too. Well, I was still young and I'd never come across anyone like you before. I simply didn't know what to look for. I'd certainly do better nowadays.... Right Jack, you stupid bastard, stupid idiot, so you left us to fend for ourselves – no, I can't forgive that, never – but, at least, I do now know why you did it.... Well, Jack, there certainly are some eerie silences on this tape, but on the whole you do still seem to be holding it together. You're still making sense, sort of. Let's see what you're like on to the seventh.*

After swapping cassettes and starting a new reel, Mary once again lay back on the bed.

*As I try to read my book, a black book, someone's hand – whose is it? – keeps reaching round and tearing the pages out just before I come to them ... all those lost leaves, that lost knowledge, falling through the air, futile....*

*Blackbirds float in the blue over Priština ... so much burnt paper.... Ravens wheel outside my window, perch on the balcony railing in black stacks, ready to fly.... Sky gone dark, papered over, black with wings.... Kids in leather jackets, jeans, flocking below ... city sparrows, trying to look hard, whistling, shrill bird-like whistling, weird....*

*Lock the door, hide behind walls of sound.... Still not safe – stains peel from the ceiling, look! Down they come, moving towards me, materialising – one, an old woman.... My dead mother? Could be, if only she looked like her.... Squats on haunches opposite, telling me everything I have to forget....*

*Last night, how did I crawl home? Remember going to the bar, yes – just off High Street.... Can see myself standing, downing the first drink or two, but nothing after.... What did I say, do? Something stupid, something terrible – something I'll always regret, can never find forgiveness for? Surely not, but I just don't know.... Came round flat out on the bed this morning, still dressed – jacket – trousers – even shoes.... Looking down, saw stains on my shirt-tail, drops of blood – mine? Someone else's? Panicked, stripped, checked every inch of my body in the mirror.... What a relief! No cuts – scratches – not a thing.... So where did the blood come from? A fight? Could be, but where's the bruises? I was drunk, dead drunk – a sitting target – just couldn't have dodged the punches.... No, must've been something else, but what? No, Christ no, couldn't be that...! I couldn't have attacked someone, unprovoked, surely – some innocent person – or molested some poor defenceless woman – girl.... Oh God, no. Look, I do get angry sometimes – lose it – but I'm no loony, psycho.... Yet what if Ultra-V*

*is locked inside me, waiting for drink's key to let it out?
No, can't be, but maybe it is, maybe it's down there in my
unconscious without me knowing.... Yes, maybe I'm a menace
on the streets, maybe I should be put away – for my own good
– for the good of others....*

*I climb to the attic – corner two mice – douse them in insect
spray, which comes out as chrome paint – the mice die (after
added blows) – when I pick them up they're so much smaller
than they should be, almost like shrews. Also spray the dog –
lift, cuddle the corpse, drowned in chrome – see it's a spaniel
– I take it to the kitchen where Mary's working – place it on
the chopping board – it's become an Albanian child, called
Qasim, who sits there and jibbers – me and Mary must go
out – put the kid in the front room – leave small window open
for air – he may escape to town – we take the risk – but he
stays behind – murders Linda, Peter – one by one – slits their
throats....*

*Got to slow this drinking down, a real dry stretch is what's
needed – trouble is can't hold out now – used to be months,
then days, now much less – after two, maybe three, hours the
old thirst's back, only stronger, and just won't go away – what
can I do but put alcohol to lip and after the first swig there's
no stopping? I'll drink and drink till there's nothing left – or
till I knock myself out....*

*God, for looseness the sausage machine's got nothing on me –
yesterday, reaching for a book on the top shelf of the library,
I shat myself – had to limp off to the toilets to clean up – big
baby without a nappy...!*

*Starting to happen more – skin begins to itch – heart to throb
– sweat breaks out on brow – pressure inside, down below,
builds and builds – then, oh yes, blessed relief – look down –
realise what's going on – a yellow stream dribbles down my
leg, darkening the trouser – first it's warm – then numbing in
the cold wind....*

*On the wagon – feel so shitty – panic about everything –
no idea why – sudden sound – shocking thought – chance*

*remark and heart starts to race, head to thump – breathe quickly, almost pant – sweating and can't stop – off in buckets – shirt soaked – pacing up and down the room – can't sit still – lie down, up again – tossing side to side – then the shakes – mostly hands, sometimes the whole body – try to hold steady, clench muscles – only helps for a short while – always slight tremors – sooner or later have to ease off – then shaking comes back stronger – just can't win – early morning worse – wake to the shakes – only one cure – another drink – and another and another – till numb....*

*Head thick – nose bulky – two florid cheeks – weak chin – greying temples – booze breath – neckless – shoulders falling – ribs through skin – beer belly – full bladder – tool redundant – buttocks flabby, spotty – wobbly stilt-legs – how can she love a body I hate...?*

*Bolt every window – lock every door – still can't sleep – hounds howl through the night – where? – never seen but they're always there, somewhere – cats, macaws screech out of sync – scratch chorus – night's so much more than the dark....*

*Wish I'd never seen the light of day – curse the father who spawned me – mother who dropped me into this world – midwife who compounded the crime – nurses who sentenced me to life – schools which squashed me in moulds that broke my bones – uni. which asked me to carry ideas no one wanted delivered – country which tells me I'll be happy if only I buy more and more – work which wants me to die at my desk – work and die – think and die – buy and die....*

*Enough of this alcohol – I've had enough – no more now – sick to the teeth of it, the taste, the smell, the after-effects – not a drop more – just water – yes, water, that's it – lovely clear water – cool water – kind water – a covering of water – yes....*

Sucking in a lungful of air, Mary rolled onto her side and paused the tape.

*Oh God, that voice: so hoarse, so harsh, so broken! That's not my Jack. It's like he's possessed – by something, someone alien. Intoning like a dead man talking and those horrible pauses, wheezes and snuffles. If I hadn't have known it was him, the voice would've been hard to recognise. And what he says is awful, so awful! The state he's in! Holed up in his flat, scared of everything outside (flocks of birds; gangs of boys), everything inside (ceiling stains coming to life; animals yelling through the night). Then there's that deep dread about himself: do I do terrible things when drunk? Am I out of control – insane? Do I need to be locked up? He's disgusted with his body – the way it looks, the way he's lost control: shitting, pissing himself, unable to stop boozing without going cold turkey or getting the shakes. Awful, simply awful! Even the dreams have got weirder, more violent.... At the end, though, he said something about water. Being covered by water. I think I saw a poem title to do with that when I flicked through. Maybe it'll reveal something, you never know. Let's check. Ah yes, here it is: 'Soaking':*

*Under warm water*
*all his winters*
*dissolve into the heat.*

*Oh, how that flickering liquid*
*life thaws into*
*relaxes the body, the mind.*

*Feeling a pinched past*
*stretch like green leaves*
*winging through summer,*

*he finds himself*
*floating in a world*
*of warmth and light.*

*Surveying the bright room*
*from tip to top,*

*he feels at ease: it is all his.*

*But, this being England,*
*his July spell cannot hold.*
*Beyond the gently-steaming rim*

*in the late September*
*of a shady corner,*
*the dark cistern –*

*another season,*
*another kind of water –*
*coolly waits,*

*ready to claim his eyes again,*
*make him recall*
*the griefs of autumn –*

*brown leaves falling,*
*green fields drowning,*
*and rain butts swallowing each grey cloud.*

*Then he'll begin to see*
*the brain as bog*
*and, all meanings flushed*

*with that first inrush,*
*the luxury of thoughtless head,*
*unfulfilled, saturated, dead.*

*Wanting to drown yourself, eh, Jack? Is that what you're*
*saying? The death wish? Heavy stuff, really heavy, if that's*
*it. In a bath, and in England too! God, must've missed that as*
*well. Were you feeling that bad when you were with me? Not*
*at the beginning – God, I hope not – but a few years in. If you*
*were, you certainly never let on. So how could I tell? I'm no*

*mind-reader, am I? True, you were always a bit of a gloomy sod – weren't you? – but I took that to be your manner, never thought it went very deep. Some people are always smiling, others just frown, doesn't necessarily mean anything – and, after all, you could always crack the odd joke.*

*'A covering of water', 'under warm water'. What's this thing with water – hot water, cold water, any water? And then those scratchings on the wall above your bed. What was it they said, exactly? It was 'Water', yes, but what else? 'Gate', that was it! I remember we wondered if you could be thinking of Watergate, but then pooh-poohed the idea. And there was another word, wasn't there? Come on, what was it? Ah yes, 'black'. That's it, 'black'.*

Feeling she was finally onto something, Mary sensed her heart quicken in rising excitement. What she should do now was leave the seventh tape and go on to the last moments of the final one, see if water was still there in Jack's mind at the very end – water generally or a particular stretch of water: a lake, a river, the Danube even! She swapped the tapes, slotting in the B side of the eighth and rewinding for a few seconds. Yet this time she decided she'd rather listen to Jack's mutterings seated in the chair. That, she thought, would somehow give her more protection against the coming storm.

*Look at you! A mess, complete waste of space! What a life! Audit-time. Now how have I fucked up? Let me count the ways: as son ... schoolboy ... student ... teacher ... lover ... husband ... father. Are there any more ways I can fail? Trying to top myself – ha! – the gas running out – rope breaking – slashed wrists closing like the Red Sea – stomach pumped of pills.... Happy days!*

*Just caught a whiff of myself – what a stink! But what can you do? Can't be arsed to wash – body – clothes – but do I smell any worse than ... Thatcher's body politic. Must admit – flat does reek – like a rhino's cage – welcome to the zoo! World of dung beetles – flies sucking from rotting flesh – dirt, decay, filth.*

*Oh, but there's always water, blue water – yes, blue Danube –*
*Blue Bayou – back today, oh wahey – bluebird, blue sky over*
*blue water, yes.... But then Black Forest – Black Sea – black*
*dog in black night – Black Death.... And grey day – concrete*
*sky – grey gates – Iron Gates – through, by, yes, under....*
*Donau – Duna – Dunaj – Dunav – Dunarea –yes.*

After rushing over to stop the cassette, Mary went to the
bedside table to get a pen and headed notepaper. After
rewinding the tape so she could hear the last three utterances
again, she restarted the machine and sat with pen poised to
note down each phrase:

*Blue Danube – Blue Bayou – Black Forest – Black Sea*
*– Iron Gates – Donnow – Dewnar – Dewnigh – Dewnav –*
*Dewnareah.*

*He's onto the Danube again, but does also mention the States:*
*that old Roy Orbison song. But where the hell's Blue Bayou?*
*Florida or somewhere? Well, I think we can definitely rule*
*out his going to the US, considering his views on Vietnam*
*and Ronnie Raygun, but what can all this about Black Forest,*
*Black Sea, Iron Gates mean? I'll just have to wait till morning*
*and ask Nuhi. Meantime, I know it's going to be torture –*
*undertaker voice, crazy notions – but I'd better finish off the*
*cassette. So, here we go:*

*Shadow on far wall – what! – peels off – starts moving –*
*towards me – I inch back – shitting bricks – will it attack?*
*No – stops foot from me – intones – what kind of voice is that?*
*Man's – woman's? Can't tell – weird neutered sounds – tells*
*me I've done something wrong, very wrong – a crime – to*
*an Albanian – word's gone out – family member will avenge*
*– that I'd better get out – out of Priština – Kosovo – Serbia –*
*Yugoslavia – the world – quick....*

*Assassin's waiting – always waiting – dark alleys – doorways*
*– stores – face behind steering wheels – on trams – trains*
*– in bars – how can I escape? – relax? – he's everywhere*
*– my eyes scanning the streets – here, there – sneaked look*
*behind – oh, for eyes back of the head! But who is this killer?*

*Kid with knife? Heavy peasant, rolling in from village – bald, paunchy, going on fifty? No idea – that's the trouble – but I know he's out there – out there somewhere – that voice never stops – reminding me, reminding me – revenge killing, voice says – for ruining family honour – but I've killed no-one's brother – stolen no sister's virginity – robbed no-one of money – work – land. OK, said stupid things to Albanians – what? Don't remember – drunk – but nothing to worry about – nothing deserving death.... But maybe I did do something – after all – some terrible thing – though too pissed to know what – my God!*

*The knife that's going to finish me – that knife – can't stop seeing it – picturing it – bread knife – boning knife – bowie knife – pocket knife – anything, but not a machete – cleaver – please! – too messy – too painful.... Blade flashing in the light – speeds towards my guts – no time to adjust – run – slide in – clothes, skin no protection – sliding in stinging, oh yes, stinging – me doubled in pain – unless – lucky – it hits the heart – life stopping on the spot – more likely, fall – writhe on ground like rattlesnake – blood leaking, leaking till there's nothing left – white corpse....*

*Taking trousers off – zip becomes teeth – begins to bite – quick, quick or I'll be singing castrato – drunken swaying but – before teeth does damage – get jeans off – trousers now on floor – safely trapped under box – no way I'm putting them on again – ever....*

*Other voices – not Shadow's – radio voices – messages – special messages – just for me – all the time – not the words, no – but beneath the words – not easy to spot – once you do, though – it's clear – call them Naggers – tell me all I've done wrong – why out there they want to kill me.... Then that voice – somewhere in my head – started while back – man's voice – posh – quiet – then louder – louder – turned Cockney – proper geezer – effing, blinding – rabbiting on this and that – all the time – can't switch off – someone controls the airwaves – who? – tuning my brain – someone wants to do me harm....*

*Can't sleep in dark anymore – giant cockroaches – scuttle cross the ceiling – mad dogs – howl in the walls – monster bats – creak through the rooms – when radar fails, feel cold slimy wings – wipe them cross my face – clutch – but too slow – down on my face cockroaches fall – huge pincers – go for my eyes – not as fast as bats – barely time to brush them off – surrounded – keep the lights on – too bright to sleep – no escape – mice, rats, fat black flies – on my bed – in my head – thrash around – ward them off – some get through – go for my eyes – can't see – where's the door? Must find the door – stagger out – ringed by stink – get away – this filthy town – the knife, where? – first the door.... Door – yes, door – then gate – Gate – Iron Gates – through gates, yes – Iron Gates – YES!*

The last word was shrieked out in an unearthly tone. Though her mind knew the depths Jack had sunk to – the imagined voices, the terror of being stabbed, the clothes and body rotting like a tramp's – Mary was still appalled by that strangulated voice and the way it forced her to relive his final state. She saw him setting out on that last journey, stumbling away from the flats, head full of lunacy, belly full of drink, carrying his stench like a calling card. His back would have been weighed down by the recorder in his rucksack. Drunk and crazy though he was, he couldn't have been so far gone he no longer knew his first stop had to be Prizren – and Liljana. And they must have let him on the coach, but how in heaven did he manage that? Maybe he got onto a virtually empty one and, for once, they opened the windows. They would've had to. She could picture the horror on Liljana's face as she opened the door to her filthy, muttering, mad-eyed lover. She'd duly cleaned him up, she said, but could get no sense out of him. And then he'd left, just as he'd used to leave her – without explanation or apology, shuffling off to God knows where.

*Jack, you stupid bastard ... poor bastard – oh Jack!*

Mary slowly regained the present and, hearing eerie static

and hoarse breathing, realised the tape was still running. Though he'd no more mad things to say, Jack must have sat there, staring at the microphone, pulling air into his lungs and forcing it noisily out. Was he thinking of the Danube with those last words or was all that just random rambling? As she listened, she began to have the spooky sense that Jack's presence had moved out of the tape and was filling the room like some ectoplasm, crowding over her, pressing down on her, even entering her head and surveilling her from inside as well out. As her heart began to drum, the breathing quickened and the mouth dried. In her panic all she could think of doing was ring Nuhi, but it was too late – too early? – and, in any case, such a move could hardly be explained away to his wife. No, she'd have to deal with this alone, tell herself to stop being so stupid, calm down and cease imagining things that simply weren't there. To start thinking like Jack was the last thing anyone needed. Ghosts, presences just didn't exist. A tired imagination, working overtime late at night, had summoned him and nothing else.

She switched the tape off: no more static, no more laboured breathing, no more Jack. What should she do to calm herself down? She thought back to those meditation sessions she'd gone to when depressed after their split-up. Some involved chanting a mantra, but incantations, for her, smelt too strongly of religion. More to her liking were those sessions that relied solely on breathing techniques because they seemed like ordinary fitness exercises. Why not try one now?

She sat straight-backed on the floor, her creaky joints only allowing a half-Lotus, rested the back of her hands on her knees and breathed deeply. She focused on the air as it was drawn into her lungs, then let out, and whenever her mind strayed back to Jack's scary 'ghost', she gently returned it to the breathing. In time, her pulse ceased to thunder in her ears and her muscles began to unstring. After a while she even found, on glancing across to the dressing-table mirror, there was a smile on her face. Who or what had put it there, she didn't know – or care. As long as it stayed in place, she'd be satisfied. Her body again felt loose. Now was the time for bed, but on lying down she found that sleep wouldn't come. Stark images of Jack's last days and his likely fate kept rising into consciousness. Though she tried centring her thoughts again on the breathing, it only worked for a while. She therefore lay on her back and relaxed her body so that its whole weight seemed to press down on the mattress. She then went round her frame, part by part, tightening, then releasing the muscles – her legs, groin, chest, arms, shoulders, neck and face. Again, however, the desired repose didn't last long. So she tried another tack, going through women singers, women film stars, women TV personalities, women writers from A to Z, rewarding each correct answer with a deep breath, but to no avail: an excess of oxygen did not drown her brain in sleep. By 3, after periods of calm, interspersed with tossing and turning, she'd become convinced she wasn't going to get any sleep.

*Maybe I should just give in and read a book. Wait, I know, why don't I do what Jack would've done – have a drink ... a couple of drinks. I know I won't feel so great in the morning, but at least I'll get some shut-eye.*

After switching on the bedside lamp, she shuffled over to the drinks cabinet.

*Let's see: beer, wine? No, something stronger. Ah lozovača! Didn't Jack mention that when going through the local spirits? Right, lozovača it is.*

Having poured a generous measure, she took her glass over to the armchair. The first mouthful was disgusting, tasting like rust, and, ordinarily, she'd have spat it out, but the longing for sleep helped her swallow. The burn in the throat became a burn in the stomach, which sent a not-displeasing warmth round her body. After the third gulp she was already beginning to feel a little tipsy and, by the time she finished the glass, she was chuckling to herself – for no reason whatsoever. Head spinning, she moved somewhat unsteadily over to the bed, slumped under the lifted covers and within minutes fell soundly asleep.

She was woken, seemingly moments later, by the phone ringing on the bedside table beside her. She felt as if she'd not slept that well, as if her mind had been frantically jumping from worry to worry. Eyes screwed up against the light flooding in from the window, she rolled over to grab the speaker.
'Yes?'
'Ah, hello ... it's Nuhi.'
'Nuhi, a bit early, isn't it? What's the time?'
'Almost ten.'
'Really?'
'I was worried about you. I kept on phoning yesterday but couldn't get a reply. In the end I came round to look for you, but you'd completely disappeared. What happened?'
'Ah, that's a long story.... Look, it sounds as if you're in the lobby.'
'That's right.' Mary quickly considered whether she looked presentable, particularly after such a troubled night, and decided it didn't matter. Nuhi would just have to take her as she was and she was confident he would.
'Well, why don't you come up?' In no time, it seemed, there was a knock on the door and Nuhi was striding in. 'Come over and give me a good cuddle. I'm not feeling that great.'
A cuddle became a kiss became many kisses and in no time Nuhi was discarding clothes and climbing in beside Mary. Soon two bodies that had been separated for more than a day were getting to know each other again. During the time of separation Mary had felt her frame fall into disconnected parts, but now loving acts were joining them together again. Though Jack had dragged her mind down to the dark, she was damned if she was going to stay there. This was just what she needed, the comforting embrace, the upward pull of light and life. It was what Nuhi needed as well. The vain searches, the completeness with which she'd vanished, had only made him

long for her more and now she was safely in his arms. She was where he wanted her to be, where he wanted to be.

Afterwards, they lay side by side, smiles on faces, replete. But, gradually, the world began to call again. Slowly, Mary's mind started to turn back to business, the business of Jack, and, propping herself up on a pillow, she began to tell Nuhi all that had happened the day before. As she was ending, she reached across for her piece of headed notepaper.

'Well, the tape finished with these odd words: *iron gates, through iron gates.* And a little before that he'd said: *grey gates, iron gates, by, though, under. Blue Danube, Black Forest, Black Sea, Iron Gates.* Then he chanted a list of – names, I think they were. It went something like: *Donnow, Dewnar, Dewnigh, Dewnav, Dewnareah.* Does any of this make sense? And don't forget, as well, he scratched "black", "water" and "gate" on the wall above his bed.'

Nuhi stretched his arms above his head and gave a smile of satisfaction. 'I don't know why I didn't get it in Jack's flat; it really couldn't be simpler. It's got nothing to do with Watergate, as we said. That's – what do you call it? – a red herring. The only water Jack was thinking of was the Danube.'

'Yes, I thought it might be.'

'The list you read out was just the different names given to the river by the countries it winds through: Germany, Austria, Czechoslovakia, Hungary, Yugoslavia and Romania.'

'But what about those Iron Gates?'

'Oh, that's just a huge hydro-electric dam, built on the border between Yugoslavia and Romania. Beyond that, the river flows into Bulgaria and breaks up into a delta that leads to the Black Sea. You know, we have this saying in Yugoslavia about the Danube: "from Black Forest to Black Sea". Jack must've come across it.'

'So, finally, we know where he was heading: the Iron Gates!'

'It does seem so.'

Looking down on a Danube that was far from blue, Mary

rested her arms on the rail. It seemed she stood at a sombre centre with the grey skies above, a grey river winding below, and a dull wetness all around. Poets, her English teacher had told her, used to pretend nature cared for us, human beings: so rain was the skies grieving for some lost soul. Could they be gently crying for Jack? After all, he might have given his body back to nature, letting the juices leech out into water.

Little more than a day had passed since Nuhi decoded Jack's cryptic messages. After the couple had tenderly soaped each other in the shower and dressed, he'd used the bedroom phone to book her a seat on the afternoon express up to Belgrade, a two-night stay at Hotel Turist and a place on one of the last Iron-Gates cruises before the winter shutdown. Then while she packed a few necessities, he'd gone off to the library to scour recent issues of *Dnevnik* for reports of a corpse found bobbing in the river; but there was no mention of any drowning, whether of man or woman, adult or child, native or foreigner. On his return, when he told Mary this, she wasn't in the least put off for she felt she had to make the journey anyway. It would, she held, be her way of coming to terms with Jack's life in all its messy detail, a kind of pilgrimage, a ritual of farewell.

So there she was on a virtually-deserted deck with her padded windcheater zipped up to the neck. The few passengers had mostly sought shelter down below and that was just how she wanted it for she was alone with her thoughts, able, in good time, to puzzle out what the tapes had told her. While listening to them, she'd felt so many conflicting emotions, but what did she feel now? Still the horror – at a mind and body she'd once loved, so systematically wrecked; but most of her exasperation, her anger seemed to have died, leaving in their stead a sadness, a disappointment that seemed to spread to everything. Was there nothing that could've been done to stop Jack drinking his life away? Could she have been of more help – not just while they were together, but after he'd run away to Yugoslavia? During all those days, those nights following his flight, she'd hated him so much she hadn't wanted even to think of him, let alone get into contact; then the hatred, she supposed, had become a habit, which had never let her find the space to think again. But now she was reconsidering. What a waste of a life it'd been! How futile, how miserable – that twenty-four-hour devotion to what was killing you! And then the paranoia – as if anyone would want to kill him – and those weird hallucinations! She shuddered inwardly as she pictured what his final days must've been like and realised, with a jolt, that this was the first time since their separation she'd wholly put herself inside his skin and felt with him, for him.

Just then a trumpeting Tannoy disturbed her train of thought with an announcement in Serbo-Croat, presumably about some passing site of interest. Fortunately, she didn't need to make sense of the incomprehensible stream of words, having picked up an English-language guide to the river on the way out of the hotel at 6.30 that morning. The waiting taxi had just managed to get her to the quay by 7. Once safely on board the *Knez Mihailova*, she'd made straight for the bow, from where she could observe the moorings being untied, the engine engaged and the boat slowly manoeuvring away from the jetty.

Now that it was in midstream, gliding past Kalemegdan, she sat herself and her shoulder bag in the middle of the front row of seats, taking the strain off her legs, but still affording herself an unimpeded view of the river ahead. Turning to starboard, she saw that the fortress' park was virtually empty; the threat of rain must have deterred all but the hardiest dog-walker. By straining her eyes upwards and almost cricking her neck, she could make out the statue of the Victor, towering over the fortress walls. Alone on his high pedestal, he looked down on the Danube like some tutelary god, but a god who now seemed to be shivering in his bronze nakedness. As the boat pushed further away from Belgrade, Mary returned to her thoughts, yet did look back, half-distractedly, at the statue in the distance, managing a small smile: its straining after the heroic was certainly not matched by the river, which, at that point, was little more than low bank, sometimes wooded, but mostly not. An hour and a half out of the capital, however, changed all that: a castle materialised eerily out of light mist and gradually rose up before the boat, ruined tower on ruined tower. This was definitely the moment to retrieve the leaflet from her shoulder bag.

*Let's see, that must be Smederevo Castle: 'a medieval fortress. Though placed in a commanding position and thoroughly fortified by the Serbs, it was nevertheless ransacked after failing to withstand the Ottomans' third assault in 1459.... During World War II it was used by the Germans as an ammunition dump. A huge explosion occurred in 1941, killing 2,500 in the nearby town and badly injuring thousands more.' God, what a history!*

Mary studied the ravaged castle: it was gloomy, perhaps even spooky, yet so peaceful; you'd hardly imagine that down through the centuries on its ground mounds of corpses had periodically lain.

Memories of suffering and death still haunted the river for, as the boat slipped further down the Danube on approaching Djerdap Gorge, a rock swung into view, standing midstream as if guarding the entrance from unwanted intruders. On it – Mary learnt from her guide – an old woman is said to have been chained by the Turks in punishment for helping rebel Serbs. As the waters rose, they begged her to repent ('Pokaj se, baba') and betray the freedom-fighters' hiding-place, but she refused and was drowned. To this day the rock is known as Babakaj. Or was it Princess Golubana who was chained there for rejecting a Turkish pasha's advances? She stopped her ears to his pleas for repentance ('Baba, pokaj se') and also drowned. So the rock is now called Babakaj and the nearby town Golubac.

*Different legends, same outcome: the woman dies. The woman always dies.*

The boat rounded the rock and sailed into the gorge, leaving martyrs behind. On either side the massive ravine cut sharply down through the cliff, exposing bare, weathered surfaces. What had seemed a reasonably-sized vessel now looked toy-like as the Carpathian Mountains to port and Deli Jovan and Veliki Krš to starboard began to soar over the deck. Straddling one headland on the Yugoslav bank from its top down to the water's edge in spectacularly-arrested stagger, Golubac Fortress hove out of a thickening mist. How did it manage to stand there so solidly, so monumentally? Surely on some fateful day, not long from now, the castle would simply crumble under the strain and its towers slide down, one after another, into the river like giant chess pieces swept into a box. And what a wave that would produce, an inland tsunami that would drown whole villages along the bank!

Before the dam's construction this stretch of the Danube had – the brochure told her – been so tricky with its treacherous currents and hidden rocks that only the most skilful pilots could navigate it. There was a series of whirlpools that, according to legend, had to be avoided at all costs for out of them a grinning gnome with devilish face, conical hat, long goatee beard and goat's ears and legs, would horribly rise to pull unsuspecting boatmen down to their deaths. Or was it a giant beluga sturgeon, twenty-four-feet long, that would drag its huge, white bulk out of the churning water and catch victims in its terrible jaws? With the rise in water level after the dam's completion, the currents had calmed and the rocks been rendered harmless beneath the boats' hulls; yet the added depth had brought its own drownings. A number of islands, great and small, had disappeared under the rising water. The largest, Ade Kale – almost two kilometres long and half a kilometre wide – had hundreds of Turks subsisting on it, marooned by history between Yugoslavia on one bank and Romania on the other. Mary tried to picture the underwater village with its mosque empty of worshippers, its bazaar no longer thronged with haggling shoppers and its cottages no more adorned with racks of drying tobacco; instead fish of various sizes nosed their way through each opening in search of food.

That image of food reminded Mary of her rushed breakfast at six; yes, she was growing hungry, wasn't she? She rose, donned her rucksack and made her way down steps that took her beneath deck. The few passengers below seemed older than her, much older – pensionable age, in fact. There were no children to be seen; they must all be back at school. Looking along the aisle between two blocks of seats, she spotted a kiosk-like structure at the far end that might well have something to eat. And indeed it did. In addition to the usual filled baps, there were cardboard boxes of cold food. The trouble was the signs were only in Serbo-Croat, both Cyrillic and Latin script. She recognised 'burek', but was unsure about the others: 'pasulj' looked like beans, 'sarma' minced meat wrapped in olive leaves, 'pljeksavica' a kind of burger and 'čevapi' kebab. To be safe (and healthy), however, Mary pointed to the 'šopska salata', which was indisputably a salad. And a good choice it proved for as she took it over to the nearest free table, she could see it was made up of large chunks of tomato, cucumber, onion and pepper, over which olive oil had been drizzled, and, having sat down and started to eat, she found that what made the whole dish delicious was its chunks of white cheese, their sharp tangy taste like the feta she'd come across in Greek restaurants.

Having wiped her lips with satisfaction, she returned to the kiosk to get a drink. 'Sok' clearly meant fruit juice, so she pointed to the carton with a drawing of oranges on it. But then she noticed the place must have been licensed for there, right at the back, stood a row of beer and spirit bottles. From nowhere, it seemed, an idea bubbled into her mind and she knew exactly what to do. As if the brain's search engine was working without her knowing it, the word 'lozovača' rose to her consciousness. Wasn't that the spirit Jack had praised and she'd recently drunk to get to sleep? She'd buy a bottle, a big bottle.

Pointing to the alcohol section, Mary said in a hesitant voice, 'Lozoh ... vatcher.' The woman behind the counter, mercifully, appeared to understand for she handed over a bottle of the transparent liquid at a remarkably generous price. Mary hid it in her shoulder bag with a guilty feeling, as if it were contraband, then 'smuggled' it past the aged passengers and up to her seat on deck. *If they'd seen it, what would they have thought? That I was an alky or something, taking it off for a lonely swig?*

She sat and took in the cliffs' splendour on either side. Mile on mile of narrow ravine followed till the gorge widened into what looked like a large lake. From her reading Mary knew they were nearing the turning-point; the dam could not be far off. Water surrounded her – from the river extending on both sides into the distance to the wet air with a fine drizzle coming on and a thick mist closing in ahead. Wavelets fell away from the prow and, aft, the propeller churned whirlpools. They were meant to loop round, but the *Knez Mihailova* seemed not to be aware of this as it thundered towards the middle of the lake, disturbing the peace. Suddenly, the Iron Gates reared from the approaching murk, wall-gap-wall in series like some gat-toothed monster. The boat seemed to be pulled inexorably towards that great grey mouth, as alcohol had pulled Jack towards the mouth of death. But surely they wouldn't smash into the dam's towers as past ships must have smashed into Smederevo and Golubac', surely they wouldn't finish, chewed up in the concrete monster's huge grey jaws. Or could the gates rise up at the last minute to let the boat through to the Danube delta and Black Sea beyond? Just then the engine ceased its noisy shuddering and they drifted silently, harmlessly forward on the still lake.

*Ah, relief, relief.... So, is this where you came, Jack, stumbling and gibbering towards these gates? What a place to end it all! It's hard to think of anywhere gloomier, but, then, you were always a sad old sod, weren't you, Jack? Oh, Jack...!*

Surrounded by league on league of water on either side and

dwarfed by a towering dam in front, Mary felt that now, in this moment of suspension before the boat came to life again and turned, was the time for a kind of ceremony. Reaching into the rucksack beside her, she pulled the bottle of lozovača out.

*Even if you're not bobbing in the water somewhere around here, Jack, perhaps you should be. Your thoughts were all on this place, on water, on being in and under water; and wasn't your life a long drowning in liquid – liquid spirits? So, only spirits, only lozovaća, can properly sum up your time on earth.*

Mary rose to her feet and, after moving over to the rail, looked down on the still water. Holding the bottle out at arm's length and slowly turning, she presented it to each of the four compass points. Then, after gently unscrewing the metal cap and laying it on the seat, she leant out and poured the transparent liquid, dram by dram, into the Danube below. It was a kind of offering to the river god, if there was one, and, more so, to Jack, who may have already offered himself to the deity, body and all.

*Firewater to water, firewater to water till there's no drop left.* She gazed as the river weakened and weakened the spirit's fatal power.

*So diluted, now scarcely a trace remains. And that's how it ought to be, how it should have been, Jack.*

The air was cooling, winter seemed not far off; light was fading, heralding dusk, black water, black rock.

*From Black Forest to Black Sea – that's what you latched on, Jack, wasn't it? But why did the saying mean so much to you? You were drawn to darkness, weren't you? The darkness of forest, deep water, black sea. Life had become a burden you couldn't carry any more. You wanted to sail into blackness, the blackness of death. Well, the dark's certainly not for me. These gloomy gates may have been your entry into death's kingdom, but for me they merely mark the point at which this boat and I stop and turn. Soon we'll be leagues from all this and that's as it should be. So, Jack, even if your black dog didn't drag you here, even if your body's lying nowhere near here, I've still got to bid you a last goodbye. You were never exactly mindful, were you? Just out of your mind, and in your distraction you chose the dark.*

The engine started firing again, the boat swung round and began its voyage home. It wouldn't be till nine that Mary would get back, yet she didn't care. Something had been settled. Though light rain blew into her face, she stayed up on deck, pulling the hood up over her dampening red hair and as she looked out at the darkening river, her thoughts leapt ahead to what awaited.

*Nuhi, Roger, Peter, Linda ... the lights of London – life!*

# The Right Connections

*She came to my door. What else could I do?*
A curt rap on its thin wooden surface – insistent, almost imperious – scattered his concentration on the marking. He winched his weary head up from scripts scrawled with red. A SUP summons? Surely not: they'd just kick the door down. So, with a tired brain that no longer made the simple connections, he moved slowly over to the door and opened it a few inches. A frame-filling frame met his gaze.
'Hi,' in a voice raw from the prairies, 'I've something real important to talk to you about.'
*My soul? If so, you needn't bother: I lost mine, if I ever had one, decades ago. You sound like a Bible-belter, but what are you doing in Kosovo of all places? Converting Commies to the true faith? Surely not.* Still he did wedge a foot firmly behind the door – just in case. 'And what would that be?'
'Right. My name's Lisa. Uh, Lisa Lutz,' pumping his hand, 'and I'm here doing some stuff for Amnesty International. You heard of it?'
He nodded, glancing beyond to a corridor mercifully empty of colleagues.
'Okay. We're looking for this guy,' flashing a blurred black-and-white photo.
'He's Albanian, a dissident who, we reckon, is being held somewhere here in Priština. We've gotten real worried. See, he's been missing these three months and no one, not even his family, has heard a thing. Nat'rally, there's been no trial – or any talk of one.'
This was, as she'd said, important, but the voice was loud and assured, too loud and too assured; it echoed confidently down the bare corridor, as if never doubting its right to occupy that space, yet was – incredibly – answered by no doors inching open. Maybe he should have brought matters to a head, demanded documentary proof or simply said he knew nothing of the case and closed the door, but his brain was too

muddled by marking to think clearly and he did feel that to leave matters there wouldn't do justice to the missing man, so he withdrew the foot and lamely let her in.

Yet as soon as she commanded his dilapidated sofa, shining face inclined towards him, plaits ready to dance in sympathy with the cause and fingers poised to point new messages in the air, he began to have his doubts. After all, how did he know the room wasn't bugged? Rumours of hidden devices had been ricocheting round the lector network ever since he'd arrived. At first he'd put them down to Cold-War paranoia and so been free to laugh them off, but, recently, the phone had been acting strangely. Whenever he raised the receiver, an odd sound –as if the call had thrown switches elsewhere –would start up and he'd sense a drop in signal strength. And then for no obvious reason – he wasn't calling from a phone box or anything – his chat would sometimes be cut short in mid-sentence. Surely if a bored telephonist had been listening in on his foreign babble, she – or he – would soon have tired of the game of breaking connections. No, it must have been something more organised. After each plug-pulling he'd rung back and joked with the caller that they could start again because the police must by then have found a new cassette, but still a nagging unease remained. Suppose they were taping each call he made or got; suppose all the talk taking place behind lounge walls was being monitored. And then it came to him how on entering his flat colleague and student alike would snaffle their tongue, become unusually interested in work-trivia and blandness, and what had been a blurred doubt at the back of his mind focused into the realisation that they all knew – or strongly suspected – his two cramped rooms were under electronic surveillance. And from that moment he'd begun to feel hemmed in, constantly monitored like some prisoner of conscience. Light thoughts – like the probability SUP's translators were former students and so wouldn't follow a word he said – failed to toss this feeling off and self-consciousness like a crammed backpack began to weigh him down.

Liza broke into his thoughts.

'Here, have a look,' passing over an Amnesty-International newsletter. 'There's a small item about this dissident on the front page.'

He located it in the bottom, right-hand corner:

### NEWS IN BRIEF – YUGOSLAVIA

*Adam Krashi, a human-rights activist in the Serbian semi-autonomous province of Kosovo, has been reported missing. The authorities in Belgrade refuse to confirm or deny that he is under arrest, but it is understood they have been angered by some of his activities on behalf of the Albanian community, which they consider 'chauvinist', 'separatist' and 'friendly to hegemonist powers'.*

This was definitely not the sort of stuff to be discussed in a possibly-bugged living-room, he decided.

'Look, I've got an idea: this flat's a bit spartan. Instead of just chatting here, why don't we go somewhere more inviting? There's this Albanian restaurant a little up the road.'

'OK. Why not?'

As they left the three-storey staff block, his eyes tracked across the ill-lit street to the campus, followed the outline of grey concrete towers, straggling up the hill in failed aspiration. There on its summit stood the main police station, lights blazing into the night, as though it were some kind of Pharos, guiding wave-tossed travellers through the city's hidden rocks. They turned left and bent into a sleety wind.

'Not exactly what you're used to, I suppose.'

'Why, no! We get this and worse in Chicago where I'm at school. The winds off the lake in winter freeze you like death.'

'Don't worry, we won't get to that stage here: there's only a couple of hundred yards to go.'

And in no time, panting from the wind buffets, they ducked off the deserted street and into the Rugovo, where their nipped ears were warmed by '*Shkon Skyferi*' and the earthy gutturals of Albanian chatter. As eyes adjusted to the dimmed lights, they saw they weren't the only ones to have sought refuge from the elements. Indeed, the place looked full, but they did eventually spot a couple of free seats at a table in one corner. While he was ordering Turkish coffee for her and a Skanderbeg for himself, Lisa scrutinised the décor with evident satisfaction.

'Real ethnic, huh!'

He nodded and dutifully scanned the local handicraft, hanging from the surrounding walls (the usual mats, embroidered slippers, wood carvings, gold filigree), finally zooming in, as he always did, on a blown-up photo of the dance that gave the restaurant its name.

Framed by a forest clearing, two rivals leapt into the air, legs bent back, left arms extended for balance, while the right waived swords high above their heads. What could have frightening was completely defused by the grin on the face of the woman, over whom the men fought. She'd placed hands firmly on her plump hips as if to hold in the laughter that was bubbling up inside. Did the dance pull her face into that smile or had she noticed the small man, inserted between the suitors, kneeling on one leg, while the other supported a drum, almost as big as himself, which he struck, eyes closed in rapt concentration on the beat? For when the airborne duellists finally landed, it seemed their swords would fall not on each other, but the hapless skullcap of the man who played – oblivious – between them?

And, leaning back in his chair, he chuckled once more at the sheer absurdity of it all: rivals in snowy turbans and off-white jackets that wouldn't have looked out of place in Ruritania; a woman in a loose, belted smock and baggy trousers, topped by a tight, Ena-Sharples headscarf; and, beyond, pairs of dancing warriors, studiously ignoring the duellists' call to arms in their determination to imitate the duck's flat-footed waddle. This was what he loved about the Albanians: their absolute refusal to be serious or formal, their rough-and-ready sense of fun.

*1 pallet, mattressless, no sheet.*
*1 stinking, crawling blanket.*
*1 slop bucket, putrid, at the far end.*
*1 bowl for washing, eating, cleaning teeth.*
*4 off-white walls, smeared with black stains.*
*1 door, no handle, locked from outside, its spy-hole always gaping.*
*1 high light-bulb, no shade, the switch beyond.*
*1 small, barred window, out of reach, its sun, sky, clouds, moon, stars speaking of     where he was not.*
*And below 1 body, bruised and expertly shocked, its strange cries sharing the night with distant groans.*

'My! Just look at those rugs!' she exclaimed, pointing a broad finger.

He cross-cut to bold saw-tooth patterns in red, black and white.

'They're mighty like Red-Indian designs I've come across in the States.'

'Yes, that's it: Native Americans in cowboy films! You know, I've been wracking my brain, trying to remember where I'd seen rugs like those before and you've solved it at a stroke! Brilliant!'

More serious matters were for the moment forgotten, but his guest was nothing if not dogged and soon re-routed the conversation to her main concern.

'You know, I've been here a day or so rooting around. Like yesterday I went to the *Rilindija* offices.'

'Oh yes ... but why?'

'To find out if its people knew where the prisoner was, of course.'

'You didn't!'

'Sure. Why not?'

He glanced at their immediate neighbours, but no one seemed to be paying them any more attention than the rare tourist on the way down to Greece would have got.

'And I asked them other questions as well.'

'You did?'

'Yeh, like if they printed stories from the other side.'

'What ... ouija boards, astral projection?'

'Hell, no. Stories criticising the government, dissident stories – stuff like that.'

'I see.'

'But they just clammed up and stood around looking guilty as hell. So I asked them if anti-communist candidates were allowed to run in local elections.'

'You did?'

'Sure, but was served the usual bull, you know the stuff they're parrot-taught in school. I just couldn't get a straight answer.'

He downed his brandy in one and waited for its forgetful glow. She ignored her coffee, even though the lees must by then have settled, and continued, 'Yes, one way or another we've been pretty busy.'

'"We"?'

'Yup! Came over with Irvin – uh, my boyfriend. We'd already decided to do Europe through to Germany this summer, so when we heard Amnesty needed to find out about this guy in Kosovo, we said, "No problem, we'll just carry on down to Yugoslavia." So here we are. Irvin's out chasing leads tonight or he'd be here. As both of us are working on this, we're sure to get some place pretty fast!'

'I wouldn't doubt it,' he replied, surveying the room and thinking of others a lot less convivial.

'But we do need your help.'

'Look, I'm only a lector here. I walk into the classroom ten times a week, try to coax a little English from my students, then walk out again. I make a policy of keeping my head down.'

'Still you sometimes hear things, surely.'

'Not really. Students only come to me to talk about essays, examinations, that sort of thing.'

'And yet you've been here one heck of a time, haven't you?'

'True, but no matter how long I stay, I'll always be a stranger.'

'Well, you still might have heard talk of this guy,' showing the photocopy once more.

Though he'd only seen the man twice, he had no problem recognising him from the poorly-reproduced features: his dark hair slicked back like an otter's, his high forehead and the thick moustache resting on either side of a sharp nose. All was as expected, except for the stupid look on his normally-intelligent face as if he couldn't quite account for the camera's sudden flash. But what the frozen image couldn't register was the recklessness of his laugh or the almost violent way his arms would orchestrate an argument.

'He's called Krashi –uh, Adam Krashi. Used to be a student here, class of '74, but majored in Albanian, not English.'

And there was more, much more.

'No, sorry, before my time.'

'But haven't you heard anything? He's real well-known.'

'Not a thing, I'm afraid.'

They locked eyes till he had to look away. The dimly-lit room swung crazily to right and left before coming to rest at the picture on the wall. That was the Albanians for him – and not Krashi and his ilk. They'd begun innocently enough with marches in favour of the Albanian language, but had recently, if rumours were correct, smuggled arms and bomb-making equipment across the border from Albania and were now busy drilling and practising firing in the hills above Uroševac. Of course, he knew about the arrested man –who didn't? – but was Lisa the right person to talk to? He'd always thought the naive American the deadest of clichés, but here was one, sitting opposite, as alive as Lady Lazarus, so sure all right-thinking people shared her views she scarcely saw those she came across, so certain error existed outside her country and herself she failed to make the humbling connections.

Most of Lisa's questions at *Rilindija* had no doubt squeezed reluctant smiles from the faces of its party hacks, but to ask about an arrested dissident was no smiling matter. Even though there didn't seem to be any police agent in the restaurant, it was still possible she was being trailed and her contacts noted. If she and her friend were caught, that wouldn't matter much to them – they'd simply be deported – but what of him? He'd be asked to leave without even his plane fare being paid – it was all down in the local contract – and what would the British Council think? After years of trying, they'd only just managed to get a toehold in the autonomous province – he was the second lector there – and they'd repeatedly advised him to keep a low profile. If he were sent home, spotlit by publicity, the university contract would probably be revoked and the British Council in its pique make sure he never worked for them again. All right, losing your job, especially for something you believed in, was no great tragedy, but in this case did he believe?

He looked down at his empty glass for inspiration. The answer, he supposed, would have to be, 'Not really'. Though he knew only too well why Krashi hated Serbs and wanted greater distance from them, he couldn't bear to watch his beloved Yugoslavia break up, its varied quilt of republics torn apart by nationalism, its nurtured cooperation between ethnic groups sabotaged by greedy Western neighbours.

True, Kosovan Albanians were ultimately controlled by Serbs in Belgrade, had Serb army units occupying strategic positions throughout the province and a police force largely manned by Serbs, but, on the other hand, they ran their own parliament, disposed its budget, and had a TV station, newspaper and education system in Albanian as well as Serbo-Croat. Things weren't perfect (they never are), but they could have been a lot worse. Nationalism was the bomb that could blow the federation apart; to prime it was at best an act of folly, at worst a crime. So, on the whole, Belgrade was wise to come down hard on anyone prepared to use those explosive tactics. But did this mean Krashi deserved prison and all that went on there? Perhaps not.

'You could have forgotten something, anything: a small – maybe you think – off-the-wall detail?'

'No, I'm sure I haven't.'

The detail he knew – and she did not – hadn't been forgotten. How could it? A week before a student friend had told him in his home that his sister, who worked as a nurse in the local hospital, had seen Krashi brought in under police guard for an emergency operation. His stomach had been cut open and two spoons found inside. It seems he'd swallowed them to escape further beatings – better the lesser than the greater pain. Did he condone this? Certainly not, but would talking to Lisa make any difference? The story might eventually surface on the international pages of the Western press, but would doubtless disappear as soon as Belgrade denied it and another story took its place. Its brief life would merely serve to illustrate the depravity of the Eastern bloc and Krashi's position would stay the same. The only change would be that if the story's source were traced, the student would find himself without a future and he without a job. He could choose to inflict this on himself, but not on someone who, as he'd left, had made him swear to tell no one of what he'd learnt. No, he had to keep the information to himself.

'So nothing to pull from the back of the brain, no last-minute connections?'

'No, nothing, I'm afraid.'

They sat only a couple of feet apart, yet as they eyed each other, ancient fault lines seemed to open at their feet, throwing them back to right and left. There was clearly no more to be said, so they rose, at the door pumped hands and parted, she to battle on through sleety wind to her hotel room, he to be blown back to his flat. And as he was bowled along with leaves and scraps of litter, he thought of the messenger who'd come to him out of the dark and whose distance from him was increasing with each step. In a few days she would put an ocean and two cultures between them. It was odd that even though he knew he would not, did not really want to turn and catch her up, he could not blank the meeting from his mind. He kept coming back to everything he might have said, but did not, each new formula further complicating the effects till his brain began to spin.

He crossed at the junction on a red light, then let the big wind carry him down the last slope to his estate. Before taking the now-tacky dirt track to his block, he looked once more across the street and up to the police headquarters, placed like a fort on its hilltop. The work of law and order was continuing in all its many forms: not one light had been switched off, nor would be, he supposed, till dawn. The building laid down a zone of light against the encroaching dark; it illuminated the higher ground as wisdom was supposed to, yet perhaps in its basement's glare Krashi was at that moment being hit in all the unwise places, his cries lost on deadened walls. He turned away in semi-darkness, stumbled over waste ground to his entrance, trudged up three flights of steps and, after fumbling for the right key, entered his flat and switched on all the lights. *What else could I do?*

# Serbia's Guts

Waiting in the dimly-lit changing room under the ring, Urim can hear through the thin ceiling the rise and fall of the crowd's response, can even make out odd shouts of support and derision. He tries to forget he'll be on next, moving round and round that ring under those spotlights with never a chance, if things go wrong, of escaping to the dark till the final bell or unconsciousness comes. Though never still, he'll be the crowd's fixed focus, the swaying, dancing pivot of its hopes. Normally, he'd revel in such attention, knowing, as he's on home turf, the first shouts will be for him, but tonight it only makes him edgy. Suppose he fights like a novice and the crowd turns against him; that'd be worse than facing the hostile rings of Serbia where insult is a matter of course. To let his own people down, a people who've suffered so much at the hands and feet of the Serbs and who've come in such large numbers tonight to see those slights redressed on his opponent's jaw, that would be unbearable. How could he face those mute, let-down looks when he sneaks from the dressing room after the fight and what could he plead as mitigation in the days to come? It just doesn't bear thinking about. Yes, the bout's become too big, both for the crowd and himself. Word of it sped round Priština and after a couple of days the few remaining tickets vanished only to resurface tonight in the touts' grubby fists. But why such interest? So many amateur scraps in the past have run their course to half-empty tiers. It can't just be because he, an Albanian, is fighting a Serb: that's happened many times before. No, it must be because his opponent's father is head of police in Peć – and a head with a history. Savaging the son tonight will allow the Albanian underdog, by default, to savage the Serb master.

Not willing to dwell on all this, Urim tries to distract his mind with the thought that there'll be no need to work himself up for this fight: already he can feel blood pumping adrenaline messages round the body; his brow's damp, but the mouth is dry and when he looks down at his feet he notices they've been tapping out an insistent rhythm on the floor – unwitting practice for the quick footwork to come or the first nervous steps of a loser's dance of fear?

He pulls his stare away, hoping to find in the room something, anything to divert him, but its half-lit, receding emptiness, broken by benches, penned in by peeling walls, provides nothing to detain him. Naked light bulbs swing in the draught; lines of rusty clothes hooks disappear down the walls; two grimy notices in Serbo-Croat and Albanian warn against leaving valuables lying about. All as expected. So he switches attention to the ceiling where damp has scrawled black blotches along much of its length, yet can spot no recognisable shapes, no heads of sheep, pigs or well-known politicians.

The crowd's roar, amplified by bowl-like seating, suddenly drops as if its power supply has been cut. A halt, clearly an unplanned one, for he's heard no bell. An official warning for butting perhaps or a glove-lace working itself loose or a hillock of jelly, over a cut, a second "forgot" to wipe away. What for the crowd is an annoying stoppage is for Urim, in his underground room, a welcome break of relative quiet. He tries to listen out for diverting sounds, but all he hears is a tap's monotonous drip and the dull murmur of chat from above and before he can detect other noises, the hubbub starts up again. He smiles grimly as his eyes pick out two dark heaps of clothes, separated by almost the room's length. Those boxers, who've begun to hurt each other at close quarters upstairs, made sure that up until the last moment they kept as far apart as possible.

Distance seems to be his opponent's strategy as well. Where is he anyway? And why isn't he changing here? Anyone would think Urim stinks or something. He lifts a right elbow, smells the pit and finding it, like the room, damp and not altogether fresh, reaches into his bag for a spray. There's going to be no excuse for the old slur of 'filthy Shiptar' that's been hurled at him, like stale burek, out of the anonymous darkness of a Serbian crowd. Probably, it's better his foe isn't here, scowling at him across the semi-darkened room, for he'll have no chance to scent Urim's fear, deodorised though it now is, and so feel more confident, but is it really better? If he were here, surely he'd betray his own nerves, then Urim would, in turn, relax. Yes, you can't hide fear; it'll waft out in unguarded signals, no matter how closely you try to smother it. And he of all people should be afraid, but by all accounts he isn't. Yet how can he not be? How can a rookie boxer just out of university think he can worst an old sweat who's learnt his trade, painfully, all over Serbia and has at 26 earned the reputation of being the best unpaid middleweight in Kosovo? Yet, it seems, he does.

A friend of Urim's, a waiter at the Hotel Grand, overheard his opponent boast to a tight circle of fellow Serbs he'd win the fight – and not just on points! Where did such cockiness come from? At first Urim put it down to slivovitz and typical Serbian mouth, but after further thought decided it was more likely the voice of ignorance: the Serb simply didn't appreciate who he was up against. Yet the man's confidence – no, arrogance – still got to Urim and, for the first time in his life, made him start to doubt himself. After all, what did it mean to be Kosovo's uncrowned amateur middleweight champion? There weren't that many other pretenders to the title. Yet to be the best, even among so few, must mean something and the Serb shouldn't feel relaxed about facing him.

Yet he did and continued to do so, for a few days after the Grand boast word came to Urim the loudmouth had repeated the performance to another group of Serbs in the university bar, proclaiming in a stage whisper as he was about to leave, 'This fight's going remind the Shiptars who really runs Kosovo!' His friends had all laughed, but Urim, listening at second-hand among the shadows of his brother's burek shop, did not.

What was he up against? A hothead? A fool? A madman? If the Serb had been searching for a form of words to make Urim utterly intent on winning and winning at all costs, he couldn't have chosen better. With this one low punch he'd taken the fight beyond a one-to-one contest into something vast and messy – like civil war or even jihad. Raising both gloves above his battered foe would now vindicate every Albanian – perhaps the Muslim faith itself.

Yet what if his opponent did know what he was doing, was a skilled tactician who understood how a mind, even a confident one, could buckle under stress? What if his boasts were, like Mohammed Ali's, part of a strategy to unsettle for it was odd how those claims, which seemed so stupid at first, got beneath his guard and threw him off balance? At odd moments of rest during the day they'd rise into his thoughts like pike, snapping threats in a cold silent language he could all too easily read or, at night, disturb his sleep with stark images of failure and disgrace.

Urim tried to fight the annoyance off with a quick series of counter-questions. Where, precisely, did the Serb's certainly of victory lie? In his physique – the weight of punch or length of reach – or in his style of boxing? As he threw out these questions, it dawned on him how little he knew about his opponent. Perhaps he was one of those tall thin boxers, human stick insects, who usually ended up in the basketball team; perhaps his arms were unnaturally long and held high like a praying mantis' as he slowly felt his way around the ring; or perhaps he was short, neckless and stocky, would come at you, head down like a bison, yet throwing a gorilla's round-arm punches. How could he plan when he didn't even know such basic information?

So he decided to quiz the town's two Albanian boxing experts. They might see this not as sensible research, but a damaging loss of nerve and spread the word accordingly, yet he had to risk that. But his efforts came to nothing for they drew only stares and shrugs from the aficionados. The Serb, it seemed, had never fought in Kosovo before and his record in Serbia, if he had one, was unknown.

What could Urim do? After days of hesitation he decided to throw over caution and plant a spy in the university gym. If his agent was spotted, the Serb would, doubtless, feel he'd won a great psychological victory and grow – if that were possible – even more confident; but if, on the other hand, he managed to sneak away unseen, Urim would surely gain the technical knowledge that would prove invaluable.

He chose as his eyes a student at the university whose mother was Albanian and father Serb, and sent him a message, asking him to look in at the burek shop next day. Urim had last come across this half-Albanian as a smallish, robust boy of fifteen, so when he saw from his position behind the vinyl counter the vaguely-remembered face bobbing above a frame that was stretched and spindly, a frame that pushed open the metal doors with difficulty and squeezed awkwardly past breakfasters squatting on stools, he gaped stupidly. The student had been chosen because his Serbian name and perfect Serbo-Croat would arouse no suspicion, but as he began to survey a body on which, it seemed, no muscle would ever have the chance to develop, he began to have doubts. This was no sportsman! What a waste of time it was for such a physique to take up weight training! But it was too late to alter plans and, besides, he didn't know of any other student from a similar background, so he proceeded to brief his agent for a mission that was rapidly collapsing into farce.

And so it proved. Urim's 'eyes' arrived at the university gym, almost set on converting his non-body to something built and went through a gruelling routine morning and evening for the first three days, but though he noticed many boxers punishing maize-balls, cracking the floor with ropes as their feet skipped furiously above, or throwing menacing combination-punches at their shadows, he didn't catch the slightest glimpse of the Serb. On the fourth morning, just as exhaustion was nearing, he decided to waive the orders about speaking to no one and, after dragging weary limbs over to a Serb-looking boxer who was noisily recovering from a painful series of dorsal raises, asked the panting figure, as casually as he could, whether he'd be fighting in the coming tournament. On learning he would, Urim's temporary right hand steered the conversation gently towards a certain middleweight, just down from university, who'd feature on the same bill. But the boxer, his breathing returning to normal, told him that though he'd heard of the fighter, he knew next to nothing of him for the Serb, it transpired, never trained at the gym – unless it was after midnight – and perhaps, difficult though this was to believe, never trained at all!

As Urim listened to the report, visions glided through his brain and returned during the shop's slack hours in troubling visitations. This was worse than ever: how could you combat a superman who didn't train, but was certain of victory? The Serb, however, kept his mystique for less than twenty-four hours. The very next day Urim learnt from an old Albanian who worked as a caretaker in the university halls that his opponent, while away from Peć, was living in a guest room on the campus. Apparently, at about two every afternoon a small blue zastava with three burly men inside drove up to the guesthouse, collected the Serb – not without squeezing – then left at great speed in the direction of the main road out of town. The old man hadn't actually seen this occur, he admitted, but he'd heard of it from a reliable colleague.

Urim greeted the news with a long smile of satisfaction: so the student had been training after all, doubtless in some makeshift gym in the heart of a Serbian enclave somewhere outside Priština. His foe now stood demystified, yet still mysterious. Did the secrecy suggest he was much less confident than he seemed in public? Was he desperately trying to figure out ways of countering Urim's unorthodox style, about which he must have heard something? Perhaps; but one thing was sure: the old man's words marked the end of Urim's search; he would never be able to smuggle an observer past the hundred eyes of a small Serbian community and into the secret training camp without being spotted.

Urim muses on his unorthodox boxing technique and, despite the pre-fight tension and closeness of his subterranean room, smiles as he remembers the reason why it is odd. The village he was born in, a village hugging a green valley in the mountains above Dečani, had never heard of boxing kit, let alone a gym. For football field it had any reasonably-flat strip of pasture, cleared of sheep; for football an inflated cow's bladder; for boots the boys' bare feet. However, when Urim was nine, one of the villagers, who'd been working as a *gastarbeiter* in Germany for as long as the boy could recall, returned with all his possessions and three thick wodges of Deutschmarks. After the main items had been unpacked for the benefit of the villagers squatting on the bare ground outside his house and their amazement began to recede, Agram, as he was called, produced two pairs of padded mittens which, with the help of much lively miming and a little explanation, were established as "gloves" in a vaguely-known sport called boxing.

For the next few days all the boys wanted to try them out, but most found that though they liked giving bloody noses, they didn't like getting them, so drifted back to the football field. Only Urim and his friend Jerdat persisted, gradually learning the sport's strategies by trial and error. On fine days the two could be seen slowly circling each other with rough unpatterned steps, throwing blows and defending in ways experience taught them to be the most effective. Jerdat was right-handed, so led with his left; Urim, though his left hand was stronger, took up the same orthodox style – not because it suited him better, but because he assumed Jerdat's was the only way. Southpaw was a stance he didn't encounter till after he'd left the village and by then it was too late: his improvised style had hardened into habit.

An unorthodox orthodox career, which had begun in the mountains above Dečani, continued in rings throughout the

Kosovan plains. Leading with his stronger fist, Urim found that while his jab could send heads jarring back, his right-hand hook bothered opponents scarcely more than ticks a rhino's hide. This would have been a real handicap had he wanted to turn professional, but didn't matter in the amateur game where keeping the other man at arm's length for nine minutes could win you the points decision. Nor did it matter that his counter-attack was clumsy: there were no marks for grace. So if he noticed his jabs were weakening the foe, he'd switch to southpaw in mid-fight and hook away at the other's head and body with all the might left in his stronger arm. During the course of a fight he'd use his right so little he sometimes fantasised he'd wake up one morning minus that arm.

Urim liked it best when he mixed it as a fighter, trading punches jaw to jaw till the bulk facing him so solidly, exuding so much insolent aggression, at last assumed that look of vagueness, began to buckle at the knees and crumple in slow motion to the canvas or till his head shot back too fast for the legs to adjust and he fell beyond consciousness to the floor.

As the bell sounds above his head for the end of Round One, Urim wonders whether tonight's bout will take the same course. Clearly, his adversary doesn't think so – or at least in public gives every sign of not thinking so. What's real about him and what fake has become too tangled, letting the Serb retain something of an enigmatic status right up till the moment of the fight.

Urim angrily recalls his last desperate attempt to learn a few hard facts. The training camp's location forced him to give up any idea of getting an eyewitness report of the Serb's boxing habits, but he decided, as very much second best, to try and catch a sighting somewhere outside the ring. This he managed, though not without risk, by turning up at the students' overcrowded *menza* – a huge, battered barnlike structure a dusty waste-ground away from the guesthouse and halls of residence. It was a Mars among refectories, warning off the weak-stomached explorer with ring on ring of unsavoury cooking smell, but Urim's resolve took him past the outer layers and into the scarcely-purer air of the hall. Once there, he gathered tray and food and sat near the centre of a vast expanse of trestle tables. Around him a fury of activity raged. The noise was more than enough for an instant headache, yet, seemingly casual at the heart of all this chaos, he began his meal and after each couple of bites made a leisurely survey of the room's compass points. Although those areas behind his head were hardest to scan – perhaps he should have gone to one of the corners – he was still able to sneak backward looks without attracting attention. As the students at his table seemed completely unaware of his alien presence, Urim continued his discreet scrutiny, but his opponent, so far as he could gather in the pandemonium, made no appearance. Perhaps he no longer ate in the dining-hall; but Urim's informant had told him he still did, and did so often.

Seated among Kosovo's brightest, Urim chewed slowly, as if to savour each tasteless mouthful, yet in no time, it seemed, he got through the three courses and was on the point of quitting when he caught sight of what he guessed to be the fighter, flanked, as expected, by his 'bodyguard' of Serb cronies. Anger at his informants' incompetence seized him for they'd misread a vital detail: even across half the hall's length Urim could tell the Serb wasn't 'quite tall' for a middleweight, but very tall indeed with – without doubt – a daunting reach.

Instantly the fight's pattern fell into place. The Serb would spend his time jabbing and retreating, jabbing and retreating, while Urim would have a mere nine minutes to reduce him to exhaustion pace. He'd need to knock his foe down, possibly out, for, when stepping inside, he'd be caught by many scoring punches. That must have been the basis for all that bragging; the Serb must have thought he could keep Urim at arm's length for three short rounds. But there he was probably wrong for he looked as if his frame was too big for the weight, so he'd have to weaken himself in sweating down to the limit.

Stamina would be his problem, especially in the final round. Urim began to feel better, even though his barely-digested food was already giving him bouts of wind.

The group of Serbs moved off with their trays to a shadowy corner where distance and weak lighting made it even more difficult for Urim to see his opponent clearly, but he did notice the Serb lift a glass of water with his right hand, which almost certainly meant he was an orthodox fighter. Well, that might make the task easier.

When the boxer and his entourage got up to leave, they wound through tables not far from Urim and, without in any way staring, the Albanian was able to get a good look. His opponent was a tall version of the Turkish-looking Serb – swarthy face with obligatory one-day growth of beard, thick black hair – but what was unusual about his height and what robbed Urim of some of his newfound belief was that the gangliness turned out to be a trick of the light. Closer up, the Serb, though by no means as stocky as Urim, seemed well capable of taking – and perhaps returning – a powerful punch. Then Urim recalled the Serb's boast about finishing the bout before the final bell. Perhaps he did have a special punch after all, something that Urim wouldn't find out about till the fight had already begun. He tried to lift his spirits by telling himself the Serb couldn't claim the bullet head, broken nose and cauliflower ears that he could as a seasoned boxer, but the thought, though in itself comforting, failed to comfort.

After this glimpse Urim applied himself even more intensely to training. Before dawn he ran faster and further, at midday attacked circuits with a gritted ferocity that finished them seconds quicker, and in the evening hit his sparring partner with a force that would sometimes send the gum-shield slithering across the ring. He'd never prepared so thoroughly and he awoke on the morning of the fight with the consoling sense that his body was fitter than it had ever been. The only snag was his mind. How could he recover that automatic assumption of victory, how sidestep fear, the fear of failure that locked the muscles, made you a standing target? The small fears were all he needed, were exactly what he needed for they made him more alert without inhibiting him, gave the toes an extra spring, the back an added suppleness. But the larger fear he'd let his people down and so lose standing in the town was one he wished he could duck. Sometimes during the day he'd dream of falling asleep in the mountains like some Kosovan Rip and wake to find the tournament and its expectations all forgotten. Why shouldn't he be able to do this? Why should his shoulders have to carry his people's hopes? Yet he knew you couldn't jump time forwards, only backwards through memory, and was in his heart glad. He must stand and face the Serb, no matter what. It was, in a way, his duty.

The bell signals the end of the second. Urim springs up and starts to jog on the balls of his feet, every so often shaking out a leg as if to dry. Soon his body vibrates into looseness and the time for more testing exercise arrives. He stands, feet wide apart, stretching the leg's inner muscles by bending each knee in turn. Having brought both feet together, he touches the floor in front and behind a score of times, and, after straightening up, clasps hands behind head and twists the torso as far as it will go to left and right. Then he wheels both arms above his head, like a butterfly swimmer caught on dry land, and feels a not-unpleasant pressure on the back and shoulder muscles, which he dissipates with a shake. Now is the turn of the neck: he revolves his head clockwise, then anti-clockwise till the tautness clicks out of the sinews. Imperceptibly, a sense of ease has stolen across the body's borders and recaptured the mind.

To sustain this feeling he now focuses on routine fight preparations, so gets ready to quit the bowels of the building, zips the kit-bag up, checks his bootlaces and, on opening the door, slowly emerges into the light. As he mounts the steps, the brilliance so dazzles him he has to stop to let his eyes adjust, and it's then that the crowd's towering roar flattens him. Wave on wave of its clamour, salted with expectation, breaks over his head, leaving him soaked with apprehension. This is the noise they make on a warm-up fight; whatever will it be like when he steps into the ring? They simply want too much, demand too much. He dislikes the Serbs as much as any of them, but shouldn't he resist swimming in that current? Not really, for wasn't it the foe and not he who'd turned the fight into a matter of race and creed? Once that had been done he'd struggled to find reasons why he should soften his response.

He remembers his time as a conscript in Belgrade, the swift, shocking change from a provincial capital that had few Serbs to a metropolis that was full of them. He made friends with a couple of Bosnian Muslims, yet there always remained a tension between them, the almost palpable sense of things not being said. So he began to spend his free time alone, but he soon realised there was no place he could go, in camp or around town, where he wouldn't run into a Serb every minute or so. In the end each turn of the head seemed to reveal a new one. His commanding officers, his fellow conscripts were Serbian almost to a man. How his barracks had rocked with laughter at Albanian jokes, as if he didn't exist or was deaf: 'When it was Kosovo's turn to chair the Central Committee and direct the country's affairs for the next two years, its leaders couldn't be found anywhere in the debating chamber, and not, after extensive searches, in the National Assembly building. Then as panic was mounting, one of the Serbian delegates' – who else? – 'had a bright idea. He went out onto Belgrade's streets, inquired among the lavatory attendants, road-sweepers and kerbside hawkers, and in no time rounded up the entire Kosovan leadership'. Ha-ha, very funny!

Then there were the legends: 'Albanian men think diseases come from contact with the air, so never remove their long johns, never wash their bodies completely, except once a year at a ceremony at which they hit themselves all over with leafy branches, dipped in water'; 'Albanian men show

how little they value their wives by prizing carthorses more highly'; 'Albanian men are primitive, quick to revenge, never forgetting an insult; they carry knives tucked into their socks and are always ready to use them in a quarrel'; and so on and so on.

He knew as an Albanian among Serbs he'd be treated with distrust and, when the wraps were off, open hostility: he'd always be first choice for the role of scapegoat. A relatively-harmless expression of this had been the way he was forever being detailed for the worst duties – cleaning out latrines or peelings potatoes at the back of the company mess. He could deal with all that pretty easily; more difficult was the threat of violence.

On one occasion a group of Serbian recruits, returning drunk from a spree in town just before lights out, tried to rough him up. That time there'd only been four of them, and he'd managed to stop any nastiness by pushing the nearest one so hard in the chest he landed on his back with his legs bicycle-kicking absurdly in the air. In the confusion he was able to escape with only the insult 'Monkey, monkey', rattling his ear drums; but on other occasions he was less lucky and still bore scars on his body to remind him of the fact.

National Service was a year and a half of slow torture. He counted down the last six months, day by day thinning his bedside calendar till at last he was free to return to Kosovo and his people, a people who didn't always like him, but who at least granted him the right to exist.

In Belgrade so many Serbs showed him prejudice he gradually came to feel every member of that race hated Albanians, all, no matter what age or sex, were equally hostile. So his last encounter with that people in the capital shouldn't have surprised him. He'd changed once and for all into civvies and, while strolling through the central railway station's main doors, felt a huge sense of release as if life could never be quite as bad again. He made his leisurely way across to the booking office, a broad grin stretched across his face, but as soon as his turn in the queue came and he asked the pretty Serbian woman behind the glass screen for a ticket to Kosovo Polje, she gave him an annihilating look as though he were some kind of loathsome insect. Her reaction was so unexpected, yet so real, that Urim was hurled from joy to rage with a speed that took him right through his carefully-placed nets.

'I'm as good as you are,' he shrieked – not just at the woman, but every Serb who'd tried to lower his self-esteem over the past eighteen months. 'I'm as good – and probably even better!'

Someone behind him laughed nervously, but the woman, her face now wearing the sourest of looks, took the matter more seriously for she simply left Urim's ticket and change on the desk and, quitting her booth, tried to catch the eye of the station policeman, who was leaning against one of the far walls, nonchalantly extracting grilled meat from between his teeth with a plastic pick. Urim, having few illusions as to what the officer would say or do, reached through the aperture, snatched up his belongings and walked swiftly out.

*Bloody Serbia! Bloody, bloody, bloody Serbia!*

From the top of the steps he delivers himself into the hot arena, cautiously entering its fluid world of light and sound. Luckily, he's come out a little to the back of one bank of seating, so is barely noticed by the crowd. Now that his eyes can make out degrees of intensity, he notes with relief that in contrast with the ring's spotlit glare he's standing in an area of anonymous light. As he moves behind the tiers, he still feels so keyed up he's hardly aware of what's going on about him. He walks in a daze, mind elsewhere. How can the here-and-now hold any interest when set against the fight to come? Without being aware of travelling any distance he reaches the weighing room where his old friend Skender jokes with him as he tapes his hands and puts the gloves on, but he barely responds, limiting himself to the odd grunt.

The bell clanging for the end of the fight momentarily brings him back to his senses, yet as he heads towards the shining ring a kind of robotic mode descends on his thoughts. He must win! He must win! He simply can't allow himself to lose! Like a watch on a chain, this idea swings through his mind, back and forth, so relentlessly it hypnotises him into that state, not far from trance, where all energy is focused on one end. Indeed so tunnelled has his thinking become the oddness of not having yet seen his opponent doesn't occur to him. He moves forward on legs, lent – in the absence of eyes – strange powers of navigation. They take him into the unforgiving spotlight where the crowd, his crowd, noticing him properly for the first time, lets out a collective roar of welcome, but he doesn't respond to it, indeed is scarcely aware of it for the noise seems to explode somewhere far off; it's as if he's hearing cheers for another boxer in another fight, someone worthier of support, some likelier lad.

Without quite knowing how, he finds himself standing next to his second, an Albanian he's seen in rings all over Kosovo, but doesn't feel he wants to talk, limiting himself to a perfunctory nod or grimaced grin. He has a fight to think about: everything else, even if coming from a friendly source, has to be blocked out. Instinctively, he jogs up and down on the spot, at times throwing punches, at others cuffing his nose with the back of the glove. After what seems a lifetime, the signal's given to climb into the ring; he crouches through the ropes, then, when straightening up, becomes aware of his foe for the first time. An image of cool arrogance fills his eyes. The Serb isn't prowling around in his corner as though the ropes are caging him in or frantically practising possible combinations for the last time or gingerly running on the spot as if the canvas is burning his feet. No, he stands leaning against the corner post, arms draped nonchalantly along the upper rope, fixing Urim with a look of contempt. Wanting to avoid the tension of a staring match, which at the time might prove something, but would in the context of the fight mean very little, Urim steps into the tray of sawdust and, when he deems his soles well-coated, dances off around his side of the ring, every so often taking the Serb's measure. What he can't miss is his opponent's tunic and shorts in Serbia's blue and white – a stark contrast with his own neutral black. Only by draping himself in the republic's flag could the Serb have become more provocative.

Well, it's too late for Urim to worry about that. He is a ski-jumper who's left behind that safe hut in the sky; his body's gaining speed down the ramp; now there's nothing for it but to go with the momentum whatever the result – whether it be controlled flight and faultless landing or a toppling forward, a desperate clutching at air and an ugly sprawling slide.

The referee comes over to inspect his gloves and boots. Urim knows him of old, an Albanian who tries to be so fair in his dealings with boxers of other nationalities he can sometimes be unfair to his own. In this case he's let the Serb get away with a day's stubble, bristling in dark tacks all over his chin and jowls. Luckily, Urim's leathery face has skin thick enough to have survived more than fifty fights without serious cuts, so he won't protest. This generous acceptance of liberty-taking makes him feel better about himself and the coming fight. All, after all, might still be well.

The referee brings the two boxers together in the centre of the ring, telling them to avoid butting, rabbit punches and blows beneath the belt. They glare at each other from less than a hook away, yet the time's too short for either to gain any advantage. They break, return to their corners, put gum-shields firmly in and await the bell.

Like a greyhound leaping through a rising trap, Urim's first out, striding, almost sprinting, into the agon. His mind, subdued to bodily imperatives, registers only what's relevant. The laziness of the Serb's orthodox guard, with the right glove lifted no higher than the collar bone, is straightway noted. This failure to protect the chin's a fault only a rookie boxer would fail to exploit and Urim, his spirits rising by the second, is no rookie.

He claims the first punch, catching his foe high on the cheekbone with a heavy jab. The Serb takes the blow easily enough, but when, seconds later, Urim connects with a series of punches to head and body, the man is visibly hurt. To forget the pain by inflicting its like, the opponent counter-attacks, bursting through the Albanian's defences with long-range jabs, then trying a big hook, which, with its path to the jaw blocked, makes glancing contact with the temple.

Though now the target, Urim is pleased with all he's seen – and felt. The other's efforts lost much of their effect through lack of co-ordination: the hook didn't follow the jab in swift succession, but arrived like a laboured afterthought. The Albanian should never have been caught, but, as if frozen by surprise, he simply stood, guard locked into place, while its awkward obviousness loomed up in front of his face. When it landed, he was almost happy he hadn't ducked. The blow, like the jabs before, didn't carry the power to ground him. Self-belief, like the Drin's bore, surges through him. His first guess was right, after all: here is no invincible destroyer; that was just a projection of his fear.

Though growing ever more confident, Urim mustn't relax: while the hook can't knock him down, it could, if landed squarely on the jaw, shake much of his strength out of him. He isn't planning to leave that bone unguarded for a second, yet he can't become complacent. The jab may be poor, but the reach is long and Urim will have to be careful when he steps inside. Although the foe can't hook, he may be better at body blows. Now is no time for a two-fisted slug.

Gradually, however, the weight of Urim's punching begins to tell and even bovine shows of resistance become more sporadic. The hook's given up, the jab scaled down from triple to solitary punches. What should have been the staple blow now arrives at longer intervals and with less effect. Such power as the punch first had has been shed in the fight's sauna till all that remains is a tap, which Urim brushes aside. The opponent who showed from the bell little wish to move, is now a fixture, never going forward, never going back, but simply turning on his axis whenever the Albanian circles him. His torso, which began with slow, barely-evasive oscillations, now stays monumentally still and his guard, which has never protected his face, is now – as the gloves lower and part – failing to protect his trunk as well.

The period for caution has passed; now's the time for an all-out attack. Urim renounces orthodoxy and, as a southpaw, hooks away at the stomach with all his uncombusted strength. Two savage punches do get right through, one sinking into the guts with such force Urim can hear the air whistling through the Serb's mouth, the other almost lifting him off the canvas and raising a look of certain pain. Though the agonist is now in agony, he does to his credit stay on his feet, while desperately trying to block further body blows. Yet just as he manages to cross-cover that area of pain, the Albanian switches to the head and when he raises his gloves to protect the face, Urim returns to the unprotected guts. Then in trying to defend two places at once, the Serb finds he can defend neither and stands in agonising doubt, the left hand more or less in front of his face, the right vaguely across the stomach.

Urim backs off an instant and, while jogging, takes stock. An extreme lassitude has settled on the Serb, adding weight to gloves already wavering in approximate positions, to head and shoulders ever on the point of drooping, and legs stiff and ready to buckle. All insolent aggression, all will to win have drained away with the sweat and saliva, and been replaced by an exhausted passivity, a mournful expectation of the *coup de grâce*. If the Serb were a bull with its stupefied head bowed beneath the matador's knife, Urim would have felt pity, but such abjectness in a man makes him angry. And when the man in question is the very one who disturbed his waking thoughts and nightly dreams by arrogantly parading his race, Urim's anger boils over into rage. That cringing object needs to be hit and hit till it crumbles, unconscious, to the floor.

In truth, the referee should step in and stop a contest that has ceased to be one, but, oddly for such a careful official, he does not, so Urim returns to pummelling the opponent's body unopposed. Redirecting his attacks to the head, he catches the Serb with a punch on the jaw which, though glancing, has enough force to knock him off balance and send him tottering back against the ropes where he lodges, stuck fast like a fly in a web. Urim, predatory as any spider, advances for the kill. Within seconds he lands half a dozen blows to head and body, any one of which would drop the opponent to the canvas did not the ropes intervene; but to the Serb, propped and tethered like a sacrificial bull, forced to endure agonising blows and wait for more, these brief metallic ticks melt in the fight's smelter and flow in burning ore round the runnels of his brain. Urim, living – like the Serb – in a dimension of time all his own, yet experiencing it as joy, pauses a moment to gulp – with relish – air, stale with sweat and smoke, then gathers himself for a final onslaught. This time the Serb must fall, but how can he when he lacks the strength to free himself from the ropes' artificial support? Urim, though vaguely aware of the problem, has no wish to puzzle it out. The fight's shape and his pulse's logic demand a knockout, however that may be achieved. If it requires a half-wrestling, half-punching of the foe through the ropes and out into the crowd, so be it.

Yet just as he's about to spring into murderous action, he feels a dragging pressure on his shoulders, which he can't account for, but instantly registers as annoying. Gradually, that weight moves round in front of him and a man's shining face floats into his line of vision, repeating meaningless sounds that buzz like a saw round his ears. He half-remembers the features, but can't understand why they're there. All he wants to do is get to the Serb and finish him off, yet this third person, not dressed for boxing, but clearly combative, is blocking his way by flapping his arms up and down in a ridiculous bird-like fashion. When he tries to push the irritating obstacle aside, it grasps him in a bear hug, wrestles him away from the ropes and only when it has him standing safely in the middle of the ring does it release its hold and raise his right arm high. It isn't till then that he connects the face, still staring at him through stupidly-goggle eyes, with the official whose role it is to save fighters from lasting injury. Slowly, those eyes lose wonder, relax into place, become human in Urim's eyes. Here is not an obstructive weight, but a fellow being, an Albanian, the referee who is even now awarding him victory.

He's won! He's won! He's actually won and not just on points! He's stopped the Serb before the final bell, before, even, the end of Round One! Praise be to Allah! Relief, like a hot shower, washes over him, unstringing from muscles the taut need to go on punching, easing his senses back to him. Lips taste sweat's saltiness. He feels his clinging, black tunic's cool wetness, once more snuffs the rank air and for the first time since entering the arena fully registers the crowd's decibels, now amplified by celebration. He lifts his gloves above his head and while striding round the ring, shakes his arms in a kind of triumphant conducting of the crowd's applause. On his circuits, however, he can't help noticing his defeated foe being untangled from the ropes and supported back to his corner on rubbery legs. He goes over to commiserate, but it's all pretence for, underneath, he's pleased with every blow he landed. His sole regret isn't that he hurt the Serb, but that he didn't hurt him more: a total thrashing would have stopped that hothead from ever opening his mouth again to boast or sneer.

His senses have returned, but not his sense. Yet after he's descended from the bright arena to the dim changing room and the cheering's subsided to the desultory chatter of departing spectators and then to eerie silence, and after a shower's battered him into warm tired submission, which slows the pulse and stems the adrenalin flow, and he's sitting on the bench again, other thoughts intrude. It comes to him that if the referee hadn't stepped between, he'd have gone on pummelling his trapped opponent till ... till what? Maiming, perhaps even death, he was so wound up. Then, oddly, for the first time in nine years of fighting he imagines what it would be like to hit someone so hard the brain ceases to function, the heart to beat, and he pictures lying motionless in the middle of the ring what had a moment ago been a living body, but is now cooling into a corpse. It lies there without hope of cure, yet still the officials fuss: although the shape's turned over, arms raised, heart massaged, not the slightest tremor can be seen. Surely no one deserves to have his life punched out of him, especially not that stupid Serb, who forced him into so much painful self-scrutiny, but who now seems barely worth thinking about.

Urim would like to congratulate himself on his new set of principles, but realises how flawed they are for they ignore the business of hurting when he felt no dismay, but a happiness that deepened with each blow. This is something he's never met before: the sheer pleasure of inflicting pain. Surely it can't be right to find your joy in another's hurt. Yet there it is. He undeniably has. Perhaps the feeling swam up with this one opponent, unique, never to resurface. Perhaps the thrill of release at a huge obstacle so easily removed carried him away and he enjoyed too much the punches that shattered the image of his terror. Or perhaps the joy is that of an Albanian underdog, granted precious moments of revenge without fear of reprisal, who loses ring discipline and gives the over-dog an over-beating.

When he emerges from the sports hall much later, the euphoria of victory has shrunk to feelings of unease. There are only a few well-wishers still waiting outside, but, as soon as they see Urim, they surround him, patting him on his back and celebrating his progress through the square with nationalist chants. Yet he moves among them like a thief, meeting their smiles with guilty scowls, their praise with grunts. He wishes he were anywhere but in the centre of that moving circle of adulation and at the first opportunity lowers his head, ducks through the admiring ring and with a sudden turn of speed disappears down an unlit alley.

Just before dawn he dreams of a long winding street, down which he walks. Every five metres or so an angry face thrusts itself from the shadows and shouts at him in a language he thinks he knows, but can't quite grasp. The words are rammed home with pointed fingers or shaken fists. He wants to ask these figures why they're so hostile for he's done nothing wrong, yet as soon as he turns to face them their forms are sucked back into the night. At first he thinks they must have mistaken him for another, so starts to feel sorry for himself, but as charge follows charge in a verbal gauntlet, he becomes enraged at the injustice of it all – what right have they got to pick on him, an innocent man? Yet after the anger's burnt itself out he begins to suspect his accusers may, after all, be right. He seems to have done something wrong; he can't remember exactly what, but his jabbing heart tells him he must flee in horror from human contact, hide himself away before he does something worse. He breaks into a sprint, arms pumping wildly, legs half staggering in the effort to push himself forward as fast as possible and just as he reaches top speed he enters an area of darkness, colliding with a obstacle which, like a punchbag, half gives under the impact, but has enough bulk to stop him in his tracks. He crumples to the road, winded. When he looks up at last, he notices the object is still swinging back and forth above him like the pendulum of a grandfather clock. He catches the material wrapped around the oscillating thing, pulls himself up and, as he does, realises he's clutching not coarse sacking, such as may cover scrap, but the woollen surface of an overcoat with buttons, sleeves, a collar and – surely not! – a body that hangs inside. He releases his grip with an instinctive recoil as if the coat were live and his hands wet. He stands back and after much squinting determines that what raises the form above the ground is a rope and that the head lolls far forward on what must be a broken neck. Mastering the desire to retch, he strains on tiptoe and pushes the head up. A face, permanently twisted in pain, stares down

at him with throttled eyes and a blackened tongue poking out
of a gaping mouth!

Urim screams himself awake. Not just his head, but the whole
body aches as if he, and not the Serb, was fisted to defeat
the night before. No elation survives; in fact, he feels more
as if he's been sentenced to death and this is the morning of
his execution. But, no, it can't be: the Serb must still be alive
and, at heart, Urim is glad, though he can't feel much relief
as he knows he carries within him, like a deadly bacillus, a
blind will to kill. How can he allow himself to climb into a
ring again? He can no longer be trusted, can no longer trust
himself. No, he must sever all links with the fighting world,
although it's been his life support for the past nine years. And
outside the ring in his daily life he must keep himself in check,
avoid any quarrels that might lead to a brawl. You never know
what might happen! He's a danger to others, to himself, no
longer the hero, more the criminal, who for society's and his
own sake has to be shut away. No, he must never put boxing
gloves on again.

For the next days, weeks, months, during a mild autumn and
bitter winter, he keeps to his resolution. So mastered is he by
fear that on his twice-daily walks to and from his brother's
shop he goes the long way round to avoid the gym that was
his second home. He feels like a recovering alcoholic: the
merest whiff of embrocation and sweat or the sound of one
short burst of speedball battering could send him back on the
road to addiction. He stops seeing boxing friends, only meets
them by chance on the streets, says a few numb words, tries
a half-hearted joke, then moves on. He can't be drawn out on
the subject of boxing anymore, not even by his brother, will,
whenever it's mentioned, abruptly change the topic or lapse
into awkward silence. Not only does he no longer watch fights
on TV, he'll even walk out of the room or abruptly switch the
set off if one comes on.

This strict regime brings its rewards. The panic lessens as he starts to feel more in control. He is after all what he always took himself to be: a good citizen, perhaps even a good man, certainly suitable material for marriage. His thoughts begin to turn to Lume, the baker's daughter and his childhood sweetheart, who, as he knows from her letters, would be only too pleased if he climbed the mountain behind Dečani up to her again.

However, his boxing fast is so severe he begins to crave the very thing that's denied. In musings through the day and dreams at night images from earlier bouts unreel across his mind, images he tries to devalue. These inner films, he tells himself, hold no glamour; though they preserve the order of punches, they're so drained of colour as to be travesties, mere film loops endlessly projected in grainy monochrome. The actual fights, he decides, are little better. The special bouts, which make training's drudgery worthwhile, come so rarely, are over so quickly – no time to savour the decisive blow – and then afterwards when the sweat's been showered off and the cuts salved and he's walking along the street or drinking in a cafe there's so little left, except the cheers, which hour by hour grow quieter in the memory. If the fight's living process could, as in a film, be freeze-framed and the mind, while still at the point of greatest excitement, linger over each shot – the glove shattering a glass chin, the head shooting back, the eyes becoming vacant and legs finding the body suddenly insupportable – then a return to the ring might be the right decision; but it can't, so he won't return.

However, this kind of thinking fails to go deep enough; parts of him still feel drawn to boxing and its images come back, with increasing allure. His body begins to tell him things he doesn't want to hear about how flabby his stomach has become, how loose his muscles. In the past large meals were burnt off in a day's training. Now he eats as much, yet does no exercise. He wakes in the morning feeling tired and sluggish, and throughout the day is unnecessarily curt with the customers.

He endures this decline for the winter, but when spring with all its compulsions arrives he feels he has to do something; he doesn't know what, but there's a pressing need to be energetic. He takes up football, tries a little basketball, but, though his muscles start to harden, he soon confirms he's too stocky for the first, too small for the second, so his thoughts about himself and the world around him remain depressed. Nothing, it seems, can take boxing's place; only that sport can bring back his vital self. And so he finds himself walking past the town's gym on his way to and from work and in the end, despite much unease, paying visits, at first briefly to exchange a few words before leaving, but later to stay and give advice on technique and strategy. It isn't long before he's in the ring again, training young boxers' reflexes by suddenly offering spar pads for snap shots or quick bursts. Eventually, the pads give way to gloves and he's once more sparring. At times – when he's hurt or hurting – the old urge comes on him and, in horror, he relives the savagery of contests, with an opponent stretched out on the canvas, all but dead. Panic then grips him and he drops his gloves and backs off like a hammered boxer, praying for the white towel; but the panic, like most other emotions, finally fades and he's left with an obsession which, day by day, spreads and sprouts.

At last, when the unrelenting summer has shortened his temper to its fuse and he can no longer ignore the daily irritations from Serbs on the streets and in the shops of Priština, he knows he's ready to box again. What else can he do? Serb army units outside town have all the guns, Serb police inside all the truncheons and dogs. Only in boxing can he discharge his anger safely. He therefore enters his name for the next tournament and soon learns, with delight, his opponent will be a Serb. He trains for the bout harder than ever, running prodigious distances before sunrise, devouring circuits at noon and sparring ferociously as the evening cools. And all the time he dreams this will be the fight when a lax referee fails to step in and he'll finally be free, free to spend all his rage on Serbia's unprotected guts.

# You Could Say So

'Teacher! Teacher!'
The shouting and banging on the door hauled Robert up from
sleep. Surfacing, he rubbed his eyes and slowly forced them
open.
*What time is it? Half-past eight! Can't a poor man get some
sleep – at least, at the weekend?*
'Teacher! Teacher! Robert! Robert!'
The banging, if anything, was getting louder. Reluctantly, he
rolled out of bed.
'What is it?' he called somewhat testily as he shuffled over the
lino to the front door.
When he opened up, he was faced with a third-year student,
Tyrhan. Ever since he'd arrived to take up his post in Prizren,
Tyrhan had grabbed every opportunity to sound him out on
this topic or that. He would do so at the end of lectures, over
coffee at the college canteen or the cafe where he hung out
with his friends, and during breaks in improvised football or
volleyball matches. He seemed to pop up with his questions
everywhere. Robert strongly suspected he'd been planted by
the secret police to check if he was a spy or was poisoning
the students' minds with capitalist propaganda. Yet he didn't
mind that for there were compensations: Tyrhan saw it as one
of his duties to introduce Robert to all that was going on in
town or the surrounding region, so he discovered a lot more
than he would have done, had he blundered round on his own.
A fair trade-off, he felt. Yet in Tyrhan's presence he did keep
a tight control on his tongue, even after – or particularly after
– a few tumblers of *raki*. All his 'subversive' views on Tito,
Brotherhood and Unity, Self-Management – not to mention
Milovan Djilas – were kept strictly to himself. If Tyrhan was
really writing reports on him for SUP, there'd be nothing
incriminating in them.
'Hi, teacher! We're going to wedding – cousin of Altan and
Demir – out in countryside. Very traditional. Wanna come

see a real Albanian wedding? Lot different from wedding in town.'

Robert found it ironic that while Tyrhan liked to show him all things Albanian, he called himself a Turk. Though he seemed to know very few Turkish words and these were pronounced, according to one of his friends who'd worked in Turkey, with a strong Albanian accent, he never seemed to have any doubts about his origins. He was, indeed, excessively proud of his lineage; it put him, he felt, above the ordinary Albanian, heir to the Ottomans who'd ruled the Balkans for so many centuries, a kind of aristocrat in a country without aristocrats.

'But I'm not even up!'

'*S'kar problem*. I borrowed car. Altan, Demir are outside now – make sure no kid scratch it.'

The brothers Altan and Demir were Tyrhan's best friends; they, like him, prided themselves on being Turkish, but, unlike him, knew no English.

'But do you mind all that translating for the three of us?'

'No, no ... happy to do it.'

*A wedding could be interesting, I suppose.* 'Well, alright then, but I'll be a while getting ready.'

'No problem. We wait.'

'OK, you go to the car and I'll be down in a few minutes.'

More than twenty minutes later, Robert was sitting in the front seat of a blue zastava, with Altan and Demir wedged uncomfortably in the back. After driving through the outskirts of Prizren, Tyrhan linked up with seven other cars at the coach station. They were all now moving en masse out of town in a kind of convoy. Looking round the rest of the procession, Robert couldn't help noticing that the other cars were filled exclusively with men.

*Where have the wives, daughters, sisters, aunts gone? How can you have a wedding of all things without women?*

Tyrhan didn't seem to notice anything odd about the entourage. In any case, his thoughts were elsewhere, focused on the coming ceremony.

'You know, us Muslims in city are like you in West. We don't go to mosque, don't believe anything, yet in end we're still Muslim. But in countryside you can still see real thing.... This wedding's gonna give you surprise!'

Soon Prizren's last vestiges were left behind and they found themselves deep in the countryside. After about five kilometres down the main road to Suva Reka, they turned off right. Tarmac gave way to dirt and they bumped over hard-baked ruts, raising a pall of dust behind. It was just as well Robert had eaten no breakfast for the constant judders, the dust drifting through open windows and an intensifying sun, shining directly through the windscreen, would surely have brought it up. Just as he was beginning to feel his stomach might, after all, be thrown into a phantom, sickless sick, the convoy drew up in what seemed the middle of nowhere. Before them stood a farmhouse, whose whitewashed upper storey and red-tiled roof could just be seen above a high stone wall that circled the property.

*Is this a remnant from the time when families had to defend themselves against brigands or is it just obsessive privacy? If the latter*, thought Robert, looking around him when the dust had settled, yet seeing little other habitation in the wide plain, *who are they guarding their privacy from?*

After a concerted honking of horns, a door in the wall opened and through it came a small, weathered man in a white skullcap. He greeted the guests in what Robert took to be Albanian, all the while gesturing for them to follow him inside. Once they'd ducked their heads under a low lintel, they were led across the courtyard under an already-hot sun to the refuge of a cool, shady room at the rear of the farmhouse. It was a long bare space, devoid of seat or table, but against the four walls cushions had been set. By squatting on haunches or sitting in modified Lotus position, the twenty-or-so men could just about be fitted in around the room's edges. To gain some support, Robert leant back against the white rough-cast wall.

Though his back was no longer under pressure, he still didn't feel totally at ease: the concrete floor was already asserting its presence through the thinly-padded cushion.

As the host plied the guests with demitasses of Turkish coffee and Russian tea, they seemed to recover from the dust and bumping, and a lively conversation – full of banter, Tyrhan informed him – sprang up. Cigarettes were handed out one by one, which Robert, apparently, could not refuse: tradition had it that the host would circle with his cigarettes and the guest simply had to accept them, whether he smoked or not. In no time Robert had built up quite a pile.

'What do I do with these?' in whispered tones.

'Don't worry. Give me later. We,' indicating Altan and Demir as well as himself, 'smoke all.'

Through the open door drifted the sounds of a highly-amplified gypsy band. From where he was seated Robert could just about make out four musicians as they played clarinet, mandolin, accordion and tam-tams in an open barn across the courtyard. Electrical amplification couldn't hide the impression of a medieval scene out of Breughel: haphazard homeliness and squalor – mangy dogs sniffing and wandering round young children, playing games or staring into the room, dirty fingers in mouths. After much tea and coffee slurping, there was a temporary lull in the conversation as two benches were brought in and laid side by side in the room's centre; over them was draped a clear plastic tablecloth. This time the wizened Albanian was helped by two younger lookalikes.

'Farmer's sons. Oldest boy's one getting married. We've not seen him.'

'But we will?'

'Hope so.'

On the improvised table a huge bowl of chicken noodle soup, surrounded by hunks of bread, another large bowl of lamb stew with beans and a dish of raw hot peppers were set. Noticing islands of grease floating on the soup's surface, Robert decided against a starter and instead ladled generous helpings of stew into his bowl, which he then took out into the shade of the yard so he didn't have to eat in a tobacco fug. He was shortly joined by Tyrhan.

'When's the wedding going to begin?'

'Oh, not yet. We have to go to bride's house first.'

'So what's happening now?'

'Groom's father showing guests – how you say? – hospitalness.'

'Hospitality,' smiling.

'Yes, soon we drive to bride's house. More hospitality, then bring her here.'

'Well, with our convoy of cars there's no danger of her being kidnapped on the way back.'

Tyrhan took off his dark glasses to guffaw.

'No, but you're right: I guess we're sort of *hajduk* band, but no guns.... You know, this wedding, parents arrange it. Bride and groom don't know the other.'

'You mean they've never met!'

'No, not once; this first time.'

'God, I hope they hit it off right from the start.'

'Usually, they learn to like, even love the other. Slowly, slowly....'

'Catchy monkey. Well, I hope so.'

When they returned to the room, the hot course had been replaced by platters of red and white grapes. As Robert was spitting his bunch's last seeds carefully into his bowl, a general shout went up and all the men rose. After shaking the host's hands and slapping him on the back to their satisfaction, they took up their positions in the cars and the cavalcade moved off again, horns blaring. Their Zastava proved slightly cooler this time, with Altan and Demir having joined relatives in a bigger car where their large bodies would find more space.

This time the Prizren convoy was accompanied by the groom in the front car and the now-non-amplified gypsy band, who serenaded proceedings from a tractor-drawn wagon. The groom turned out to be a broad-shouldered lad in his early twenties. The constant physical demands of the farm had clearly built up a strong body. There should be no problem when it came to hanging blood-stained sheets from the bedroom window next morning. Potency was in the air as the clarinettist's wild notes and the pulsing tack-tack of tam tams lent a Dionysian note to the groom's progress.

At last they came to another high-walled farmhouse, just outside Suva Reka. Having parked in the field, the men ran a happy gauntlet at the wall door, shaking hands with the bride's father and four brothers, and then, once inside, sat on benches that had been arranged in a shaded circle beside a broad tree. Packets of cigarettes and cream wafers were given to all and, as they smoked and ate, a small drunken gypsy wandered in. He was clearly the local joker, playing tricks on the guests, stealing and producing hats, wallets and keys, and exchanging quips involving lots of gestures and laughter. All was conducted in a good-natured manner, yet after a while the father intervened and led the gypsy gently and with smiles to the edge of things. While these capers were going on, Tyrhan informed Robert, the bride was being collected.

'But aren't we going to accompany her?'

'I think not.'

'Or even see her?'

'Maybe not. You know, not even the groom sees her – not till later.'

'Wow!'

'Last two, three days she looks on no man. Stays alone in bedroom, cared for by mother and sisters.'

'In purdah!'

'That how you call it?'

'Yes, but it's not our word: we borrowed it, stole it – from India, I think.'

'All these days bride wears wedding dress, makeup, but face's hidden.'

'Oh, covered with a veil?'

'That's right. Not easy, you know: sit there whole day, talk little, get hot with all those clothes.'

'Sounds a real torture. Poor girl!'

'Yes, she is girl – sixteen, I hear.'

Robert pictured the bride on the bed, twisting uncomfortably in the midday heat, little drops of sweat under the veil smirching the white face powder as they ran down her cheeks. And all those questions whirling round her head! Will my mother-in-law treat me well or like a slave? Will my husband be gentle or beat me? Will he be happy with me or reject me, say I'm not a virgin and send me home in disgrace? And as Robert imagined her seesawing between hope and despair, he saw how vulnerable she was, a mere child, tied to the track, waiting for maturity to hit her like a train.

'Guest told me her car to go first – in fact, probably gone.'

'There's no turning-back for her now.'

'No, she was in one family, now she's in another.'

'A successful transfer of "property"!'

'Ha, sort of.'

So a quarter of an hour after being piped in by the gypsy clarinettist, they were duly piped out. The cars turned round in the field, let out a last long blast on the horns and set out for the groom's home.

On getting back to the farmhouse, Robert and Tyrhan came across an empty Zastava already parked outside.

'Bride's car. Now she's getting wedded.'

'What! Aren't we going to see any of it?'

'Oh no, *hoxha* – you know, er, priest – goes over to women's part of farm and does wedding.'

'So we just wait.'

'Yes, just wait.'

By the time they re-entered the courtyard, the ceremony seemed to be over for from beyond the fence that segregated women from men they could hear spirited voices singing in rough unison.

'They praise wedding.'

'OK, but what happened before all this singing kicked in?'

'Oh, not much. *Hoxha* stands at end of room, parents sit round side. First, groom comes in, then *hoxha* – how you say? – "sings".'

'Chants, probably.'

'Chants some Arab words to boy ... who doesn't understand, then bride comes in, maids behind and stands next to groom. *Hoxha* says more Arabic ... which bride, groom don't understand, but gets them wedded. Then groom moves across, lifts bride's covering. This is first time sees her.'

'Not exactly a love-match then.'

'Well, could be – in time they can grow to love.'

Though Robert had been moved by the generosity of the two families, providing for the guests the best they could in copious quantities, he couldn't help feeling disappointed. He'd spent most of the day at a country wedding, yet had seen nothing of it – not even a glimpse of the bride, close-up or distant; but he wasn't destined to miss everything for some other event was about to start in the women's quarters – Tyrhan couldn't quite gather what – and he as 'esteemed stranger' was to be the sole guest to go behind the barrier and discover what it was.

The groom's father led Robert without interpreter up to the fence door and after rapping smartly on it, stood back, as it was partially opened, to let the Englishman squeeze through. Once inside, Robert encountered a portly, middle-aged matron, holding the handle, who he took – for no reason other than association – to be the groom's mother. Just as he was beginning to feel he'd entered a secret, forbidden territory, a place where no man should set foot, the woman gave him a broad smile, straightway putting him at ease and making this side of the courtyard equally welcoming. The women who'd been singing raucously were now milling around in groups, quietly chatting and chuckling. Among them the bridesmaids stood out like something not quite human – replicants, perhaps – dressed to the hilt, as they were, in white and so over-made-up they could be taken for living dolls. Running around the groups and shouting or tugging at the women's skirts to get their attention were even more children than in the men's section. The scene's simple intimacy made Robert suspect the children lived there with the women; but what about the boys when they got older? Would they go over and join the men once puberty came?

The matriarch guided Robert through the throng and over to a room at the side of the farmhouse with double doors that opened onto the yard. On stepping through, he saw the *hoxha* seated resplendently at one end in a red tasselless fez above a prodigious grey beard and flowing white robes. He gestured to Robert to come over and pointed to the cushion next to his. Clearly, he was to have the place of honour, but from that privileged place what was he about to watch?

He didn't have long to wait, though his smiling in response to the words of the mullah, none of which he could follow, lasted long enough, he felt, to make him look like a grinning idiot. A few minutes after taking his seat, a boy of perhaps ten, his sunburnt face pale and taut, was led in by a tall, lean man. Many of the women and some of the few men seated round the room nodded approvingly: here was something, it seemed, they wanted to witness. The *hoxha* chanted a brief formula – in Arabic or Albanian, Robert was not sure – and the rite began.

The man loosened the boy's trousers so that they fell to his ankles, exposing a lack of pants. Though two women held a sheet in front of the lad, Robert, from his angle, could still see all that was going on. The man, who must have done this often, so nonchalantly did he perform his duties, got hold of the boy's penis and pulled the foreskin over the head, holding it in place with a sort of tweezer in his left hand, while the right brandished an old-fashioned cut-throat razor such as Robert had come across in the barber shops of his youth. Though its long blade shone, it seemed not totally free of rust – or, at least, serious tarnishing. Was it sufficiently sharp? Robert wondered, a doubt that only deepened his nervous tension. While he had no wish to look, he found his gaze helplessly trapped in a vice of horror. Try as he might, he simply couldn't avert his eyes.

The hand came down and the razor proved its sharpness, slicing cleanly through the skin. Blood welled up, but the man was ready, swiftly wiping his blade clean and placing the same tissue on the injury he'd only just caused. After a few seconds of shock, the boy felt the full pain and his face, which had been white, turned the brightest red. Yet though in agony and half-naked in a room of adults, he was determined not to cry. His face, however, eloquently registered the struggle to keep tears back. One of the women who'd held the sheet led him over to a mattress of cushions in an adjoining room. Observing through an open door, Robert saw that although more tissues were applied to staunch his blood, the boy seemed to feel no relief for he rolled from side to side, occasionally, despite his efforts to control himself, letting out a stifled moan. Seeing and faintly hearing the suffering boy, Robert started to feel smothered as if all the oxygen was being sucked out of the room and, to avoid suffocation, he needed to gasp for air.

The next boy, a child of four or five, had no such truck with trying to be stoic in all things. As he was led in, he struggled against the lean man's guiding hand and tried to hold on to his trousers when they were being pulled down. His foreskin proved to be not of any length, yet still capable of giving great pain, when removed, for, as the blade cut through, the boy let out a howl of pain like a wolf cub caught in a trap, then wailed and wailed and would not be comforted. He was still bawling as tissue was put on his bleeding skin and he was carried over and laid on cushions next to the older boy.

Robert's eyes had again been clamped in horror on the scene, no amount of willpower letting him look away. And this one had been so much worse to witness. His heart was still thumping and stomach churning at what the little boy had suffered and these, added to the lack of air, made him feel sick. Yet as he surveyed the room, he could find no one else looking in the least queasy; indeed all he could see were triumphant smiles on the faces of the adults. 'Rejoice,' they seemed to say, 'two boys are now on the proper path to manhood.'

Dressed, despite the weather, in a three-piece suit, a man sitting on Robert's left – later revealed as a teacher – leaned towards him, 'That was hygienic! Boy need it! You know, tourists – many – come see this.'

Robert doubted that, but was in no fit state to argue. The food of the day was inching inexorably up from his stomach. Setting aside all worries about showing insufficient respect to his hosts, he rushed, with hand over mouth, from the stuffy room and out into the courtyard, drawing in and expelling great lungfuls of fresh air. He was going to keep calm, he told himself, but that would be no easy task. Stark images of razor cuts kept returning. Then, as the food continued to rise, a forgotten memory, painful, long suppressed, rose in tandem: a faint image from his earliest days of his own wounding, the tight foreskin surgically removed, that non-religious circumcision. A loss of sensitivity at the penis head would now be the boys' lot as it had been his. Cleaner their members might now be, but not as responsive.

Upsetting as these thoughts were, he was determined they would not make him throw up. Such an outcome would be equal to retching over all the hospitality he'd received. As the food reached the back of his throat, he could taste its bitterness, but for a reason he did not know – perhaps his resolve, his growing calm or the air lock he periodically placed on his throat – it did not climb any further.

Ironically, as if his precipitous exit were a cue for all to leave, the assembled adults duly followed him out and, as he paced the courtyard, taking and holding deep breaths, they grouped themselves in a circle to perform a celebratory dance. The gypsy band, which had been brought in from the men's section, struck up a stately, slightly swaying rhythm, and the women and a couple of men joined hands and started moving slowly to left and right, occasionally freeing a hand to wave a white handkerchief. As he wandered on the periphery, well out of the way of the dancers, Robert looked across at the celebratory ring, circling in the sunlight, and thought of other rings – rings of skin – now discarded in a waste bin's depths.

Pleased to have kept his food down, Robert latched on to the two men, who, having finished their dance, were filing back through the barrier. Though he rejoined Tyrhan on the other side in reasonable spirits, he was loath to answer questions on what had happened, keeping his replies as terse as possible. He needed to think of other, happier themes, so started to talk of Red Star, Belgrade, Partisan, Leb i Sol, Pekinška Patka and Riblja Čorba. In the end, however, Tyrhan brought him back to the subject.

'Older boy, you know, when better, comes to this side – men's side – eats here, sleeps here.'

*As I thought: a rite of passage, but what a painful one!*

Evening drinks and snacks were being provided in the yard to the accompaniment of the newly-returned gypsy band. While Robert wisely declined any of the refreshments, Tyrhan, unhaunted by images of bloody blades, piled his plate with kebab, burek and baklava, and poured himself large plastic mugs of orange juice.

'Waiting makes man hungry.'

'So I see.'

'Well, at least you didn't miss all Albanian customs.'

'Maybe it would have been better if I had.'

'Forget it, anyway.... Look, I meet someone you should talk to. Speaks English.'

He pointed to a guest, whose loud voice could be heard from the other side of the yard. Still chewing baklava's sticky remains, Tyrhan led Robert over to the man, who was introduced as the boss of a small trucking company in America. His stockiness and the way his bullet head ran down to shoulders with hardly a neck between suggested he'd little trouble enforcing his authority over the drivers – no doubt resorting to physical means, if needs be. As they were nearing, Robert noticed the man reach into his jacket's inner pocket and, having produced a flask, take a quick swig. He clearly had no time for the soft drinks on offer, preferring his own *raki*. It seemed he'd been indulging quite a while for when Robert reached him, he could tell from the man's red face and noisy animation that he was no longer sober. While Tyrhan moved back to his food and drink, the drunken man clutched Robert's shirt collar with his left hand, as if this were the prelude to a right-arm smash, and launched into a lurching monologue. His narrative swayed from the perils of Route 66, through his truckers getting round restrictions on driving time, to the back roads you have to take in smuggling drugs from Mexico, but whatever interest it might have originally possessed for Robert was marred by the fact that he was, literally, being collared. After what seemed like many minutes of this, Tyrhan, taking a moment from stuffing his face to look across, grasped Robert's plight. Setting down his mug and plate, he came over to rescue the Englishman, though not without difficulty. The man simply did not want to let go of the shirt and, when he did, he shouted after Robert and Tyrhan.

'You two, don't you dare leave early – or I kill you.'

They did; he didn't.

As Altan and Demir had decided to stay overnight, Tyrhan and Robert drove back alone. By the time they reached Prizren, the evening heat had worked up a thirst, so they made for the cafe overlooking the Bistrica. From the open window next to their table the sound of water falling over rocks in a series of cascades floated up to them and soothed their tired minds, while glasses of cool lager did the rest.

'You going on holiday this summer?'

*Is he checking my movements?* 'I don't know. I haven't got round to thinking about that yet.'

'Me, Altan and Demir go to Black-Sea coast. Near Varna, there's good camping site. Last year we did same.'

'You must like it.'

'We do, but sometimes we have trouble.'

'Oh, yes?'

'Last year, we drink too much one night. Bulgarian police stop our car and took it. We had to go police station. Anyway we pay the fine, but police still not give car back. We get angry. Police say, "You're not in Yugoslavia now, argue more and you get two weeks in jail." So we gave them more money.'

'What, a bribe?'

'Yes, a bribe, that's right word. Don't look like that, Robert! Everybody does it – in Yugoslavia, Bulgaria, Romania, Hungary I think, all over Balkans. Anyway we get car again, so all's fine in end.'

*Is he happy with what they did? Does he find it funny or is he testing me to see if I approve of law-breaking?*

'Talking of police, you know, my father's in police – and when I finish university, I go to SUP.'

*Just as I supposed: the secret-police connection!* 'So, you'll be dealing with my file, eh?'

'Ha-ha, you joke.'

'Yes, yes, only joking.' *Or am I? Change the subject.* 'If you had all that trouble in Bulgaria, why go again?'

'Girls, girls, girls! Here it's difficult ... too strict.'

'But not in Varna?'

'No, no, you get lot of East-German *fräulein*. Work hard in factory all year, looking for good time. Also some girls from West.'

'That's a surprise: I didn't know Black-Sea holidays were popular in Europe.'

'Oh only few go – socialists, I guess, or people looking for cheap stay. Last year I met Western family in bar. I was little drunk, thought they were Germans – East Germans – but they were Dutch.'

'Well, Dutch is a German dialect, but I don't think they'd be happy to be confused with Germans.'

'Anyway, this family's happy with me, very happy. Got friends with daughter – sixteen, beautiful. In the end moved in same hotel. Family said they pay my ticket to Nederlands, give me room in their house. I was interested, but couldn't go. Problems with my passport on Dutch side, then Yugoslavia said I had to do soldier-training.'

'Military service.'

'Yes, eighteen months. Good thing about if I go to police, though: don't have to do military service. They have own training in guns and how to defend yourself without guns.'

*Let's get off that subject: the police, the secret police – don't want to think of them, of their surveillance ... He's been testing me, I think. How about me testing him?* 'So you had an interesting time last summer?'

'Yes, great: East-German girl, Britta from Dresden, Pavla, Bulgarian girl, then the Dutch girl, Suus.'

'What would you think if your sister went to Varna and had a good time?'

'Afërdita?'

'Yes.'

'What, sleep with East-German men, Bulgarian men?'

'If she wanted to.'

Tyrnhan, no longer smiling, stared into the distance, then looked back at Robert with fiercely-angry eyes.

'I kill her!'


Later that night, lying on his bed, Robert reviewed the day's events. For all his urban sophistication, Tyrhan, when pushed, had reverted to village type. And what about that all-but-empty countryside he'd visited earlier – what was going on now in those scattered farmsteads? He thought of the newly-circumcised boys and the teenage bride. Was the younger boy still crying? Would the girl in a far room be groaning in pain as her hymen was torn and the bedsheets stained suitably red? He feared for her, having heard Albanian colleagues in their cups talk of how husbands on wedding nights liked to rudely force their brides' virginity as a first lesson in who was boss. The boys would eventually get better, but would the girl? Would this hurt be just the start of a lifetime of pain for her:

serial childbirth, back-breaking drudgery, a husband's slaps and kicks, the aches of old age? Of course, the boys would also have it tough, eking out a living on that dusty plain, but, at least, country mores gave them power, power over women, the power to demand their wives were always on hand, no matter how hard a day they'd had. So on one night in the future would those boys, their members long-healed, also enter their new brides with unnecessary pain?

Staring out of the window at the black, almost starless night, Robert recalled how Tyrhan had looked across to him with an ironic smile, when driving the car back, and declared, 'Country customs – quaint, yes?'

You could say so.

# First Light

Typical, thought Marko! It was just like Biljana to choose that of all times to leave: the day of Tito's death! But was it really the day? Rumours had been pin-balling round Skopje's narrow streets for weeks, claiming he'd already died or was being kept artificially alive on a support machine. According to these, the authorities hadn't been ready to tell the whole truth (so many things needing to be put into place); they'd simply thought Yugoslavs weren't ready to hear it. So a policy of gradual leaking had been decided on: first, hints of irreversible decline, then, at last, the full disclosure, all in the hope the first seismic shock would settle into mild after-tremors. Still the old marshal may have died on the day his relationship did.

After seven tedious, tiring hours at the gallery, checking the proofs of his guide to Sveti Pantelejmon, Marko trudged back through the estate, each concrete block looming in shadow like a huge domino upended in some intergalactic game he could neither grasp nor join. At last he reached his own high-rise, entered its battered lobby, but, finding both lifts out of order, had to haul his lanky body up seven flights of steps before he could rest, panting, on the landing. When turning the key and prodding the door open with his case, he was met with an eerie silence as if in his absence the flat had contracted to a cell and he were its prisoner. It was certainly strange how his calls seemed to lose themselves on suddenly deadened walls. Biljana was usually 'home' on Thursday evenings and could be so still: perhaps she was playing that game she loved to surprise him with in earlier days, of hiding behind a door, ready to spring out with cries of laughter the moment he went by, but empty room followed empty room and as he was completing a circuit of the flat, he caught sight of a note, lying neatly folded on the kitchen table, its edges yellowed by the sun's last rays.

This was unlike her. Not that she was ever to be found in the hall, arms spread on either side of an apron, waiting to hug him home. No, that wasn't her style, nor did he ever want it to be. What he treasured most about Biljana was her free spirit, which made its own decisions, led its own life. So when she came to you, it was because at that moment you were the one she most wanted to be with. Such a woman couldn't be expected to stay with you all the time, would, quite naturally, be taking herself off somewhere to do something now and then. The precise nature of that something was, like another's diary, none of his business; if she wanted to open its pages, all well and good; if not, that was her right. He therefore left her free, but did suggest it would be useful if she sometimes scribbled a message before leaving, nothing elaborate, just a few words giving some idea of when she'd be back. It wasn't that he wanted to keep tabs on her, simply that by getting a sense of her movements he could clear up such small domestic details as what they should do about eating. But she saw the suggestion as snaffling her movements. After all, they weren't hands in a factory, even a self-managing one, were they? So a clock-in, clock-out system was hardly what they needed! Well, was it?

Why then leave a note? A change of heart? Unlikely. Or on unfolding it, would he learn of a visit to Ohis, Treska or Štip for well-paid translation work or to a friend's for babysitting or her mother's for care and consolation? Or were the contents scarier? Had she suddenly been taken ill? Was she right now lying on a hospital bed, attached to drips? Surely not! He'd have been contacted at work and in any case if she'd been rushed off in an ambulance, she wouldn't have had the time or presence of mind to leave an elegantly-folded letter.

In fact, the note contained none of these:

*Dragi Marko,*

*I've begun to feel we don't seem to be getting anywhere and this feeling has grown stronger and stronger of late. I'm not even sure we make each other particularly happy any more. So I've decided to leave. Let's face it, our characters are so different, aren't they? That used to be a turn-on, but now just seems to get in the way. For instance, you prefer to stay at home – just the two of us, nice and cosy – but I want to get out and meet people. That sort of thing charges me up, challenges me, and I really need the buzz it gives. You must admit we're on very different paths, so in the end we'd eventually be prised apart, no matter how hard we tried to stay in touch. Look, I've lately been wondering a lot why I'm here. I feel you don't really see me, maybe never have. It's as if at our first meeting you made your own image of me and ever since, whenever you've looked at me, it was that you saw and not the real me. But I'm not just one more of your icons, Marko.*

*Ciao,*

*Biljana.*

*PS*

*Thanks for all the old times!*

So their years together were already 'old times' and he was like used tissue, tossed into some corner bin. Biljana had warned him – half jokingly, he thought – that one day he'd return from work to find her gone, and though his mind had more or less got used to that, his feelings obviously had not for a spreading numbness rooted him to the spot. How long he stood by the table, right hand foolishly clutching the illuminated text, he couldn't tell, but as life's motions slowly returned, shock gave way to weakness. His right hand dropped the letter as it gripped the table, while the left pulled a chair scrapingly across, and as the last light drained from the sky he slumped down, burying his face in his hands.

Past words, past events, from the beginning – the end? – sped, like videos, back and forth through his brain without ever reaching the right place. His head ached with a confusion which seemed, if anything, to be growing. Some relief, any relief, had to be found. He thought of phoning friends and lessening the grief by sharing it, but who should he call? Slavko? No, there'd always been a competition in their friendship, and though he'd try to console, he'd still betray the smug sense that his still-surviving, six-years with Marika had been more successful than Marko's four with Biljana. What about Vlado? He was a good friend for socialising, would sympathise, but, ultimately, he was only really interested in himself. After a few minutes he'd be relaying his own troubles, perhaps even hinting they were the more serious. Maybe a woman then. Jana? No, she was closer to Biljana than to him and would assume he was only ringing to wheedle information out of her. Or Bogdana? Perhaps, but didn't Biljana once say she fancied him? It could have been a joke, but he didn't want her misinterpreting his call as an attempt to get to know her better, now that he was 'free'. Going through the rest of the list, he found objections of one sort or another to each name, so in the end decided to hold his peace till he'd gained more control over his feelings.

He tried to find comfort by telling his all-too-willing brain that the break wasn't necessarily final, that she'd have to return to collect her things and when she did, he'd have a chance to persuade her to come back. Yet, gradually, he sensed why the flat had seemed so odd, so prison-like: Biljana had already taken her stuff, but so neatly his tired mind had failed to register what the eyes had intuitively seen. He levered his frame up from the chair and groped across the darkened room to the switch. A quick check of the flat confirmed his fears. Her romance dictionaries – all those fat tomes! – and presentation copies of her translation of de Beauvoir's *Second Sex* had gone from the lounge bookcase. Its loose shelves which she'd often asked him to fix were now exposed for all to see. How had he missed that? The wardrobe door in the bedroom opened to bare, unstable hangers, jangling tinnily – all those quirky coats and dresses, each so laboriously acquired and now, like Djilas, so effortlessly removed! The bathroom revealed cabinets bare of perfume, powder, oil and cream; not even the smallest bar of scented soap remained. And in the hall – how on earth did he miss that? – her naive prints by Generalić and Rabuzin had both been taken down.

That rooms could be so emptied of a presence that it seemed never to have existed there was the painful riddle. The flat felt desecrated, like those churches he wrote about, after the Turks had whitewashed the frescoes and filled the naves with alien chants.

He remembered the writing desk. Surely she'd have left that untouched, since none of her papers were stored there. He rushed to the lounge and over to the desk's central drawer. After some impatient rummaging, found, as he'd hoped, a tied stack of photos. On untying the string, he went through the pile one by one poring over every detail. The shots came so profusely and so randomly that any sense of development was lost and her changes stood before him in a radiant present: the changeling of twenty-five, blond and curly locks set off by a black parting; the twenty-one year old he'd first known with black hair falling to olive shoulders; the woman of twenty-four, locks in henna spikes like an angry chrysanthemum; and the student of twenty he wished he'd known, looking seriously from out of horn-rimmed glasses, face innocent of makeup, black hair pulled severely back to a ponytail. That last snap was one of Biljana's and there was another of hers which had somehow found its way into his collection. He didn't like it nearly as much – in fact didn't like at all. It showed her arm-in-arm with a well-built man against an urban backdrop he didn't recognise. Turning it over, he saw in Biljana's flowing hand: 'With Todor in Ljubljana'. Who was this Todor? Had she run away to be with him? Was she with him now? No, she'd always been perfectly straight with Marko and, in any case, he didn't want to get stuck in the quicksand of jealousy, especially as he'd no evidence to support his suspicions. He was determined to take Biljana's letter at face value.

Returning the photo to the scanned pile, he flicked through the remainder, noticing all the different styles: a red mini revealing her marvellous legs and green baggy trousers – her Eastern look! – covering them up; a loose lace dress – her pregnancy smock, he'd jokingly called it – vaguely suggesting a body beneath and the tightest of flannel frocks leaving little to the imagination. She put more thought than she'd like to admit into her choice of clothes and when they all came together in a perfect blend she could imagine herself – she once told him – a walking, talking picture.

With each new image the style changed, but what remained constant was her expression: in pink party dress or brief bikini, glancing up from a book or standing in a nave of trees, she'd greet the camera with the same look of challenge in her large brown eyes, a look that warned the unwary that here was a woman of substance, of depth. Her receding hinterland might take a lifetime to explore, as he'd found out, for even after four years he still stumbled on new, untrodden paths, twisting out of sight. But, presumably, she didn't see him in the same way. She must have felt she'd plumbed his shallows early on and wanted, instead, to explore the 'deep blue sea'.

From all that rich archive he selected one of Biljana in traditional costume, her lustrous black hair caught in a yellow scarf, her white blouse held tightly by a woollen belt, while her linen apron and skirt unfurled loosely around her legs. For a woman of few words, her mouth was unusually open, singing a Macedonian folk song at an open-air concert in Skopje. He'd forgotten almost everything about that Sunday afternoon, except the song for its title was her first name. The public performances, a survival of student days, were slowly given up, but she'd still burst into private song at odd moments of the day, producing those raw throaty sounds in solidarity with Slav girls sold to the Turk as slaves, bricked up alive in the foundations of bridges or lamenting over the bodies of brothers killed in battle. Occasionally, as here, her face would relax into a smile as she celebrated the love of a Macedonian boy and girl, and that untypical look was why he chose the shot.

On carrying it reverently over to the mantelpiece, he lit two candles in front of the upright picture and, switching off the main lights, stood silently before her image, noticing how it seemed to absorb each radiant flicker until its surface shone like those icons in Sv. Pantelejmon. Let his parents pray to the Blessed Lady at their household shrine; here was his place of worship, the only altar he'd show devotion to. True, it was just Biljana's picture he was worshipping, but that was all he had. The letter of hers had some truth in it, yet was ultimately wrong: she wasn't just an image to him; she was much, much more.

After an indeterminate track of time he tore himself away and looked down from his seventh-floor window. There was a thin scattering of people on the pavement below, some striding towards appointments or assignations, some strolling in linked pairs, others simply gossiping in huddles. Next day the whole area, indeed the entire town, would be densely packed with grieving people. Skopje, stretching along its narrow airless valley under an unremitting sun, was bad enough on the best of summer days; tomorrow it would be intolerable and, except for his scarcely-bearable flat, there'd be no refuge from the stifling streets: by decree all workplaces would be closed, each cinema, every cafe shuttered and locked, and public transport at a complete halt. In their place martial music would pursue you balefully from each street corner, and around each picture of their dead leader, fringed with black like icons on Easter Friday, people would throng, sobbing or simply standing in silence. No, it would be all too much. He just had to get away.

That was it. The front-door lock clicked firmly into place. Biljana had thought leaving would be easy, a clean break. Yet as she looked at the door's nondescript laminate surface for the last time, memory began to upload files of images, with feelings attached, images of Marko's long body, the way he pulled his ear lobe when he had something awkward to say, but, most of all, the smile that always soothed her fears, telling her that, despite so many things outside being wrong, all would be alright inside, in their world. To avoid messiness, she'd decided against a face-to-face farewell; instead she'd move out long before Marko came back from work. Was this cowardice? Maybe, but he was sure to get too emotional, particularly when he saw she was set on leaving, and she didn't want to have to cope with all that. Had her letter been unnecessarily harsh? Perhaps, but she needed to be certain Marko wasn't left with any hope. He had to see there was no chance of them getting together again.

So the sinking feeling in her stomach as she descended the stairs surprised her. Tiredness from heaving all those belongings down seven flights to the car clearly had something to do with it, but, beneath that, she sensed a sadness spreading. The expected elation of starting a new life seemed – for the moment at least – some way off. She'd only just managed to get her things into the Zastava's boot and back seat. Her books had been wedged in the space between front and back seats and the mere sight of them there reminded her how impractical Marko was, how she'd often asked him to mend the book shelves, but he never had. After looking one last time up at the flat, she turned briskly and climbed inside the car, checking she had a clear view in all her mirrors. Luckily, the temperamental engine spluttered into life with the key's first turn, allowing her to drive out of the building's shade and into the sun's full glare. She left her old life behind.

The plan was to deposit her possessions with Jana and, taking only essentials, get away for a few days to her friend's dacha, a converted hunting lodge high up in the Šar mountains. Up there in the thin air she should be able to see things more clearly. Turning twenty-five this March had stopped her short, making her think about how she'd been drifting through her days. That shock reminded her of what Simone had said about bourgeois wives' lives, how snug they were, yet mediocre, drained of aspiration or desire, enduring aimless year on aimless year, without struggle, as they fell in sequence down to death. She wasn't going to allow herself to get caught in that bind. Simone was right: if a woman was lucky enough to find herself able to be self-supporting and therefore economically free of men, she should choose a life of adventure, pushing back the frontiers of the possible, seeking wisdom and new feelings wherever they could be found. That was the sort of liberated woman she wanted to be and she couldn't achieve that with Marko.

In relationships, her friends were always telling her, you had to make compromises, and that's exactly what happened when she and Marko first came together. He was older than her and she'd been a little in awe of him – he seemed so clever, so good at everything; but gradually she began to notice flaws, to realise, to her surprise, that she was better than him in quite a few areas. So why should she still have to adapt herself to him? Why couldn't he adapt himself to her? As months became years she gradually decided she didn't want to compromise anymore. This and the weight of deadened habit were what drove her to leave. Sex wasn't the problem. She and Marko had lived Simone's ideal: two equal partners without pride or predation, freely interacting in bed. Mind you, Marko wasn't the best lover she'd ever had – *Todor!* – but he certainly wasn't the worst either. No, her dissatisfactions grew outside the sheets. And perhaps it was partly her own fault. She was self-absorbed, it was true, possibly too self-absorbed to share a life with someone else. Well, if that were the case, she was surely better off by herself.

Thankfully, Jana lived on the ground floor, so it was relatively easy to carry her things in and place them, as discreetly as possible, around the flat. On leaving, she pushed the borrowed key under the door. She kept the other one, the key to the mountain hut, a hut which would help her make a complete break from Skopje. Without phone or postal service to bother her, she'd be free to sort herself out. With this thought she smiled inwardly as she drove away with only her smallest case in the boot. Certainly, she'd no regrets about leaving behind those boring business documents she translated for a living, but the idea of bringing along Simone's fourth novel, *The Mandarins*, which she had struggled to put into adequate

Macedonian for the past year and a half, had nagged at her mind. In the end she decided a barely-converted peasant's hut was not the proper place to do justice to the great Frenchwoman. The brief note Simone had written, thanking her for the Macedonian translation of *The Second Sex*, would always be her most treasured possession.

Crossing Golce Delčev Bridge, her hidden smile surfaced and creased her cheeks. Joyful cries through the open window made her look down at a knot of boys diving from the quay into the onrushing river, only be swept in an eye-blink a hundred metres downstream. Throughout her childhood she'd been a tomboy, bored with girls' games, preferring boys' rough-and-tumble: climbing trees, kicking footballs, playing Slav versus Turk, partisan versus German; but, best of all, joining them by the river for a bit of 'Vardar bombing'. It held some danger – you had to avoid being swept away by keeping close to the bank – but the pure thrill of giving yourself up to the current, being mastered by, then mastering it, just couldn't be bettered. Blissful, thrilling freedom! That's what she longed for now.

She pulled the visor down to shade her eyes, but the midday sun still stupefied and she'd have worried her reactions would slow dangerously had it not been that Popovo Šapka was only thirty kilometres down the E65. In no time she was through Tetovo and climbing way up above sea level to the little town at the mountains' foot. Paradoxically, Popova Šapka was most alive in the dead of winter when it reinvented itself as a ski resort and all its chalets filled. Now, as Biljana pulled up in front of the largest one, an all-wooden three-storey affair with a flattened chevron of sloping roofs, she found the resort desolately empty. This chalet, like all the others, was boarded up, abandoned presumably until its reason for being there – the snow – returned. Absolutely no one seemed to be about: no tourists, no staff, not even an off-season caretaker.

You couldn't drive to the hut; you had to walk up a mountain path winding above the chalets. Jana had told her the resort, rather than the town below, was the safe place to leave the car, but, just to be sure, Biljana clamped the steering wheel. Funny, she thought, for who on earth would steal her beaten-up machine? The only thing she now needed to do was stroll down the rutted road to the town for the provisions, and that meant not only food and drink, but gas for the primus and oil for the lamp.

Finding in the small market square below a general store, she set the bell ringing as she pushed the door open. She stooped to pick up an empty basket and, humming a folk tune to herself, joyfully went in search of all she wanted: bread, slabs of burek and feta cheese, palacinka, pasulj, salami, eggs, coffee and enough fuel for a few days. In no time, after carefully avoiding the newspaper-and-magazine section – this had to be a complete retreat – she carried her load over to the checkout, but was halted by a sight that lowered her newfound high-spirits: an aged woman, squatting behind the till, all in black, her tired eyes wet with tears.

'Are you alright?' she asked.

The small, shrivelled *baba* looked up in hurt surprise.

'You mean ... you haven't heard?'

'Heard what?'

'He's dead.'

'Who's dead?'

'Tito, of course.'

'*Bože!*' she exclaimed, more from decorum than shock. Tito had been slowly dying for weeks – or so the papers had hinted – but now he was officially gone, she did feel real loss. After all, he was like the sun you looked up to every day: there'd never been a moment of her life when the old Marshal wasn't up there, shining down on her, and now that sun had forever set. Despite her wishes, she found herself thinking of affairs beyond those linked with the mountain hut. Though she'd had reservations – who hadn't? – she'd fully shared her leader's belief in a federal Yugoslavia, made up of republics living together in peace. But what would happen to *Bratstvo i Jedinstvo* now? Who would stop the republics warring against each other? Slovenia and Croatia were already complaining about their hard-earned money being wasted on Kosovo and Macedonia in the poor, corrupt south. And what about the outside powers sniffing around? Austria had its eyes on Slovenia and Bulgaria, of course, wanted to get its hands on Macedonia again. So how would we survive?

In sober mood she paid and, having just managed to cram her things into two carrier bags, walked pensively back up to the car. It was, Jana told her, a further ten-minute climb from there to the hut. She didn't fancy doing that twice, so, after extending the case handle to bring the wheels into play and gripping the two bags with her stronger right arm, she started off up the steep track. Ironically, the haul must have taken up almost as many minutes as two journeys for every so often she had to stop to regain her breath, but at last she reached the hill's brow and Jana's wooden shack came into view. Small and utterly undistinguished though it was, it could still boast at being the valley's only building. On setting her things down gratefully at its front door, she turned and surveyed the scene. To her left the mountain rose to a spectacular peak that, even in summer, was still white. Along its lower slopes sheep, dotted to the distance, browsed on the stone-strewn grass. To her right the ground gradually swelled to a hill with a glimpse of dark green – a pine forest perhaps – beyond. Beneath her feet the valley fell steadily to a stream that gurgled through the length of it. She sucked in a lungful of bracing air and expelled it forcefully. True, her leader was gone. True, there would be hard times ahead, but, setting all that – for the moment – aside, who could not be content with this place?

After a night of fitful sleep Marko found himself early next morning down at the coach station. A quick wash, a holdall stuffed with clothes and money for a long weekend, and Biljana's photo in the jacket pocket, and he was ready for the long walk to the centre. He reached the ticket-office just in time to get one of the few remaining seats on the 9 o'clock to Ohrid, the last Proleter to make the journey south before the general shutdown. This good fortune and a breakfast of burek and yoghurt momentarily lightened his mood, but as the bus crunched the cinders of the station forecourt, then crossed Golce Delčev Bridge, his black dog began to bark again. Looking out toward the hump of the old stone bridge, he caught sight of the usual herd of sunburnt boys, one by one disappearing from the quay into the swift-flowing current only to be spirited way downstream. Ordinarily, he would have smiled at the happy reciprocity of youth and age, weakness and strength, but the glass barrier cut him off not only from the delighted cries, but from sympathy as well. Why, after all, should they be enjoying themselves when he, when the whole nation, were grieving?

They drove past the ruins of the old station with the clock forever stopped at 5.17. The general air of dilapidation – grey walls cut in zigzags to the ground, bits of Doric column, odd bricks crazily exposed to the weather – fitted his humour better. He'd been only a few blocks away when the building crumbled and the memory had never left him, invading his dreams and odd moments of melancholy. He, with ten thousand other sleepers, had been buried by the stronger second tremor, which quickly followed the first. Those, like him, who woke, woke to darkness and the distant thunder of collapsing buildings. He'd lived in the night for two days, unable to move in his rubble coffin, till he was dug out into blinding light, coughing and spluttering with the dust that coated mouth and lungs. He came from eerie silence to the sounds of excavation and keening. He was lifted into the demolished city miraculously whole, able, after food, medicine and an improvised wash, to walk away from his burial on unbroken legs. He met grieving parents everywhere, but his, when reunited with them, rejoiced: they'd lost the flat and most of their possessions, but their bodies had survived with nothing worse than a broken wrist for his father. His schoolboy mind, fastened on the family's fortune, simply could not at first grasp the scale of what had happened, but as he wandered through the devastated city and shared bread and soup with mourners in their village of tents, the size of the tragedy had slowly come to him. This time when a different kind of earthquake had hit his country, he'd understand everything from the off: the public grief (real and pretended), the obligatory black clothes, the strained faces, the oppressiveness. Yes, he simply had to get away from Skopje and seek solace in a quieter place.

Soon they were into the suburbs, leaving behind the streets he and Biljana had strolled down, arm in arm, on so many summer nights. As whitewashed houses with red-tiled roofs gave way to groves of dusty cotton, he could feel something inside him stretch and snap into the certainty that she was never coming back. Nothing could now bridge the gap between them. After an hour the road began to rise between white-flecked mountains, following the Vardar back to its source, but the ascent into cooler air was too gradual to defeat the intensifying sun. Blow on blow of its golden hammer through thin net curtains stunned the passengers into stupor. Only the little boy in front of him jumped up and down, excitedly celebrating Šar mountain dogs, a boarded ski resort and shadows he took for bears; but even he was eventually stilled when a partly-digested breakfast, which his young stomach couldn't hold, pumped in gushes over his shirt and shorts. His mother did her best to clean up, but the smell of sick still hung thickly around the seat. To take his nose off that, Marko stared out the window, studying how green groves gave way to branch on branch of blood-red apples. Though he and Biljana had spilt very little blood, their relationship, it seemed, had bled itself dry. Tito, unlike other Eastern-bloc leaders, had tried to avoid the shedding of blood, but he had spilt his own diseased blood in a series of transfusions. Jesus, it was said, sweated blood on the cross for our sins, yet his creed now clung anaemically to the Macedonian land.

Out of respect for the dead leader the roads were left clear of lorries, cars and carts, so they made swift progress, but, on entering Tetovo, were slowed to walking pace by crowds which, having overpopulated the pavements, sought space on the streets. The faces they inched past looked genuinely shocked or lost as if their daughters' long-garnered trousseaux had been stolen in the night. Cheeks shone with real tears and they, looking down, would have responded in kind had it not been for the sun's gavel and the unreality of glass which made them think of outside as no more than images projected on a screen.

The coach stopped briefly at the station before edging through the crowd and dust again. At length it could move at proper speed past mosque, Dervish monastery and Turkish baths before reaching the suburbs where tobacco wreaths were hung on house gables as if in Muslim mourning for Tito, their smoker of fat cigars.

In trying to find a more comfortable position for his long legs, Marko disturbed the ancient *baka* asleep next to him and apologised.

'That's alright, son. I'll have time enough to sleep when I'm gone. At least I'm still alive – unlike our leader!'

'Yes indeed.'

'He was a good man – a good man – good for us Macedonians. A Croat, yes, but he didn't let the Croats or Serbs or Slovenes push us around. He wouldn't even allow any of them call us Bulgarians.'

'No, not at all.'

'We know our language, our culture's not the same as the Bulgars', don't we?'

'Well, yes.'

Marko wasn't so sure about the last point, but, not being in the mood to talk, stared out of the window and noticed that the coach, having left the outskirts behind, once more had a clear run. As it climbed steadily, he turned back to look down Polog Valley to Tetovo's red roofs, glowing serenely in the sun, all sign of grief swallowed by distance. When he returned to scanning the window to his right, he spotted the

Šar Mountains' highest point, renamed after Liberation Tito's Peak, flowing into view. Even in death, even in this remote rocky landscape, he seemed to look down on his people like a god.

At the valley's end they gained a plateau. On that platform among the mountains could Marko rise above his sorrows and forget them? No, for in Gostivar's main square, between whitewashed spire and town hall grieving crowds had also massed. Most of the crush were Albanians, mourning as much for themselves as for their late leader: Tito, Yugoslavia's wily Croat, had protected them from the Serbs and Macedonians, but what would the future hold? In their white skullcaps and off-white jackets the Albanians looked like skeletons in some macabre festival of death, yet, after the briefest of stops, the bus did manage to inch its way through that square of dry bones and on a mountain road above the town pulled up for refreshment at a roadside tavern which was, mercifully, still open. Soon trestle tables were creaking under the weight of grilled meat, beer and *sok*. Shaken by the coach's jolting and numb from the sun, they made little noise apart from the clink of fork or glass, but above the awnings, shading their heads, invisible bird formations sang of what summer meant to them, while behind the inn a mountain stream gurgled mischievously over stones and once behind green walls of pine Marko thought he heard the raw confident bark of fox.

They returned to the coach with renewed zest for high passes. After zigzagging along the bare sides and over the top of the Plakeska mountains, the bus stopped in Kičevo to let a few passengers off, crossed the Treska, then there was liberation in the air. They skirted Slinovo, where the first Partisan brigade had been formed, and entered Debarca, the earliest Macedonian region to be freed from the Germans. And he was now free, but to do what? Be solitary, yes, but also gain distance, reassess. The mountains gradually lost touch with the clouds, the passes were less strenuously reached and though they still climbed and at times climbed high, he could sense their ultimate direction was downwards. They were descending towards the summer heat. Peaks flattened into hills, pine became beech and oak, and then the hills themselves split into a valley, down which their coach and a river sped towards Ohrid.

That river, tired of slicing through the landscape, eventually slowed to a meander and as the road followed one of its long curves they caught a glimpse of blue, but had it snatched from sight by a looming wooded ridge. It was frustrating, yet they travelled in hope, knowing that somewhere just out of sight a stretch of water lay glinting in the sun and that they should eventually break free of the valley and find themselves at rest beside it. The stony outcrop did finally give way and they turned through the gap into the outskirts of Ohrid, but after forking right at a mosque and freewheeling down Boris Kidrić Street, they drew up at the station without any sign of the lake. Marko lumbered from the coach on stiff legs, sun-battered but satisfied, and, after claiming his holdall, staggered down the road like a man from a bar made drunk by fresh air. Still he could see no blue but that of the sky, yet people strolling by were dressed as if this were a resort and they'd just come from the water. Their draped towels and bright swimwear over sunburnt bodies, their flip flops, shades and quick white smiles ordered the day. Miraculously, the black of public mourning, which seemed to have covered Macedonia as fully as Our Lady in the frescoes, had left the southern edge uncovered: he smiled as he took in the open shops and crowded restaurants all around him.

The pavement rose in steady incline, denying any chance of seeing what was beyond, but on reaching the summit he had to stop, put down his grip and stare open-mouthed like any heavy peasant. Although he'd seen many pictures, they were nothing like the real thing. Before him stretched league on league of deep blue water till at the far horizon white mountains joined it to the lighter blue of a sky that darkened as it climbed. The lake seemed large enough for a sea, yet was calm as any municipal pond with moorhens receding at intervals into the distance. And all that homely immensity was held by a light so soft and silky it hinted at degrees of peace yet unknown to him. This vast inland lake, contained by mountains, spoke of such quiet permanence that his problems, which, before, had loomed so hugely in his mind, began to seem less important, even small. Lifting his bag, he walked towards the water and, as he did, sky, mountains, ducks and all the scintillations of the lake rose to greet him; stretch on stretch of clearest blue shook his mind, like a hand, welcoming him to repose.

She'd woken to the rush of water and now, rucksack on back and boots tied firmly over feet, she pushed the hut door shut and set out in the strong morning sun for the tablelands stretching above her head. The ultimate goal was Crno Jezero, but to get to the Black Lake she had first to go down to fertile valleys of thick grass and alpine flowers. Soon, however, she was hopping from rock to higher rock with a chamois' deftness, climbing against streams' downward flight. Valleys opened out to exposed rocky terrain, sparsely covered by light brown or reddy-purplish grass. Though the air was a little cooler up there, the sun still beat down on her bunned hair and bare arms. Yet the heat didn't really bother her and she found her mood as bright as the landscape she walked through. In this high country her life's tangled connections seemed to unknot, leaving her mind and body free to go wherever they wanted.

The grass might be rarely green, yet, on reaching one plateau, she was met by a flock of sheep dotted round a small farmstead. A skull-capped Albanian farmer came out to greet her and his headscarved wife brought a round loaf, cheese and yoghurt to the table outside. Although they couldn't speak much Macedonian, the couple still clearly conveyed how hard their life was, less through their stumbling words than the deep lines and weathering on their faces, roughened by sun and snow to the texture of cracked leather. After thanking her hosts and ruffling the ears of their sturdy Šar sheepdog,

Biljana left, replete and with renewed vigour for the uplands. Her enthusiasm was rewarded within an hour for, as she was rounding a boulder, so huge it screened all that lay ahead, she heard louder and yet louder static as if some vast radio were disturbing the air, and, when the stony barrier at last gave way, stared in awe at mighty torrents surging through a cleft in a cliff high above her head, leaping clear of the rock to churn the deep pool below. Such dynamic energy, such overwhelming sound tossed her spirit under, seeming to drown it, but, instead of being suffocated, it gradually gained second wind and, finding itself stronger, kicked for the surface. Yet the lure of pure energy was still there and, as if by a charm, she was drawn, running, arms outstretched, towards the thunder, but she kept sufficient presence of mind to come to an abrupt halt at the pool's edge, while cool spray slowly baptised her.

As she grew damper and colder, the reverie receded, and she began to take in her bearings: Krivosijski Vodopad; so Black Lake couldn't be that far above. Yet, having scaled the ridge over the waterfall, she found she'd still have to climb quite a way up through dense pine forest. In doing this, she'd need to keep her wits about her: who knew what wild beast might be lurking in the undergrowth? She'd heard tales of walkers setting out on these hills alone and never returning. In the event nothing happened. In fact, apart from the gradient and the thinning air, which made her pant more heavily than usual, the whole experience was a joy with a cooling breeze whispering through the pines and from somewhere off to her left a mountain stream modulating the fall's roar to a pleasing rustle. At length, the twisting path took her up through a cluster of trees until she came out onto a ridge and stopped, astonished at what she saw below: the Little Lake stretched out, then narrowed to an isthmus, through which water flowed to join the large lake beyond. The Black Lake! And black it literally was with much of its length covered by shadows from the mountains and bluffs surrounding it. Yet after she'd clambered down to the water's edge and scooped a handful up, she could see it was as clear and pure as water could be. She sat her pleasantly-weary body down and took in all that was around her. What moved her most was the lake's shape: a figure of eight. Yes, she really had found a sort of infinity. The lake, the times, yes, life itself might be black, but all this endless dark seemed somehow contained by the solid immensity of rock, ridge and peak.

The pines, of course, were far from static; they rustled gently in a light wind; and after a half an hour or so she was back among them, plunging down forest paths. Why, she did not know, but she began to sing her favourite folk song, which shared its name with her: 'Biljana'. The words raised a smile as they brought back memories of student days when life had seemed so simple. Something, however, stopped short all that singing. She thought she caught the sound of movement ahead, down the twisting path and round behind a dense clump of pine. But when she halted and listened carefully, nothing, apart from the whish of branches, reached her ears. Surely only something big, a large body, could have made such a noise! But, look, forests could so easily make you nervous with their snapped twigs, odd calls and furtive scurryings. No, she shouldn't give way to fear; she'd probably imagined it all. Nevertheless, she did proceed cautiously, looking from side to side as she descended into the forest depths, and when she came to the clump, she inched round it till she had a clear view of what lay ahead. Nothing. An empty path. There you are, silly you, she thought. There was, after all, no reason to be afraid. Yet just as she was about to set off on her hiking stride, a huge brown shape lumbered out of the tree cover and in zoo stink loomed before her – so high it seemed to block out all the light.

'*Bože! Bože!*'

A mountain bear and behind a smaller brown body! A mother with cub, protecting her territory! That must be why she was standing so scarily on hind legs, pawing the air with her massive arms, snorting, blowing and popping her jaw. In deep panic, all Biljana wanted was to turn and flee, but just before she did an inner voice, coming from stores of knowledge she didn't know she had, spoke to her, *Whatever you do, don't run! Pretend to be brave: look the bear in the eye, if you can, and, speaking calm words, walk backwards up the path you came down. If you turn and bolt, she'll outrun you....*

Desperately trying to stop her voice from cracking or rising to a shriek, Biljana spoke in her most reassuring tones, 'Well... yes...I'm just...going...to go back...leave you...in peace... let you...carry on...as you were...before I came....all alone... with your child....'

She knew if this didn't work, you were meant to stun the bear with a spray, but she didn't have one to extract as gently as she could from her rucksack. Why, on earth, had she forgotten to bring the spray? How could she have been so stupid?

Yet, miraculously, her soothing words and fixing of the eye had an effect for as she slowly retraced her steps, the bear allowed the distance between them to increase; but, suddenly, without warning, her large body crashed to the ground and she began to beat the earth with her fore-paws. Terror freeze-framed Biljana, each bear blow shaking her to the heart, but, worse still, as soon as the beast stopped pounding, she crouched, then made a violent lunge. Was this the prelude to a charge? And, if it was, would she just stand there while the bear tore her apart with its huge yellow claws? Was this the way her life would end – killed and eaten like any forest prey, mere carrion? But the bear, instead of breaking into a run and bringing those savage paws down on her unprotected chest, checked its momentum, swayed back and, while glowering at the terrified woman, let out a long, hoarse roar.

Unable to move, Biljana stared and stared at the bear in utter horror; yet nothing happened and as more precious seconds ticked by, she started to sense that all this might have been bluff to warn her off, that the beast had never really meant to kill her. This, mercifully, now seemed to be confirmed as the mother turned to see what her cub was doing behind her. Biljana felt tears sting her eyes. She was still alive, yes – panting, with heart pumping, it was true – yet still alive!

Although the bear may have been merely trying to frighten her, she still couldn't take any chances, so as soon as control of her muscles returned and she was able to move, she slowly paced backwards, continuing to face the beast and laying gentle words on the air. Yet it wasn't till she'd rounded the clump in reverse and the bear was screened from sight that she turned and broke into a sprint. What started as panic, mixed with relief, gradually, as the bear and all the horror receded from her flying feet, grew into exhilaration. How wonderful it was to live in flesh, snuffle air and send oxygen coursing round the body from pumping arms to pounding legs. But she couldn't keep the pace up for long – she was no athlete, had never even jogged – and as she reached the forest edge she slowed, exhaustion overtaking her, and at the first chance slumped down on the sparse grass. She threw the rucksack off the shoulders of her sweat-darkened T-shirt and, lying on her back, panted as if her lungs would burst. That panting gradually slowed to steady breathing and she became aware she was looking up at pure blue air. Noticing a few scattered clouds, she began to follow their serene progress across the sky. Steadily, their calmness became her calmness and, from relaxed depths, laughter, like a subterranean stream, gurgled up till it so filled her she found she couldn't stop. Yes, life was a joke, wasn't it? One moment a waterfall, a lake could raise it to the sublime, the next a bear plunge it down to the point of extinction. She felt complete solidarity with the sisterhood of whatever species, yet a female bear, a mother defending her cub, had nevertheless seen her as the enemy and almost killed her. Simone was always going on about women as the prey of men; well, she'd come very close to being the prey of a woman, a she-bear. The trick was to relish life's joke, no matter how black, while it was being told. And for the first time in months, she began to think excitedly of what she'd do next day and in future days. Todor? No, not from one man to another. Paris? Maybe. A further step towards freedom, existential freedom. Having come so near to death had already made her feel differently about life. Every moment was absurd, yes, yet precious. Savour them all. So now she'd find another route to wind down to the hut and, while she did, she'd praise each rock, each tree, each living creature she passed, enjoy her simple supper, as if it were a feast, and lie down on her hard pallet to blessed sleep, all the time longing, yes, longing for first light.

Following the lake's curve down Marshal Tito Quay, Marko found that the first red-tiled guesthouse he came to had a free room – pokey and Spartan, it was true, but with windows opening onto the lake that promised lullabies of faint lapping when sleep wouldn't come. He paid for three days and, after laying out his few things and showering, left without food or nap, but with an alert hunger for what the town could offer. On reaching Moša Pijada, a pedestrian street that climbed steeply through the old business district, he ran into a *korzo*, snaking its way up and down the cobblestones, reminding him – if the declining sun had not – that the afternoon was far advanced. He squeezed through two of its happy, laughing coils to craft shops on the other side. After inspecting the wares of coppersmith, weaver and goldsmith in leisurely fashion, he followed street signs which directed him to the right, then left down a narrow alley till he issued out into Kliment Ohridski Street. He knew that somewhere along its length he should find St Clement's and at the end of a lazy climb he did indeed come across the church, almost hidden by a detached bell tower and steeply-rising courtyard.
After walking gingerly over random cobbles, trying to land on the grass sprouting between, he mounted rough-hewn steps before ducking to enter the low-roofed church. Once inside and standing upright in a darkness only partially relieved by the cool dusty light of high windows, he found himself as

ever overwhelmed by presences. It never failed; he'd felt the same when he first visited Sv. Pantelejmon just outside Skopje and would undoubtedly feel the same later that day when he entered Sv. Sophia.

On every wall, on each square column, from the flagstones beneath his feet to the cupola arching over his head tier on tier of tall, elongated figures, saints and holy warriors, looked out at him and, had he been raised to their level, through him. All expressed the expressionless, communicated by refusing to, displayed haughty hieratic gestures he could take or leave. He preferred to leave them, but in the dome's upper reaches he found something more to his taste: a huge Mary, swaddled in dark, sea-blue robes, her face half-hooded, standing on a golden plinth, arms opened and palms upturned to reassure the faithful all was well. But Marko liked to think she was spreading arms wide to welcome her ghostly lover. This deliberate misreading let him like this Mary more than Sv. Pantelejmon's, unceremoniously cut off at the waist, and Sv. Sophia's, seated too demurely on a throne. Yet, ultimately, Marko felt sorry for Our Lady of Sv. Kliment: divinely impregnated under wraps, then bursting with god, the confused woman accepted, as she was told, a carpenter for mate and thirty years of motherhood. Such a lot could hardly have been less like Biljana's, whose body, feelings, course of life, were always in her sole control; but this reluctant mother, so dignified in her indignity, moved him, as Biljana in other ways had done, her calm, serious eyes seeming to see a purpose in our random world. As he left, he again stooped at the lintel, St Mercury on the pillar opposite, sword drawn over scarlet battle gear, granting his exit a silent farewell. He issued from intense darkness to soft light, from the life beyond to his sort of life and Ohrid all around him.

Marko descended from high ground to what should have been the heat of narrow backstreets, but found himself walking down cool corridors of shade under leaning buildings, whose roofs almost met above his head. Timbered storeys overhung ground floors of local stone and were themselves overhung by oriel windows. What could have been oppressive floated away above him in successive projections of whitened wood. The shady avenue of airborne timber widened, at length, into a square, at whose far corner he spotted the town museum. A real hard-luck tale persuaded the old man, squatting in the ticket office, to let him in for the last few minutes before closing, and he made straight for the top of the building where, the sign told him, hung those icons he'd met in reproduction, but never face-to-face.

Why was he so drawn to icons and church frescoes, he often asked himself, when he was no believer. Why did they always speak to him and speak to him so regularly that they became a part of his life? Maybe it was the figures' restraint, matched by the restrained palette, or the implied intensity or the way potentially-tragic conflict was resolved into satisfying patterns. Beyond this, it could be the lack of any stylistic evolution, the favoured motifs staying the same over the past thousand years. Despite his sympathy for communism, maybe he was a bit of a conservative. Yes, these pictures did stand for stability, reassurance and – something he couldn't say in his booklets – local excellence. That was it: though he fully agreed with Tito's stamping down on any expression of nationalism, he was at heart something of a nationalist – no, patriot. Macedonia wasn't, as many thought, a cultural backwater; it could produce an unbroken line of wonderful, though largely anonymous, icon painters, painters that were as fine as any in Russia or Greece.

On entering the room, he found himself sucked once more into a pocket of strange calm. A semi-circle of head-high faces met his: Jesus, his mother and local saints all swam, like unruffled swans, in a uniformly golden light. Floating in radiance, Jesus' long Slavic face looked back with serene assurance; Mary in black impassive robes heard the angel's astonishing message with no more agitation than a vaguely lifted hand; while Clement and Naum, the saints who'd brought Orthodoxy to Ohrid, regarded Marko impassively, raising Buddha hands to bless. Even the crucifixion scene reined in all strong emotion. Its foreground was quartered by a large brown cross with two angels, minute yet confident, flying out of the upper corners, heads held high, while in the lower Mary and James balanced them on either side of the cross, but with shoulders slumped and heads bowed towards the earth. Embodying these opposing forces with apparent ease, Jesus lay back – almost comfortably – on the cross, palms spread upwards towards the departing angels as if, even in defeat, he still commanded all, yet the head slumped beneath a setting halo. The arrangement of figures and masses caught the scene's sadness exactly, but expressed it with a dignified restraint. Would he in his grief for Biljana be as restrained, would Macedonians in their grief for Tito?

He left the museum, his heartfelt thanks momentarily halting the attendant's good-natured grumble, and, as he did, noticed all the heat had gone out of the day. Dusk couldn't be long in coming, yet he continued to stroll from the centre. He'd no meal time to keep, no partner, no friends to meet. He could just wander and so he wandered, coming eventually on Sv. Sofia, which he'd earlier glimpsed from above. Even though its wooden doors were now locked and his cupped hands at the windows had failed to reveal the huge Madonna with surrounding saints, he knew he'd see her tomorrow. Outside, boys were playing football in and out of the logia and a local priest stood, stroking his long black beard as he listened to parishioners' complaints, yet every so often casting glances in the direction of the game to make sure it didn't get too boisterous, but never once intervening to still the happy cries. Cheered by such restraint, he sauntered past the church and out into open ground where workers between banter were erecting a stage for the Balkan Folk Festival. He smiled at their rallies of friendly insult as he strolled through Tsar Samuel's ruined fortress at the back to a narrow lane. The grass rose abruptly to a lip of earth on the right and, to the left, fell sharply away in stony ground to the lake. With the town and all its noises now truly left behind, he began to hear other sounds, sounds of unhurried labour. Approaching the edge, he peered down. There in a large cove, sheltered from the elements and the town's curiosity, lay a tiny fishing village. Old men sat on the backs of upturned boats, mending nets, while women in traditional costume – Biljana! – dried flax at the water's margin. In the middle, helping the older women, a teenage girl laid cloth out on the shore. Looking down at her, he found his mouth opening as if in surprise and, despite himself, he started to sing, brokenly at first, but with greater fluency as he realised what he was doing:

*Biljana, drying linen*
*by the springs of Ohrid,*
*cried to the vintner riding by,*
*'Careful where you're going*

*with that cart, your grace,*
*or my cloth will become nothing*
*but wheel mark and dust –*
*then where would my dowry be?'*

*'Don't worry, my beauty,'*
*Replied the laughing vintner,*
*'For each ruined piece I'll more*
*than repay in wine and song.'*

*'You can keep all that, old man!'*
*said the girl. 'Look over in the shade.*
*The boy gazing from under his fez*
*will surely be the only one for me.*

This was the song Biljana had been singing in his chosen picture, the song she sometimes sang at home to tease him about his age or the fact that she'd never marry him. Smiling as he patted the photo in his back pocket, he continued down the winding path, its bleached brownness increasingly enriched by banks of yellowcress and the occasional poppy, sprouting between mossy grass. At the point where the land dropped sheer to the beach, the path was cordoned by a beige wall of local stone. He pursued it round on a sharp curve and as it was about to straighten out, the hill also fell away, flattening itself, as if in sympathy, to reveal a rocky promontory, at whose tip a small compact church stood, its glowing light-brown brick and red-tiled roofs surrounded on three sides by the lake's deep blue. Though complete in itself, the building directed his eyes, like a pointing finger, to immense stretches of untroubled water beyond. One moment his spirit was standing above it all, looking down, and the next, like a diver, piercing the heart of it and breaking the surface to see ripples slowly stretching to the distant shore. Time widened from present into deep past and distant future, and he sensed that here, if anywhere, he could devolve to fins and swim undisturbed in a world of water, or the last man could retreat to these shores, this inland sea and find moorhens still bobbing in the kind light and breathe again its deep calm.

Sv. Jovan Kaneo was as durable, as unpretentious as the community it served. Fixing eyes on it, as on a lodestar, he followed the wall down and entered church land through a gateless gateway, open at all times to sheep and the elements. It was weather-beaten like the church it introduced with its plaster fallen away in several places to reveal the stone skeleton beneath. His path opened out to a courtyard with a wooden bench, shaded by cypresses, looking across stone flags to the bust of the partisan poet, Kočo Racin, and past to still water and white mountain. He stood and contemplated the poet of poppies and white dawns till his gaze was pulled back to the church with its rugged steps overgrown with grass and roofs interlocking like a terracotta collage; but in time his eyes renounced these rough subtleties for the fine simplicity of lake water, its uncomplicated blue stretching to the far horizon.

This was the land's end and would, for that day at least, be his journey's end too. He'd arrived at that resting place without having or meaning to. No plan had led his steps that way, just a winding path through yielding air and the promise of healing vistas. And the lake, headland and birds had not disappointed. They, unlike woman or god, could reject no one, so did not reject him, offered, as they had to, whatever they owned to whoever took the trouble, and he had done that.

Turning his back on the church, as Biljana had on him, he walked slowly over the paving stones, sat on the shaded seat and stared past the bronze poet to the stuff of poetry and belief. As the sun began to touch the mountain tops, its light weakened and the darkening promontory was blessed with a halo of liquid gold. The glowing outcrop called to mind an icon's craggy-headed saint, yet demanded no submission. Just before setting, the sun threw fiery jags above the white peaks, turning the golden lake a burning red, then molten copper. Soon all colour would drain from the landscape, but till then his eyes thirsted for each modulation, drinking in the last evidences of the lake as the lake had earlier drunk in all the rays of the sun.

He sat there in the stillness, knowing that less than a republic away stood an empty flat, its genius forever fled, and encircling it, like after-tremors an epicentre, a country shaken leaderless, knowing too that all he'd felt during the day might have been no more than a trick of the mind, conjured by travel and shock, knowing these things, knowing them only too well, yet, as dusk thickened and the world's objects became indistinct, longing, yes, longing for first light.

# What Was Yugoslavia?

Jeannie McEwan glanced across at the classroom windows, her attention drawn by the tinny patter of hail against the glass. Beyond, she could make out ice-pellets hitting the playground with such velocity they bounced up an inch or so before landing again, only to dissolve into standing pools. Sighing inwardly, she gazed at her class. *What a day! Awful dreich! There's precious little chance now of letting the bairns out for morning break: they'll only get themselves soaked. Policing duties then. No quick cuppa in the staffroom. Oh, well. Right ... now's the time for my big speech!* She cleared her throat: even the rebels and the shy ones at the back must hear what she had to say. 'OK, children, as it's the first week of Spring term, we have to start to think, as we do every year, of projects. These projects are going to keep you busy for the rest of January, so they're very important ... yes, very important to you as well, Ben. Stop talking! Now ... we're islanders, aren't we? As British citizens we live on one of two islands. What are those two islands?'

A girl at the front immediately raised her hand.

'Yes, Aesha?'

'The one with England and Wales on.'

'You've left a country out.'

'Oh, yes, sorry, Scotland.'

*Don't forget Scotland! Never forget Scotland, even here in East London.* 'And what about the other island?'

The hand of the girl sitting next to Aesha went up in hesitant stages. 'Is it the one with Northern Ireland on, Miss?'

'That's right, Jyothi, well done. So ... we live on an island, but that doesn't mean we have to cut ourselves off from everyone else, does it? We're part of the wider world and, because of that, we need to know not just about Britain, but also what's happening in other nations, other continents as well. To help towards that, we're going to ask you to choose a country outside the UK that you'd like to write about.'

Thirty of the thirty-three faces staring back at her didn't seem especially excited by the idea.

*Ach well: not a great start! When I was little more than a lass and still in love with teaching, I'd have no trouble getting bairns excited with whatever I suggested. So what's gone wrong? Mebbe I'm just losing it – running short on adrenaline, lacking the youthful fizz that gets a class on your side. Or mebbe it's simply I've just done this project thing once too often. Yet from the look on their faces, I'd say they're not so much bored as tired. Course, a lot are on free school-meals. Lunch's the only proper food they get all day! I must admit they do seem a bit peeky this morning and it's only half-past nine! Wouldn't be surprised if some of them haven't eaten much – anything? – for breakfast. And then there's those that have had to get up at dawn for paper rounds. Poor wee souls!*

Though she really liked her girls and boys and felt for them in their difficulties (she had, after all, been brought up in an Easterhouse tenement), Jeannie was still irked by their attitude to lessons. They were only final-year primary pupils, yet most had already decided school wasn't for them, was, instead, something they'd just have to endure for a few more years. With the ending of car production at Ford and the financial crash last year jobs were scarce, but that didn't stop these kids from chafing at their educational bits. All they wanted to do was escape the borstal of school and start earning money in the real world. Little did they know work would turn out to be another kind of prison. Schooling wasn't like that in Scotland, oh no – nor in Ilford. She smiled as the image of her previous class flashed across her mind: a room of mainly Asian kids, attentive, eager to learn – well, most of them. That school, though only a mile or two down the road from Dagenham, was so different! These largely white, working-class kids seemed to see education as some sort of conspiracy, practised upon them from above by sinister forces.

Only three of the pupils regarding Jeannie with largely quizzical looks were not white: Aesha and Jyothi in the front row and Leroy, a black boy who seemed to feel more comfortable at the back.

*Wonder why this is one of East London's last white 'manors'. You can easily explain the few non-whites in Wanstead with its sky-high house prices, but Dagenham! It's almost all estates. Mebbe the council panicked when it noted the locals' sympathy for Thatcher's views on race and doctored the waiting lists.*

Unlike her previous pupils, these had to be pushed and pushed to get anything out of them. Observing the rows of drawn, vacant faces, two by two, Jeannie found it all-too-easy to guess what was going through their minds, *Oh no, not another stupid thing to do and this one's going to last for weeks! How's finding out about some stupid country hundreds of miles away gonna help me get a job in a garage, factory or shop?*

But resistant looks weren't on every face. She was pleased to notice the usual three exceptions: the Indian girls and a small boy with an Eastern-European name. This trio, by far her brightest kids, paid attention to every one of the lessons as if Jeannie might, after all, have something worth saying and, true to form, Aesha, Jyothi and Josip sat there with alert faces, waiting for what they'd hear next.

'Now ... you're free to choose any country, any country you want. It could be one your parents have a family connection with or one you've visited on holiday.' *But how many of these kids have actually ever gone abroad? A day-trip down to Southend's more like it? Mebbe Aesha and Jyothi have flown back to Bangladesh and Josip to his homeland, wherever that is.* 'Or it could be a country you've heard about in the news, a country that's caught your attention.... Jack, stop whispering to Charlie. Turn round and face the front! Jack, you're still smirking. I really don't know what you find so funny. Perhaps you can share the joke with the rest of the class.'

'Sorry, Miss. It was nothing, Miss.'

'Now, any questions?'

A timid hand raised itself inch by inch above a row of heads. A girl, never known for enquiring about anything, seemed finally about to ask a question.

*Success, success! I've actually got a response – and from someone I'd never have guessed! Mebbe my words did get through, after all!* 'Yes, Jenny?'

'Can I be excused, Miss?'

*I should have known!* 'Can't you wait till the end of the lesson?'

'No, Miss.'

'OK, but be as quick as you can.'

'Yes, Miss.'

'Good. Right, back to our projects. Can you open your exercise books and make a list of countries you might like to write about? When you've finished that, turn to the classmate sitting next to you and talk to them about which countries you chose and which one, you think, you'll finally go with. Then they'll tell you about their list. But, children, while you're explaining your choice, I want you to talk quietly, ever so quietly; I don't want to hear anyone shouting! Is that clear?'

A minute or so of preternatural silence fell on the room as the children lowered their heads to write, but in no time a hubbub started up.

*Wheesht, wheesht!* 'Alright, alright! Calm down, just calm down!'

To back up her point, Jeannie moved her open palms repeatedly downwards, as if she was trying to press the din to quietness. When this only half-succeeded, she walked round the class, placing forefinger to lips whenever she caught the eye of a noisy kid. While passing Charlie's desk, she snatched a glance beyond his shielding elbow to what must have caused his earlier mirth: a rough sketch of herself, wearing a black conical hat and flowing robes, her long nose extended as far as Pinocchio's. Under the image a single word was scratched: 'Witch'.

*Well, at least he spelt it correctly.* She smiled, a smile

prolonged in wrinkles round her eyes, then moved on. *In the old days he'd have got a good skelp, mebbe even a tawse over the hand! Now you're sued just for touching them.... Still, I didn't know Charlie had it in him – that hidden creativity! Well l never!*

Once the voices had been reduced to a level that wouldn't trouble the headmistress down the corridor, Jeannie let the exchanges go on till most of the pupils had run out of things to say.

'OK. What countries have you picked?'

'Ireland ... Spain ... Portugal ... Wales!'

'No, you can't have Wales, Anne – or Scotland either, or Northern Ireland. Do you remember why not? We mentioned the reason a couple of minutes ago. Anyone? Aesha's got her hand up again. Can anyone else answer? No ... OK, Aesha.'

'They're all part of the UK, Miss.'

'That's right!' *But mebbe not forever. Roll on independence, independence all round!* Well, at least *we got a bit of enthusiasm over the choice of country – or was that just an excuse for making noise?*

'OK, any more?'

'Australia, Miss.'

'Why Australia, Ned?'

'Dad's always saying I ought to go there when I'm finished with school.'

'Why's that?'

'He thinks I'll get a chance there.'

'But not here?'

'No, Miss.'

'So you want to find out what Australia's got to offer?'

'Yes, Miss.'

'Good. Right, anyone else?'

'Argentina, Miss.'

'That's an unusual choice, Jimmy. Why Argentina?'

'It's where Maradona's from, Miss,' in indignant tones, as if he'd said something that everyone, who wasn't stupid, would

– should – know.

'Oh, yes, of course, I forgot.' *Lies, lies.*

A small, fair-haired boy with a half-regrown crew-cut raised his hand hesitantly.

'What about you, Josip?'

'Well. Miss, can I do ... Yugoslavia?'

'Now class, if you asked anyone on the street outside about what Josip wants to do, they'd say, "That's really odd!" Girls and boys, can anyone – apart from Josip, of course – tell me what's so odd about his choice?'

Blank faces, even Aesha's and Jyothi's.

'No. Well, OK Josip, can you explain?'

'Because there isn't a country called Yugoslavia anymore.'

Puzzled faces, even Aesha's and Jyothi's.

'Don't worry, class; it's not a made-up place like Hogwarts or Oz! No, there used to be an actual state called Yugoslavia – and not so long ago either. Josip, have you often visited this country that's no longer on the map?'

'I was born there, Miss, but I've never been back.'

'Never, really! But you know lots about it, don't you?'

'No, Miss – almost nothing.'

'Well, this'll give you a chance to find out more, won't it?'

'Yes, Miss, thank you, Miss.'

'But, Josip, we don't want to hear about all those horrible things that happened at the end. They're just too nasty, too sad. Go more into what it was like before. OK?'

'Yes, Miss.'

'And Josip, if you don't mind me asking, what sort of family connection do you have with Yugoslavia?'

'My dad's from Zagreb and my mum's from Novi Sad, Miss. He's a Croat, she's a Serb.'

'Oh I see: an interesting combination!' *The two main warring tribes. No wonder they got out!*

Jeannie knew Josip's subject might prove controversial. It wasn't long ago that the front pages were full of haunting pictures: the staring eyes and jutting ribs of Croat prisoners, the traumatised faces of raped Bosnian girls, the corpses of fathers, mothers, grandmothers, lying on Sarajevo streets, picked off by Serb snipers up in the hills above the town. Though she well knew the authorities liked teachers to avoid any topic that might cause offence, in the final reckoning she no longer cared. This was her last year before retirement; if the headmistress didn't like it, tough!

After all, she'd grown to love Yugoslavia from those holidays she'd had during teacher-training and just after, and had been sickened   by the way the country broke-up. Summer in Yugoslavia had become almost a yearly ritual back then, observed with college friends and later her future husband. It was a break she could afford, and the clear skies and hot sun were a wonderful antidote to Glasgow's rain and general gloom. Though the sun certainly shone more often and more strongly down in London, it rarely reached the pure, paradisal light of a Yugoslav summer, a radiance that simply made you feel happy to be alive the moment you woke. And then there was the political side, which she always got a taste of while she was there: the most liberal of the worker democracies, the clever balance of republics, the self-managing factories, the reasonably-free press, the open borders, all that sort of thing. She'd sometimes wondered if Britain could have followed suite, but Thatcher and Reaganomics put paid to all that, and now things had drifted so far that just to think of such an outcome seemed pure fiction. Even the Labour Party had become Tory Light, so what hope was there? Still, capitalism had screwed up again with the Bankers' Crash last year, so maybe something good might come of it – maybe, but probably not. Britain was more likely to go to the right than left. Yet, with the help of Josip, Jeannie could at least haunt the Old Yugoslavia again and celebrate its socialist past, which probably now only survived in traces that got paler by the year.

'Right, children, I expect you've all chosen your country. Anyone who hasn't?'

No hands went up.

'Good. What I want you to do now is learn as much as you can about that country. We're all going off down the corridor to the library now. You should be able to find something there. It could be a book about your country's geography ... or climate ... or history ... or customs ... or language ... or pop music – anything.'

Jeannie sensed a silent collective groan emanating from the children as they began to realise the type of effort the project would involve, but she plunged on regardless.

'Now, you've all joined the local library – remember doing that last term? I also want you to go there in your spare time and see what they've got. If you can't find anything in the children's section, go to the adults'. And if you can't find anything there either, go and ask a librarian. They'll tell you where a book is, if they have one. It could, you know, be hidden away in their reserve stock and not be on the shelves. If they haven't got anything anywhere, they can always borrow a book from another branch or another London borough. It's called an inter-library loan ... inter-library loan, remember that! Can you all write that down, please, in case you have to ask for it?'

She duly spelt out the term, letter by letter, on the whiteboard. 'So, while you're in the library, gather and then jot down in your exercise books as many details as you can. You'll need a lot because the project is a big piece: one thousand words long! Don't just take out books, take DVDs or CDs as well. Also, see what's on the internet: if your family's got a laptop at home, work on that; if not, use one here in the school library or the local library. So, if you come across an interesting picture online, save it: they like projects that are nicely presented and pictures will make your work look good. Beyond that, if you're struggling for material, ask me, but, more to the point, ask your parents. They're sure to know a lot more about your chosen countries.'

She surveyed the rows of not-exactly-energised pupils.

'Any problems?'

No response.

'Oh yes, I almost forgot. The school chooses the best project – sometimes the best two – and the pupil or pupils get invited to the Barking and Dagenham Reading Day. It's held in Barking Town Hall at the end of every February and all the local primary schools go along. The judges there will choose the best project – also the best short story and poem – from the whole borough. If you win, you get £70 in book tokens; come second and you get £20; third, £10.'

The whole class was finally impressed, but she could read the frustration behind their excited expressions. *£70! Wow! Wicked! But book tokens! What can you do with book tokens? You can't buy a bike with them or trainers or a month's supply of sweets.*

'OK, class, let's go to the library, but make sure you're quiet in the corridor!'

So keen was Josip to tell his parents about the new project that he ditched his usual dawdling and got down to the dinner table first. During the previous hour, while he'd flicked through comic after comic before finally settling on sticking the remaining loose cards into his Premier-League album, the long, minute hand on his watch had seemed to move so slowly he wouldn't have been surprised, had it not been for the busy second hand, if time hadn't stopped altogether. After the last lesson of the day he'd mined the rockface of time, as he always did, kicking a football round the playground. He was the best player in the school by far, captain of Barking and Dagenham Under-11s and it was rumoured he'd been watched by West-Ham scouts. Though no approach had yet been made, he still strongly believed he'd become a Hammer one day. Whenever doubters like his PE teacher, Mr Knowles, said he was too small, not 'physical' enough to make it as a midfielder, he always gave the same reply, 'What about Luka Modrić at Spurs? He wasn't tall or strong, but he hasn't done so badly, has he?' His father humoured him in his daydreams, knowing full well that of the many boys who went through the club's youth systems, few got contracts and of those a fair proportion had their careers cut short by broken legs or torn ligaments or by managers who lost faith in them. No, as far as his father was concerned, the best thing Josip could do was get down to his studies, so he could go to college and qualify for a job that would support him, and possibly a family, for the rest of his life. If football could be fitted into that, all well and good. It was, after all, possible to do both for he'd read somewhere there'd been a number of footballers over here who'd also held degrees, though he could only remember one: West Ham's Slaven Bilić. But if it proved too hard and the choice was between football and study, football would always have to give way.

Josip knew he was lucky to be honing his skills each weekday morning and afternoon in such a large playground, the largest in Dagenham. Wadham Road, his father had told him, was an old Edwardian school, whose playground was originally divided into a Boys' and Girls' section. As if to prove the point, his father had pointed at the lintels above the entrances at the main building's opposite ends, which still had carved on them the inscriptions 'Infant Boys' and 'Infant Girls'. But when co-education came, the net railings separating the two parts had been pulled down, revealing a wonderfully-long expanse of asphalt.

Josip's special ability, threading a ball through a defensive line or finding a winger on the other side of the pitch without seeming to look up, meant that when it came to picking teams, he was generally made one of the captains or, if not, was the first player to be picked, and today had been no exception, the team he captained leading 7-4 when his father had come over to usher his mates out and lock the gates behind them. While his father had gone off with a fat bunch of keys jangling from his belt, Josip had scooped up the plastic ball and, feeling pleasantly tired, trudged with it under his arm across to the caretaker's pebbledash cottage beside the school. Once inside, he'd run up to his room where he looked for things to pass the time as he waited for the dinner bell.

Now that he was seated at the side of the kitchen table, he watched his father, summoned by his mother's call, wedge his stomach, with some difficulty, into his place at the head. Laid out before them was a large steaming bowl of Josip's favourite food: mussels and squid with rice. What always got him was the way the squid ink turned the rice a deep black, making it look eerie, almost otherworldly. Zombie food! He thought of his schoolmates; they never seemed to eat anything like this: takeaway burger and chips or pizza was more like it or, if they were lucky (unlucky?), meat and two veg.

His mother joined them, sitting, as always, opposite his father. He looked from mother to father and back again. When she spoke, his mother pronounced words in a way that couldn't be said to be foreign, but even before she opened her mouth, it was clear she wasn't quite English. Although she had the sort of pleasant round face with dark hair down to the shoulders that you might see on any high street, her skin, despite nine years of English cloud, was still distinctively tanned – and not an orange sun-lamp tan at that. His father, who spoke with a strong Slavic accent, looked even less English. His partially-regrown crew-cut was what you'd come across in boys, not fully-grown men in their thirties. There was also the way he left his stubble in the shape of a goatee, keeping his cheeks and the rest of his jaw closely shaven.

Though Josip wanted to broach his topic right away, he decided to wait till the meal was over, when his parents would be free to give him useful suggestions, undisturbed by the business of eating. To bring that moment closer, he wolfed down his rice dish, declining a second helping, and scoffed only four of the lemon dough-balls that followed. In the absence of anything else to do he quietly tapped his spoon on the table's formica surface, waiting impatiently for his parents to finish and, at last, they did, allowing him to make his big announcement.

'Mum ... Dad, we started doing our projects today.'
'Oh yes.'
'Miss asked us to write about a country, any country. Well,' grinning broadly, 'I picked Yugoslavia.'
His father's face instantly turned the reddest he'd ever seen it, straightway freezing the smile on his own face and before he knew it, his father was actually shouting at him and shouting in such a scary manner – as if he'd completely lost control and in a mad fit was about to tear him limb from limb.
'No, no, no! You can't, no! Stupid boy, don't you know it's not possible? What do you think? Stupid, stupid, stupid! No, I even don't want to look at you! Don't want to see your stupid face! Go upstairs now! Go to bed! Get your stupid face out. I don't want to see you! Get out! Go, go!'
Josip was so stunned by this unexpected turn of events he didn't cry, didn't even say a word, but, instead, swivelled on his heels and, white-faced, fled upstairs, slamming the bedroom door behind him.
Later, after the father had calmed down and was lying in bed next to his wife, she turned to him and quietly said, 'The boy didn't mean any harm. He just didn't know.'
'But he sees the way are things, surely. We talk of Yugoslavia never, never go to holiday there, never phone, write to family. When he's home, we speak English, only English, even don't say one or two words of Serbo-Croat. Look, tonight we eat Croat food, but never call it *crni rižot* or *fritule*. Even in bed we speak English in case he hears something through the wall. Isn't he seeing this?'
'He's only a child, Slavko, doesn't pick up all the hints. Maybe he thinks we cut ourselves off so we can become more English.'
'Maybe, maybe. I guess, thinking of it, you're maybe right. Look, I get angry quick, too quick. Sorry for that.'
'It's OK: you were taken by surprise. But perhaps it's time to talk to Josip. Why don't we make the project our chance to tell him a bit about why we carry on as we do. We can't keep

things secret forever. We have to explain one day, so why not now?'

'You think so? But isn't he young, too young?'

'Maybe. He's still a kid, yes, but in many ways he's quite grown-up for his age. What do the English say? Ah yes: an old head on young shoulders. That's him.'

'You know, I think you're right, Mira. We can't go on saying, "Next year we tell him." Then, "Next year, next year".... Oh, I get so angry, why? You know, it's *me, me* is the stupid one!'

'Come on, you're not stupid at all, dear! So, why don't we start off from tomorrow – after the evening meal – say something about what happened in the old country.'

'Yes, but only little, little.'

'And I'll tell him at breakfast he can do his project after all.'

Seated at the dressing table, Jeannie stared intently at her reflection in the mirror.

*The kids must think I'm some sort of ancient crone, dried up, 'witchy' even. OK, I've got a long nose and jutting chin, can't deny that, but I'm no witch. The cheek of those two wee eejits! Still you have to laugh: that sketch was clever – the pointed hat, the black robes, the broomstick to fly away on. Hasn't always been my nose and chin, mind you; when I was younger, it was the neck, my long neck. There were those drawings at my first school – weren't there? – of me as an ostrich or giraffe with a human head. I can still mind confiscating them. Hurt me then, now I just laugh it off. My ex. once called me a witch, ha, but that was meant to be a compliment – back from when he still fancied me. Later, I guess, he got bored with me and I certainly got bored with him, so we drifted apart. Now he's gone and I'm all on my lane – boo-hoo, boo-hoo! But it's not like that really. No, this is the way I want things. I've had more than enough of men for one lifetime and I've got no children – that wasn't possible. Sad, but mebbe just as well: I wouldn't have made a good mum. Now I'm really content, and if I ever start feeling sorry for myself, as I sometimes do, there's always my pals to take me out for a meal and a good natter; they never let me down.... It's funny, though, this getting old. You just don't care what other people think of you anymore. All that seemed so important when you were young; now you just can't be bothered. They don't like me – who cares? But will it change after I retire when all those work ties undo? Ha, retirement, old age-pension! Well, you certainly do look your age, Jeannie McEwan: that white streak along the middle parting, the bags beneath the eyes, the loose skin under the chin ... my turkey wattle! Ha! Now that's an idea for another classroom sketch!*

A clank in the radiator made her turn her head and, as she did, her eyes rested on the chest of drawers with its framed photo of her younger self, sunbathing in a bikini on a Croatian beach.

*Ach, if only I could look like that again. No, no, mustn't think that way: you've just got to accept how you are. Still, I must admit I was a skinnymalinkie in those days! Now even my face's rounded out – a right bawface you've got, Jeannie. Wait, where was that picture taken? Och aye, Trogir? I was with my teacher-training pals, Steph and Nicci. That's right, it was just before I started going with Jack. Cor, did we have a merry old time! The local lads couldn't get enough of us – hotel staff, waiters in the cafes, lifeguards on the beach! It was great! Never been so popular! Course, they didn't speak much English, but that didn't slow us down. We were all on the pill by then, so why not enjoy yourself? I mind Goran, I think it was – aye, that's it, a bartender. He certainly knew his way round town. Knew his way round a woman's body too – better than Jack did, much better, but then Jack did have other plus points. Oh, those Croat days and, more, those nights when Yugoslavia was still Yugoslavia and we were young! Ach, wheesht! What's all this? You're not going soft in your old age, are you? Yugoslavia, aye – now what about young Josip and his project? Bet he's had a great time over dinner, sitting with his parents, hearing all those stories about the good times – and there were good times.*

The following evening Josip sat with his parents in the narrow
lounge, he on a low stool, they together on the sofa as if to
present their son with a united front. For once the TV had
been switched off for something other than homework. The
stage was set for serious talking. Josip's head ached as he'd
slept poorly the night before. Images of his father's staring
eyes, his face scarlet with anger and the huge gap of his mouth
as he roared demonically kept flashing across his mind like
stills from some horror movie. Not only did they terrify, they
made him feel guiltier as well. He'd obviously said something
unforgivable, something with the force to turn a usually-mild
father into an ogre; but what could that have been? All he'd
done was mention his project and there couldn't be anything
wrong in writing about Yugoslavia, his parents' old homeland,
surely. But everything seemed to change by the morning. His
mother told him over breakfast he could, after all, go ahead
with his chosen country. They'd explain everything, she
added, after they'd eaten that evening.

His father cleared his throat. 'Look, son, sorry for last night:
I shout too much!'

'No problem, dad.'

'But there is reason. You know we leave Yugoslavia.'

Josip nodded.

'Well, we don't want to, but we have to. So we come to
England. You know why?'

'No.'

'This is most far from Yugoslavia – and still stay in Europe.
That's joke, but bit of it's true. No, real reason is your mother
speak English, good English.'

'Yes, but it's OK over here, isn't it?'

'"OK!"' almost losing his temper again. 'Look in Zagreb we
have good life: nice city, capital of Croatia; I work in university
library; your mother teaches English in local school. We do
fine: flat big enough; go to restaurant one time a week, even

holidays out of Yugoslavia.'

'Sounds good.'

'Yes, it was, but we have to get out – and what we have here? I'm professional, two library degrees, but UK doesn't like them – and your mother? Nobody needs learn English here: all speak it? So we look for jobs, any jobs. I do many bad ones. My job now, school caretaker, best I have, but it's long hours, not much pay. Good thing is, though, we get free house, no rent. Your mother's also professional, trained teacher – and what she doing? Part-time at ASDA. So we make nothing with our lives, but we want you to do good. That's why you have to study, get exam passes, *English* passes.'

'Yes, dad. I'll try my best.'

'We know, son, you're good boy.'

Slavko paused. He'd already decided what to mention and what to leave out, but he tried for the final time to arrange the remaining details into their best order. 'Now, how to start? Look, I'm Croat, your mother's Serb. You think it's odd we have nothing with our old republics?'

'Maybe – just a bit.'

'Well, your mother and me are lucky. We grow up when our great leader, Marshall Tito, is president, president of six republics. You know them?'

'Well, there's Serbia and Croatia....'

'Other four were Slovenia, Montenegro, Macedonia and Bosnia and Herzegovina. Tito's clever, makes sure big ones don't bully small ones and rich ones give money to poor ones and none say nationalist things. His message: always think of country, not your republic. His idea has big effect on mum and me: first we are Yugoslav, far second: Croat (for me), Serb (for your mother). You know how Croats and Serbs are in past?'

'No.'

'Well, many times fight – old enemies – but mum and me don't worry to get married. We forget all that: we're new generation; our two peoples will live like one; no more problems. We have big hopes.'

'That's why when you were born, during our last year there, even though things had already gone wrong, we still called you Josip. You know why?'

'No, mum.'

'It was President Tito's first name: Josip Broz Tito!'

'Oh, yes.'

'But after he dies, good idea dies. Rich republics say: "We give money to poor ones and politicians just put it in their pockets." Big republics want more power and to get it they stir up people, make them full of nationalism, hate. In no time we're fighting: Serbs and Slovenes; Serbs and Croats; Serbs with Croats and Bosnians; Serbs and Kosovans. Horrible, too horrible!'

Slavko scrutinised his son's face to see how he was taking it.

'Look, Josip, I say much. You want to stop?'

'It's a lot to take in, but I guess I'm OK, dad.'

'Good. Now, of course, worst fighting for mum and me is Serbia with Croatia. Terrible things happen. Maybe we tell you later, not sure. In end, you couldn't be Yugoslav any more. You must be Croat or Serb; if not, you're traitor. Day on day harder to live. On Zagreb streets and at school mum gets bad words: dirty Serb – Serb killer – Serb trash. It's too much; we have to get away.'

Josip's eyeline had been gradually battered to the floor by blow on blow of his father's catalogue, but now he looked him straight in the eye. He knew he had to say something, but was unsure exactly what.

'Sorry, dad. I didn't know any of this. I see now I made a mistake.'

'No, no, we're wrong, not you. We need to tell you before.'

'So, Josip, from today your father and I are going to start talking to you about Yugoslavia – not just what happened at the end, but the good times as well before that.'

'OK. Thanks, mum, thanks, dad. I think I need that.'

Friday's last class had finished, the school week was finally over. The scrape of seats and excited chatter of liberated souls had given way to a low electronic hum that pervaded every room of the building. Jeannie looked up from collecting her red and black board-markers and the pile of maths test-papers, which she hoped were largely correct this time round, to see one child left behind: Josip. He was packing his satchel with uncharacteristic care.

'Not off to football? You usually shoot out to the playground the moment the bell goes.'

'Well, funny enough, Miss, it's football I want to talk to you about.'

'Oh, yes?' warily.

'You know the project about Yugoslavia.... Well, I want to write about the football: you know, the top league, the cups, the clubs, the national team, all of that. Is it alright, Miss?'

'I could have guessed! Well ... yes, I suppose so.'

'Great, Miss.'

'But, remember, not everyone loves football as much as you do; put in some bits to interest those that don't.'

'What sort of bits, Miss?'

'Oh, I don't know – maybe how the nationalities show their different characters through the way they play football.'

'Yes, that's good, Miss.'

'And ... oh ... the part of town you find the grounds in – the rich part or poor part – and – what else? – the colours of the shirts and socks maybe, that sort of thing.' Jeannie rarely became personal with her pupils, but for some reason she started to reminisce. 'You know, Josip, I used to go to Yugoslavia – the Croatian coast at least – quite a lot when I was younger.'

'Did you, Miss? You must have really liked it there.'

'Oh yes, the sun, the people, the food, everything.'

'You like Yugoslav food, do you?'

'I did then, but haven't eaten any for a long, long while.'

'Well, why don't you have dinner with us some day? You can come over after class: we're only just across the playground.'

Jeannie thought for a second. Normally, she would have found an excuse which would keep work and leisure neatly apart, but this time – perhaps because she was retiring soon anyway – she decided not to.

'Thanks, I'd be happy to – but, Josip, check with your mum first to see if it's OK.'

'It'll be no problem, Miss, no problem at all.'

'Yes, but check anyway. So, off you go, off to your kick-about.'

Josip needed no further prompting.

The table had been moved from kitchen to front room. With its garish plastic top covered by a white tablecloth that Mira found in Poundland, it had been transformed into something presentable. True, it was rather small for four people, even if one was a child, yet the cramped conditions only seemed to make the meal cosier, and the fact that Miss McEwan insisted on being called Jeannie added to the ease.

When Josip first broached the subject of dinner with his mother, she'd panicked and scolded him for putting her in such an impossible position. How could she ever impress his teacher on her tight budget? But as soon as she'd calmed down, she began to see it wasn't so much of a problem after all: she could easily do tried-and-tested dishes, which would be staple fare for Slavko and Josip, but, hopefully, new to Miss McEwan. On her holidays to Istria she'd probably come across only Croat food, so Serb recipes would be something different, possibly even exciting. Mira had therefore started the meal with a nicely-steaming tureen of chicken-and-noodle soup, from which she'd ladled generous helpings, followed by sauerkraut-and-pork casserole and, finally, thick squares of quince jelly, topped with cream. Now they were free to retire to the lounge.

'That was great, Mira! I've haven't eaten any dishes quite like those before. All very tasty! Well done!'

Jeannie had indeed thoroughly enjoyed the meal, as well as the accompanying small talk. The only blip had come when Mira referred to her son as 'Yosip', pronouncing the 'J' as a

'Y', and it suddenly came to Jeannie that she'd been saying his name wrong all this time. She, rather self-consciously, followed suite, vowing to continue that version in class for the rest of the school year.

'Thanks for your kind words, Jeannie, but, really, I'm a very average cook.'

'Well, if you're average, I don't know what I am! Bottom 10%?'

'No, no, you're just being modest. I'm sure you're a very good cook, especially those Scottish dishes.'

'What, you mean haggis? No, can't do that: too fiddly; but my kedgeree's not too bad – oh, and my cock-a-leekie soup.'

For some unknown reason – perhaps the conviviality and that lovely sense of being sated – she decided, once again, not to keep her distance. 'You must all come round some time and try them. I promise not to poison you.'

'Ha, I'm sure you won't. Well, thanks, we'd love to.

Slavko sensed it was time to leave the table. 'We go to back room now? Has soft seats, good for chat.'

'Yes, let's?'

'You drink Turkish coffee, Jeannie?'

'Oh, I used to years ago on my Yugoslav hols. You know, I can still remember the whole business. It was a bit like some religious rite: sitting expectantly outside the cafe under a sunshade; the waiter threading through the tables to bring across a tray of coffee, then ceremoniously putting down those little open pots – copper, I think, they were – with long handles and the tiny cups. Yes, and the coffee was so strong, like espresso, you had to have a glass of water with it.'

'Oh, you think of *dzezva*; that's traditional way. Well, we haven't got pots here, but we have small cups – and lots of water.... And what about alcohol? You like rakia? We have slivovitz.'

'Better not, Slavko, thanks: I'm driving.'

While Mira went off to make coffee in the tiny kitchen, the other three moved pleasantly-full bodies in leisurely fashion to the back room where Jeannie and Slavko took a place on the sofa, while Josip squatted on a stool.

'So I hear from Josip,' making sure she got the name right this time, 'you're helping him with his project.'

There was a long pause.

'Well, at first, we say no, he can't do it. You see, very bad things happen in Yugoslavia. We don't even want to think, less talk, about them. Just forget. But we change and, you know, now we're happy we change: so many things we love deep in hearts (language … friends … customs … places) come back to mind.'

'Is football one of those things?'

'Oh yes. When I was boy, Josip's age, in Zagreb I love Dynamo. Best club in Croatia. As I help Josip, all come back: Dynamo shirt I wear in park when I play kickabout; Sunday afternoons when I go to stadium for match. You see, me and friends go very early, hour and half early, stand near tunnel, wait for players to come out and practice before match. Then we see who get most … what you say: footballers writing names in notebook?'

'Signatures.'

'*Da*, signatures. Mostly I win. I'm not shy, you know, not at all.'

Mira brought the coffee in and set it on the small table by the window. Slavko immediately jumped up and fetched a hardback seat from the front room.

'Go on, dear, you sit with Jeannie. I sit here,' placing his seat next to Josip.

'My, my, did you catch the excitement in Slavko's voice, Jeannie? When he talks football, he's like a boy again.'

Her husband chuckled, lowering his head as if to hide his embarrassment.

'But, you know, it's not just him who's excited. We've been bottled up for so long, years and years; but now we've popped the cork, all the thoughts and feelings are bubbling out.'

'Getting drunk on them, eh?'

'Oh, yes. So, now at home we talk in Serbo-Croat, hoping Josip will pick up a word or two. And as we remember the old times, we find we're smiling. And, you know, this year we're even thinking of changing our holiday plans and maybe going to Croatia of all places!'

'Oh, really.'

'It's amazing how different we feel! We didn't realise at the time, but we've both been carrying around a heavy weight and now it's fallen off. We're like new people.'

'That's wonderful, Mira! But I do feel a bit bad. You know, when I agreed to Josip's project, I never thought it would cause a family crisis.'

'No, no, no, it was our fault: we kept putting off the moment of telling Josip – cowards we were, I suppose. It had to happen one day and, funnily enough, this has proved to be the right time. Josip now knows of some of the bad things – well, roughly. And, on top of that, we've come to a big decision: this project's only going to be a start; Josip needs more. Look at him: there's little Yugoslav about him, apart from his name. So, you know what?'

'What?'

'I've decided to teach him Serbo-Croat! It's ridiculous: Serbia and Croatia now say they've two distinct languages, but we know better. The only real difference is in the writing: Croats like Slavko use the Latin script and I use Cyrillic – you know, the letters are a bit like Russian, a bit like Greek. I'll get Josip to read and write in both. You know, if we left teaching him for a few more years, he'd never become bilingual and that's what we now want.'

'So, Josip, you won't just be finding out about Yugoslav football; you'll also be learning a new language. Excited?'

'Well, sort of, Miss.'

Mira smiled. 'At the moment he sees it as a lot of extra work, hard work, but as it gets easier, we hope he'll start to enjoy it.'

'I'm sure he will. You know, I was thinking of learning a new language myself when I retired this year.'

'I didn't know you were retiring! So this is your last year?'

'It certainly is, then freedom!'

'But you must be sad to be giving up teaching after all that time.'

'Well, yes and no. Sad to leave the kids (they keep me young – in spirit, if not body); but happy to get a proper rest at last.'

'I heard British people like to retire to the coast? Are you thinking of that?'

'I did for a while, but if I retired to, say, Eastbourne, who would I know down there? And then somewhere in Scotland would be too cold for me now. I've got used to the soft South.'

'Croatia's much warmer than both, you know. Why don't you buy a holiday home there? It's still pretty easy to find cheap ones; we looked into it. That's another thing we decided. From now on we're going to save all the money we can and when we retire, buy a house in Croatia, probably on one of the islands. But you could divide your time between here and Croatia, get the best of both worlds.'

'Well, I must say I've never thought of going abroad – Spain, that sort of thing. But, look, if I lived in Croatia for any time, I'd have to learn the language, wouldn't I?'

'It'd help, of course, just basics, but the kids are now taught English in schools – not like in my day. It was Russian then.'

'And I suppose the cheap places would require a lot doing to them.'

'Not all ... and if they do need a bit of repair, labour costs are very reasonable.'

'You know I somehow always pictured myself ending my days in this part of London where I've got friends, but you've certainly made me think....'

The talk then turned to Jeannie's memories of Hvar, Zadar, Korčula and Split. Slavko recommended Dubrovnik and sang the praises of the Zagreb he knew as a child. Mira, in turn, fondly described Novi Sad, where she'd grown up. 'A beautiful Austro-Hungarian town on the banks of the Danube,' she called it. Not to be outdone, Josip excitedly informed them of the Yugoslav clubs and players he now liked best. After an hour Jeannie took her leave, thanking her hosts again for their hospitality. At the door Mira stayed her momentarily with a last remark. 'You never know, but we might even run into each other in Croatia next summer.'

'Stranger things have happened.'

The following evening Josip sat restlessly on the stool, waiting for his mother to finish tidying the kitchen and join him in the back room. She'd said she'd some background stuff for his project, but what could that be? Although he'd racked his brains, he'd come up with no likely answer. After all, his mother knew nothing about football – and was there anything else of interest? Five minutes seemed like hours, but at last his mother did hang her pinny up and enter the room, clutching a couple of pieces of paper. Josip's first response was one of disappointment. Surely nothing exciting could come from those printed pages.

'I want to tell you about something too many Serbs believe, I'm afraid. It's a real event, but it's become a myth, you could say. Now you need to know this because it helps explain why Serbs did what they did in the 1990s, why it was so easy to turn them into nasty nationalists. But we have to go through a bit of history first. Ready?'

'It's not going to go on and on, is it?'

'Don't worry, I'll make it short and sweet. Right, think of the end of the fourteenth century – medieval times. The Ottomans – they're Turks, basically, Muslim Turks – have built up a huge empire in the east and now they're beginning to look to invading Europe. And who is the first to try to stop them?'

'Yugoslavia?'

'No, no, there wasn't a Yugoslavia then. It was the Serbian kingdom. And the place it tried to stop them at was Kosovo Polje – Kosovo Field. The Battle of Kosovo Polje was one of the big battles of the Middle Ages, but it wasn't an equal battle. The Serb army, led by Prince Lazar and Vuk Branković, was outnumbered and, as you'd expect, lost. But they so weakened the Ottomans that in the years to come, though they went on to beat the Hungarians at the Battle of Mohacs, they were in the end turned back from the gates of Vienna. Western Europe was saved. Are you following?'

'I think so.'

'But, though forced back, the Ottomans did keep control of Serbia. For five hundred years Christian Serbia was ruled by Muslims. Croatia stayed largely free of the Ottomans and was in the end swallowed up by the Austro-Hungarian Empire.'

Josip shifted position on his stool.

'OK?'

'Is there a lot more?'

'No: lesson's almost over. So, Serbs like to see themselves as both heroes and martyrs. They sacrificed their kingdom to keep Europe Christian and, as a result, suffered for centuries. Through the long years of occupation they cheered themselves with ballads, praising the heroes of the battle and cursing the villains. Now, you should get an idea of what these ballads are like, but you can't read Serbo-Croat yet and I couldn't find any translation. So what I've done is make my own free version in English with bits taken from many ballads and bits made up. Well, here you are!' handing over the poem. 'Hope you like it.'

'I'll have a go, mum,' somewhat half-heartedly.

Noticing this, Mira realised she had to add more colour.

'Look. Imagine a medieval battle: chainmail, cavalry charging down a hill, lances drawn, archers sending off flights of arrows, opposing flags waving in the air, hand-to-hand fighting: broadswords, axes, hacking, slashing.'

Josip was already paying more attention.

'And remember, too, that in those days most Serbs couldn't read or write, so these ballads were learnt by heart and passed down by poets, bards. They used to travel from village to village, performing the poems. They carried with them a musical instrument we call a *gusle* – it's – what? – a kind of lute, a kind of mandolin – and these bards used to chant or sing the ballads as they moved a bow back and forth across a single string. It must have drawn quite a crowd! Can you picture all this – the battle and the poet's performance?'

'Sort of.'

'Now, what I want you to do is take this away. See what you make of it. Go on, go to the kitchen and have a read, while I check if there's anything good on telly. OK?'

'OK, mum.'

If the pages had shown pictures of Yugoslav footballers, Josip would have moved quicker, but, eventually, he was seated at the kitchen table, looking down at the poem's title, printed in capitals: *'THE BATTLE OF KOSOVO POLJE'*. Then his eyes lowered to the first line:

*They rode down from Prizren town, armour flashing*
*In the sun, rode down from that white city*
*To the green fields of Kosovo: Old Jug Bogdan*
*And his sons, the Jugovići, with a thousand men,*
*Three Mrnjavčevići lords – King Vukašin, Duke Gojko*
*And the Despot Ugleša – with two thousand men each,*
*Vuk Branković with his five thousand, and, at the front,*
*Vuk's father-in-law, Tsar Lazar, with twelve.*
*Sultan Murat had challenged Tsar Lazar,*
*Hoping to bully him: 'We can't both reign in Serbia,*
*So hand me the golden keys to your cities,*
*The keys of Prizren, Priština and Kruševac,*
*And add to them the gold from seven years of taxes.*
*If you don't like this idea, come to Kosovo Field*
*And let our armies decide which of us deserves to rule.'*
*Tsar Lazar didn't like the idea, so came to Kosovo Field*
*With all his men, and sent ahead the Serbian lord,*
*Ivan Kosančić, to spy out the Turkish host*
*And on his return Kosančić told the Tsar,*
*'Their army is large, sire, yet most of the soldiers*
*Are boys without beards or doddery old men*

*Or dim-witted muezzins.' But when he ended his report,*
*He turned to Miloš Obilić and whispered in his ear,*
*'There are so many of them – five thousand Janissaries,*
*Eight thousand holy warriors, twelve thousand cavalry,*
*Fifteen thousand archers and thirty-five thousand*
*Vassal troops – so many that even if every one of us*
*Became a grain of salt, there still wouldn't be*
*Enough to season their next meal.*

*Now when they got to Kosovo Field, Tsar Lazar*
*Pitched tent and in front of it knelt with all his nobles*
*And received from the Patriarch of Peć the bread*
*That was Christ's body and wine that was His blood.*
*And Tsar Lazar dedicated the coming battle*
*To the Pantocrator. Yet that evening as he was sitting*
*Outside his tent, a grey falcon flew down and said,*
*'Great ruler, tomorrow you must choose*
*Between the Kingdom of Earth and the Kingdom*
*Of Heaven. If you choose the first,*
*Gather all your men and rush on the Turks*
*For not one of their soldiers shall survive.*
*But if you choose the second, build a church*
*On Kosovo Field, made not of stone, but silk,*
*And consecrate it, for you and all your men shall die.'*
*Tsar Lazar thought over the choice and finally*
*Decided an earthly kingdom would soon fade,*
*But the Kingdom of Heaven last forever.*
*So he chose the heavenly kingdom, trusting that,*
*Though he and his men would perish,*
*The Turks would be halted there on Kosovo Field.*
*So in Zagreb, Ljubljana, Venice and Rome*
*Masses would still be sung and not one muezzin*
*Heard calling the faithful to prayer.*

*Thus, next morning, Tsar Lazar, Old Jug Bogdan*
*And his nine sons, King Vukašin, Duke Gojko*

And the Despot Ugleša rode out to their deaths.
And Jug Bogdan and his sons killed seven Pashas,
But when pursuing the eighth, they themselves
Were overwhelmed and killed. And the three
Mrnjavčevići princes killed eight Pashas,
But with the ninth were themselves overpowered
And killed. And Tsar Lazar slew nine Pashas,
But against the tenth he was himself outnumbered
And killed. Only Vuk Branković – may his soul
Rot in hell! – with his five thousand men
Came home alive from Kosovo Field,
Came safely away for, seeing the Serbs
Being pushed back, he refused to fight
And withdrew his troops. Yet while curses
Must forever fall on Branković and his kin,
Praise must never cease ringing out for Obilić.
Seeming to surrender, to renounce his faith,
He was taken to Sultan Murat's tent
And, once inside, pulled out a hidden dagger
And thrust it into the belly of the Turkish general,
Moving the blade quickly upwards towards the heart.

Now when the battle was lost – and won –,
The Maiden of Kosovo walked on the Field
Among the dead and dying. The dead
She wept over, closing their furious eyes;
The dying she washed in cool water,
Giving them the wine and the bread
Of last rites, and all the while she searched
For three men: Duke Miloš Obilić,
Ivan Kosančić and Milan Toplica.
For Duke Miloš had said, 'If I survive,
I shall marry you to my sworn brother,
Milan, and be your kum.' And Ivan Kosančić
Had said, 'Were I to return alive,
I should marry you to Milan, my sworn brother,

*And I should be your stari svat.'*
*And Milan Toplica had said, 'If I come back*
*From the Field, I shall marry you*
*And you will be my beloved bride.'*
*Among the wounded was one, Pavle Orlović,*
*Tsar Lazar's standard-bearer, and when the Maiden*
*Asked him if he knew of the three men,*
*He sorrowfully replied, 'Dear sister, look*
*Where the mountain of bodies stands tallest,*
*The river of blood runs deepest. There you shall find*
*Ivan Kosančić and your Milan Toplica.*
*But as for Miloš Obilić, he, single-handed,*
*Killed Sultan Murat and, in revenge,*
*His severed head looks down from a Turkish spear.*
*So go home, go home, dear maiden,*
*Or you will soil your skirts and sleeves*
*With our blood.' So, reluctantly, the Maiden*
*Stumbled back home, crying out all the way,*
*'O Serbia, Serbia, whatever will become*
*Of you and what will become of me?'*

Eager to hear Josip's reaction, Mira turned the TV off as soon as he returned. Writing the poem had been a real surprise for she believed herself totally free of nationalist feeling, yet found herself a little moved, stirred even, despite knowing what carnage had just a decade ago resulted from such a sentiment.

'Well, what do you think?'

'Better than I'd thought it'd be, but sad.'

'Yes, it is, though, you know, Serbs have used this story to feel sorry for themselves, to say they're not getting what they deserve.... Did you understand it all?'

'Bits. Some of it was very hard – the leaders' names ... the Yugoslav words I didn't know. Look, I marked them.'

Mira focused in on his underlinings.

'Yes, maybe I should've added notes. Let's see ... *kum* and *stari svat*: they're important people in a Serb wedding. There's nothing quite like them over here: *kum*'s a sort of godfather, *stari svat* a sort of best man, but the duties are a bit different. Right, what else? Ah, 'pantocrator': the Serbs aren't Catholic, you know, like the Croats, but Orthodox; so while Croats look to Rome, Serbs look to Russia. Now 'pantocrator' is a term the Orthodox use for Jesus; I think it means 'ruling everywhere'. A 'patriarch' is a priest high up in the Orthodox Church, like a Catholic archbishop. But 'muezzin' is a Muslim term; it's the man calling from the top of a minaret – you know, the tower in a mosque. Oh, yes, there's one more: 'pashas' – it's what Ottomans called governors and generals – an honorary title, I guess. Does that help?'

'Yes, I think I get it a bit better. But can I have the poem back?'

'Of course,' smiling broadly.

'I want to read it again before going to sleep.'

'Careful it doesn't give you nightmares.'

'Don't worry, it won't.'


'Oh, look! Over there! It's turned and now it's rushing down the runway.'

The other three women followed the direction of Jeannie's pointed finger across the stretch of water to a small executive jet, gradually building up speed for takeoff.

'A planeload of German bankers, no doubt, scurrying back to their safe piles of Deutschmarks. Bye-bye,' waving an ironic hand as the Lufthansa rose steeply into the grey October skies above City Airport, its roar pleasantly modulated by distance and the restaurant's thick glass.

Jeannie was in high spirits. Though it was Sunday-lunch time, a time when local Chinese families liked to eat out en masse, she'd managed, without having to queue on the stairs, to get not only seats, but a small round table for herself and her three friends, and a table not hidden away in the depths, but in prime position right next to the picture window that ran from floor to ceiling along the dining-room's length. And what a view they had, with the planes, taking off every five minutes or so just beyond the Albert Dock, seeming to rise miraculously out of water like large shiny birds!

'And look down there!'

Just below them on the Quay bobbed two dragon boats, inside which a striking mix of Chinese and English, men and women, young and old, were vigorously digging the water with their paddles, practising, no doubt, for some future race. 'Those dragon heads on the prows – aren't they exotic? Like an Oriental version of Viking long-ships.'

'Oh yes, but they don't look nearly as menacing. More friendly, I'd say.'

'Yes, I think they're even smiling.'

And Jeannie was smiling too as she surveyed the restaurant, happy to have chosen Yi Ban. Mae, her old Ilford colleague, had once given her a piece of advice, which for some reason stuck in her memory: look through the window before going into a Chinese restaurant; if it's full of Westerners, tourists particularly, stay outside; but if you see a lot of Chinese in there, even if the place appears tatty, go in; that means they serve proper Chinese food. And Yi Ban *was* full of Chinese families, enjoying their Sunday treat. Being in Silvertown, not Mayfair, the restaurant's attitude to behaviour and dress was relaxed. Two tables down a small Chinese boy had brought along his own birthday cake. While his family were on their feet, giving him a rousing chorus of 'Happy Birthday to You', he sat there, looking up and beaming, and the passing waiters and waitresses, carrying dishes in, beamed too. The customers, seated round the long room, seemed to see little need for 'Sunday Best'. Most wore casual clothes – woollies, T-shirts, slacks, jeans, trainers – though a few were a little more formal, enough to make Jeannie feel that she and Jada in their dresses and Amy in her skirt more-or-less fitted in. Molly, by contrast, didn't seem to belong to either group for while she wore trousers, hers were of proper material. Ten types of dim sum on small plates or in bamboo steamers, a large platter of crispy duck and a pot of green tea were already spread out round the table in front of the four. *That's the beauty of Chinese restaurants*, thought Jeannie: *you never have to wait long for your food.*

'Come on, girls, let's tuck in; it's getting cold.'

'You know I just can't can get the hang of these chopsticks, Jeannie.'

'Don't worry, Moll, use your spoon instead.'

'Or your fingers.'

'Ha-ha, very droll!'

Fried pork dumplings, steamed prawn dumplings, dofu-skin rolls, white crepe rolls, red barbeque pork, spare ribs, sticky rice balls in lotus leaves, black-bean buns, turnip cake and wonton soup all called to the women with their various textures and colours. Or should they start with the duck and have a go at making their own pancakes? In no time they were sampling whatever took their fancy, relishing the different juices as they burst over the palate.

'Well, you two "youngsters", as you know, Amy and I will be retiring this June.'

'Not a moment too soon!'

'Thank you, Moll. So we'll have a lot of free time. Any suggestions on what we should do to fill it?'

'Why don't you do what I do: get yourself a camera and go round taking photos?'

'I don't know, Jada. Make me feel a bit self-conscious, snapping total strangers. What if they don't take kindly to it?'

'Go for landscapes then: hills and trees never complain. But, seriously, you don't need to worry. For God's sake, I'm black and I still manage to blend in OK – well, in London anyway – so you'll have no trouble. Look, last Sunday I went to Epping Forest – High Beech, it was. There were loads of rockers there, parked near the church; seems they've been going there for sixty, seventy years or so – not the same ones, course, but rockers anyway. And you know what? I took pictures of the greasers, lots of them, some close-up. No problem at all. Course, there's always a bit of banter, but as long as you give as good as you get, you'll be fine.'

'Well, that does surprise me. I mean, I'd have expected a bit of aggro.'

'Look, most people couldn't care less about being photographed – long as it's not the police or MI5 on rooftops! Couple of weeks ago I went to Valentines Park – you know, in Ilford. They have a park run every Saturday morning – nothing professional: most people trundle round just above walking pace. On this particular Saturday there was a dirty great mist – almost a fog – and know what? I got some wicked pictures of runners, suddenly stepping out of the white. Most smiled when I snapped them, some even waved. No one got angry.'

'OK, I'll think about it, Jada. But, you know, what I really need to take up is cooking, go on a course, study it properly. Jack was always grousing about my meals. Maybe that was why we split up – well, that and the fact that we couldn't get on with each other any longer. But how about you, Amy, what sort of reaction do you get with your cooking?'

'Oh, Brian seems to like it.'

'Incidentally, Amy, why isn't hubby here?'

'Not his scene, Moll: the only man, no one interested in darts or football. He thought he'd get in the way of the conversation; better for us to stick to things we're really in to.'

'So what's he going to eat, all on his lonesome?'

'Oh, don't worry about him. He'll rustle up something. Might surprise you, but he does a mean stir fry – English-style, mind you.'

Having removed all the empty steamers and plates, the waiter was now carrying the dessert dishes in: egg tarts, chewy sesame balls with red-bean filling and a large bowl of tapioca pudding.

'You know, a funny thing happened to me the other day and it was all to do with retiring....'

'Sounds like the start of a joke! So what happened? You

decided to carry on, after all?'

'Not on your life, Moll! No, I was chatting with the school caretaker and his wife – their son's in my class. Husband's a Croat, wife's a Serb. Well, we were talking about this and that – you know, retirement, pensions, free time, that sort of thing – and as soon as they learnt I used to go on holiday to Croatia when I was a student, they said, "Why don't you buy a holiday home out there?" Well, I didn't want to hurt them, so I pretended to go along with the idea, but my immediate reaction was, "No way!"'

'So what's so funny about that?'

'Hold on, I'm coming to that. Well, a couple of days later I began to think about what they'd said and you know what I did?'

'Bought a place.'

'Steady on, Moll. No, I rummaged round in the lounge cupboard and finally found what I'd been looking for: my old photo album, chock-full of holiday snaps of Croatia. I also turned up, right at the back, this tattered Serbo-Croat phrasebook and *Teach Yourself Serbo-Croat*. You know, I'd totally forgotten I had them. Well, as you'd guess, when I leafed through the album, all the old memories flooded back. So I began to think more and more about those times, and you know what? I logged on to this Croat property site and checked holiday homes. The couple said you could get them cheap. Well, the amazing thing is you can buy a whole house for as little as £40,000!'

'Ah, but there's no electricity or running water, and it's at the top of a mountain.'

'Cynic! No, they have all the mod-cons, don't you worry, and some of the places aren't that far from the sea. So though I was still uneasy about taking a place a local might want, I did think, *Maybe, yes, maybe I could, after all.*'

'Come this summer, then, we'll all be visiting you in Croatia!'

'Well, it's still a long shot, but you never know, you never know.... Anyone for coffee?'

'So, son, how's project going?'
Slavko, Mira and Josip were spaced round the lounge, digesting the dinner in leisurely fashion.
'Good. I know all the clubs now. I know where they play ... their colours ... the nicknames....'
'Then you know about my team – Dynamo, Dynamo Zagreb?'
'Well, I know they play in Zagreb....'
'Yes, Maksimir Stadium – very big, can be 60,000 fans, more!'
'And they wear blue shirts and blue socks and they're called The Blues. Oh yes, and their big derby's against Hajduk Split.'
'That's right, good. And how many times win league?'
'Dunno.'
'Four, I think. And Tito Cup?'
'Can't remember.'
'Six, maybe seven. Good cup side, you see.'
'And what about my team?'
'Come on, Mira, you're no fan. You even don't like football.'
'True, but my father was always telling me what a good side we had. You know, he took me along one time.'
'You never tell me.'
'You never asked. But it all ended badly. You see, I'd no idea which team was which and while we were chatting after the final whistle, my father found out I'd been supporting the wrong side. Well, you can't imagine how upset he was. Anyway, he never asked me to go with him again.'
'So you just see one match.'
'Well, that was quite enough; the ninety minutes seemed to take a long, long time.... But anyway, Josip, I'm sure you'd never make the same mistake, now would you? So what do you know about my local team?'
'The Novi-Sad team! Wait, it's coming. Yes, Vojvodina, that's it ... and their shirts are red and white halves ... and they're called the Red and Whites!'
'That's right, and also the Tulips and the Old Lady.'

'And they won league two times. Not bad for small team! So now what you doing, Josip?'

'Finding out about the best club players – oh, and the national team.'

'National team, yes, national team – so sad! I tell you, at end of 1980s-beginning 1990s we have great, great team. 1987: we win World Under-20 Championship. 1990: we get to last eight of World Cup. No luck, we lose to Argentina – penalties! 1991: Red Star win European Cup – first, now only, Communist team to win. You see, we have great team and great players: Jarni, Stimac, Prosinečki, Boban, Suker, Bokšić, Stojković, Mihajlović, Savićević, Katenac – best in world, I think.'

'Sounds all good, dad. So why are you sad?'

'War, son: republic start fighting republic; Yugoslavia break up and FIFA say, "You don't play in any cup." We qualify for Euro 92, but they ban us. In our place Denmark – we beat Denmark in group stage. Well, with Laudrup, Michael Laudrup, Denmark win final. But if we play, we win, I'm sure, not just Euro 92, but maybe 1994 World Cup. Look, only Croat players from Yugoslav team get Croatia third place in 1998. Then the national team has as well four great footballers from Serbia, one from Montenegro, and one from Slovenia!'

'Ah yes, if only, if only. But you know, Josip, it wasn't just football. When me and dad were growing up, there were some great rock groups as well – and they were spread all over the country: *Buldožer* in Slovenia; *Bijelo Dugme* – that's White Button – in Bosnia; in Serbia *Riblja Čorba*, which is Fish Soup....'

'Though there's other meaning too.'

'We won't go into that... Now in Macedonia we had *Leb i Sol* or Bread and Salt – you know, in the old days visitors to Macedonian homes were given freshly-baked bread and salt on arrival.'

'Who did you and dad like?'

'Well, your father in Croatia was, typically, into hard rock: Dado Topić's *Time;* while, across in Vojvodina, I was a bit of a punk.'

'I don't know that.'

'Before your time, dear. Yes, I used razors to slash holes in my jeans and, once, dyed my hair bright green. Didn't last long, though. Teachers made me change it back: wasn't what socialist youth should look like.'

'Have you got a photo of yourself back then, mum?'

'Afraid not.... But, anyway, in Novi Sad we had this great punk group, *Pekinška Patka*, 'Peking Duck'. It's funny, but their lead singer, Nebojša Čonkić, was also a teacher and he worked at the Mihajlo Pupin High School where I did my teaching practice. I got to know him well.'

'Not as boyfriend, I hope.'

'Don't worry, dear; he was already with Marija, but, I must say, I did rather fancy him. He was always the rebel, always doing naughty things. But, unlike me, Professor Čonta, as us punks used to call him, has done really well for himself since the war: emigrated to Canada and he's now teaching Computer Science at Seneca College, Toronto.... If only I'd studied science, like Nebojša, and not English....'

'You've done OK, mum.'

'No, I haven't, I haven't.... But, anyway, you should listen to these groups, Josip. We've got the records and cassettes packed away somewhere upstairs.'

'Thanks, but I won't understand anything, will I?'

'Oh, don't worry about that: I'll write down the lyrics for you and put an English translation underneath – well, of the clean ones at least. It'll be a good way to learn Serbo-Croat: study mixed with pleasure.'

'OK, I'll give it a go.'

'You know, a lot of these groups had strong links with London. They used to come over, listen to the latest sounds in the clubs, then go back and make their own versions. Look at Nebojša. He told me he visited London and took in all the punk and two-tone groups he could – the Clash, Glenn Matlock's Rich Kids and, I seem to remember, the Specials. Another time I asked him about his group's name and he said it came to him while he was at a Chinese restaurant in Soho, looking at what the table next to him was eating: Peking Duck!'

'Not all by yourself, Jimmy. In twos. Stand next to Mary.'
With help from a couple of parents Jeannie was chivvying her class into some sort of line. Once the coach had drawn up outside the William Morris Gallery, the children had spilled out higgledy-piggledy. Rain, falling steadily over Walthamstow, made the task all the more urgent.
'Come on, class, or we'll all get soaked. Now pay attention. Before we go in I just need to remind you of a couple of things. Jack, that means you as well.'
'Yes, miss.'
'Behave yourselves today. No shouting – there'll be grown-ups in there and the last thing they'll want is noise. No running around, particularly in groups. Above all, no, absolutely no touching: what they've got in there is very, very valuable. You damage one of them and you'll be paying back for the rest of your lives. Now my helpers and me will be going from room to room and if we catch any of you messing about, you'll be back in the coach with the driver before you know it, twiddling your thumbs for the rest of the morning. Is that understood?'
A collective 'Yes, Miss.'
'And don't forget: some of you are in uniform. People can see which school you're from and you don't want them saying, "What a bunch of horrors this lot are!" OK, let's get out of the wet!'
More or less in twos and more or less quiet, the children snaked through the iron gates, across a wide courtyard and up the steps of the large Georgian mansion. In the foyer they found the curator, waiting for them, rubbing her hands together as if in eager anticipation.
*God, pick 'em young these days, don't they? She can't be more than – what? – thirty. And she just glows with energy, enthusiasm – youth, I suppose it is! Aye, but wait till she gets*

*to my age. That'll take the gloss off her. Now, though, she'll have no trouble getting these bairns' full attention. I've lost that, I guess – mebbe for good. Just as well I'm getting out of teaching. Still, glad to be back at the old Gallery, showing solidarity. All those opening hours the council cut last year and that talk of closing the place down for good! But we ran a great campaign, got Chris Smith on board and now things look altogether rosier, what with the Lottery grant. You know, mebbe someone from the Gallery is beavering away on a redevelopment plan, somewhere in the basement, right at this moment. Hope the bairns appreciate what's been saved for them – well, not now, but when they get a wee bit older.*

'Welcome to Water House, children. Lovely to have you all here. Let me tell you what we're going to do today. First, there'll be a quick tour of the gallery, so you'll know who William Morris was and what he did. Then we'll give you a little Spot-the-Animal quiz. You'll have to go round the Gallery again, with pens and clipboards this time, and hunt for different animals pictured on the exhibits. A warning, though! Some are a bit difficult to find because they're almost hidden in all the detail. You'll have to look very hard or you'll miss them, but the eagle-eyed among you, who spot every one, will get a small prize.'

Murmurs of appreciation filled the foyer.

'Oh and what would that be, Miss?'

'Don't you worry about that now, Jimmy. You just wait and see.'

'So, yes, a small prize. After the quiz we'll all go upstairs to the study room and you can enjoy yourself, doing some drawing. I do hope some of you will do a picture of something you've seen today, when going round the Gallery…. Right, children, let's begin our tour in the room over there.'

Like a flock into a pen, the children were funnelled into Room 1, Jeannie and the two parents sheepdogging at the back.

'Now William Morris came from a rich family.'

Jeannie raised an amused eyebrow. *Unlike us. Isn't that what you mean?*

'His father made lots of money in stocks and shares. Well, children, you won't know what they are, but it's funny his father got his riches that way because later in life when William became interested in social problems, he turned on the whole business of stocks and shares, calling the Stock Exchange, "Swindling Kens" and its rooms "gambling booths".'

*Oow, politics right from the go! Daring!*

'So in 1834 William was born into a very comfy world. He was a local boy, living first at Elm House, here in Walthamstow, then moving in 1840 to Woodford Hall, a huge building with acres of ground in Woodford, and finally returning to this house in Walthamstow after his father's death in 1847. Though they were downsizing, the Morrises still had it easy. For instance, if you look behind the Gallery, you'll see a large park, Lloyd Park, with long walkways and a big duck pond. Well, the Morrises owned all that too! Pictures of the three houses can be seen on the wall over there.... Now, William had four brothers and two sisters. Any of you come from a large family?'

Aesha raised a timid hand. 'I have two older brothers and three older sisters, Miss.'

'There you are, so you know what it's like – sharing toys, getting hand-me-downs, things like that. Well, despite all this and despite his father dying, William had a very happy childhood. Walthamstow and Woodford weren't built-up then as they are now, but little villages on the edge of Epping Forest and close to the unspoilt Lea Valley. He really loved this area.'

*Ay, but he got a bit snotty later, didn't he? What did he say: 'terribly cocknified and choked up by the jerry-builder'? Ooow, get you, Mr Morris!*

'When he was about your age, he was given a little suit of armour and he used to go out into the forest, imagining he was a knight on some adventure for King Arthur. Has anyone heard of King Arthur?'

Sean, unexpectedly, thrust a hand up. 'He had knights –

Lancelot, Gawain, others as well. Twelve it was, I think, but can't remember their names. Anyway, they used to ride out from ... er, Camelot, was it? ... to kill dragons and rescue ladies. Oh yes, and Arthur had a round table and the Knights of the Round Table broke up in the end. They started fighting each other when the Queen – what's her name? Oh yeh, Guinevere – went off with Lancelot.'

'Very good, very good, but how did you know all that?'

'Well, there was this series on the telly a while back and I really got into it, watched every part.'

'Good, but do you also know this legend: that Arthur's not really dead, but sleeping under the hill and when England's in her greatest danger he'll wake up and save the country?'

Sean shook his head.

*Steady on, steady on! Arthur was originally a Celt, wasn't he? So what about saving Wales or Cornwall or the Isle of Man or Ireland or even Scotland, all those edges of the British Isles the Sassenachs drove us to?*

'It was this area around Walthamstow that first got William interested in those magical stories about knights, ladies, magicians, monsters and damsels in distress. In one of his lectures he remembers the 'lasting impression of romance' Queen Elizabeth's Hunting Lodge, 'by Chingford hatch, in Epping Forest', made on him when he visited it 'as a boy'. In a short story he imagines the Lea Valley of his childhood with 'a little girl sitting on the grass ... eyes fixed on the far away blue hills, and seeing who knows what shapes there; for the boy by her side is reading to her wondrous stories of knight and lady, and fairy thing, that lived in ancient days'. Such stories filled William's mind not only as a child, but into adulthood and in this room and the next you can see him using these subjects again and again in paintings, drawings, wall-hangings, book-illustrations and so on. Look over there at those two small stained-glass windows that Morris made when he was 28. You have a young king, probably Arthur, in one and a young lady – is it Guinevere? – in the other, both

wearing typical medieval clothes. Listen and I'll give you a clue for the quiz: if you look closely at the king's robes, you might just spot an animal woven on them. Do you see it...?'
The children crowded even closer around.
'Now, let's go through to Room 3.'

As Jeannie shepherded the class, with the help of parents, through two rooms to the third, she began to feel with increasing confidence that it had, after all, been a good idea to bring the kids to the Gallery. They hadn't become fidgety, whispery or obstructive, as she'd feared, but seemed to be swept along by the curator's enthusiasm.

'Now, children, we move from William Morris the dreamer to William Morris the businessman. He joined up with a group of friends in 1859 to form the Firm. They decorated a lot of buildings with wall-paintings, wall-hangings and stained-glass windows. They also made books, printed and hand-written, as well as wallpaper. When the Firm broke up in 1875, Morris carried on alone, calling his business Morris & Company. He introduced new products like carpets and tapestries, but what he was most famous for was the wallpaper, and you can see lots of examples on the walls around you. Do you notice that they're all in different colours, deep colours, but they all have the same style? What can you find in all of them?'
'Flowers, Miss!'
'Yes. Anything else?'
'Leaves!'
'Branches!'
'That's right. Morris wanted to make bold, beautiful designs and he thought the best thing to do was copy nature. Notice how the flowers stand out, but when they're repeated, the stems become woven into the ones next to them to make a dense pattern. But it's not all petals and leaves and branches; sometimes he puts birds and creatures in. There's one wallpaper design – which you'll need to find for your quiz – where he has an animal from children's stories that you probably all know: the Uncle Remus tales.'

*Ach, no. We don't do those anymore. "Reinforces racial stereotyping!" Pity! I really used to like them.*

'Morris wanted his wallpaper to be not only beautiful, but also hand-made by craftsmen and craftswomen who enjoyed what they were doing. He said, "My work is ... pleasure to me .... Why should not my lot be the common lot?" He thought machines had turned workers into joyless slaves and that factory owners' never-ending race for profit had resulted in the production of too many things, things nobody really wanted or needed. Think about your own parents' jobs, children. Do they enjoy their work? Do their jobs allow them to express themselves? Are they doing work that is necessary and useful?'

A good half shook their heads.

*Come on, that's hardly fair! Most of their parents can't pick and choose the work they do, now can they?*

'Morris wanted us to fill our homes with practical, but nice-looking products. He said, "Have nothing in your houses which you do not know to be useful or believe to be beautiful".'

*Ay, but his beautiful things were too pricey for ordinary folk, weren't they?*

'While we're here, I'll give you another quiz-clue: look at that tapestry, hanging over there; around the edge it says, "I once a king, now am the tree-bark's thief". It shows a tree where the one-time king, turned into a thieving bird, sits among the apples. For your quiz answer you have to find out what sort of bird he's become.... Now, let's go on to the last room, Room 4. There we can see Morris in his late forties, getting interested in political ideas: first Socialism, then, just before his death, Communism. Now these are very long words, children, but does anyone know what they mean?'

Sharon, for one, seemed to know the answer for not only did she put her hand up, but she waved it from side to side to get the curator's attention.

'Yes, the girl over there,' pointing.

'Socialists and Communists, Miss, don't want posh people

over ordinary people. They want everyone to be the same. Be
paid the same. Have the same sort of houses.'
'That kind of thing, yes. But how did you know all this?'
'Oh, me dad's always going on about it ... he's a – what do you
call it? – shop steward ... that's right.'
*Steady on, steady on! We can't be polluting the bairns' minds
with all this bolshy stuff, now can we?*
Still engaged, but happy the tour was coming to a close, the
kids needed little encouragement to troop to the last room.
The curator led them over to a long central desk, running
from end to end.
'For someone to start off as a rich child and end up preaching
communism on street corners is an amazing journey, but
that's the road that Morris took. He became more and more
unhappy with the way England was divided into people who
had a lot and people who had nothing. Take a look here at
this engraving! It's at the start of a book called *A Dream of
John Bull*. Now John Bull's not a real person; he stands for
something. Does anyone know what he stands for?'
Silence.
'Well, it's England. He's usually pictured as a fat, red-cheeked
man, wearing a top hat. This engraving here's not very big, so
can you all crowd round, please? I hope you can make out that
it's a picture from the Bible. Can you see Adam, digging the
ground, and over there Eve, spinning yarn, and playing around
her feet their sons, Cain and Abel? Notice what's printed in
bold capitals underneath: "WHEN ADAM DELVED AND
EVE SPAN/ WHO WAS THEN THE GENTLEMAN?"'
Jeannie spotted a smirking Jimmy, elbowing Johnny as he
pointed out the mother of mankind's naked breast, and with a
well-aimed prod stopped him in his tracks.
'Morris was beginning to dream of an England not divided
into rich and poor, an England where everybody was equal;
and in his novel, *News from Nowhere*, he imagines what that
England might be like after a revolution. As you'd expect, no
one is above or beneath anyone else and, unusually for the

time, women have as much power as men.'
*Ay, but he does suggest women are best occupied running houses or bearing bairns.*

'After the revolution London goes back to the sort of rural suburb Morris knew as a child here in Walthamstow. What you'd like about Nowhere is that children don't have to go to school; they only study if they want to. But I think you'd also find some of the changes funny. For instance, the Houses of Parliament are no longer used for politicians' speeches, but as a 'storage place for manure'. Also, though this is a little sad as well, Morris set *News from Nowhere* in the future – the 1950s and 60s – by which time he confidently expected the revolution to have taken place. Everything that happens to the novel's hero happens when he's asleep, but at the end he wakes up and asks himself, "Was this just a dream or a vision of things to come?"'

*Well, a dream so far, though the dream did come true – briefly – in Slavic countries – and stayed true longest in Yugoslavia ... aye, but even there it didn't last ... alas!*

Sunday morning, so Slavko didn't have to rise at dawn. Eleven had struck, breakfast been lingered over and now father, mother and son were all seated in the lounge.

'You know, Josip, I was a bit of a poet back in Yugoslavia. Never told you that, have I?'

'No, mum. Did you put out any books?'

'Only one, a very slim volume: *Pod Grčkim Nebom*. Not that good really, looking back at it, but still I'll show you it one day when your Serbo-Croat gets a little better. You know, the title, *Under a Greek Sky*, comes from a holiday dad and I had in Athens and Delphi. It's strange, but writing that poem must have sparked something for, look,' brandishing a couple of sheets, 'I've produced another one, this time about a later "battle" at Kosovo Polje!'

Josip looked startled, not exactly pleased.

'Don't worry: it's all in English. Are you up for it?'

'I guess so,' slowing his sigh so his mother wouldn't pick it up. 'Good. Now it takes place in exactly the same spot, but six hundred years later. Slobodan Milošević – he's the Serbian President – flies down to Kosovo Polje to speak to a huge crowd of Serbs, there to remember the six-hundredth anniversary of the medieval battle. He's in a strong position because he's just forced Serbia's two half-free mini-republics – that is, my Vojvodina, which has lots of Hungarians and Romanians in it, and Kosovo, which is mostly Albanian – to be swallowed up again in Serbia. You'd think with the battlefield being right in the middle of Kosovo and there being very few Serbs left in the area, not many people would show up, but they came from all over – from other parts of Serbia, from Serb Krajina, from Bosnia, Macedonia, Montenegro, Slovenia, even from abroad. There must have been half a million, probably more. Are you following?'

'Think so.'

'Well, Milošević, knowing how unhappy the Serbs have become, has two choices: one, to carry on Tito's policy of avoiding any talk of nationalism; or, two, to play on Serb fears. I want you to look over the poem and tell me which you think he chose and what happened as a result.'

Josip put the two sheets on his knees in a slightly wary manner as if they might burn him with their difficulty. Nevertheless, he did lower his eyes, as instructed, and begin to read:

## THE SECOND BATTLE OF KOSOVO POLJE (28 June 1989)

*He flew down from Belgrade town, rotor blades*
*Flashing in the sun, flew down from that white city*
*To the green fields of Kosovo. A chartered express*
*Followed him down, yet all that folk along the route,*
*Standing at level crossings, saw was a ghost train,*
*Full of absence. Where was the West? Where were*
*The ambassadors of France, Germany, Japan,*
*Of Britain and the United States? Why weren't they*

*Sitting with interpreters in their assigned seats*
*As the train rattled down to Priština? Could it be*
*Some kind of joke, a joke of fate, that, on board,*
*The only legate, the only one to sit through*
*The President's speech on the ancient battlefield*
*Of Gazimestan, the 'Place of Warriors', was a Turk,*
*Smirking heir of Ottomans, Seljuks, who'd carried*
*The Field of Kosovo six hundred years before?*
*Sarcasm, snub: that's all you get from the West,*
*Thought Milošević. And when you need them most,*
*They're two-faced, sniggering behind their hands,*
*Or nowhere to be found. In dark suit, white Teflon shirt*
*And red tie – that small souvenir of socialist ways –*
*Slobodan Milošević slowly mounted the stage*
*Beneath the backdrop of a towering capital I, as if*
*A vast exclamation mark greeted his entry,*
*And, pinned on the huge I, a white medallion*
*Reminding every Serb on that muddy field just what*
*They were honouring: '1389/1989, 600 Years' –*
*But six hundred years of what? Sorrow? Suffering?*
*Or simply self-pity? Yet, fixed at the medallion's base*
*A contrary tug: behind Milošević's head a sprig*
*Luxuriantly spread, recalling, through its red leaves,*
*His late socialist leader, Tito, nationalism's lifelong foe.*
*But Milošević did not look back, looked instead ahead,*
*Looked at the far horizon, then looked right and left,*
*And everywhere he looked, even in nooks and crannies,*
*He spied thick knots of Serb heads, army-hatted or hatless.*
*Half a million, more, there might have been. Now*
*If every head were a grain of salt, thought Milošević,*
*We'd have more than enough to season the meze*
*At the start of outdoor feasts in every Serb town.*
*The president looked down, beyond the seated rows*
*Of local dignitaries, at the milling men, noticing*
*How many clutched pictures of him in one hand*
*And of Prince Lazar in the other. though this*

*Was hardly surprising for the day of remembrance*
*Coincided with St Vitus Day. The half-million had come*
*Not just to see him affirm, at last, those myths*
*Of Serbian hardship and persecution, but also*
*Honour the Christian dead, honour St Vitus,*
*Martyred by Rome, and the saintly Lazar,*
*Martyred on Kosovo Field. Milošević laid*
*His speech on the lectern beneath banks*
*Of microphones and stared long at the printed lines.*
*Yes, he did hate giving speeches, but he knew*
*Full well that if he played this one right, he'd soon*
*Become the new Lazar, Serbia's Warrior-Saint,*
*Tito's true successor. Yet, raising his eyes*
*Again he could see, scattered here and there,*
*Serbs brazenly sporting Četnik insignia,*
*Hated emblems of the monarchist thugs*
*Who'd spent the war, harassing not Nazis,*
*But Tito's partisans. Just then realisation,*
*Like a falcon, swooped down on his mind*
*And he saw how fateful was the choice*
*He had to make for from its cracked shell*
*A greater or lesser Serbia would emerge.*
*Should he ditch the speech, rehearse*
*For what must be the six-hundredth time*
*Tito's tired old creed of Unity, Brotherhood?*
*Or should he read it, word for word, and*
*Knowingly unleash Serbia's Rottweiler rage,*
*Even to the last snarl or snap? Much*
*As he'd like to hold the line for Socialism,*
*Its red walls were falling all over Europe,*
*And the West was scarcely likely to buttress*
*His country's crumbling defences, even though*
*Its communism was growing pinker by the day.*
*Slovenia and Croatia were already stoking fires*
*Of division, so why not Serbia, why not Slobodan?*
*Thinking back two years to his last time in Kosovo*

*He smiled grimly as he recalled what he'd told*
*Protesting Serbs, beaten by batons, the batons*
*Of Albanian police, 'No one shall dare strike you*
*Again.' For too long he'd played the eel,*
*Sliding between socialist and chauvinist stances,*
*Never making his position clear. Now was the time*
*to stop all that slithering. With resolve his piggy eyes*
*Stared down at the text and, having unblocked*
*His throat, he squealed his message out, clear words*
*Above mud, the mud of the Field. 'The Battle of Kosovo*
*Stands as a symbol, a glorious symbol of heroism,*
*That Serbs still commemorate in songs, dances*
*And legends. And now, six centuries later, we face*
*New battles, not battles with arms, though arms*
*Cannot be ruled out.' And arms were not ruled out*
*For Milošević's amplified words echoed not only*
*Round that vast field, but through the heart*
*Of each Serb listening there. And the half-million*
*Let out a roar, a mighty roar of released fervour,*
*A roar that said Serbs would fight to the death*
*Anybody stupid enough to try to stop them*
*Claiming their national rights. And soon enough*
*Milošević did have them fighting, fighting first*
*With Slovene, then Croat, Bosnian and Kosovan,*
*War upon bloody war upon bloody war.*
*And he set the mad dogs free – Arcan, Soselj,*
*Karadžić, Mladić –, free to slobber over*
*Every trace of Brotherhood, Sisterhood, Unity,*
*Free to ethnically cleanse, gang rape, massacre,*
*And starve in concentration camp. In Srebrenica*
*Those seven thousand unarmed men and boys*
*Slaughtered as if cattle in an abattoir! No wonder*
*NATO bombed Belgrade and brought Milošević,*
*'Butcher of the Balkans', on charges of genocide*
*To his Hague cell. The night before his heart,*
*Never strong, at last gave way, his wife came to him*

*In a dream. Mira, 'The Red Witch of Belgrade',*
*Stood by his bed in her nightgown, hair unloosed.*
*Though no sound escaped her moving lips,*
*He caught each word she said. 'Slobo, dear,*
*You know they called you hen-pecked. Well,*
*They were wrong. The truth is you didn't listen*
*To me enough, didn't listen when I praised*
*Our country "where Serb, Croat and Muslim*
*Can all live side by side", didn't listen when*
*I turned on rabble-rousers, calling Karadžić*
*A "Četnik" and Soselj "less than a man"*
*For "inciting wars he was too scared to fight in".*
*But, dear, above all else, you didn't listen when*
*I spoke to your better nature, telling the world*
*And in telling it, telling you, "No educated man*
*Can be a nationalist and my husband is certainly*
*Not one. I fight for the left, have always done.*
*Do you really think I could live with a chauvinist?"'*
*And having mouthed her message, Mira*
*Shrank back down the black hole of night*
*And Milošević awoke with a start. He shook*
*His head as if to rid it of his wife's words,*
*But they wouldn't budge. They buzzed round*
*His brain like ticks a bull. So, giving in,*
*He wearily replied to a wife, no longer there.*
*'Yes, you were right, you were always right.*
*Mira ...'Peace'. Even your name advised me*
*What to do, but I didn't listen, never listened.*
*All I brought was war and all that war brings:*
*Torn bodies, maimed minds, death howls,*
*An earth stained red and spoil heaps*
*Of rotting corpses.*

'So, what did you make of it?' as soon as Josip looked up from
the printed sheets.
'That was hard, very hard, mum. I think I only got a bit of it.'

'But did you understand which side Milošević chose?'

'Not sure, but I think ... the nationalist one.'

'That's right! Well done!'

Josip looked relieved as if his was a fifty-fifty choice.

'And what happened after that?'

'Well, a lot of fighting.'

'Yes, and, you know, dad and me were caught up in all that, really caught up. We did tell you something of it before, but we left a lot out. Now, I think, is the time to fill in some of the gaps. But I've got to warn you: what we're going to say isn't at all nice. Are you ready?'

'Guess so.'

'Well, as the war between the Serbs and Croats got worse, our two families fell out. In fact, they slowly began to hate each other. They'd say to dad and me, "You can't be on both sides; you've got to choose: it's either them or us". My father even told me, "Best thing you can do, Mira, is get a divorce. We don't want to see that Croat husband of yours around here anymore." Course, I replied, "Slavko's not a Croat and I'm not a Serb, we're both Yugoslav and we're staying together." As you can guess, there was quarrel after quarrel – so many, always angry, always ending in shouting. So seeing they couldn't change us, our parents finally said to both of us in almost identical words, "Never come near our house again; we don't want to see you, hear from you ever again. To us you're now dead!"'

'That's awful, mum!'

'And it got worse. I had a younger brother, Marko, and when fighting with Croatia began, he suddenly told us he was thinking of joining a paramilitary group – that's like a gang of madmen and thugs with guns – basically, fascists. I just couldn't understand it: I'd always thought Marko had the same ideas as me. Well, I talked to him down the phone from Zagreb so many times, urging him to stay at home, arguing that his worst fears were being exploited by unscrupulous politicians, but he just wouldn't listen. It was as if his brain had been washed clean of all I thought we shared, as if he was no longer my brother, just a robot. He kept spouting the same old lies; I just couldn't stop him. So he went away to fight and got killed less than a month later – a sniper's bullet in the head.'

Josip looked at his mother in horror.

'But that wasn't all: Dad also had a brother, an elder brother, Goran, and he fought for the Croats against the Serbs and was captured and put in one of those terrible concentration camps where prisoners were wedged together like chickens in a factory farm, hardly able to move, given virtually no food and beaten every day. He almost died in there and when he came out, he was so weak and thin, his father said all you needed to knock him over was the lightest of winds.'

*It gets worse and worse*, thought Josip. *Maybe I should cheer things up a bit!* 'Well, I guess it's lucky I chose to write about something nicer – football.'

'But you know, football doesn't come out well either. In fact, football was part of the problem. Why don't you tell him, Slavko!'

'Yes. Look, you can say our war start on football field. Stadion Maksimir, my stadium. 1990, I think it was. Dynamo Zagreb, my team, play Red Star Belgrade. They're big, big rivals, enemies: it's like Croatia vs. Serbia. But politics make it worse. Croats just vote for independence. 'Freedom' Party's now biggest in parliament. Lots of Red-Star fans there, maybe 3,000, led by Arcan.'

'He's one of the paramilitary thugs I mention in my poem.'

'Match is in Zagreb, but for some reason security is Serb police. They dress like soldiers: helmet, sticks, big boots. In stands Red Star fans sing: "Zagreb is Serb", "We kill Tudjman" (you know, Croat President). So Dynamo and Red Star fans start to fight in stands. Things get very bad: lots of injuries. Dynamo and Red Star fans run on pitch. Serb police run after them, but hit Dynamo fans only. Players all go off, except our captain, Zvonomir Boban, best player in team, best player in

Yugoslavia. He see one policeman beat Croat fan very bad. So he run over, kick him right in face. Dynamo fans immediately stand as wall round him, make sure he get off the pitch OK. But later police charge him and Football Federation ban him.'

'Oh I see now ... so that's why he didn't play in the 1990 World Cup!'

'Yes and why Yugoslavia don't win. But Boban thinks he do what he must do. Later he say something like, "That day I risk all: life, career, fame, but it is for one thing – Croatia!"'

'So he was like Milošević ... a nationalist.'

'Well ... yes, but he kills nobody, just one kick.'

Josip's face bore a perplexed look. To him it was all violence, merely a difference in degree. His mother noticed his puzzlement.

'What's the problem, Josip?'

'Nothing, nothing.'

'That match, in a way, started all the trouble. Arcan said, right after, that he could see war was coming. So he began to organise and what he organised was the most brutal of all the paramilitary groups, the Tigers, and to do that he turned to football. He got together the worst hooligans from Red Star and Partisan – roughly a thousand of them. They liked nothing better than – to use an English term – sticking the boot in, but they had no discipline. So Arcan had their hair cut, stopped them drinking, and got them marching in ordered ranks. He turned them into a killing machine and did they kill – not just enemy soldiers, but anyone they could get their hands on? I can't even bear to think of what they did. It's just too disgusting. But, you see, it all began with football – football hooligans, it's true, yet still something football produced.'

Josip stood up, his brain aching from all the examples of suffering and hate colliding in his head.

'I want to go out for a bit.'

'What – to kick a ball around?'

'No, not this time.'

There they all were, sitting in the room of honour: the chosen pupils, accompanied by teachers, a couple of local authors, even the lady mayor herself. Jeannie always enjoyed the Barking and Dagenham Reading Day. It was such a welcome break from teaching. And this day had so far proved a carefree one: Wadham Road could boast of only one winning student this year, Josip, and he was never any trouble. All the borough's primary schools took part and with a teacher from each coming along it gave Jeannie a great chance to meet up with colleagues, compare work hassles and swop gossip. Then there was the setting. The event always took place in the town hall and whenever she walked across the square towards the rectangular, brown-brick building, its strikingly-steep clock tower, looming up above her, made her think of nothing so much as a lighthouse, placed there to guide storm-tossed citizens through the borough's choppy seas. And, as ever, they'd been given the town hall's poshest room: the council chamber with its two semi-circles of plush, upholstered seats, both faced by narrow, matching semi-circles of wooden desk tops for writing notes or speaking into microphones. Jeannie smiled with satisfaction as she eased back into the unresisting chair and let her arms relax on the padded rests. Facing her, seated on the largest of three high-backed wooden 'thrones' and flanked on either side by her jury of local writers, the lady mayor had just finished praising the fine work done by the borough's primary schools, as reflected in the varied creativity of their chosen pupils. What more, Jeannie asked herself, could Barking and Dagenham do to show how much it appreciated its teachers?

The lady mayor was now reading out the three winners of the short-story competition in reverse order. After each announcement the pupil would stand up and recite a short extract, learnt by heart, from his or her tale before walking to the front to receive book tokens. While the lady mayor was shaking the hand of a small girl with a ponytail, whose story, 'A Day I Shall Never Forget', had been judged the best,

Jeannie leant towards Josip, his body almost lost in the large seat next to hers, and whispered, 'Right, projects next! Are you ready?'

As he nodded, Jeannie noticed how tense his face had become. 'Well, I dunno,' putting on her comic voice, 'the last item on the programme! They make us wait and wait, don't they? Just typical!'

Josip managed a small smile.

'Look, no need to worry: your project was the best in the school by far. It's sure to do well.'

The lady mayor cleared her throat and adjusted the microphone nearest her.

'Now, last but not least: the project prizes. In third place we have Sharon Hicks, who's written on America.'

When a tall red-headed girl rose to recite, Jeannie showed Josip the crossed fingers of both hands and said softly from the corner of her mouth, 'One down, only two to go!'

Josip's face remained set; this was clearly no smiling matter. He looked on tensely as the girl finished her recitation, went up to the 'thrones' to be congratulated and returned, carefully clutching her token.

'In second place is....' Irritatingly, the lady mayor paused for effect, as compères do on TV quizzes, just to increase the suspense. 'Josip Horvat of Wadham Road. His project's all about football in Yugoslavia.'

Forcing his set facial muscles into the semblance of a smile, Josip got slowly up and spoke in a voice that faltered at first, but soon became fluent as his confidence grew.

'This … is … how my project … starts: "Yugo … slavia? What is … Yugoslavia? Well … it used to be a country. Now in its place there are seven countries: Slovenia, Croatia, Serbia, Montenegro, Macedonia, Bosnia and Kosovo. But less than twenty years ago they were all joined in one country, called Yugoslavia, the Land of the South Slavs. And in the late 1980s and early 1990s Yugoslavia had a very good football team, perhaps the best in the world. They were as good as England

in 1966. England had Geoff Hurst, Martin Peters, Bobby
Charlton and Bobby Moore; but Yugoslavia had Davor Suker,
Robert Prosenecki, Zvonimir Boban and Siniša Mihajlović.
And there were other great players in the team as well. But
they didn't have the same success as England because of a
tragedy. In the 1990s the Yugoslav republics started fighting
each other and the football team, like the country, fell apart.
It's a sad end to the story, but I want to look at the happy times
before that.'"

Enthusiastic applause, swelled by the clever mention of two
local heroes, Bobby Moore and Martin Peters, greeted the end
of the recitation. Jeannie, for good measure, added her loudest
clap and the occasional whoop. Though slightly abashed by
his reception, Josip still managed the broadest of smiles as
he shook the lady mayor's hand, a smile that was caught by
a local reporter's camera and later appeared in *The Barking
Recorder.*

'And now here's what you've all been waiting for: first place
goes to Mary Keogh, who wrote so brilliantly on Ireland.'

Seated again, Josip had resumed the crestfallen look that had
surfaced when he learnt he'd 'only' come second.

*He must have worked so hard and now, I suppose, thinks it's
all wasted. Just shows how competitive he is. I didn't realise
that. Normally, he's such an easy-going boy; that was what
must have fooled me.* 'Come on, cheer up, Josip. Second's no
disgrace. And for your information, I read all three finalists
and thought you were the best. But the judges, clearly, didn't
agree. Decisions, you know, aren't always fair. You just have
to take it on the chin.'

'Yes, Miss.'

Having seen the last prize awarded, the audience was just
about to rise from their seats when the lady mayor jumped up
and waved both arms above her head. 'Before we leave, can
we all show our appreciation for Mary Shannon from Wood
Street Primary, who organised this event, for my two fellow
judges, Joyce Smith and Rose Bailey, who gave up some of

their valuable writing time to be here today, and, once again,
for all you wonderful pupils?'

Loud applause followed, made up of genuine appreciation,
but also relief that everyone was at last free to leave.

'Well, I really enjoyed that, Josip: bit like the Queen's Birthday
Honours, but more democratic. Now I want to chat with some
of the other teachers here, but, first, I'll take you down to your
mother and father.'

Leaving the council chamber, teacher and pupil descended
the worn stone steps of the central staircase to the front door
and out onto the darkening square where a group of parents
were patiently waiting. Jeannie managed to pick out Mira and
Slavko from the huddle of bodies and waved. The mother, full
of anticipation, was the first to reach them.

'Well, how did it go, Josip?'

'Not so great: second!' holding up his £20 token.

'No, that's fine, second's fine. You know, you can't always
win, as you seem to do in football.'

'Funny as it may sound, Mira, but football might be the reason
he came second. Maybe the judges just don't like sport.'

Mira laughed. 'I'm sure that wasn't it, but, talking of football,
Dad's got something to tell you, Josip…. Sorry about this,
Jeannie.'

'No, no, go ahead.'

'Yes, son, scout come to see me today, says wants you to play
in Under-12 team.'

'A West-Ham scout?'

Slavko shook his head.

'Spurs?'

Another shake.

'Arsenal?'

And yet another.

'No: Leyton Orient.'

'Oh!'

Jeannie saw the lightning change on Josip's face: for the
second time that day he looked poleaxed.

'But that's good, isn't it?'

'Well, I was hoping for a bigger club, Miss ... but I guess it's local. Their ground's nearly as close as the Boleyn.... Yes, and with the club being small, I've got a good chance of getting into the first team.'

'Yes, and in first team scouts from big clubs will come, watch you. It's shop window.'

'So maybe, Miss, it hasn't turned out so bad after all.'

'That's the spirit, Josip.... Now, I've got some news for you too. You'll never guess, Mira, but you know what?'

'What?'

'I've gone and bought a flat in Pula, bought it outright!'

'Wow! You haven't?'

'Certainly have. All the mod cons and not far from the sea. It's great!'

'So you're going to stay there all summer?'

'No, no, I'm getting too old for that, can't take the heat as I used to. No: spring and summer in England, autumn and winter in Pula. It's much milder there than in London.'

'That's great, Jeannie, but it's also a bit of a pity!'

'Oh, why's that?'

'Well, we've got an announcement of our own. We've decided, for the first time since coming to England, to go back to Croatia for a holiday this year.'

'But that's no problem, is it?'

'Ah, but ours has to be in early August, so it seems we won't run into you.'

'Oh, I see what you mean. That's sad, yes, but now there'll be enough room for you to stay in my flat.'

'No, no, we couldn't.'

'Sure you could. Otherwise, it'd be empty and I'd rather it was used.'

'Well, if you're really sure, that'd be great. I can't thank you enough. It would get us out of a bit of a hole. You see, we still can't stay with Slavko's parents or his sister, we're still not talking.... But we must pay you.'

'Don't be ridiculous! No chance. You'll be guests.'
'That's so kind of you.'
'Don't mention it. Just tell me the exact dates, so I can make sure there are no clashes: you see, a few of my friends said they'd like to stay there some time this summer.... Anyway, I'm really looking forward to settling in.'
'And after you've done that, you can explore the town. There's quite a lot to check out, you know: Roman ruins, the beach, the food (it's a mixture of Italian and Croat), not to mention the many festivals.'
'Yes, I've got all those on my list, and, after that, I'm going to treat the flat as a base: explore the coast and islands – from Pula down to Dubrovnik; then turn inland and have a look at your Zagreb, Slavko, as well as Belgrade, the Danube, maybe even up to your Novi Sad, Mira. That done, I might venture further afield: you know, somewhere like Macedonia – Lake Ohrid perhaps.'
'Well, it'll certainly take a good few autumns to get round to all those.... Ha, you know, I've just thought: if you do go through every "republic", you'll have recreated through your travels the Old Yugoslavia.'
Jeannie looked up at the town-hall tower, so solid in its solidarity, then back at Mira. '"Recreated ... the Old Yugoslavia", yes! Wouldn't that be wonderful! Trouble is it's now just a memory. Yugoslavia's no more than a country of the mind for that's all that's been left behind.'